Critical Acclaim For Madeline Baker's previous bestsellers:

LAKOTA RENEGADE

"This latest addition is as rich, passionate and delicious as all her award-winning romances"

—*Romantic Times*

APACHE RUNAWAY

"Madeline Baker has done it again! This romance is poignant, adventurous, and action packed."

—*Romantic Times*

CHEYENNE SURRENDER

"This is a funny, witty, poignant, and delightful love story! Ms. Baker's fans will be more than satisfied!"

—*Romantic Times*

THE SPIRIT PATH

"Poignant, sensual, and wonderful....Madeline Baker fans will be enchanted!"

—*Romantic Times*

MIDNIGHT FIRE

"Once again, Madeline Baker proves that she has the Midas touch....A definite treasure!"

—*Romantic Times*

COMANCHE FLAME

"Another Baker triumph! Powerful, passionate, and action packed, it will keep readers on the edge of their seats!"

—*Romantic Times*

THE WILD AND THE INNOCENT

Warning bells rang loud and clear in Matt Drago's mind. It was time to stop. She was just a kid, he reminded himself, new to passion, intoxicated with pleasure. She didn't know what she was doing to him, what he wanted to do to her.

With an effort, he pried her arms from around his neck. "Lacey...." His voice was low and edged with the pain of wanting her.

"Please, Matt," she murmured breathlessly.

"Lacey, you don't know what you're asking for."

"Show me," she begged, and pressed her lips to his again, certain she would die if he didn't kiss her again.

It was a temptation no man could resist. Knowing it was wrong, Matt lowered Lacey to his blanket....

MADELINE BAKER

LACEY'S WAY

LEISURE BOOKS NEW YORK CITY

A LEISURE BOOK®

Published by
Dorchester Publishing Co., Inc.
276 Fifth Avenue
New York, NY 10001

ISBN 0-8439-4587-7

To the Laddies of the "Belles" and the "Classics"
at the Friendly Hills Bowl
—a *striking* bunch of women!

And especially for JOAN CHANCEY,
who made our '89 summer team fun!
(Go, Batman!)

CHAPTER 1

Lacey Montana stared blankly at the empty courtroom, her ears still ringing with the resounding bang of the judge's gavel as he sentenced her father to twenty years in the Yuma Penitentiary. Twenty years, she thought numbly. Her father would be an old man when he got out. If he ever got out. Royce Montana was not in the best of health. His heart was bad, the doctor had told her only a few months earlier; might give out at any time. How would her father survive the hardships and deprivations of prison life?

It was an effort to make her legs move, and Lacey walked stiffly out of the courtroom, her eyes filling with tears. Her father was her only kin left since her mother died five years ago.

What would she do without him? She was not quite eighteen years old and she had no money to speak of. No close friends to turn to for help. No family.

She walked slowly down the main street toward the south end of town, and then kept walking, hardly aware of her surroundings. Only a few weeks ago, everything had been wonderful. Her father had had a steady job as cook at the Double L cattle ranch, and Lacey had helped out in the kitchen on weekends and after school. For once, her father's future seemed secure, and Lacey had been looking forward to finally staying in one place for longer than a month or two. She had been thrilled at the idea of making friends, of settling down and becoming part of the community. Life had been good at the Double L. She'd had a room of her own, a horse, a growing wardrobe. The housekeeper, Mrs. Drebin, had been teaching Lacey how to sew, and Lacey had made herself two dresses she was quite proud of. She had met several girls her age at church and had been certain that, in time, she would be welcomed into their circle. Yes, life had been good and had promised to get better.

And then, in a moment, it was all over.

Lemuel Webster, owner of the Double L, had caught Royce Montana drinking on the job. There had been a heated argument. Angry words. A fight. Her father had hit Mr. Webster over the head with a whiskey bottle. And killed him.

Lacey choked back a sob as she sat down on a broad tree stump. Her father had promised on his word of honor that he would not take another drink. It was a promise he had made at least two dozen times in the last five years. But this time she had believed him. He'd been dry for over a year. And now this.

She stared into the distance, not seeing the stark beauty of the land around her, unaware of the clump of yellow wildflowers growing at her feet. The last few weeks had been awful. Visiting her father in jail, seeing the guilt and remorse in his eyes, hearing him beg for her forgiveness because he had failed her again. Then sitting through the trial, seeing the pity on the faces of people she knew . . .

The sun had slipped behind the distant hills when Lacey began the long walk back to town. She had been spending her nights in the loft of the livery stable since her father's arrest. She had been too ashamed to return to the Double L to collect her few belongings, too ashamed to face Mrs. Webster and the others who had been kind to her. Consequently, she had nothing to her name but the clothes on her back and her horse, Cinder.

The wind began to blow, and Lacey shivered as she ducked down the alley and made her way to the livery barn. Climbing up the ladder that rested against the west side of the building, Lacey pulled herself through the narrow window of the loft and nestled in the hay. It was warm and fragrant inside the barn, quiet save for the soft snorts of the horses in the stalls below. Her own mare was corraled behind the stable.

With a sigh, Lacey closed her eyes. Tomorrow they were taking her father to the territorial prison. Until now, she had not known what she was going to do, but in a lightning-like decision, she decided she would follow the prison wagon to Yuma. Perhaps there was a rooming house near the penitentiary. Perhaps she could find a job there, cooking or cleaning or making beds. At least then she would be close to her father. Perhaps she could even visit him occasionally.

She fell asleep with that thought in mind.

It was in the cool gray hours just before dawn when Lacey crept out of the loft and made her way through the town's back alleys until she found a pair of boy's pants hanging from a washline. They looked to be about her size, as did the plaid flannel shirt hanging beside them.

Her conscience bothered her as she tucked the stolen clothing under her arm and darted back down the alley. Her mother had taught her that stealing and lying and cheating were wrong, and that nothing ever made them right. But Lacey needed a change of clothing and she didn't have any money. What other choice did she have? She couldn't go back to the Double L and ask for charity, not after what her father had done. No one in town would give her credit, and her pride would not let her beg from people she hardly knew.

Running lightly, Lacey went back to the loft and quickly changed out of her blue cotton dress into the pants and shirt. The pants felt strange. They hugged her legs and thighs like a second skin. She knew her father would be scandalized if he saw her in such an outrageous outfit. No decent lady ever wore pants, but there was no help for it. Riding across country in a dress was out of the question.

Coiling her long, russet-colored hair into a knot on top of her head, she pulled on her hat, carefully tucking the loose ends of hair under the broad brim. Lastly, she pulled on her boots. Hopefully, no one would notice she was a girl. Hopefully, from a distance, she would be mistaken for a cowhand, or a drifter on the move.

Saddling Cinder, Lacey mounted the mare and rode down the main street toward the jailhouse. It was still early and no one was out on the street yet. She slowed her horse as the sheriff's office came into view. The prison wagon was just pulling away from the board-walk. She could see her father, his face pale and haggard, his eyes downcast, sitting on the narrow wooden bench that ran the length of the heavy iron-barred wagon on both sides. He looked old, she thought sadly, old and ashamed.

One other man caught Lacey's eye. He appeared to be in his early thirties. His hair was long and black and straight, his eyes dark. He was staring out of the bars, a decidedly sour expression on his face.

Two uniformed guards sat on the wagon's high spring seat. One held the reins of the four-horse team in his gloved hands, the other held a sawed-off shotgun across his lap. Two deputies rode alongside the wagon, both heavily armed.

Lacey waited until the heavy prison cart had a good start; then, with a look of determination on her face, she touched her heels to Cinder's flanks and set out after the wagon. She had no money, no clothing other than what was on her back and the simple blue cotton dress stuffed inside her saddlebag. But she had plenty of food, thanks to her nimble fingers. She had managed to steal quite a good supply of beans, hardtack, beef jerky, and canned peaches from the general store. She had a canteen filled with fresh water.

Lacey grinned ruefully. If her name was

written in the Lord's Good Book in Heaven, there were likely a number of black marks beside it now. But it couldn't be helped. She had needed something suitable to wear for her journey, and she had needed food to eat along the way. Perhaps at some future date she would be able to make restitution for the items she had stolen. If not, she would just have to trust that the good Lord would understand her motives and forgive her.

Belatedly, she wished she had thought to steal a kerchief to keep the dust out of her nose and mouth.

Ordinarily it was only a five-day ride to Yuma, but the prison cart was heavy and cumbersome and traveled slowly, doubling the travel time, and after four days in the saddle, Lacey began to wonder if they would ever reach their destination. She knew little about Yuma, only that it was a small town near the Colorado River in the southeast corner of Arizona, and that temperatures often reached over one hundred degrees in the summertime.

She was bone weary by the end of each day. The guards halted the wagon only once each afternoon to rest the horses and eat lunch. Lacey's heart went out to her father, knowing that the long hours he was forced to spend caged in the wagon must be miserable. The only time the prisoners were allowed out of the cart was at night, and then they were shackled to the wagon wheels to prevent any escape attempts.

Lacey slept fitfully at night, afraid the wagon would leave before she woke in the morning, afraid she would be left behind, lost and alone in the trackless Arizona desert. There were snakes in the desert, and she was deathly afraid of snakes. During the day, she was careful to keep a goodly distance between herself and the wagon, leery of getting too close to the prison guards for fear they would make her go back to Salt Creek.

The guards were mean-spirited and cruel, free with their fists if a prisoner did not immediately do whatever he was told. She had watched in horror as one of the guards struck her father for not climbing out of the cart fast enough to suit him. Another time, one of the guards had kicked one of the prisoners in the stomach because he spilled a cup of water. The two deputies who were accompanying the wagon never interfered, apparently feeling that the prisoners deserved whatever they got.

On the evening of the fifth day, Lacey climbed wearily from the saddle. Her legs, back, and shoulders were a constant throbbing ache. She was a good horsewoman, skilled and knowledgeable about horses and horsemanship, but spending almost ten hours a day on horseback was eight hours more than she was accustomed to. She had ridden often at the Double L, but only for pleasure, never like this.

Smothering a yawn, she stripped the bridle and saddle from Cinder, slipped a halter over the mare's head, and tethered the animal to a stout tree. With that done, she sank down on the ground and pulled off her boots and thick wool socks. With a sigh of pleasure, she wriggled her toes, yawning again as she did so.

Sitting there, contemplating a cold meal and another night spent on the hard ground, she fell asleep.

She woke with a start to find the sun high in the sky. Alarmed, she jumped to her feet and uttered a cry of dismay when she saw that the prison wagon was gone.

Muttering under her breath, she pulled on her socks and boots and quickly saddled her horse. Reluctantly she climbed into the saddle. Pulling a hunk of jerky from one of her saddlebags, she gnawed the tough strip of dried meat as she followed the deep ruts left by the heavy prison wagon.

Absently she noted that the desert was in bloom. Cactus flowers made bold splashes of color against the dun-colored sand. The palo-verde trees were flowering, and the gray-green

9

ironwood trees were crowned with beautiful pale violet blossoms. The flowers of the ocotillo were as red as flame, the blooms of the yucca as white as snow. Once, she passed a giant saguaro cactus that stood over forty feet high.

But she was too busy watching the trail of the wagon and keeping an eye out for snakes and scorpions to really give heed to the wonders of nature. While living at the Double L, she had not given much thought to the wildlife of Arizona, but it was frequently uppermost in her mind now. Besides snakes and scorpions, there were poisonous spiders in the desert. And a poisonous lizard, as well. She had seen only one Gila monster in her life, and it had been dead, but she had been repulsed by its chunky black and orange body.

An hour passed. Two. The wagon left deep ruts that made the trail easy to follow, and for that Lacey was grateful. She breathed a sigh of relief when, at last, she saw the wooden cart far ahead.

Matt Drago grunted softly when he saw the small cloud of dust rising from the southeast. So, the mysterious rider was still trailing them. He wondered, not for the first time, who the rider was, and what he wanted. Was it a friend of one of the prisoners? A father or a brother, perhaps, hoping for a chance to spring his kin before the wagon reached Yuma?

Matt shrugged. Whoever the unknown rider was, it had nothing to do with him. He had no friends in this part of the territory, no family to speak of.

He swore under his breath as he contemplated the heavy iron shackles on his hands and feet. Their infernal clanking was a constant reminder of the precious freedom he had lost. He had spent the last five years wandering across the southwest, never staying long in any one place, keeping to himself as he roamed from town to town. After the misery and deprivation of the war, it felt good to roam at will, to be his own man again. He rubbed his wrists, noting they were chafed and red from the constant rubbing of metal against his flesh. Damn. He'd go crazy if he had to spend the rest of his life behind bars, doing hard time for a crime he was certain he hadn't committed. If only he could remember what had happened that night.

Closing his eyes, he let his thoughts wander backward in time, back to the very beginning of his life. . . .

He had been born deep in the wilds of the Sierra Madre Mountains. His father, Saul Drago, had been an itchy-footed wanderer, roaming far and wide in search of fortune and adventure, returning home to Virginia from time to time, staying just long enough to get his wife pregnant again, then riding off to explore mountains and valleys he had never seen. One year, Saul had gone West. In his travels, he had acquired an Apache squaw to warm his blankets and had quickly gotten her with child. Matt Drago was the result of their union. The squaw had died in childbirth. Saul had contemplated letting the squalling brat he had so carelessly sired die with the mother, but, in the end, he had taken his newborn son home to Virginia. Leticia Drago had raised the boy as if he were her own. She had been a devout Christian woman, and although she spent the rest of her life hating Saul Drago for what he had done, she had not blamed the child for the father's sins.

Matt had grown up in poverty. He had hunted the verdant hills for game to feed his family from the time he had been old enough to lift a rifle. It had been evident to everyone from the beginning that Matthew Drago was a born marksman. In his spare time, he had practiced shooting with an old Walker Colt that belonged to his older brother, Abraham. Matt had a natural feel for guns, a steady hand, and a keen eye. No one in all Virginia could outshoot him.

As he grew to manhood, Matt had often wondered why he looked so different from his two brothers and his sister, who were all blond and fair while he was dark-skinned and had hair as black as midnight. He had been sixteen when Leticia Drago told him the truth about his parentage. It had been a hard thing to accept, being a half-breed and a bastard, harder still to learn that the mother he had idolized was not his mother at all. After that, he had pestered his father for information about his true mother, but Saul had insisted he didn't know anything about her except that she had been a Chiricahua Apache, pretty as a spring flower, and that her name had been Hummingbird. It hadn't been until Matt met old Smoke Johnson that he learned anything about the Apache people. Smoke had lived among the Apache and admired them. They were a proud and fierce people, Smoke had said, loyal to their friends, deadly to their enemies. There was no shame in being a half-breed, Smoke had remarked, no shame at all so long as a man was true to his word and loyal to his kin and country.

For a time, Matt had toyed with the idea of going West to learn more about his mother's people. The stories Smoke Johnson had told him excited him, making him anxious to see the mountains where he was born, to lie under a desert sky and listen to the night wind sigh across the face of the land. But then the war had come and he had gone to fight for the South. Smoke Johnson had joined up, too.

The war had been hell. Matt saw men blown to bits, felt his stomach churn as he heard horses and men scream in agony. He suffered hunger and fatigue, marched through the snow in his bare feet, ate food that would make a hog puke. His two brothers were killed at Vicksburg, and his sister entered a convent. Leticia (he never called her Mother again after he learned who he was) died of smallpox. Saul Drago had gone to war and was never heard from again, no doubt long dead and buried in an unmarked grave.

After Lee surrendered, Matt headed West, settling in Texas for no reason other than he'd never been there before and was eager to start a new life in a place that held no memories. There he met Claire Duprey. He fell for her the minute he saw her alighting from her father's carriage, a vision of loveliness in a fashionable gown of the palest pink satin and lace. He idolized her for months, always from a distance, of course. After all, she was a lady of quality, and he was just a no-account wrangler. She was rich and beautiful and well-educated, everything he was not, and he never dreamed she would give him a second look. And then, one soft summer night at a church social, she had noticed him, seemingly for the first time. Encouraged by the angelic smile she had bestowed upon him, Matt had taken his courage in hand and asked Claire to dance. Things had progressed beautifully after that. He had walked her home, mesmerized by her charm and elegance, by the slightly haughty tilt of her chin. Many carriage rides and dances and barbecues followed in the months ahead, and he had been a happy man, secure in her love. And then, out of the blue, she had changed her mind.

"I'm sorry, Matthew," Claire had said in her soft Southern drawl, "but I've decided to marry Ross."

Well, who could blame her? Ross Kilkenny was a rich young man, well-mannered, well-bred, handsome as the very devil.

Matt hadn't argued with Claire's decision. He wasn't one to beg, or one to hang around where he wasn't wanted. He had no one in Texas, no reason to stay. He quit his job as head wrangler at the Dawson ranch the next day, packed his few belongings, hopped on his horse, and rode away without looking back. He had a good horse, money in his jeans, and that was all he needed, all he'd ever needed. He had headed West, drinking and gambling his way from one cow town to another, cursing all women in general and one raven-haired beauty in particular.

He had been drowning his sorrows in an Arizona town no bigger than a postage stamp

15

when he drank his way through one bottle too many and passed out cold. When he woke up, he was in jail, accused of murder . . .

Matt Drago shook his head ruefully. He'd always had a quick temper and he was a fast hand with a gun, but he'd never gunned a man down in cold blood, not even during the war.

He lifted his head and stared out the back of the wagon. The dust cloud was still there, and now he could make out an indistinct shape on a dark horse.

Matt scowled bleakly as his thoughts drifted back in time once more. As luck would have it, the man he'd been accused of killing had been the only son of the local sheriff. In court, three men had taken the stand and testified, under oath, that Matt Drago had rousted young Billy Henderson, harassing the boy, calling him names. And when Billy wouldn't agree to a shoot-out, the man known as Drago had shot him down in cold blood and then passed out.

Matt had expected to be hanged, but Sheriff Henderson had taken the judge aside and asked that Drago be sentenced to life in prison instead. A hanging would be over too quickly, the sheriff had said, and he wanted the man who had killed his son to suffer for a long time.

Matt let out a long, discouraged sigh. How could he have killed a man—a boy, really—

16

and not remember it? He couldn't have been *that* drunk. Damn!

He glanced at the four men who shared the prison wagon with him. The prisoner on his left was just a kid, no more than seventeen or eighteen. He had been convicted of robbing the bank in Salt Creek. The two men sitting across from Matt were brothers. They were the last surviving members of the Belmont gang, a notorious bunch of men who had terrorized trains and stage coaches across the Southwest. The last train they had robbed had been filled with heavily armed lawmen instead of frightened passengers.

Matt slid a look at the man sitting on his right. He seemed old to be an outlaw. He never spoke, just sat there, his head cradled in his hands, a morose expression on his weathered face. The guards called him Gramps and kidded him about being the oldest first-time con they'd ever met.

Matt shook his head wearily. They'd been on the trail for six days now and every day seemed longer than the last. The wagon bounced and jolted over the rough terrain, raising clouds of dry yellow dust that irritated his eyes and clogged his throat. The shackles on his hands and feet clanked with each movement, the sound mocking him like evil laughter. His temper was frayed to the breaking point, and when one of the Belmont brothers accidentally bumped into him, he lashed out, his knotted fist driving into the man's face. Only the intervention of the prisoner called Gramps kept Matt from beating George Belmont to a pulp. Thereafter, the other men kept away from Matt as best they could in the confined space.

He felt as if he were going mad. It was galling, being in chains, having the guards treat him like dirt. And things would only get worse. In another four days, the doors of the Yuma pen would slam shut behind him. He had never liked small enclosed places. How could he spend the rest of his life in a cramped, iron-barred cell? Damn. He'd grow old and die there, his only hope the slim possibility of parole. And that was a slim hope indeed. Rehabilitation was not one of Yuma's objectives. Their main concern was preventing escapes and riots. The guards were brutal and corrupt. There had been so many escape attempts in the last few years that Gatling guns had been installed to discourage prisoners from trying to go over the wall. Yuma was the most feared and hated prison in the Territory. A lot of men had died behind the grim gray walls, unable to survive the cold winters and sweltering summers, the hard work, the whippings, the unpalatable food, the scummy water.

At dusk the wagon came to a halt alongside

a high yellow bluff. Matt stood up, eager to get out of the cart and stretch his muscles, which were cramped after so many hours of sitting on the hard wooden bench. He swore under his breath as the guards took their own sweet time about unlocking the door. Climbing out of the wagon, Matt jostled the arm of one of the guards, causing the man to spill the drink in his hand.

"You clumsy ass!" the guard snarled, driving his fist into Matt's midsection. "Why the hell don'tcha watch where you're goin'?"

Matt choked back the angry words that sprang to his lips, knowing anything he said would only bring more of the same.

A few minutes later one of the deputies herded the prisoners a short distance away from the cart so they could relieve themselves. Matt scowled, irritated by the lack of privacy, and by the way the lawman kept his rifle aimed steadily in his direction.

Thirty minutes later the prisoners sat down to a lukewarm meal of red beans, greasy bacon, and cold biscuits. When dinner was over, they were shackled to the wagon's wheels for the night.

Matt lay on his back, his head pillowed on his free arm as he gazed up at the stars that twinkled overhead like a million tiny lights in a dark house. Four more days until they reached Yuma, he mused bleakly, and shuddered with dread as he imagined himself caged behind cold iron bars for the rest of his life, never again to ride across the prairie with the wind in his face. Never to savor the taste of good whiskey, or the delights of a bad woman.

With an effort, he shook the dismal thought from his mind and stared out into the empty darkness, wondering where the mysterious rider had bedded down for the night.

Lacey woke early the following morning. She had slept badly, afraid she would awake to find the wagon gone again. They were riding in canyon country now, and she had to stay closer to the prison cart for fear of losing sight of it.

Rising, she pulled on her boots and began saddling Cinder. The horse was beginning to show signs of the long ride, too, Lacey thought as she affectionately stroked the mare's sleek black neck. Cinder was used to short, quiet rides, not long, arduous treks across wild, unbroken country.

Lacey was about to swing into the saddle when a ferocious cry rent the still morning air. Turning, she felt her blood run cold as she saw a dozen painted Indians swarm around the prison wagon.

The prisoners had been released from the wagon to stretch their legs and relieve themselves. Now they scrambled for cover under the cart while the guards and deputies fired at the shrieking Indians. Their cries were more animal than human, Lacey thought in dismay, and covered her ears with her hands as shivers of fears raced down her spine.

She held her breath as the battle raged some forty yards away, gasped as one of the guards slumped to the ground, an arrow quivering in the center of his back. Too frightened to move, Lacey huddled behind the mound of boulders that screened her from sight, one hand covering Cinder's nose to keep the horse quiet.

Time seemed to stand still as Lacey watched the awful scene of life and death being enacted before her eyes. Two of the Indians had been wounded, a third lay unmoving on the ground. The three remaining guards put up a good fight, but they were outnumbered and, one by one, they were cut down, until only the prisoners remained alive, still huddling under the wagon for protection.

Abruptly, one of the convicts rolled out from under the prison cart, scooped up a rifle lying on the ground, and began firing at the Indians. It was a brave but foolhardy move. Two of the warriors swung around, returning his fire, and the prisoner was knocked to the ground as their bullets slammed into him.

As the wounded convict struck the ground, three of the other prisoners panicked. Scram-

21

bling from beneath the cover of the wagon, they ran blindly across the desert, their steps hindered by the chains hobbling their feet. With wild shrieks of delight, the Indians gave chase, quickly catching and killing all three men.

Lacey bit down on her lower lip as the Indians rode back to the wagon. Her father was there, and she watched in helpless horror as Royce Montana crawled out of his hiding place and faced the Indians. One of the warriors fitted an arrow to his bow string and sighted down the feathered shaft. Lacey watched, her eyes filling with tears, as she waited for the warrior to kill her father. Time seemed to slow, and she was aware of every detail. She saw the black paint smeared across the lower half of the warrior's face, the eagle feathers tied in his long black hair, the mocking grin on his swarthy face as he prepared to draw back the bow string. The arrow was striped in black and red. For death and blood, Lacey thought dully, and turned her eyes to her father once again. His face was drained of color; his hands, bound with chains, were tightly clenched, the knuckles white. But his head was high and his shoulders were back, and she felt a wave of pride sweep over her. She knew he must be terribly afraid, knew his heart must be pounding with fear as he stared death in the face, but it didn't show. Not one bit.

The other warriors were waiting, their dark eyes glinting with eager anticipation as they waited for their companion to take the old man's life.

Royce Montana did not flinch, though he was more frightened than he had ever been in his life. Still, if he was going to die, he thought he would rather die here, out in the open under a blazing summer sun, than die a little each day locked up behind the cold iron bars of the Yuma prison. Head high, he returned the warrior's gaze. And, inexplicably, the warrior lowered his bow. He spoke a few words to the young brave beside him, and the young warrior leaped gracefully from the back of his calico pony and walked toward the white man.

Royce Montana held his ground, the hair prickling on the back of his neck as the Indian came to stand in front of him. With a curt nod, the young brave dropped a rope around Royce Montana's neck, vaulted onto the back of his pony, and rode away. Royce Montana followed in the wake of the calico pony, his leg irons clanking with each hurried step.

The remaining Indians did not bother with the dead white men. They quickly rounded up the four-horse team that had pulled the wagon, as well as the two saddle horses the deputies had ridden, collected all the guns, rifles, and ammunition, and left the scene of the slaughter with the dead warrior tied face-down across the back of his horse.

Fearful of discovery, Lacey held her breath until the war party was out of sight. Only then did she feel it was safe to breathe again. Absently, she stroked Cinder's neck. What was she going to do now? Her father was alive, but for how long? Did she dare follow him? How could she not? Perhaps she could find a way to help him escape. The odds were against it, she thought bleakly, but she had to try. She quickly formed and rejected a half-dozen ideas, and then she laughed bitterly. What could she possibly do against a dozen armed warriors? And yet, she had to try to free her father. She couldn't stay out here alone, and she couldn't just ride away and leave her father in the hands of those savages, never to know what happened to him.

With her mind made up, Lacey stepped into the saddle and rode toward the wagon. Perhaps she could find some food and water to add to her dwindling supplies.

She swallowed hard as she urged Cinder toward the wagon. She had never been so close to death before, never seen anyone who had died violently, or seen so much blood. Already vultures were gathering in the distance, drawn by the scent of blood and death. Cinder pranced beneath her, nostrils flaring and eyes rolling as they neared the wagon.

How quickly a life could be snuffed out, Lacey thought sadly. One moment these men had been alive, filled with hopes and dreams and fears, and now they were dead.

Lacey shivered, the food she had hoped to find suddenly unimportant in the face of such carnage. Better to go hungry, she thought, than linger here a moment longer.

She was about to leave when a low moan reached her ears. Lacey cocked her head. Was she hearing things? She glanced at the bodies lying on the ground, and quickly looked away. They were all dead, and she felt her heart begin to pound. She didn't believe in ghosts, but she was suddenly afraid. And then she heard it again, a muffled cry of pain. Dear God, someone *was* alive. She urged Cinder closer to the wagon, her eyes darting from one body to the next. Was it one of the guards, she thought hopefully. Or one of the prisoners?

Dismounting, she walked cautiously among the bodies, her heart in her throat. What if it was one of the convicts? He might be a murderer, a molester of women and children, anything.

The man was lying on his back. Drawing closer, Lacey recognized him as the man who had charged the Indians. His eyes, dark as a midnight sky, were open and clouded with pain. He gazed up at her, opened his mouth to speak, and fainted dead away.

Lacey stared at him for a long moment. What was she going to do? If she stayed to help him, she would probably lose any chance she had of following her father. On the other hand, she couldn't just ride off and leave the man to die in the desert alone.

With a resentful sigh, Lacey knelt beside the injured prisoner. Unbuttoning his shirt, she contemplated his wounds. The first, high in his left shoulder, was bleeding profusely. Lifting him was an effort, but she was relieved to see that there was an exit wound in his back. The bullet had passed cleanly through his shoulder. The second wound was in his left arm also, just above the elbow. The bullet was lodged in the meaty part of his arm.

Lowering the man carefully to the ground, Lacey searched through the camp gear until she found a sharp knife, a bottle of rye whiskey, and a clean undershirt that she ripped into long strips for bandages. Then, kneeling beside the unconscious man once more, she soaked a strip of the cloth with whiskey and began to clean his wounds.

The man moaned and began to thrash about as the fiery liquid seared his flesh. One of his elbows caught Lacey full in the stomach, knocking the wind out of her. Mouth set in a determined line, she placed her hands on the man's shoulders and held him down until he lay quiet once more. Then, teeth clenched, she quickly bound the wound in his shoulder with a strip of whiskey-soaked cloth, wrapping the bandage just tight enough to stop the flow of blood.

For a moment, she sat back on her heels and stared at the wound above his elbow; then, with a grimace, she began to probe for the slug. Thankfully, it was not embedded too deep in his arm and she had it out in a matter of moments. She let the wound bleed for a moment, and then doused the shallow wound with whiskey. Deep lines of pain etched the man's face as the liquor penetrated his torn flesh.

Lacey let out a sigh of relief as she bound the wound with a strip of cloth. Thank God, that was done. Now there was nothing to do but wait.

To pass the time, she rummaged through the supplies loaded on top of the wagon. Her efforts were rewarded with a sack of coffee, a side of bacon, some hard biscuits, a couple of red apples, several cans of peaches, a good supply of red beans, a loaf of dark brown bread, and a dozen eggs.

Lacey's stomach rumbled hungrily, reminding her that she had not eaten since the night before, and she quickly scrambled down from the wagon, built a fire, and fried up some bacon and eggs, washing it down with two cups of hot coffee heavily laced with canned milk and sugar.

Feeling much better, she gathered up some blankets and covered the dead men. Then, head bowed, she murmured the Lord's Prayer and the Twenty-Third Psalm over the bodies, giving thanks all the while that her father was still alive.

A low groan interrupted Lacey's prayers, and she glanced over her shoulder to find the wounded man staring at her. Lacey hesitated a moment before going to him, a little fearful of getting too close. He was a convicted felon, after all, and while she was fairly certain he was in no condition to do her any harm, it wouldn't hurt to be careful. There was no telling what horrible crime he had been accused of, what foul deeds he had committed.

Matt Drago blinked several times, not daring to believe his eyes. Surely the young woman standing beside him was a figment of his fevered imagination. Even decked out in boy's clothing, there was no disguising the trim feminine shape of her, the soft curves. Her hair, swept away from her face, was a deep reddish-brown. Her eyes, wide-set and heavily lashed, were the color of warm chocolate. There was a smattering of freckles across

28

her cheeks and over the bridge of her tip-tilted nose, a beguiling dimple in her chin.

"How are you feeling?" Lacey asked.

"Rotten." Matt Drago glanced at the make-shift bandages on his arm and shoulder. "Thanks for patching me up."

"You're welcome," Lacey mumbled, disturbed by his steady gaze. Earlier, she had been too busy tending his wounds to give any thought to his appearance, but now she noticed he was quite handsome.

She realized with some embarrassment that she was staring at him. "Would you like something to eat?" she asked, drawing her gaze from his face.

"No."

"You really should eat something," Lacey urged. "You've lost a lot of blood."

Matt nodded. He wasn't hungry, but the girl was right. He needed nourishment. He felt as weak and helpless as a day-old pup. Not only that, but his left arm ached as if all the fires of hell blazed inside.

In an effort to ignore the pain, he watched the girl as she began to fry up a batch of bacon and eggs. She was a pretty little thing, and his eyes lingered on the provocative swell of her breasts and her shapely bottom as she knelt beside the fire. He wondered absently how old she was. Not more than seventeen or eighteen, he decided. Young. Much too young.

He dutifully ate the meal the girl prepared, drank several cups of strong black coffee, and then fell asleep.

When he woke again, it was night and the girl was sitting beside him.

Lacey smiled tentatively when she saw the prisoner was awake, but frowned when she noticed he was shaking.

"Cold," he husked.

With a nod, Lacey spread her blanket over him, then added another as chills continued to wrack his body. She thought of the blankets she had used to cover the dead men, but she could not make herself go to them in the dark, could not leave them lying dead and uncovered. Her eyes filled with concern as violent tremors shook the prisoner. Matt tried to smile reassuringly, but a low moan escaped his lips instead. His left arm and shoulder throbbed mercilessly, and he was cold, so cold. Lacey sat there for a few minutes and then, with a shrug, she crawled under the blankets and lay beside him, warming him with the heat of her body.

Later, the fever came, and he tossed fretfully, throwing the blankets aside. Lacey replaced the covers time after time, becoming more and more frightened as he began to mutter incoherently. Once he stared, unseeing, into the distance, his face a dark mask of rage as he cried, "I didn't kill him! Dammit, why won't anyone believe me?"

Another time he called for someone named Claire. Over and over again he murmured the woman's name, his voice sometimes soft and tender, sometimes filled with anger and bitter regret.

Not knowing what else to do, Lacey kept him covered as best she could. In his quiet moments, she forced him to drink as much water as he could hold, afraid he might dehydrate from the fever and from the amount of blood he had lost.

It was the longest night of her life. Thoughts of Indians and wild animals preyed on her mind, and she dozed sporadically, only to wake with a start each time the man cried out. She prayed fervently that he would be better in the morning. Her nursing skills were minimal at best. She had always been squeamish in the face of pain, and blood made her queasy. If his fever got worse, or his wound became infected, what would she do? Ride for help and leave him out here alone, prey to scavengers? Or sit by and watch him writhe in pain until he died?

With the coming of dawn, he fell into a deep sleep. Exhausted mentally and physically, Lacey stretched out beside him, and in moments she, too, was sleeping soundly.

CHAPTER 2

Matt Drago opened his eyes to find the girl pressed close beside him, her head pillowed on his right shoulder, her reddish-brown hair feeling like silk against his beard-roughened cheek. For a moment he did not move, hardly daring to breathe as he lay there studying her face for fear she would wake up. She wasn't as breathtakingly beautiful as Claire had been, he mused dispassionately, but she was a decidedly pretty girl. Her mouth was wide and generous, her nose finely chiseled with a slight upward tilt, her eyebrows a delicate arch over wide-set eyes, her lashes long and thick.

He felt a faint stirring of desire as she snuggled closer to him, her breasts pressing against his side, one slim leg slipping between his.

Matt swore softly. He had not had a woman in a long time. Claire had been a lady of quality, and he had never touched her other than to give her a lingering kiss in the moonlight. Since Claire, he had occasionally found relief for his masculine urges in the arms of women whose morals would not bear close scrutiny.

Cautiously he raised his shackled hands and stroked the girl's cheek. Her skin was warm and smooth beneath his fingertips, soft and undeniably feminine.

His touch jolted Lacey awake. For a moment, they gazed into each other's eyes. Lacey felt a peculiar shiver deep in the core of her being as his midnight blue eyes held her own. They seemed to be asking questions she was afraid to answer, yet she could not draw her gaze away from his. She noted that his lashes were short and thick and sooty black, that his eyes were the darkest blue she had ever seen. They seemed to be probing the depths of her heart, stealing her soul. . . .

With a wordless cry, Lacey scrambled to her feet, her face flushing bright crimson as she realized she had been practically lying in his arms.

Matt grinned up at her, his eyes glinting with mirth until he saw she was genuinely upset. "Sorry," he said soberly. "I didn't mean to alarm you."

"You didn't," Lacey lied, not quite meeting his steady gaze. "I . . . it was time to get up anyway. I . . . how are you feeling?"

"Better, thanks to you."

"It was nothing."

"You probably saved my life. That's something. To me, anyway. I'm in your debt."

Lacey shrugged. She did not want this man indebted to her. He was a convict, and the less she had to do with him, the better. Besides, she did not like the way he was looking at her, or the way her insides turned to soft mush whenever his eyes met hers.

"How about finding the key to these cuffs?" Matt asked, holding up his shackled hands.

Lacey took a wary step backward. "No."

"Why not?"

"Because I . . . because."

Matt sat up, his head cocked to one side. "You're not afraid of me, are you?" he challenged.

"Of course not," Lacey replied quickly. Too quickly.

Before he could argue further, she went to start breakfast. She *was* afraid of him, she admitted to herself, but not in the way he thought. She didn't think he would harm her physically, but there was something about him that disturbed her deeply. He aroused feelings within her that she was not certain she cared for, feelings she could not put a name to. Feelings she was afraid to examine too closely. She felt her cheeks redden as she recalled the way he had gazed into her eyes, his own eyes dark and turbulent with some emotion Lacey could not identify.

Breakfast was a silent meal. Lacey's thoughts were centered on her father. Was he still alive? How could she ever find him now? What would she do without him? She had nowhere to go, no one to turn to. For the first time, it occurred to her that she was all alone in the world. It was a scary thought, knowing there was no one to care if she lived or died, no one who would mourn her, no one to cherish her memory.

She stole a furtive glance at the man sitting across the fire from her. How much longer would she have to stay with him before he was well enough to make it on his own? Did she dare just ride off and leave him out here, alone and on foot? He was in no fit condition to make the long trek back to Salt Creek. Of course, when the prison wagon didn't arrive at the penitentiary at the scheduled time, someone would likely come looking for it. Would he be able to survive out here alone until then? Probably not.

Darn her soft heart! She could not bring herself to leave him out here alone. But then, she had always had a tender spot in her heart for orphans and wounded things. Stray dogs and cats, birds with broken wings, injured rabbits and squirrels—she had always taken them home to nurse until they were well enough to return to the wild. Maybe her father had been right. Maybe she should have been a nurse after all.

"Who's Claire?" Lacey asked abruptly.

Matt Drago frowned. "How do you know about her?"

"You called for her when you were unconscious."

"Oh."

Lacey waited for him to go on, but he didn't seem inclined to elaborate.

"Is she your wife?" Lacey asked, knowing it was none of her business, yet unable to curb her curiosity.

"I'm not married."

"Your sweetheart?"

"She's nothing to me," Matt answered curtly. "Just a girl I used to know."

"I'm sorry. I didn't mean to pry," Lacey said, unable to explain why she was so pleased to learn he wasn't married or engaged.

"What's your name, anyway?"

"Lacey," she answered somewhat shyly. "Lacey Montana."

"Matt Drago." He looked at her curiously. "Why were you following the wagon?"

"My father was on it. The Indians took him away. As soon as you're . . . as soon as someone comes for you, I'm going after him."

"After your father?" Matt exclaimed in surprise.

"Yes."

"You can't go traipsing off after those Apaches by yourself," he scoffed. "They'd grab you so fast, it would make your head spin."

"I don't care!" Lacey replied hotly. "They have my father, and I intend to help him in any way I can."

"It's your life," Matt muttered. "I guess you can throw it away if you want. It's up to you. But you won't be able to save your old man, and you'll just end up getting yourself killed, or worse, if you try."

"It's no concern of yours," Lacey retorted. But Matt's words were so near to her own thoughts, she felt a sense of hopelessness. And then she brightened as a new thought occurred to her. "When the men from Yuma come looking for the wagon, perhaps they'll help me find my father."

Matt Drago frowned. The girl was right. When the prison wagon didn't show up at Yuma, someone would come looking for it. And for him, as well. He scowled at his shackled hands. Well, he for damn sure didn't intend to be sitting around waiting for them.

37

No, sir! He was heading back to Salt Creek to find out who set him up for the murder of young Billy Henderson just as soon as he could travel.

Matt sipped the last of his coffee thoughtfully. The Indians had taken the wagon team and the lawmen's horses, but the girl had a horse, a good-looking quarter-horse mare. He stared into his empty cup. Of course, he couldn't very well take the horse and leave the girl out here alone. She had saved his life, after all. Well, there was no help for it, she would just have to go back to Salt Creek with him whether she liked it or not. Maybe Sheriff Henderson would help her track her old man.

He would rest up another day or so, Matt decided, and then be on his way long before anyone from Yuma arrived on the scene. And woe to the men who had falsely accused him of killing Billy Henderson.

He slept most of the day. Once, upon waking, he saw Lacey brushing out her long, russet-colored hair. He watched, mesmerized, as she pulled the brush through the heavy silken mass. It was a decidedly feminine gesture, graceful and innocently provocative. He remembered how soft her hair had felt against his cheek earlier that day, and he had a sudden urge to run his fingers through her hair, to massage the back of her slender neck, to taste those pouting pink lips.

Feeling his gaze, Lacey turned to find Matt staring at her, his dark blue eyes alight with a mysterious inner fire. What was he thinking, she wondered. Unaccountably, her insides began to tremble under the force of his gaze.

"What's wrong?" she asked.

"Nothing." His voice sounded strange in his ears.

Self-conscious now, Lacey put her hairbrush away. Rising, she walked away from the wagon until she was out of sight behind some scrub oak. Why had he looked at her like that? And why had she reacted in such a peculiar way?

Abruptly, she recalled the way some of the men back at the ranch had looked at her, their eyes bright, intent, as they watched her. She recalled the way they had smiled at her. And she remembered her father warning her to stay away from the men, saying they only wanted one thing from a girl. She knew what he meant by that. Her mother had told her all about men and women and the intimate side of life.

"Hang onto your virginity, Lacey," her mother had admonished. "It's a rare prize, and one that should be saved for your husband. No other man deserves it. And no decent, God-fearing man will try to take it from you."

Was that what Matt Drago wanted from

her? The thought repelled and excited her even as she vowed to stay out of his reach. Perversely, it warmed her to think he found her desirable.

Troubled, she sat down on a log, her elbows resting on her knees, her chin cradled in the palms of her hands. He was quite a handsome man, she mused idly. His hair was as black as ten feet down, his eyes as dark as the sky at midnight. His mouth was full-lipped, sensuous; his jaw, strong and square, was covered with thick black bristles, giving him the look of a Barbary Coast pirate. She recalled, with a blush, that his skin was smooth and unblemished, and that his arms were corded with muscle. His belly was as flat as a tabletop, his chest was covered with curly black hair. . . .

Lacey quickly pulled her thoughts away from such unladylike musings. The man was a convicted felon, and the sooner she got away from him, the better.

She was about to slide off the log and return to camp when she saw the snake. It was coiled in the sun only a few feet from where she sat, its triangular-shaped head facing in her direction, its eyes black and menacing. A warning buzz of its tail held her frozen in place.

Swallowing hard, Lacey glanced over her shoulder, thinking she could climb over the log and escape, but a thick tangle of thorny brush blocked her path. Fighting a growing sense of panic, she looked at the snake again, let out a small scream as its forked tongue darted toward her.

Matt Drago was searching through the pockets of one of the slain deputies, looking for the key to the handcuffs, when he heard Lacey's cry of alarm. Cursing under his breath, he delved into the lawman's shirt pocket, his stomach churning as the smell of decaying flesh filled his nostrils. He uttered an exclamation of relief as his fingers closed around a ring of keys, and he quickly removed the irons from his hands and feet. Each movement sent a stab of pain jolting through his wounded arm, but he ignored it as he quickly followed Lacey's tracks, cussing mightily because he didn't have a gun. A hell of a lot of help he'd be if she was in real trouble, he mused sourly. No gun and a bum arm. Damn! Leave it to a woman to get into trouble a hundred miles in the middle of nowhere.

He found her sitting on a log, her legs drawn up under her, her face as pale as death as she stared at the rattlesnake poised within striking distance.

"Don't move," Matt said quietly. "When he realizes you're not food and you're not a threat, he'll leave. Just be patient."

Easy for you to say, Lacey thought wryly. She continued to stare at the snake in fascinated awe. It looked so menacing, its black

41

eyes staring at her, unblinking, its forked tongue darting out to test the air. She recalled the time when one of the men on the Double L had been bitten. He had been found hours later when it was too late for anyone to help him. His leg had swollen to twice its normal size and turned black. He had died a horrible death.

Frozen with fear, Lacey could not take her eyes from the snake. Terror older than time itself held her in its grasp, and then she heard Matt's voice again, deep and soothing, tinged with a slight Southern accent.

"Don't panic, Lacey. Just sit tight and you'll be fine, I promise."

Lacey nodded, not really believing him.

"Look at the flowers, Lacey. Over there, behind the snake."

Lacey shook her head, certain the snake would attack her when she wasn't looking.

Matt frowned thoughtfully, wondering what he could say to take Lacey's mind off the rattler, and then he grinned.

"The Apache are an interesting people," he mused. "For instance, they believe that any Apache who marries a Ute will turn into an owl when he dies."

"An owl?" Lacey said, still watching the snake.

"Yeah. And if an Apache marries a Navajo, he'll turn into a mountain lion. Worst of all would be marrying a Mexican. Any Apache who married a Mexican would be reborn as a burro, and if he married a paleface, he'd come back as a mule."

Lacey looked at Matt, a tremulous smile on her face. "You're making that up."

Matt shook his head. "No, it's true."

"It's nonsense."

"Maybe, but it makes the young Apache bucks and maidens think twice about marrying out of the tribe."

Lacey chuckled, the snake momentarily forgotten.

"It's okay now," Matt said as the snake slithered into the underbrush.

Timidly, Lacey placed one foot on the ground, her eyes focused on the spot where the snake had disappeared, her whole body tense. Perhaps the snake was only hiding, waiting for her to move so it could strike.

"It's okay, Lacey," Matt assured her. "Trust me."

Cautiously she placed her other foot on the ground, then stood up and ran toward Matt, who suddenly seemed like the only safe haven in all the world. His arms closed around her, strong and supportive, and the fear slowly drained out of her limbs. His hand lightly stroked her hair as he quietly assured her that the danger was past.

It felt so good, standing in the shelter of his

embrace. His voice was low and soothing, his breath warm where it brushed her cheek. She felt so safe, so protected, as though nothing could ever hurt her again.

Matt felt the stirrings of desire as he held Lacey in his arms. The scent of her filled his nostrils, her hair felt like fine silk in his hand, her breasts were warm against his chest. He felt his muscles begin to tense as he fought off the urge to lower her gently to the ground and cover her face with kisses. Only the throbbing ache in his arm, and the fact that she trusted him so completely, kept him from possessing her.

Gradually, as her fears subsided, Lacey became aware of Matt's ragged breathing, of the tension in his arms.

"I . . . thank you," she murmured, drawing away from him. "I'm terrified of snakes. I saw a man die from a rattlesnake bite once. It was horrible."

Matt nodded, and Lacey thought he looked suddenly pale. "You shouldn't be up," she admonished, her voice sharper than she intended. "You're still weak."

"I'm alright."

Arms akimbo, Lacey looked at him, her eyes filled with doubt.

"I am a little tired," Matt confessed. "Think you could help me back to camp?"

"Of course."

"Good." Smiling at her, he draped his right arm around her shoulders. It was only then that Lacey realized he had somehow managed to remove the shackles from his hands and feet.

Walking back to camp, she was very much aware of Matt's leg brushing against her own, of the length and breadth of him beside her. He was quite tall, taller than she had imagined. Her head barely reached his shoulder. But he was more than just tall. He was big-boned and broad-shouldered, making her feel small and helpless.

"You make a good crutch," Matt remarked when they reached his bedroll.

"Thanks," Lacey muttered. "How long do you think it will take for the men from Yuma to get here?"

"I don't know," Matt replied curtly. "And I don't aim to wait around to find out."

"What do you mean?"

"I mean I'm leaving. First thing in the morning."

"Leaving? Where will you go?"

"Back to Salt Creek. I've got some unfinished business there."

Lacey frowned at him. "You don't mean to walk all that way?" she exclaimed. "Not in your condition."

"I don't intend to walk."

Lacey mulled that over for a moment, then

gasped as realization struck her. "Oh, no," she said, shaking her head at him. "You're not taking my horse."

Matt nodded slowly. "Your horse. And you."

Lacey shook her head again. "No. I'm going after my father. I don't care what you do."

"I'm afraid you don't have any choice in the matter," Matt said firmly.

"Oh, really?" Lacey retorted. "Well, we'll just see about that." And so saying, she ran toward Cinder, grabbed the halter rope, and swung onto the mare's bare back, intending to ride away from Matt Drago as quickly as possible.

She screamed in bitter protest as Matt's hands closed around her waist and yanked her from Cinder's back.

"Put me down!" Lacey shrieked, pummeling Matt's face and chest with her puny fists. "Put me down this instant!"

Matt's hands tightened around Lacey's waist as he tried to avoid her angry fists. He swore under his breath as her fist smashed into his nose. Lacey gasped as she saw a thin trickle of blood oozing from Matt's nostrils. Good Lord, had she broken his nose? Well, it served him right!

"Let me go," she demanded, and when he still refused to release her, she began to kick him, her booted feet slamming into his shins.

"Damn you, you little hellcat!" Matt

growled. "Cut it out before I take you over my knee and teach you some manners."

"Manners! Oh, I wish I were a man, Matt Drago! I'd teach *you* some manners," she cried petulantly, and when he still refused to unhand her, she lashed out at him, her fist striking his wounded shoulder with all the force at her command.

Matt released her immediately, a vile oath erupting from between his clenched teeth as bright shafts of pain danced up and down the length of his arm.

Lacey's moment of triumph quickly turned to remorse when she saw how pale Matt's face was, and noticed the bright red blood seeping from under the bandage on his shoulder.

"Oh, Matt," she murmured, instantly contrite. "I'm sorry. Here, sit down and let me look at your arm."

He didn't argue, only sat down heavily, his lips compressed into a tight line, his dark eyes glazed with pain.

"Does it hurt?" Lacey asked anxiously.

"What the hell do you think?" Matt rasped.

With gentle hands, Lacey removed the sodden bandage. The wound was bleeding again, and it was all her fault. Silently chastising herself for taking unfair advantage of him, she made a clean dressing and pressed it firmly over the angry wound, then wrapped it with a strip of clean cloth.

"I'm sorry, Matt," she said again. "Truly I am."

"I'm sorry, too," Matt grated, and before Lacey was quite aware of what he was about, he had caught both her hands in one of his and tied her wrists together with the bloody bandage she had removed from his arm.

"Oh!" Lacey cried in exasperation. "You're despicable, you swine! I hope they hang you! Twice!"

"I need that horse, Lacey," Matt explained calmly. "I can't leave you out here alone. And I don't intend to spend the rest of my life cooling my heels in the Yuma pen for something I didn't do."

Lacey made a face at him. "Don't *all* convicted men claim they're innocent?"

"I guess so," Matt allowed wearily. "I don't know about anyone else. All I know is that I didn't kill that kid." He shook his head ruefully. "At least, I'm pretty sure I didn't."

"Pretty sure?"

"I was drunk. But, dammit, I couldn't have killed a man and forgotten it. I've never been *that* drunk."

"What are you going to do with me?" Lacey asked, tugging against the cloth that bound her wrists together.

"I'll take you back to Salt Creek with me, and then you're on your own."

Lacey shook her head, tears welling in her eyes. "No, Matt, please. I've got to go after my father. Don't you understand? I've got to find him. He's all the family I have left in the world. I can't spend the rest of my life wondering what happened to him, wondering if he's dead or alive."

Matt felt a tug at his heart as he looked at Lacey, her cheeks stained with tears, her hands bound with a bloody rag, her eyes wide and pleading. How could he refuse her? She had saved his life, after all. What if it was *his* father the Indians had taken? Wouldn't he move heaven and earth to try to rescue him? Why should Lacey Montana feel differently just because she was a girl?

With a sigh, Matt gave in. "All right, Lacey. I'll help you look for your father. We'll start at first light."

"Thank you, Matt," she said sincerely. "Will you untie me now, please?"

"No."

"No?"

"No. I think I'll rest a mite easier knowing you can't pick up and leave in the middle of the night."

Lacey ranted for several minutes, calling Matt Drago every vile name she could think of, but he refused to change his mind, and in the end she sank down on her blankets and fumed in angry silence. The gall of the man! Tying her up like she was some kind of criminal.

Her eyes blazed with silent fury when he solicitously covered her with a blanket.

"Sleep tight," he murmured, and smiled when she stuck her tongue out at him.

CHAPTER 3

Matt Drago dismounted and studied the ground, his eyes narrowed in concentration. The trail was three days old, but still clear. The Indians were moving at a slow but steady pace, always heading south. Royce Montana was still on foot. Still alive. So far.

Matt frowned as he swung back into the saddle. They were on a fool's errand, he thought darkly. Even if they found the Indian camp, they had little chance of rescuing Lacey's father. They had no weapons other than a knife Matt had found on one of the dead lawmen, and he was doubtful if one man armed with a knife and one little bit of a girl would intimidate the Indians. The Apaches were as hard as nails, ruthless as a cornered lobo. They had little respect for anyone or anything that was not of the Dineh, the People, as they called themselves. Their men were among the most savage, the most warlike, of all the tribes in the Southwest. They had little regard for horseflesh and often ran a horse to death, then ate the carcass. Only children seemed to hold a soft spot in Apache hearts, and the Indians welcomed young ones of any race into the tribe, treating them as their own. Apache women owned the lodge and all its belongings save for her warrior's weapons. She raised the children, and she often fought at her husband's side, as valiant and fearless as her man.

Matt shook his head ruefully. He had been a fool to agree to take Lacey after her father and yet, he had been like putty in her hands. One look into those wistful brown eyes and he had been hooked and helpless. She was so young, so damned innocent. So vulnerable.

They rode for several hours, not talking much. Lacey rode behind Matt, her arms around his lean waist. She tried not to touch him any more than necessary, but every now and then her breasts rubbed against his broad back. Once, she dozed off, only to wake with her cheek pillowed comfortably on his back. Embarrassed, she had straightened up immediately. She thought she heard him chuckle softly as she pulled away, but she couldn't be sure.

He was a hard man, she thought, hard and unforgiving. She had expected him to bury the dead men before they left the site of the slaughter, but he just shook his head when she suggested it.

"They never did me any favors," he had said laconically.

"But—"

"But nothing. My arm's sore as hell as it is. I'm not gonna make it worse by digging a grave for those bastards," he had explained coldly, and then he had grinned at her. "Besides, the wolves and the vultures have to eat, too, same as the worms."

Matt reined Cinder to a halt shortly after noon, and while he took care of the horse, Lacey prepared a quick, cold lunch.

"Do you think we'll find him?" Lacey asked, hoping for some reassurance.

Matt shrugged. "I don't know. It depends on how well the trail holds up." He took a deep breath, let it out slowly. He didn't want to discourage her, but she needed to be prepared for the worst. "Listen, Lacey, your father's chances are pretty slim. The Apache aren't the most forgiving people in the world, and the whites have been treating them pretty bad over the last few years. They might . . . I mean, your father could be in for a rough time. He might even be dead. I think you'd best be prepared for that."

Slowly, Lacey shook her head. "No. He's all right. I know he is. He has to be."

"I hope you're right, for your sake," Matt replied kindly. He gestured toward her saddlebag. "You don't happen to have a gun in there, do you?"

Lacey stared at him. She *did* have a gun. She had forgotten all about it until now. Her father had given it to her when they moved West. He had patiently taught her how to load and clean the weapon, and instructed her in how to fire it if necessary. Occasionally she had even hit what she aimed at. But she did not like firearms, and she had only kept the deadly little weapon because it made her father feel better to know she had it if she needed it.

"I . . . it's just a little derringer," Lacey answered. "My father gave it to me."

"Is it loaded?"

"Of course it's loaded. What good is an unloaded gun?"

"Not much," Matt muttered. "Mind if I take a look at it?"

"Help yourself. It's in my saddlebag."

Matt Drago's spirits lifted about 110 percent as he rummaged around in Lacey's gear. The gun was just a little two-shot over-and-under derringer. It was obviously a lady's

54

weapon. Lightweight, small in size, with carved pearl handles. It fit snugly in the palm of his hand.

"Any extra shells?"

"A box," Lacey said.

Matt found the extra ammunition and dumped a handful into his pants pocket. At least they were no longer totally defenseless, although the gun wasn't much good for long-range shooting. Still, it was better than nothing.

After lunch, Matt picked up the trail again. He swore under his breath as the tracks changed.

"What is it?" Lacey asked anxiously.

"Your old man's not walking any more. Either they've put him on a horse because he was slowing them down too much, or . . ." He didn't finish the sentence.

"Or they've killed him," Lacey said in a small voice.

Matt nodded. It was what he had been afraid of all along, and his eyes swept the countryside, searching for some sign of a body. The Indians wouldn't bother to bury Lacey's old man. If he were out there on the desert somewhere, there would be vultures in the sky if the body was fresh, scattered remains if the scavengers had finished with him.

"He couldn't straddle a horse with shackles on his feet," Lacey said. Her eyes, big and brown, looked to Matt for a thread of hope, no matter how tenuous.

Matt couldn't stand to see the hurt in her eyes, or the way her slight shoulders sagged in defeat. "They might have dumped him face down over the back of a horse," Matt ventured, injecting a note of cheerfulness into his tone. "It's not the most comfortable way to travel, but it's a possibility. It doesn't seem likely they'd haul him all this way and then kill him before they reached their destination."

"That's true," Lacey agreed, brightening. "Oh, Matt, let's hurry."

They rode until nightfall. Lacey thought constantly of her father, praying that he was safe. In spite of his drinking, in spite of his many failings, he was her father and she loved him dearly.

That night they made camp in the shelter of a grove of stunted cottonwoods. Lacey made dinner while Matt unsaddled and curried the mare. Lacey watched Matt from the corner of her eye as the beans and bacon simmered over the fire, noting the way he talked to the horse, the gentle way his hands moved over Cinder's coat as he ran the brush briskly over her sleek black hide. He checked the mare's legs, cleaned her feet, ran his hands skillfully over her shoes to make sure they were still tight.

He was a remarkable man, Lacey mused.

She knew his arm must still be sore, but he never complained. He rode effortlessly, tirelessly, and she had to admire his strength and stamina, as well as his knowledge about surviving in the wilderness. And he was a handsome man, more handsome than any man she had ever known. The firelight danced in his black hair, and she could not help but notice the rhythmic play of corded muscles beneath his shirt as he gave Cinder a vigorous rubdown. He had been awfully kind, Lacey thought. Perhaps he wasn't such a bad sort after all. And yet, he had been accused and convicted of killing a man. Probably he was guilty. If so, why wasn't she afraid to be out here in the middle of nowhere with him? She should be scared out of her wits, afraid for her very life, but she wasn't. She was certain that Matt Drago would protect her from any harm that threatened her, just as he had protected her from the snake.

Some of her confidence waned when he came to sit beside her. He was so tall, his shoulders so broad, his arms thick with muscle, that she felt dwarfed sitting beside him. He was so virile, so terribly masculine.

She didn't quite meet his eyes as she handed him a plate of beans, bacon, and biscuits, then busied herself with her own meal. She could feel Matt's eyes watching her, and color washed into her cheeks. Why was he staring at her like that? What was he thinking?

"That's a good horse you've got there," Matt remarked, hoping to ease the tension building between them.

"Yes. Mr. Webster gave her to me for my birthday."

"Webster?"

"He owned the ranch where my father worked before . . . before he was arrested."

Matt didn't pursue the matter. He could see by the expression on Lacey's face that she didn't want to discuss it further.

Matt poured himself a cup of coffee and filled Lacey's cup. She sipped the hot, bitter brew slowly, and he watched her surreptitiously. She was quite a girl. She hadn't complained once since he'd met her. Not about taking care of him, not about the long hours they spent in the saddle, not about the sameness of the food they ate or the hard ground they slept on.

Feeling Matt's gaze, Lacey glanced up. Why was he looking at her like that, as if she had done something wonderful? Her stomach started to flutter in the most peculiar way, as if a million winged creatures were trapped inside. Warmth flooded her limbs and crept up into her cheeks, and she licked her lips nervously, wondering why her mouth was suddenly so dry.

"I . . . I'm going to turn in," she stammered. "I . . . it's been a long day."

Matt nodded. "Good night, Lacey."

"Good night."

But, tucked snugly beneath her blankets, Lacey could not sleep. Her gaze was drawn toward Matt, and she watched from behind the veil of her lashes as he banked the fire, then walked slowly around the perimeter of their camp, his dark eyes searching the shadows, his ears listening to the sounds of the night. Satisfied that there was no danger lurking nearby, he sat down on his bedroll and checked the derringer.

Lacey continued to watch him, fascinated by his hands as they moved knowingly over the gun, then slid the weapon back into his pocket. His hands were large, with long fingers. They were remarkably gentle hands at times, she mused, and felt a tickle of excitement in the pit of her stomach as she recalled how soothing those hands had been as they lightly stroked her back the day she had encountered the rattlesnake. There was strength in Matt's hands; strength and comfort. She experienced a sense of shame as she found herself wishing he would hold her in his arms again. Hold her and kiss her and . . . she pulled her wayward thoughts away from such wicked daydreams. What would he think if he knew she was yearning for his touch? Likely he would laugh, or, worse yet, take advantage of her.

She held her breath as Matt's gaze swung in her direction, her cheeks flaming because of what she had been thinking.

Matt smiled faintly, and then he crawled between his own blankets. "Go to sleep, Lacey," he called softly.

Wordlessly she let out her breath in a long, angry sigh. He had known all along that she had been watching him! Humiliation washed over her, making her feel as if her very soul had been laid bare to his mocking eyes.

Sleep was a long time coming.

Lacey stared at the remains of the Indian village, her expression one of utter dismay. "Where have they gone?"

Matt shrugged. "Beats the hell out of me. Likely moved on toward their winter camp."

Dismounting, he walked through the deserted campsite. Nothing was left now but the remains of many campfires, a few lodgepoles, the skull of a deer, a few scraps of rawhide, and mounds of waste.

Matt chewed his lower lip thoughtfully as he wandered through the abandoned village. There were many pony and travois tracks, and he followed them for some distance, then cursed aloud. The Indians had split into two groups, one bunch heading south toward the border, the other heading toward the Territory of New Mexico. Why had they split up? Were both groups Apache, or had the Apache spent the summer with another tribe? He studied the divided tracks, hoping to find some clear moccasin prints, but to no avail.

"Well, that's it," he muttered. "We'll head back to Salt Creek first thing in the morning."

"Head back?" Lacey exclaimed. "Why?"

"Because the Indians have split up, that's why," Matt retorted. "There's no telling which bunch has your father."

"But—"

"But nothing," Matt interrupted irritably. "We tried to find him and we failed. Personally, I'm tired of hauling my ass over half of Arizona. Tomorrow we're going back to Salt Creek, I'm going to clear my name of that murder charge and get on with my life."

"But we can't give up now," Lacey argued stubbornly. "We're so close."

"We're no closer now than we ever were. I told you before, your chances of finding him were slim, and they're worse now."

Lacey squared her shoulders. "Listen to me, Matt Drago, we're not turning back, not until we find my father. You promised. But if you want to turn back, you just go right ahead. Of course, it's a long walk back to Salt Creek."

Matt scowled at her. Stubborn ornery female. She wanted everything her way. But it was true he had promised to help her find her father.

"Please, Matt."

He glared at her, his anger slowly draining away when he saw the expression on her face. Damn! She looked like a little girl who had just discovered there was no Santa Claus.

Muttering an oath, Matt gazed into the distance. Assuming that both sets of tracks belonged to the Apache, which group had Lacey's father in tow (assuming he was still alive), the small group headed for the border, or the larger group headed for New Mexico?

"What is it?" Lacey asked, coming to stand beside him.

Matt gestured at the tracks. "There's no way to tell which bunch has your father."

"What are we going to do?"

"Beats the hell out of me. We can't follow both trails, and while we're following one set of tracks, the other's going to get cold." Matt glanced northward. "It'll be winter in a few more weeks."

"And the rain will wash out all the tracks," Lacey said, finishing his thought.

"Right."

"Well, we've got to do something."

"Yeah." Matt walked along one set of tracks

for several yards, then crossed to the other. "I don't know," he muttered, shaking his head. "He's your father. You decide."

"Which direction would you go?"

Matt shrugged. "The Apaches generally spend the winter across the border, and they usually travel in small groups. I'd say go south."

"South, then," Lacey agreed.

Matt nodded. Moments later, they were riding toward the border.

Three days later they reached the outskirts of a small town. Lacey objected to stopping, wanting to stay on the trail while it was clear and easy to follow, but Matt was adamant. They needed food. He needed a horse and a better weapon than Lacey's little derringer. And they were going to need some warm clothing.

Lacey grimaced as they rode down the narrow dusty street. It was an ugly little town. The buildings were run-down and shabby, the paint peeling and faded. She counted four saloons on one side of the street, two on the other. A single hotel was situated in the center of town. There were no houses in evidence, nor did there appear to be a law office, or a church.

"I don't suppose you've got any money?"

Matt remarked, and Lacey regretfully shook her head.

"Well, then, we'll just have to pawn your saddle and hope my luck's good at the card table."

"Are you a gambler?" Lacey asked in surprise.

"Only when I have to be."

"Are you any good?" Lacey asked dubiously.

"Good enough."

"And what happens if you aren't good enough? My father paid a lot of money for that saddle. I don't want to lose it."

"We're doing this for your father," Matt reminded her. "Come on, let's see how much we can get for your rig."

Lacey followed Matt into a dingy store between two small saloons. She stayed near the doorway while Matt bargained with the owner, a ruddy-faced man with a bulbous nose and yellow teeth.

They haggled for quite some time. Matt was muttering under his breath when he stalked out of the building.

"Damn thief," he growled. "Come on, let's go get some grub."

There was a tiny restaurant wedged between a saloon and a vacant building near the end of town. Lacey was terribly self-conscious as she followed Matt into the place. No lady would ever dream of appearing in public wearing pants, but Matt had given her no opportunity to change.

She kept her head down as he ordered steak and potatoes for the two of them. The woman who took their order gave Lacey a look of disdain, but she was all smiles when she looked at Matt.

"After we eat, we'll get a room and get cleaned up," Matt said, thinking aloud. "And then I'll go find a card game while you get some sleep."

"I'm not staying anywhere in this town alone," Lacey informed him. "I'll bet the whole place is crawling with outlaws."

"You're probably right," Matt allowed, "but ladies don't frequent saloons."

"They don't ride astride or wear pants, either," Lacey retorted.

Matt glared at her across the table. What a stubborn creature she was, always wanting things her own way—and getting it.

Their dinner arrived a few minutes later and Matt attacked his steak with a vengeance. It was the first decent meal he'd had in months. The food back in the Salt Creek jail hadn't been anything to brag about. Considering the circumstances, he supposed he had been lucky the sheriff had fed him at all. He had spent six weeks in that damn cell, waiting for the wagon that would transport him to Yuma. It had been a long six weeks. Nothing to do but pace back and forth, or sit on the edge of his bunk and count the bricks in the wall. Time and time again he had thought about that night in the saloon. And, thinking about it now, he wondered if someone had deliberately set him up to take the fall. He had been a stranger in town. There had only been five other men in the saloon that night: the three men who had accused him, young Billy Henderson, and the barkeep, all long-time residents of Salt Creek. Henderson was dead, and the barkeep had refused to testify except to say he hadn't seen anything. But the other three men had said enough. More than enough.

Lost in thought, Matt finished the rest of his meal without tasting it. They could have drugged his whiskey, killed the kid, and laid the blame on him. He frowned as he tried to recall that night. Vaguely he remembered talking to Billy Henderson. The kid had been a loud-mouthed braggart, overly proud of his iron, a flashy blue-steel Navy Colt with inlaid pearl handles. Matt remembered telling the kid that a fancy gun didn't make a gunfighter, and the kid had started boasting about what a crack shot he was. Already killed a man, he had said smugly, and Matt had thought he looked more than ready to kill another one. . . .

"What?" he glanced up as he realized Lacey was speaking to him.

"I said I'm ready to go."

"Yeah, me too." Matt dropped a few coins on the table, flashed a smile at their waitress as he picked up his hat, and followed Lacey outside.

"What were you thinking about in there?" Lacey asked. "You looked like you were a million miles away."

"Nothing," Matt said.

After leaving Lacey's mare at the livery barn, they walked along the dusty street to the hotel. The lobby was large and bare. Faded blue and gold wallpaper that might once have been pretty covered the walls. A stout man wearing a red shirt, dirty brown twill trousers, and a black bowler hat stood behind the reception desk. An old Walker Colt was shoved into the waistband of his trousers. A large black cigar was clamped between his teeth.

"Help you?" the man asked in a bored tone.

"I'd like a room," Matt replied. "And a bathtub, if you've got one."

"There's a tub in Room 17," the man said. He took a large brass key from a peg on the wall behind the desk and tossed it to Matt. "It'll cost you an extra two bits for the tub, and

67

another two bits for hot water. Payable in advance."

"Fine." Matt tossed the man fifty cents.

"I'll have Rosa bring the water up when it's hot." The man jerked a calloused thumb toward the staircase. "Your room's at the top of the stairs on the left."

"Obliged," Matt said.

Lacey felt her cheeks grow hot as the man behind the desk leered at her. Of course, the man had no way of knowing that she and Matt were not married, but *she* knew. She hurried up the stairs after Matt, wishing they had never come to this place. Everything looked so sleazy, so temporary.

Room 17 was small and square. There was no furniture other than a sagging double bed and a scarred oak commode. The tub stood in one corner, hidden by a garishly painted screen. A cobweb fluttered in one corner of the ceiling.

With a look of disgust, Lacey sat down on the edge of the bed. The barn back in Salt Creek had been cleaner and smelled better than this place. Removing her hat, she ran her fingers through her hair. It would be so good to take a bath and wash her hair. She had never been so dirty in her whole life. Pulling off her boots and stockings, she stretched her legs and wiggled her toes. It was wonderful to sit on something other than a horse or the hard ground for a change.

Looking up, she saw Matt watching her. For a moment she had forgotten he was in the room, but it suddenly dawned on her that she was actually in a hotel room alone with a man who was not her husband—and that there was only one bed. A guilty flush stained her cheeks. No unmarried woman was *ever* alone with a man. Lacey's mother had drummed that into her head time after time. That she had been alone with Matt out on the prairie for the last week did not seem near as shocking as the thought of spending one night with him in a hotel room. The bed, the four walls that surrounded them, all conspired to make this setting far more intimate than sharing a campfire.

Matt grinned roguishly at Lacey. It was easy to see what she was thinking. Her consternation at being alone with him in a sleazy hotel room was plainly written across her face.

"You're the one who said she wouldn't stay anyplace in this town alone," Matt reminded her, "but I'll get another room if it will make you feel better."

Lacey shook her head. Better to defy convention and spend the night with Matt than spend the night alone in a strange hotel room in a strange town.

Moments later, a rather plump Mexican woman entered the room carrying two buckets of hot water. Two sturdy young boys trailed at her heels, each bearing a bucket of water.

The woman glanced at Lacey, then at Matt, and smiled a knowing smile before leaving the room. The boys followed on silent feet.

Lacey gazed longingly at the steaming bathtub, and then glared at Matt. "Well?"

"Well, what?"

"You don't intend to stay in here while I bathe, do you?" Lacey demanded indignantly.

"I thought you didn't want to be alone," Matt replied, stifling a grin.

"You could wait out in the hall," Lacey suggested hopefully.

"I'll wait on the bed," Matt decided. He was sitting down as he spoke, pulling off his boots and socks, wriggling his toes. "The screen will protect your maidenly modesty."

"But—"

"I won't look, I promise."

With an exasperated sigh, Lacey stepped behind the screen and began to undress, listening all the while for the sound of Matt's footsteps sneaking up on her. Could she trust him to behave like a gentleman? She almost laughed out loud. A gentleman, indeed! The man was a convicted felon, a gambler, and Heaven only knew what else.

Reluctant as she was to trust him, the call of the water was too strong to resist, and she sank down in the tub, closing her eyes as the deliciously hot water covered her. Never had hot water felt so wonderful. She soaked a long while, bathed leisurely, and then washed and rinsed her hair. Belatedly, she realized she had neglected to bring a towel behind the screen with her.

"Matt?"

"Yeah?"

He sounded drowsy and she wondered if he had been napping.

"I need some towels."

"Oh."

Was it her imagination, or did he sound suddenly wide awake?

"Could you please throw me a couple?"

"Sure, Lacey."

"You won't look!"

"Not if you don't want me to," he answered with regret.

"Thank you, Matt."

"For what?"

"For being so understanding."

"Yeah." Matt tossed two towels over the screen, trying not to imagine what Lacey looked like in the bathtub. There was a splash as she stood up, and a sudden heat suffused him as he pictured her standing in the tub

71

drying off, her skin all smooth and sleek, her hair trailing wetly down her back.

Suddenly restless, he began to pace the tiny room, his hands jammed deep into his pockets. How could he spend the night cooped up in this little room with Lacey and not touch her? He hadn't had a woman for so long, he could probably qualify to be a monk.

Minutes later, Lacey stepped out from behind the screen dressed in her trail clothes, her hair wrapped in a towel. Her skin, washed clean, glowed a healthy golden tan. Her eyes, brown as mother earth, were shy when they met his.

"The water's still warm," she said. It was difficult to speak when he looked at her like that, his dark eyes dancing with a deep inner fire that she was reluctant to recognize.

"Thanks." He stepped past her, careful not to touch her. Damn that outfit! It clearly defined every sweet curve of her body. The pants hugged her trim legs and thighs and softly rounded bottom like a second skin, while the shirt clearly outlined her full breasts. His palms were sweaty when he sank into the tub, willing himself to think of something else.

He sat in the bathtub until the water was cold, hoping it would cool his wayward thoughts. Telling himself all the while it was only lust he felt for her, nothing more. Reminding himself that he was far too old for her, and that he was an escaped convict as well.

Nothing worked. The simple fact remained that he wanted her more than he had ever wanted any woman he had known. If only she were older, wiser in the ways of men. But she wasn't. She was sweet. So damned sweet. And so trusting. It was the only thing that saved her.

He sat in the cold water until the visible evidence of his desire for her was gone. He was in a foul mood when he stepped out of the bathtub and pulled on his shirt and pants.

"I thought you'd drowned," Lacey remarked when Matt finally emerged from behind the screen.

"Sorry to disappoint you," Matt muttered irritably.

"I didn't mean it like that," Lacey snapped, piqued by his tone.

They glared at each other for a long moment, the electricity between them a palpable presence in the dingy little room. Without quite realizing what she was doing, Lacey found herself admiring the width of Matt's shoulders. He was so masculine, so handsome now that he had shaved off a week's growth of whiskers. His jaw was strong and square, his

nose straight as a blade. And his mouth . . .
she flushed and looked away lest he guess
what she was thinking.

Matt sat down on the edge of the bed and
pulled on his boots. "You sure you don't want
to stay here?" he asked, not looking at her.

Lacey glanced around the ugly little room
and shook her head. "I'm sure."

"Then let's go find a card game," Matt said
curtly, and headed out the door. He had to get
out of that little room and away from its very
large bed, he thought darkly, away from Lacey
before he dragged her into his arms and did
something they'd both be sorry for.

Lacey stared after Matt, but he didn't slow
down and he didn't look back, just stalked out
of the room like a man possessed. Fearful of
being left behind, Lacey slammed the door
and ran after him.

Matt passed by three saloons before he
turned into one called the Red Ace. Lacey
swallowed hard as she followed him inside.
She had never been inside a saloon before,
and she could not suppress a rush of excitement as she glanced around. A long plank bar
took up most of one side of the room. There
were rough-hewn tables scattered around the
floor, most of them occupied by men playing
poker or faro. Lacey blushed when she saw
the painting hanging over the bar. It was of a

plump woman with long red hair, bare breasts and long legs.

Lacey quickly looked away, and saw three women she had not noticed before. Saloon girls, she thought disapprovingly, and could not help staring at them. They were all young, dressed in short red skirts, low-cut silk blouses, black net stockings, and high-heeled slippers. One was a blond, one a brunette, and one a redhead. The blond was sitting on a man's lap, nonchalantly smoking a cigar.

"It's not polite to stare," Matt whispered, giving Lacey a sharp poke in the ribs. "Behave yourself."

"But she's smoking!" Lacey exclaimed. "A cigar!"

"Do you want one, too?" Matt queried, his voice faintly mocking.

"Don't be ridiculous."

"Stay close to me," Matt warned, serious once more. "And keep your mouth shut. This is a rough bunch, and I don't want any trouble if I can avoid it. Understand?"

"Yes," Lacey answered sullenly. "I understand."

Matt nodded. Then, releasing a long breath, he walked over to the nearest table. "Mind if I sit in?" he asked, nodding at an empty chair.

"Help yourself," invited a thin man in a light blue shirt and denim pants.

"Obliged," Matt said, and slid into the chair. Reaching into his pants pocket, he pulled out their meager bankroll and placed it on the stained green baize tabletop.

Lacey stood behind Matt, nervously twisting a lock of her hair between thumb and forefinger. Besides Matt, there were four other men in the game. She felt terribly out of place standing there. Around her she could hear a loud hum of conversation, punctuated now and then by a shriek of high-pitched feminine laughter, or a crude oath as one man or another lost a great deal of money on the turn of a card.

Lacey watched Matt as he put a dollar into the middle of the table. She had no idea how to play poker. Her father had played often, but he had forbidden Lacey to watch, and had refused to teach her how to play when she asked. "Poker's a man's game," her father had declared firmly. "Women and cards don't mix."

Matt placed ten dollars in the pot, and two of the men tossed their cards into the middle of the table. With a shake of his head, a third man tossed in his cards, and now only Matt and the man in the blue shirt were in the game.

Lacey peered over Matt's shoulder. He was holding three kings and two aces, and she decided it must be a pretty good hand by the way he was betting on it.

The man in the blue shirt scowled blackly as Matt slid another five dollars into the pot. Muttering an oath, Blue Shirt threw his cards into the center of the table, face down. Wordlessly, Matt raked in the pot.

He won four hands out of the next six, and Lacey was suddenly aware of the tension building at the table. Matt had won a sizable amount of money, and the other men didn't seem to like it.

"You're awfully lucky, stranger," remarked a tall, thin man sporting a black eye patch.

Matt nodded. "Tonight I surely am," he agreed affably. And then he smiled. "But I'm due. Lady Luck's been avoiding me the last few months."

The man wearing the eye patch grunted as he dealt a new hand.

Lacey glanced across the table and her eyes met those of a man wearing a red hat. He looked at her for a long time, his gaze filled with what could only be described as lust, and then he slid a glance in Matt's direction, his expression thoughtful. Lacey quickly took her eyes from him, and thereafter carefully avoided his gaze, but she could feel him watching her over his cards. It made her feel dirty, the way he stared at her, as if he were trying to imagine what she looked like un-clothed.

Matt won another hand, and then another, and the men at the table began to grumble about his so-called good luck. The man in the red trapper's hat glared at Matt.

"You're a little too lucky for my taste," he growled, his hand stroking his bearded jaw.

"Maybe you'd do better if you kept your eyes on your cards and off my woman," Matt suggested gruffly.

Red Hat shrugged. "I think maybe you're helping Lady Luck along."

"Are you accusing me of cheating?" Matt asked. His words were softly spoken, but the whole saloon was suddenly dead quiet.

The man in the red hat pushed away from the table. "I'm accusing you of being a little too lucky," he replied ominously.

Matt's eyes bored into those of the other man, his thoughts racing. He could not risk a shoot-out, not here, not with Lacey standing behind him, directly in the line of fire. Nor could he take a chance on getting himself killed and leaving Lacey to face this ragtag bunch of men alone.

"There's no crime in being lucky," Matt said with a shrug. "But if it bothers you, I'll leave."

The man in the red hat nodded. "Do that."

He stood up slowly, his hands dangling at his sides. "But leave the little lady here."

Lacey swallowed hard. Surely the man was kidding!

Now Matt stood up. "I'm afraid I can't do that," he said, his voice deceptively mild. "She's my wife, and I'm kind of attached to her."

"Leave her," Red Hat insisted, "or she's gonna be your widow."

"Lacey, go outside and wait for me," Matt said, not taking his eyes off Red Hat.

"No."

"Do as I say!" Matt said curtly.

"Please, Matt."

"Dammit, Lacey, I don't have time to argue. Get the hell out of here!"

Frightened, Lacey turned and walked toward the saloon's double doors. No one tried to stop her. She halted just outside the doorway, refusing to go any further. Whatever happened between Matt and the man in the red hat, she intended to be there. Standing on tiptoe, she peered over the batwing doors.

Matt and the man in the red hat were glaring at each other. The atmosphere inside the saloon was charged with morbid anticipation as the spectators waited to see what would happen next. There was little doubt that there would be a shoot-out because of the woman, and one of the two men would die. A man in a striped vest made his way to the bar and began taking bets on the outcome.

The other three men who had been seated at the table with Matt and the man in the red hat moved away, out of the line of fire.

The tension and the waiting seemed to stretch into eternity.

Matt cursed softly under his breath. He couldn't back down now. Vainly he wished for a better weapon than the two-shot derringer shoved in the waistband of his pants.

Lacey held her breath as she waited to see what would happen next. She did not have to wait long. The man with the red hat made a grab for the gun holstered on his left thigh. Matt drew his derringer in the same instant, and there was a long rolling report as both weapons were fired simultaneously. The smell of gunpowder filled Lacey's nostrils.

For a timeless moment no one moved, and Lacey had the feeling that everyone in the saloon had been trapped in some mysterious limbo between life and death. Then, as though all the bones in his body had melted, the man in the red hat slowly sank to the floor. It was then that Lacey noticed the dark red stain blossoming across the front of his shirt.

Matt took a step back, his gun still in his hand, his eyes narrowed as they swept the room in a long challenging glance. "Anybody else think I was cheating?" he asked in a hard tone.

No one spoke up. The man in the blue shirt shook his head vigorously.

The man wearing the eye patch shrugged. "There's no crime in being lucky, just like you said."

"You," Matt said, speaking to the man nearest him. "Hand me his gun."

The man quickly did as bidden, and Matt shoved Lacey's derringer into his pocket as he took hold of Red Hat's .44. It was a new Colt, and it felt good in his hand.

"I'll be leaving now," Matt said curtly. He gathered his winnings from the table and stuffed the greenbacks into his pocket. "Don't anybody follow me."

Slowly Matt edged toward the door, his cold blue eyes sweeping back and forth as he crossed the room.

Outside, he grabbed Lacey by the arm and pulled her into the alley behind the saloon.

"Matt—"

"Be quiet."

He stood there, listening, for several moments until he was certain they weren't being followed. "Let's go."

They followed the alley to the livery barn. Matt paid the man at the stable for putting up

Lacey's horse, bought a tall bay gelding for himself, and then, riding side by side, they went to retrieve Lacey's saddle.

"I guess we won't be spending the night here after all," Lacey remarked as Matt saddled the mare.

"No. We're going to buy some grub and ammunition and get the hell out of here."

She did not have to ask why. Matt was worried that the dead man might have friends, and that they might come looking for revenge.

Lacey stayed with the horses while Matt bought provisions. In addition to food and ammunition, he bought a deck of cards, a pint of whiskey, a black Stetson, and a sack of tobacco, and then they were riding into the desert. Lacey strained to hear some sound that would indicate they were being followed, but she could hear nothing but the sounds made by their own horses.

"Relax," Matt said. "Nobody's following us, at least not yet."

They rode for over an hour before Matt reined his horse to a halt in a shallow draw.

"We'll bed down here for the night and pick up the trail first thing in the morning," he said, dismounting.

Lacey nodded, suddenly overcome with weariness. She hadn't realized how tense she had been the whole time they were in that squalid little town until now. Spreading her bedroll on the sand, she crawled under the blanket and closed her eyes. She could hear Matt unsaddling the horses, hobbling them nearby, then getting into bed.

She closed her eyes, but sleep would not come. A niggling question kept repeating itself in the back of her mind. She had to know.

"Were you cheating?" she asked, sitting up.

Matt cocked an eyebrow at her. Then, without a word, he pulled a deck of cards from his saddlebag. He shuffled the deck several times, then dealt the cards. He gestured for Lacey to pick up her hand. She had a full house, jacks over tens. She glanced up at Matt, a question in her eyes, and Matt turned his cards over. He had a full house, aces over kings.

Matt looked at her, one black eyebrow arching upward as he scooped up the cards, shuffled them, cut them, and dealt her another hand. This time she had four kings; Matt had four aces.

For the next fifteen minutes he shuffled the cards, making the ace of spades appear on the top of the deck time after time, and then he dealt two hands. Lacey had a full house, queens over jacks. Matt had four aces.

Lacey tossed her cards on the ground. "You didn't answer my question," she remarked, although the answer seemed obvious now.

Matt shook his head. "I wasn't cheating, but I would have if it had been necessary."

"Oh." It troubled her, his knowing how to cheat at cards like that. What other nefarious talents did he have? Did she really want to know?

Matt Drago stared into the darkness long after Lacey was asleep, his thoughts troubled. It was never easy, killing a man. Had he been alone, he might have turned and walked away from the fight, but Red Hat wore the look of a man who would have shot him in the back without turning a hair. Matt couldn't risk that, couldn't take a chance on leaving Lacey alone in a strange town, at the mercy of men who had little or no regard for a decent woman.

Loosing a long sigh, he closed his eyes. He had tried gambling for a living once, but it had been a rotten way of life. Spending most of his waking hours in crowded, smoke-filled saloons, depending on the luck of the draw, or his own nimble fingers, to earn his keep. Having to defend himself when he was accused of cheating. And he had faced that accusation more times than he cared to recall, because he was lucky at cards, just plain lucky. Like tonight. So he had given up gambling and earned his living breaking horses, working at one ranch or another until he had enough money to move on, drifting until his money ran out, and then working again.

He drifted off to sleep, his dreams haunted

by the faces of the men he had killed over a game of cards. Red Hat's face was there, too, only this time it was Red Hat who cleared leather first. Matt uttered a strangled cry as he saw Red Hat's finger squeeze the trigger. Time slowed and the images warped and he saw the bullet leave the barrel of the gun and head straight toward him.

"Matt. Matt!"

Lacey's voice penetrated his nightmare, and he woke to find her kneeling beside him, a worried expression on her face, her long russet-colored hair falling over her shoulders.

"Are you all right?" she asked anxiously.

"Yeah." He looked at Lacey, at the horses resting near by. It had only been a dream after all.

Lacey sat back on her heels, a quizzical expression on her face. "Were you having a nightmare?"

"Yeah." He hated to admit it, it seemed so childish. Damn! It had seemed so real.

"Do you want to talk about it?"

"No."

"It might help."

It might at that, Matt thought, but how could he tell her about the nightmares that plagued him? He was a grown man, not a little boy frightened of the dark.

"Go back to bed, Lacey."

"Not until you tell me what's troubling

you," she argued, and then, out of the blue, she knew what was bothering him. "It was that man you killed, wasn't it? That's what your nightmare was about."

"Yeah."

"Do you have bad dreams often?"

"No."

"Just when you . . . when you kill someone?"

"Lacey—"

"Have you killed a lot of men?"

"I don't know," Matt replied sarcastically. "How many men makes a lot? Two? Four? Ten?"

"Have you killed ten men?" Lacey asked, awed by the thought.

"No. Just four, counting the one tonight."

Numbers were a relative thing, Lacey mused. Four cents didn't seem like much, but four dead men seemed a high number.

"Why did you kill them?" She had not meant to ask, but her curiosity got the best of her.

Matt shrugged. Sitting up, he stirred the ashes and placed the coffee pot over the glowing coals. It was obvious he wasn't going to get any sleep until he told Lacey what she wanted to know.

"I used to be a gambler," Matt said, gazing into the distance. "I've got a way with cards, I guess. Always been lucky. Too lucky. When you win too often, most men can't believe you're not cheating. There's always a few who want to shoot it out. So far, I've been lucky there, too."

"Oh." Lacey watched Matt's hands as he lifted the blue enamel coffee pot and poured himself a cup of coffee. His hands were large, capable. The fingers were long, the nails short and square. It was easy to imagine him in a dark suit and flashy brocade vest, sitting at a green baize table in a noisy saloon. She remembered how at home he had looked back in the saloon, how nimble his fingers had been when he shuffled the cards. So, he had been a gambler. "Why did you quit?"

"The last man I killed was just a kid. He lost every cent he had in an all-night poker game. He accused me of cheating and demanded I return his money. When I refused, he pulled a gun on me, and I killed him." Matt shook his head. "I didn't find out until later that he was only seventeen, and that he had stolen the money he'd lost from his mother."

"How awful for you."

"Yeah, awful. I haven't picked up a deck of cards since, until tonight."

Lacey felt a rush of sympathy for the man sitting beside her. He had turned his back on gambling, determined never to play cards again. But he had done it for her, because they needed food and supplies to go after her father and gambling was the quickest way to get it.

"Matt . . ." her voice trailed off as she realized she didn't quite know how to put her feelings into words, nor was she sure just what those feelings were. She knew only that Matthew Drago no longer seemed like a stranger. She felt remorse because she had caused him to do something he had turned his back on, and affection because he had done it for her.

"Go to bed, Lacey," Matt said wearily.

Lacey placed her hand on his arm and gave it a squeeze, wanting him to know how grateful she was. "Thank you, Matt."

He nodded, his eyes moving over her face, his skin growing warm where her hand rested on his arm. She was so lovely in the moonlight, so damn lovely.

With a low groan, he pulled her into his arms and kissed her, his mouth drinking in the sweetness of her lips, one arm holding her tight while his hand caressed her back. Lord, she was sweet.

For a moment Lacey was too stunned to move, too startled to think. She was only aware of Matt's lips on hers, of a sudden warmth rushing through her, as if her blood had turned to fire. She knew she should be outraged by Matt's ungentlemanly conduct, and she fully intended to let him know how she felt, but first she wanted him to kiss her just a little longer. It was such a gloriously intoxicating feeling. Shivers of excitement shook her body, making her feel weak and a little light-headed. No one had ever kissed her with such passion, such fierce intensity. Breathless, she kissed him back, her arms stealing around his waist, her body pressing against his.

It was only when she felt his hand begin to stroke her thigh that reality came crashing down. With a cry, Lacey pulled out of Matt's embrace and jumped to her feet.

"How dare you!" she said with what she hoped was the proper amount of righteous indignation.

"Lacey, I'm sorry."

"You should be," she replied haughtily, although she knew she was just as guilty as he.

"I said I was," Matt snapped, feeling his own anger rise. What the hell was she so mad about, he thought irritably. She had kissed him back, after all. If she hadn't liked it, why hadn't she said so sooner?

Without another word, Lacey turned on her heel and flounced back to her own blankets. Crawling under the covers, she pulled them up to her chin, then gazed into the darkness, too keyed up to sleep. Lifting her hand, she ran a finger over her lips, remembering how Matt's kiss had felt. The memory had warmed her clear down to her toes.

Smiling into the darkness, she fell asleep.

CHAPTER 4

They picked up the trail early the following morning. There were times when Lacey could see nothing at all to indicate that anyone had passed by, but Matt seemed confident they were heading in the right direction and she took comfort in that.

When they stopped at noon to eat and rest the horses, she asked him where he had learned to read trail sign.

"During the war," Matt replied. He bit off a piece of jerky and chewed it thoughtfully for a moment. "Old Smoke Johnson was in my outfit. He'd been an Army scout out West before the war, but when he heard the Yankees were marching through Georgia, he came home and joined up. Old Smoke was a talkative cuss, and he must have told me everything he knew about tracking and Indians and the fur trade. When he wasn't yapping at me, he was teaching me to read sign, and how to navigate by the stars. Between battles, he used to go off into the woods and I'd see if I could pick up his trail. He ran into a half-dozen bluebelly scouts one night when I was following his tracks." Matt laughed with the memory. "That was a hell of a fight. I don't know who was more surprised, those six Yankees or me and Smoke. Anyway, we recovered first and killed four of them. The other two ran like scalded cats. Smoke took a bullet in the leg, but he said it was no more than he deserved, since he'd walked right into their hidey hole."

"Where is Mr. Johnson now?"

"Dead. He was killed at Chickamagua."

"I'm sorry," Lacey said softly. "Were you born in the South?"

"Yeah. Virginia."

"Why did you leave?"

"Too many bad memories. My brothers were killed at Vicksburg. My stepmother died during the war, and my sister entered a convent. There was no reason to stay, so I decided to see the country and I lit out for Texas when the war was over."

"I've never been there. Was it nice?"

A picture of Claire Duprey flashed through Matt's mind: soft white skin, hair as black as sin, eyes as green as emeralds. "It was all right," he said with a shrug.

"Why did you leave Texas?"

"It's time to go," Matt said brusquely, and rising to his feet, he stepped into the saddle and gigged his horse into a trot.

There was nothing for Lacey to do but climb onto her horse and follow him. In his present mood, she feared he just might leave her behind.

Matt was withdrawn and quiet the rest of the day. Lacey slid several sidelong glances in his direction, but he seemed oblivious to her presence. His face was set in hard lines, his eyes were dark and sullen, as though he were remembering something unpleasant. Apparently talking about Texas had reminded him of something he wanted to forget, but what?

She puzzled over the matter all that day, her imagination running wild.

That night they bedded down in the shadow of a tall sandstone bluff. Lacey held her peace until after dinner, and then, while they were sipping a last cup of coffee before bedtime, she said quietly, "I'm sorry if I made you angry this afternoon. I didn't mean to pry into something that's none of my business."

"It's all right, Lacey," Matt said. "I shouldn't have snapped at you like that."

"Then you're not mad?" Somehow she could not stand to have him angry with her.

"No."

Lacey smiled at him, and Matt felt as though he had stepped into a pool of sunlight. The warmth of her smile seemed to engulf him, and he was conscious of a sudden heat flooding through his veins. He was reminded of the kiss they had shared the night before, the way her body had molded to his, the way she had trembled at his touch.

"Good night, Lacey," Matt said abruptly, and crawled into his blankets, knowing if he didn't get away from her, he would grab her and ease the awful longing that was tying him in knots.

"Good night, Matt," Lacey murmured. Tossing the last drops of coffee into the fire, she slipped under her blankets, baffled by Matt's behavior. If he wasn't mad, why did his voice sound so gruff, and why had he gone to bed so abruptly, as though he couldn't stand to be near her? It was most peculiar, but she was too saddle weary to fret for long and she was soon asleep.

Matt Drago remained awake for some time, acutely aware that he had a real problem on his hands. And that problem was Lacey, or, more specifically, his growing desire for her. Certainly he had known women who were more beautiful, better educated, more lady-like than Lacey, but he had never met a woman who had tempted him so deeply, or one he could not resist if he put his mind to it. He wasn't sure what was so special about Lacey Montana, but she had certainly captured his attention. Riding beside her every day, hour after hour, was hell. He tried not to look at her, tried not to notice the way her brown eyes glowed when she saw a deer grazing on a hillside or a bear playing with its cubs. He tried to ignore the sweet curve of her thigh, and the swell of her breasts beneath the thin fabric of her shirt. He tried not to notice how the sun danced in her hair, and the merry laughter bubbled in her throat when they raced up a hill.

Turning on his side, he gazed at Lacey, sleeping across the fire from him. Her eyelashes made dark crescents against her cheeks, her hair framed her face like a thick red-gold cloud. Her chest rose and fell with each soft breath and he tried not to think of the sweet feminine shape nestled beneath the rough blanket, but all he could dwell on was the way she had kissed him the day before, her lips sweetly yielding, her lush body molding to his, warm and soft and desirable.

Damn, but she was lovely! So lovely, and so young, surely not more than eighteen. Far too young for a man pushing thirty. But it wasn't just the difference in their ages. She was innocent in the ways of the world, and the ways of men. Innocent and vulnerable. She still believed in miracles, still believed that wanting something badly enough would make it happen. Had he ever been *that* young, he mused sardonically, that trusting?

Muttering an oath, he rolled onto his back and stared out into the inky night until, at long last, he fell asleep.

Lacey smothered a yawn as she urged Cinder across a shallow stream. Sometimes she thought she was becoming permanently attached to her saddle. Matt did not seem to mind the long hours they spent on the trail. Indeed, he never seemed to get tired at all.

It was late in the afternoon almost a week later when Matt drew his horse to a halt and gestured for Lacey to dismount and stay quiet.

Lacey quickly did as bidden, her eyes watching Matt as he ground-reined his bay and dropped to his belly, snaking his way to the top of a brush-covered slope. He stayed there for a long time, and Lacey's heart began to pound with excitement. Had they found her father at last?

Some twenty minutes later, Matt made his way back to Lacey. "Well, we've found some Indians," he said in a low voice. "There's about twenty lodges just over that rise."

"Did you see my father?" Lacey asked, her eyes wide with excitement and hope.

"No, but that doesn't mean anything. Come on, we've got to get out of here before someone spots us."

With a nod, Lacey followed Matt away from the slope toward a thick copse of trees.

"We'll lay low until nightfall," Matt explained, "and then I'll go scout around and see if I can locate your old man. No fires," he added.

Lacey nodded again. They were finally here. For the first time, she realized the danger they were in. There was no telling what might happen if the Indians became aware of their presence.

It seemed as if the sun would never go down. Lacey gnawed on a piece of beef jerky to ease her hunger. Matt rolled a cigarette, but didn't light it.

As darkness dropped over the land, Matt took Lacey's hand in his. "Listen to me. You stay here, no matter what. Understand? If I'm not back by the time the moon is over that tall pine, you jump on your horse and hightail it outta here."

"But, Matt—"

"Don't argue with me. If I'm not back by then, it means I'm not coming back. You get on that horse and ride like hell. If you head due south, you'll come to a little mining town in a day or two. You can't miss it."

Matt reached into his pocket and pulled out a roll of greenbacks. It was what was left of the money he had won in the card game. "This should be enough to take care of you for quite a while."

"Matt, I . . ." Her voice seemed weak, her throat tight. He talked as if he doubted he would return to her. She had been so eager to find her father, so anxious to have everything her own way, that she had never given any real thought to the danger involved. Until now.

"Take it." Matt pushed the money into her hand; then, with a sigh, he put his arms around Lacey and kissed her gently. Her mouth was soft and warm, sweeter than life itself, and what began as a chaste token of affection quickly turned into a burning kiss filled with passion and desire.

For a moment, Lacey stood rigid in Matt's arms, stunned by the force of his kiss, and her reaction to it. His kiss, at first no more than the mere pressing of his lips against hers, suddenly became urgent, and Lacey clung to him as the only solid thing in a world spinning out of control. Her legs began to tremble and her heart began to pound a quick staccato in her breast. Heat from his lips coursed through her, filling her with a raw hunger that was new and wildly exciting. If only he would kiss her thus forever.

Abruptly, Matt released her, and Lacey swayed on her feet, her lips bereft, her legs weak.

"Wish me luck," he said laconically, and then he was gone.

Lacey stared after him, shaken to the core of her being by the force of his kiss, and by the stark realization that he might well be killed and it would be all her fault.

She shoved the wad of greenbacks into her pocket, hardly aware that she had done so, then sat down, her fingers drumming nervously on the ground, her heart sending urgent prayers to Heaven, beseeching an all-knowing God to protect Matt from harm.

Five minutes passed. Ten. Twenty. Where was he? What was taking so long? She peered into the darkness, hoping to see him striding toward her, but she saw only shadows and the outline of a lonely tree silhouetted in the distance. Ears straining, she listened to the night, hoping to hear Matt's footsteps, but she heard only the soft sigh of the wind and the occasional screech of an owl searching for prey.

The minutes dragged by, and her stomach knotted with tension. Where was he?

* * *

Matt Drago hunkered down on his heels in the shadow of a large boulder, his eyes sweeping back and forth as he scanned the Apache camp for some sign of Lacey's father. There were about eighty Indians in the camp, mostly women and children. But there were more than enough warriors to make a good fight.

He sat there for over an hour, but there was no sign of Royce Montana, no way of knowing if Lacey's father had ever been there at all. Of course, it was possible that Royce Montana had been killed long ago, or that they were trailing the wrong bunch of Indians. It was just as possible, though doubtful, that Lacey's father was inside one of the lodges. Apaches weren't known for their hospitality to those considered the enemy.

Matt grimaced as he changed positions. Below, the Indians were getting ready to turn in for the night. The women hustled their young ones off to bed, the men put their pipes away and left the community campfire for the warmth of their lodges.

Watching the scene below, Matt found himself thinking of Lacey, of how she felt in his arms, the way she had kissed him back. Kissing her had been a grave mistake. He had not meant to touch her again after that first time. She was a nice girl, too good for him by half, and too damn young. Yet he kept remembering the pressure of her breasts against his chest, the little sigh of pleasure that had escaped her lips when he held her close, the fragrance of her hair and skin that was hers and hers alone.

He was telling himself all the reasons why loving her would never work when he felt the sharp prick of a knife below his right ear.

Matt froze, his gun in his hand, as two other warriors materialized out of the darkness.

The warrior holding the knife against Matt's neck reached around and plucked the gun from his hand.

"Stand up, white man," he said in a deep bass voice. The Indian spoke stilted English. He was short and stocky; a long scar ran from his left temple to his jaw line.

Matt stood up slowly, his fists clenched at his sides as one of the other warriors searched him for weapons. The warrior uttered a little cry of satisfaction when he withdrew the derringer from Matt's hip pocket.

"Go." The Indian with the scar gave Matt a shove in the direction of the Indian camp, and Matt obligingly made his way down the hill. It was all over now, he thought bleakly.

When they reached the Apache camp, one of the warriors tied Matt's hands behind his back, lashed his feet together at the ankles, then dropped a rope around his neck and tethered him to a stout sapling on the outskirts of the village.

101

The warrior with the scarred face grinned at Matt as he drew a finger across his throat. "Tomorrow, white man," he said menacingly. "Tomorrow you will die."

"Go to hell," Matt retorted with more bravado than he felt, and was rewarded by a swift kick in the stomach. He doubled over, fighting the urge to vomit, as the other warriors lashed out at him with their hands and feet, driving Matt to the ground as they rained blow after blow to his face, chest, ribcage, and back.

Gritting his teeth against the pain, Matt curled into a tight ball in an effort to protect his face and stomach. Blood oozed from his nose and mouth and pounded in his ears as he fought to stay conscious.

Abruptly, the beating came to a halt. Spitting blood from his mouth, Matt risked a glance at his captors.

"You have a fighting heart, I think," Scarface said grudgingly. "Tomorrow we will find out which is stronger, the knives of the Mescalero or the heart of a white man."

"Would you kill a brother?" Matt rasped, clutching at a straw of hope.

"I see no brother," Scarface sneered. "Only a foolish white man."

"My mother was of the Dineh."

"What tribe did she belong to?" Scarface asked, interested in spite of himself. "What was her name?"

"Her name was Hummingbird. She was of the Chiricahua."

Scarface shook his head. "I have never heard of her. Who was her father?"

"I don't know," Matt answered, and the tiny shred of hope that had surfaced quickly died.

The three warriors spoke to each other in rapid Apache, and then Scarface knelt beside Matt.

"We do not believe you are of the Dineh, white man. Do not lie to us again." Scarface studied Matt for a long moment. "What are you doing in the land of the Apache?"

"Just passing through," Matt replied through clenched teeth.

"Alone?"

"Yeah."

"On foot?" the warrior asked skeptically.

"My horse broke a leg a couple of days back. I was hoping to steal one of yours."

Scarface nodded. To steal a horse from the enemy was a worthy accomplishment, one the Apache regarded highly. Was it possible the white man possessed Apache blood? His hair was as black and coarse as an Indian's, his skin was dark. It was possible, perhaps, that the white man was of the People, and yet a man would say anything that might save him when his life was at stake.

Scarface had not yet made up his mind about the prisoner when he rose to his feet and walked toward his lodge. Tomorrow would be time enough to decide what to do with the white man.

The other two warriors stared at Matt for a few minutes, their eyes fathomless, and then they, too, went to their lodges.

Matt watched the Indians out of sight. He had not really expected them to believe he was half Apache. It had simply been a last-ditch effort to save himself from a long and painful death, and it had failed.

Muttering an oath, Matt made himself as comfortable as possible on the hard ground. He was hurting. The rawhide binding his wrists had been tied tight and soon his hands grew numb, but the pain in his wrists was small compared to the dull, throbbing ache that wracked him from head to foot. There was the taste of blood in his mouth, but stronger than the taste of blood was the brassy taste of fear. He was afraid, and he didn't like it. Of course, he had been afraid before. No sane man went into battle without experiencing fear, but at least then he'd had a fighting chance. He hadn't been trussed up like a sacrificial offering, helpless to defend himself. A cold sweat broke out across his forehead as he contemplated what lay ahead. Better to rot in the bowels of the Yuma pen than die a slow and agonizing death at the skilled hands of the Apache.

He shivered convulsively. He was afraid. Afraid of the pain to come, afraid of behaving like a coward in the face of the enemy. He had always thought of himself as a brave man, but he'd never really been put to the test. What if he cracked under the pressure? Everyone knew that the Apache were the unchallenged masters in the fine art of inflicting torture and pain. How did a man know how much agony he could endure? He had no desire to die screaming for mercy, or whimpering like a child afraid of the dark. Damn!

He tried to shift to a more comfortable position, and the movement sent a fresh wave of pain through him. *Get used to it*, he thought morbidly. *There's worse to come.*

Matt gazed up at the midnight sky. Each breath caused new waves of pain to ripple down his left side, and he wondered if Scarface had broken a rib or two. At least the Indians had not gone to scout his backtrail. He could be grateful for that. Lacey was safe. If she had obeyed his instructions, she would be heading south by now. With any luck at all, she would make it to safety without any trouble.

Lacey. He wished he had made love to her just once, and he felt a rush of envy for the man, whoever he might be, who would be lucky enough to bed Lacey the first time, to see her beautiful brown eyes glaze with passion, hear the quickened intake of her breath as she experienced fulfillment in the arms of the man she loved. He felt a peculiar emptiness in his heart when he realized he would never see her again. So many things he had not yet done, would never do. . . .

He focused his attention on the North Star, trying not to think about alabaster skin and pouting pink lips; trying not to think about what lay waiting for him the following day, but, unbidden, came the stories of torture and treachery that old Smoke Johnson had related with great delight, tales of men who had been disemboweled, or burned alive, or covered with honey and buried up to their necks in an ant hill. Matt could not suppress a shudder of revulsion as visions of a long and lingering death danced in his mind. Was that what the future held for him?

Lacey felt a shiver of apprehension slither down her spine as the moon crawled across the sky. It was past midnight now, and still Matt had not returned.

Too nervous to sit still any longer, Lacey stood up, uncertain as to what to do. Matt had told her to leave if he hadn't returned at the specified time, but she could not bring herself to ride away and leave him. They had traveled together for several weeks now. She had tended his wounds, perhaps even saved his life. And now he was risking his life to search for her father; indeed, even now he might be dead, and it would be all her fault. She might never see him again. The thought hurt more deeply than she had dreamed possible.

After another ten minutes of indecision, she began to walk toward the Indian camp. She had to know if her father was there. She had to know if Matt was dead or alive.

She walked slowly, putting each foot down carefully lest she step on a dry branch that might betray her presence to any Indians lurking in the darkness.

Twenty minutes later she was lying on her stomach at the top of the rise. The Apache camp was spread below, dark and quiet. At first she couldn't see much of anything, but then her eyes picked up a faint sign of movement near the far edge of the village. It was a man tied to a tree. Was it Matt? Her heart lurched in her chest. Perhaps it was her father!

Moving as fast as she dared, Lacey went back to the grove of trees and collected the horses, then made her way through the shadows toward the prisoner. Sweet relief washed through her when she saw that it was Matt, and that he was alone.

Taking a knife from her saddlebag, Lacey left the horses ground-reined out of sight and crept toward Matt. Hardly daring to breathe, she dropped to her hands and knees, inching closer and closer to the sleeping village, every nerve in her body stretched taut, her eyes and ears straining for any sound that would indicate she was no longer alone.

Matt was on the brink of sleep when he heard someone whisper his name. Glancing over his shoulder, he saw Lacey creeping up behind him. His first emotion was one of relief. Thank God, help was on the way! And then he grew angry. Stupid girl! What the hell did she think she was doing, prowling around an Apache camp in the dead of night. Didn't she realize the danger she was in?

"Lacey, get out of here," he hissed.

Wordlessly, she shook her head and began sawing through the rope binding Matt's wrists. The knife was sharp and quickly sliced through the rawhide, freeing Matt's hands. Keeping one eye on the camp, Matt hurriedly untied his feet and removed the rope from his neck.

He was about to grab Lacey by the hand and make a run for it when a low growl sounded behind him. Turning, he saw a large yellow hound staring at him, lips curled back to reveal sharp white teeth.

"Don't move," Matt warned Lacey as the dog growled again. "If he starts barking, he'll rouse the whole damn camp."

Lacey nodded, her eyes fixed on the dog. Seconds passed like hours. *They'll find us here in the morning*, she thought bleakly, *unmoving as statues*.

"Lacey," Matt whispered. "Pass me the knife."

She was too frightened to ask questions. Moving as slowly as she could, she slipped the knife to Matt. She was unprepared for what happened next. Without warning, Matt lunged forward, his left arm in front of his face, the knife in his right hand. His sudden movement startled the dog, who let out a low growl and attacked, his jaws closing over Matt's arm. Matt was ready, and when the dog attacked, he drove the knife into the animal's throat, killing it instantly, soundlessly.

Jerking the blade free, Matt grabbed Lacey's arm and ran into the darkness beyond the camp, gritting his teeth against the pain in his arm.

"This way," Lacey whispered urgently, and led him to where the horses were waiting.

In seconds they were riding away from the village, slowly at first lest their hoofbeats be heard, and then at a gallop.

They rode all night, wanting to put as much distance as possible between themselves and the Apache.

At first light, Matt reined his lathered gelding to a halt. Lacey drew rein beside him, her eyes growing wide as she saw the dried blood caked around his nose and mouth.

"Matt, what happened?"

"Apache hospitality," he answered ruefully. "Don't worry, it's not as bad as it looks."

"Maybe not, but that dog bite looks bad. Let me clean it for you."

"I'll take care of it. You look beat."

Lacey nodded, too tired to reply. He was alive, and that was all that mattered. All the tenseness, all the worry of the last few hours drained out of her like water through a sieve, and she suddenly went limp, practically falling out of the saddle.

Jumping to the ground, Matt caught her before she collapsed.

"You little fool," he scolded. "Didn't I tell you to hightail it outta there if I didn't come back? You might have been killed."

"Yell at me tomorrow, Matt," Lacey mumbled. "I'm too tired to argue with you right now."

Matt stared at Lacey in disbelief as her eyelids fluttered down. She was actually asleep! Muttering an oath, he held her in his arms, unable to believe that she had risked her own life just to save his. Then, with a sigh, he untied her bedroll from behind her saddle, spread it on the ground as best he could with one hand, and placed Lacey on the blanket.

Feeling tender and protective, he covered her and then, too tired to spread his own blankets, stretched out on the ground beside her and fell asleep.

Lacey tried to turn over, then frowned. There was a heavy weight across her chest, and another across her legs. Turning her head, she gave a little gasp of alarm when she saw Matt lying beside her. One of his arms was flung across her breasts, one of his legs was resting over hers. She relaxed when she saw that he was sound asleep.

He looked very handsome, lying there peacefully beside her. Even with one eye black and swollen, and his jaw covered with bristles, he was beautiful. His nose was slightly crooked, as if it had once been broken. She had never noticed that before, she mused absently. His mouth was full and wide, and she had a sudden impulse to run her fingers over his lower lip. The mere idea made her warm all over. Would he awaken if she dared?

She was trying to summon the courage when she realized that Matt was awake and watching her. Embarrassed, she pushed his arm off her breast and sat up, clutching the blanket to her chest even though she was fully clothed.

"What are you doing here?" she demanded.

"I was too tired to spread my bedroll," Matt explained. And then he grinned roguishly. "Besides, since you were willing to risk your life to save mine, I didn't think you'd mind if I shared your bed."

"Well, you thought wrong!" Lacey exclaimed. "I . . . I only saved your life because I . . . because I was afraid to be out here alone."

"Another hope crushed," Matt lamented.

"Did you see my father? Was he there?"

"I didn't see him, Lacey. I think he must be with that other bunch."

"Oh." Her disappointment showed in her eyes. She had been so certain they would find her father. She had wanted it so bad. Now they had to backtrack and hope that Matt could still pick up the trail of the Indians who had gone toward New Mexico Territory.

"I'm sorry, Lacey," Matt said tenderly.

She nodded, too close to tears to speak.

"How about something to eat," Matt suggested, "and then we'll see if we can pick up that other trail."

"All right," Lacey said, "but first I'm going to take a look at your arm."

Matt didn't object, and Lacey quickly heated some water and gently washed Matt's arm. The dog bite wasn't deep and there was no sign of infection, but she rinsed it thoroughly.

Matt washed the dried blood from his face with the leftover water, grunting as the movement jarred his injured rib.

"What's wrong?" Lacey asked.

"I think one of my ribs is cracked. You got anything I can wrap it with?"

Lacey nodded. Going to her saddlebag, she pulled out her petticoat and ripped several strips from the hem. At Matt's direction, she wrapped the material tightly around his middle.

"Thanks," he said, smiling at her. "That feels better."

Lacey was subdued as they rode back the way they had come. The chances of picking up a cold trail were slim, even for a tracker as experienced as Matt appeared to be. She wondered if her father was still alive; if so, was he being treated well, or was he being abused and tormented? She glanced at Matt. His face was swollen and discolored. Apache hospitality, he had said. Was her father being treated the same way? He was too old, too sick, to endure such cruelty for very long.

The plains spread out before them, seemingly flat and barren save for an occasional stand of timber and patches of gray-green scrub brush. The sky began to grow dark as clouds gathered, and within thirty minutes the sun had been blotted from sight by thick black clouds. A stiff wind began to blow, and Lacey shivered, wishing she had something warmer to wear than her cotton shirt. Matt was no better off. In the rush to leave town after the gunfight, they had neglected to buy warm clothing.

A few large drops of rain fell intermittently, and then the heavens opened, unleashing a downpour that soon had Lacey and Matt soaked to the skin.

Matt swore under his breath as his eyes searched the bleak landscape for shelter. He squinted into the distance. Was he imagining things, or was that a cabin up ahead? He reined his horse toward it, and felt a surge of relief when he saw that it was indeed a building of some kind. As they drew nearer, he saw that it was a shack, poorly built and in need of repair but good enough to provide them with some degree of shelter from the raging storm.

He grimaced with pain as he dismounted. His left side was still sore, but he was grateful his ribs weren't broken. Hitching his gelding to a rotted tree stump alongside the shack, he reached up to help Lacey dismount.

"Get inside," Matt shouted. "I'll unsaddle the horses."

With a nod, Lacey ran to the front door, turned the knob, and gave it a shove. The door refused to open, and she gave it a hard push, then practically fell on her face as the door flew open.

The inside of the shack was dismal, gloomy, and cold. There was no furniture, only a rusted iron stove and a fireplace with a cracked hearth. But at least it was dry.

She was standing in the middle of the floor, shivering, when Matt came in carrying their saddles. He dropped their gear on the floor inside the door, removed his hat, and shook the water from the brim.

"Not much, is it?" he mused, glancing around the shack's single room.

Lacey shrugged. It was better than riding in the rain.

"You're cold," Matt remarked. "Get out of those wet things and wrap up in a blanket." He looked around the room, hoping to find something that would burn, but to no avail. Untying Lacey's bedroll from behind the cantle of her saddle, he tossed her a blanket. "Get bundled up before you freeze to death."

"Would you mind turning around, please?"

"Sure." Matt turned toward the opposite wall, rubbing his arms with his hands while Lacey hastily undressed and wrapped up in the blanket. "My turn," he said when he figured she was through, and began to strip off his wet shirt.

Lacey stared out the shack's only window. Lightning slashed through the heavy black clouds, great jagged bolts of brilliant white light. The rain was very loud on the wooden roof, but not loud enough to blot out the sound of Matt undressing behind her. She had never seen a naked man before, and she did not want to see one now, but she could not help remembering the days she had tended Matt—the sight of his bare chest, the width of his shoulders, the muscles rippling in his arms when he moved. She sent a silent prayer to heaven, praying that the rain would not last long. Somehow she had felt less vulnerable when they had been outside. The shack, drab as it was, hinted at intimacy, and while she didn't know much about men, she knew that Matt found her desirable. If he decided to attack her, she would be at his mercy. He was too big, too strong, for her to resist.

"Come and sit down," Matt called, and Lacey slowly turned around to see him sitting on his saddle blanket before the cold hearth. He patted the floor beside him. "Come on, sit down. Might as well be comfortable."

Lacey nodded uncertainly. The blanket Matt was sitting on offered little padding, and as she sat down beside him, she could feel the cold floor beneath her. But she was more aware of Matt at her side. Though they were not quite touching, she could almost feel the heat of his body. If only they were married. At least then she could curl up in his arms and get warm. Just contemplating such a thing provided a few moments of warmth as she imagined what it would be like to be Matt's wife, to lie beside him in the night. An embarrassed flush warmed her from head to foot at the mere idea. She hardly knew the man. Certainly he was not the type of person she would want to marry. He was a criminal, after all, a man accused of murder. But she was so cold. . . .

Matt slid a sidelong glance at Lacey. She was shivering uncontrollably, and he wondered if he dared put his arm around her. Bundling would make them both warmer, but he wasn't sure Lacey would approve.

A gust of chill wind shook the cabin walls, and Matt shivered some himself as a draft of icy air swept in around them.

"Lacey, we'd both be warmer if we sat closer together," Matt suggested, trying to make his voice even and businesslike. "What do you say?"

She was too cold to argue. A quick nod, and Matt was pressed against her, his arm around her shoulder. Lacey was instantly warmer, but it had nothing to do with Matt's body heat. Indeed, the sudden warmth came from within herself as she realized that only two pitifully thin blankets separated her bare flesh from his. It was a shockingly provocative thought, and she was suddenly glad that the shack's dim interior hid the crimson flush spreading across her cheeks.

The minutes crept by, and Lacey's eyelids began to grow heavy. The steady patter of the rain on the roof, the gathering darkness, the warmth that now engulfed her, all combined to lull her gently to sleep.

Matt's arm tightened around Lacey as her head lolled forward and her body relaxed. Poor kid, he thought. She'd been through a lot in the last few days. Gently he lowered her to the floor, careful to keep the blanket wrapped snugly around her though he was sorely tempted to peek through the folds and see if her body could possibly be as beautiful as he imagined.

Drawing his own blanket tighter, he stretched out beside Lacey, his body pressed close to hers, the saddle blanket covering them both.

Outside, the rain fell and the wind blew, but inside the dismal little shack, all was peaceful and still.

CHAPTER 5

Lacey woke slowly, roused by the sound of the rain falling on the roof, and by a movement next to her.

Opening her eyes, she was suddenly jolted wide awake by the sight of Matt Drago lying close beside her. Sometime during the night they had rolled out of their separate blankets and were now lying side by side beneath their combined covers, as cozy as two people could be.

She stared at the black head nestled comfortably on her shoulder, then let her gaze drift to the long brown arm curled around her waist. For a moment, she remained completely still, hardly daring to breathe for fear he might awaken and find them in such a compromising position.

As her initial shock at finding herself lying in Matt's arms passed, another reality struck home. Not only was Matt stark naked under the covers, but so was she!

All Lacey's senses sprang to life, and she was suddenly, keenly, aware of the coarse hair on Matt's legs, the day's growth of beard on his strong square jaw, the smell of leather and sweat and maleness, the fact that the length of her body was in direct contact with his from shoulder to ankle.

What was she going to do now, she thought frantically. Would he awaken if she moved? She would be mortified if he woke up. What if he thought she had purposefully slept so close to him? What if he woke up and saw her naked? Oh, she would die of shame.

Matt Drago didn't move. He knew Lacey was awake, knew she must be suffering miserably to find herself lying so close to him. She was such an innocent, so shy and modest. Personally, he found lying beside her most enjoyable, though he knew Lacey must be horrified. But, Lord, she felt good lying there beside him, her skin smooth and warm against his own, her hair soft and silky where it brushed his cheek. He felt the stirrings of desire begin to make themselves known and he thought, wryly, that if Lacey didn't roll out of those blankets pretty damn quick, she would know without a doubt that he was awake. Awake and thinking about something besides breakfast.

Drawing a deep breath, Lacey took hold of the top blanket and quickly rolled away from Matt, taking the blanket with her. Jumping to her feet, she wrapped the blanket around her, tucking the ends between her breasts before sending a quick glance over her shoulder. She had expected to find Matt grinning at her, but he appeared to be sleeping soundly. For a moment Lacey stared at him, wondering if he was all right. On the trail the slightest movement or sound had awakened him in an instant. With a slight shrug of her shoulders, she began to pull on her clothes, shivering as she pulled on the cold cotton jeans and shirt —hurrying because she did not want him to awake and find her in a state of undress.

Matt watched Lacey through narrowed eyes. Her back was smooth and unblemished, her legs long and shapely, her bottom nicely rounded. It was all he could do to keep from reaching out and touching her, and he cursed under his breath as he closed his eyes. She was even more beautiful than he had imagined, he mused glumly, and he had imagined quite a bit.

He stretched and yawned hugely as Lacey reached for her boots.

"Good morning," Lacey said, somewhat breathlessly.

"Morning. Still raining, huh?"

"Yes."

"Did you sleep well?" Matt asked.

Lacey slanted a probing look in his direction. Was there a hint of laughter in his voice, or was she imagining things? "Yes, thank you. Are you hungry? There's some jerky left. And an apple."

"Fine," Matt said, though what he really wanted was a cup of coffee. Sitting up, he stretched again.

Lacey quickly averted her eyes as the blanket fell down around Matt's hips, exposing his heavily muscled torso, long sinewy arms, and broad shoulders. Rummaging through one of the packs, she tried not to remember the thick mat of black hair that covered his chest, or the way it tapered to a thin line before disappearing below the concealing folds of the blanket.

"Would you mind throwing me my pants?" Matt asked.

Lacey picked up his jeans as though they might bite her. Not meeting his eyes, she tossed the pants in Matt's general direction, then quickly turned around, her cheeks flaming with embarrassment at the wayward turn of her thoughts.

Chewing on her lower lip, she tried to concentrate on the apple she was slicing. She could feel Matt's eyes on her back. Knowing he was watching her made her clumsy, and she gave a little cry of pain as the knife's sharp blade sliced into her finger.

"What is it?" Matt asked.

"Nothing. I cut myself."

"Let me have a look," Matt said, coming to stand beside her.

Lacey held out her hand, and felt her stomach churn at the sight of the blood oozing from her finger.

"Hey, that's a bad cut," Matt exclaimed. Taking a bandana from his hip pocket, he wrapped it around Lacey's finger, then held the cloth in place with his thumb and forefinger. "Are you all right?" he asked. "You look a little pale."

Lacey laughed self-consciously. "I . . . I could never stand the sight of blood," she confessed.

"You weren't all pale and shaky when you patched me up," Matt remarked.

Lacey shrugged. "It doesn't bother me so much when it's not my blood."

"Oh." He unwrapped the bandana and checked the cut. "The bleeding's stopped, but we'd better wash it out and disinfect it," he decided. "We wouldn't want it to get infected."

Lacey nodded. Catching her lower lip between her teeth, she tried not to flinch as Matt

123

doused her injured finger with water from the canteen.

"This is going to sting like hell," Matt said as he laid the canteen aside and picked up the whiskey bottle.

Lacey nodded. Holding her breath, she stared at the cobwebs hanging from a corner of the ceiling as Matt tilted the whiskey bottle over her hand. In spite of her resolve to be brave, she gave a cry of pain as the alcohol seeped into the wound, making her finger feel on fire.

Matt swore softly as he wrapped the injured digit in a bit of cloth ripped from his shirt tail. The sight of blood, his own or someone else's, had never bothered him in the slightest. He had seen men blown to bits during the war. He had helped one of the Army doctors amputate a man's leg and never turned a hair. He had buried men who had been hacked to pieces in a bayonet charge, or been blown to bits by cannon fire and remained calm, but seeing Lacey's finger oozing with blood and hearing her small cry of pain tugged at his heart in a most peculiar way.

Feeling suddenly light-headed, Lacey swayed unsteadily on her feet. Immediately Matt reached out and grabbed her, pulling her close to him.

"You okay?" he asked anxiously. "You're not gonna faint on me, are you?"

"I don't think so." Lacey gave a little sigh as Matt's arm slid around her waist, holding her tightly, protectively. It was nice to have someone look after her. It felt so good to stand in Matt's embrace, to feel the security of his arm around her. Without thinking of what she was doing, she closed her eyes and rested her cheek against his chest. It was such a comforting chest, she thought dreamily, hard and strong and solid. She could hear his heart beating, steady and sure beneath her ear, and that was comforting, too.

Tenderly, Matt held Lacey to him. Poor little thing, he thought affectionately, and began to stroke her hair. Bending, he kissed the top of her head, his lips moving softly in the heavy silken mass of her hair. She felt good in his arms, as if she belonged there.

Wordlessly he drew her closer to him, his hands moving to caress her back. It had been hell, living with her all these weeks, wanting her, and yet not daring to touch her for fear of frightening her with the intensity of his desire, or, worse yet, incurring her hatred. She was innocent in the ways of men, and he yearned to be the one to teach her the joys and pleasures that a man and woman could share. Nevertheless, he had been taught from childhood that a gentleman did not force a lady. A gentleman took his base desires elsewhere, for there were plenty of women who were

125

more than willing to satisfy a man's lust for the right amount of money.

Matt frowned. He had seen his share of prostitutes during the war, women willing to sell themselves for the price of a meal, camp followers who had bartered their virtue for food or clothing or shelter. Women of easy virtue were never hard to find. They were always there, lingering in shadowy hotel doorways or in smoke-filled saloons, waiting. Always waiting, always willing.

Matt gazed at the top of Lacey's head. Was that all he felt for her, just lust? He wanted to make love to her, that was true enough, but he also wanted to care for her, to protect her from harm. Surely those emotions were of a higher, more noble caliber than mere lust for her sweet flesh. Was it possible he had fallen in love with her?

Lacey stirred in Matt's arms. Lifting her head, she gave him a shy smile. "Thank you," she murmured. "I feel better now."

She was so beautiful, Matt thought. So darn beautiful. Her hair was like a dull flame, her eyes were wide and innocent. Cupping her chin in the palm of his hand, he lowered his head and kissed her gently. He was not prepared for the heat that shot clear through him as his lips touched hers; heat that turned his body to flame and then settled in his loins, urging him to take that which he had been yearning for since the moment he opened his eyes and saw her hovering over him. He kissed her again, his mouth hungry.

And Lacey kissed him back. Feeling suddenly shameless, she pressed herself against Matt, wanting him to kiss her, wanting to feel the hard masculine length of his body next to hers, his arms tight around her. He was the only sure thing in a world of strangers, the only source of comfort and security. Her only source of strength. She yielded her mouth to his, her lips parting as she surrendered to the heady warmth that surged through her limbs, making her knees weak, turning her blood to fire.

Matt's tongue gently probed the recesses of her mouth, savoring the secret sweetness within, igniting a never before known feeling of excitement in the very core of her being, a feeling of such wonder and delight that she shivered with the sheer pleasure of it. Her heart was beating a wild primal rhythm as her arms twined around his neck, drawing him closer, wanting to absorb his essence into herself.

Matt groaned low in his throat as Lacey's lips parted beneath his. His whole body felt alive, tingling with sensation and desire. His kiss deepened as he sought to draw her closer still. Heat washed through him, driving him to the brink of madness. Her breasts were flattened against his chest, soft and warm, exciting him still further. His hands slid down her back, cupping her buttocks, molding her hips to his, letting her feel the visible evidence of his desire.

"Lacey." Her name was a groan on his lips. The blood pounded in his brain, roaring in his ears like the crash of distant thunder as the fire of his desire spread through him. Dimly, the faint voice of reason warned him that if he didn't release her soon, he never would.

He started to pull away, but Lacey refused to let him go. Her arms tightened around his neck as she kissed him ardently, passionately. She was trembling with an emotion she did not understand, but it was incredibly sweet, drugging her senses, mesmerizing her with pleasure, and she knew only that she did not want it to end. Not now, not ever.

Warning bells rang loud and clear in Matt Drago's mind. It was time to stop. She was just a kid, he reminded himself, new to passion, intoxicated with pleasure. She didn't know what she was doing to him, what he wanted to do to her.

With an effort, he pried her arms from around his neck. "Lacey . . ." His voice was low and edged with the pain of wanting her.

"Please, Matt," she murmured breathlessly.

"Lacey, you don't know what you're asking for."

"Show me," she begged, and pressed her lips to his again, certain she would die if he didn't kiss her again.

It was a temptation no man could resist. Knowing it was wrong, Matt lowered Lacey onto his blanket. His tongue plundered the sweetness of her mouth as his hands gently massaged her belly and thighs.

Lacey moaned with delight as a sudden rush of warmth filled her. All her senses were attuned to Matt. Her lips tasted his, her hands touched his flesh, her nostrils were filled with his scent, and her ears heard only the harsh rasp of his breathing as his mouth moved over her face, raining kisses on her eyes and nose and mouth. Closing her eyes, she surrendered to the magic of his hands, the rapture of his kisses. Waves of sensation washed through her, making her forget everything but the touch of his hands and mouth on her all too willing flesh.

She was hardly aware that he was undressing her until she felt the cool air whisper over her bare skin. She gasped with surprise as she felt his tongue slide over her breast, teasing and tormenting. She tried to stop him, but when the first shock passed, she urged him on, driven by a hunger that was new and frightening in its intensity, certain she would shatter into a million pieces if he did not satisfy the alien need raging through her. Her hands moved restlessly over his broad back and shoulders, delving under his shirt to stroke the hard-muscled flesh beneath. His skin was moist and warm and exhilarating, his eyes bright with desire as her fingers curled in the thick pelt on his chest, following it down, down, until it disappeared inside his trousers.

Matt uttered a hoarse cry as her hand stopped at his waist. Somehow, without quite letting her go, he managed to shrug out of his jeans and shirt, and now they were lying side by side, bodies and mouths fused together.

Outside, the rain fell in icy sheets. Thunder rolled across the darkened skies; lightning split the angry clouds. A gust of wind rattled the door of the cabin and howled above the roar of the rain.

We're all alone in the world, Lacey mused. *Just me and Matt and the storm.*

She was ready for him when he rose over her, ready to give him whatever he asked of her if only he would satisfy the fierce desire that plagued her. She knew a brief moment of fear when he parted her thighs. There could be no going back now, she thought, and experienced an unexpected wave of panic.

Matt sensed the change in her, saw the sudden fright in her eyes. He should stop then and there, he knew. She was a virgin, an innocent child, and he had no right to touch her. But he needed her. Lord, how he needed her. And so, knowing it was wrong, he lowered his head and kissed her fervently, his lips tender yet insistent, and as she kissed him back, he drove into her, sighing with pleasure as her womanly warmth closed around him.

Lacey hardly noticed the brief stab of pain as he possessed her. She was lost in the wonder of his kisses, the magic of his touch.

She whispered his name as his life surged within her, filling her with delicious warmth and a feeling of endless peace. . . .

Later, she was ashamed. She had given herself to a man who was not her husband, a man who had never even said he loved her. A man who was an escaped felon. How would she ever face her father again? How would she live with the shame of what she had done? She had sold her virtue for a few moments of pleasure in the arms of a stranger.

She didn't move or say a word, but Matt felt her drawing away from him. "What's the matter, Lacey?" he asked, frowning. "Did I hurt you?"

Wordlessly, she shook her head. He *had* hurt her, she thought bitterly, but not in the way he meant.

"Lacey . . ." He reached out a hand to comfort her, and she batted it away.

"Leave me alone."

"Lacey, what is it?"

"Just leave me alone!" she repeated vehemently, and burst into tears, sobbing as though her heart would break.

In spite of her plea to be left alone, Matt gathered Lacey in his arms and held her tight. For a moment she struggled against him; then, with a sigh that seemed to come from deep inside of her, she went limp in his arms.

"Lacey, what's wrong?" Matt asked tenderly. "You can tell me."

"I'm so ashamed." The words were barely audible, but they were filled with guilt and remorse.

Matt patted Lacey's back as one might comfort a hurt child, his mind and heart accusing him of being the lowest form of scum. Of course she was ashamed. She was a nice girl, not some cheap tramp. He should never have touched her. She was young and innocent, unaware of what she was getting into, easily carried away by the newness of passion, the wonder of discovery. He had known she would regret the deed as soon as the magic dissolved and reality set in.

"Lacey," he said slowly. "I didn't mean to shame you. I never meant that."

"It wasn't your fault," she said in a small voice. And that was the worst part of it, she thought miserably. It wasn't his fault. The blame was entirely hers.

"I could have said no," Matt replied with a wry grin.

"I practically raped you," Lacey blurted, and then flushed crimson from head to heel.

Matt tried not to laugh, but the idea of Lacey taking advantage of him was so ludicrous he couldn't help himself.

With a wordless cry, Lacey wriggled out of his arms, more humiliated than she had ever been. For weeks, she had worried that Matt might abuse her, and when it finally happened, it was all her fault. She had behaved like a shameless hussy, and now he had the nerve to laugh at her.

"Lacey, I'm sorry," Matt apologized. "I wasn't laughing at you, honest. You must know I wanted you, too, that nothing would have ever happened between us otherwise."

Lacey glared at him, her brown eyes sparkling with tears.

"You're a beautiful young woman," Matt said sincerely. "It's been hell, trying to keep my hands off you. If anyone's at fault, it's me."

"Do you really think I'm beautiful?"

"Very beautiful," he said huskily. "And very desirable."

His words warmed her right down to her toes, taking some of the sting from her shame.

Matt patted the floor beside him. "Come here."

Lacey's heart fluttered wildly as she returned to his side. Sinking down beside him, she rested her head against his shoulder.

Matt let out a long breath. The tears shining in Lacey's eyes pricked his conscious. He had never deflowered a virgin before and he felt guilty as hell.

"Listen, Lacey, I . . . as soon as we reach a town, we'll get married." The words were out before he quite realized what he'd said.

Lacey looked at him, blinking in disbelief. "We will?"

"I promise."

"Do you *want* to get married?"

Her question caught him off guard. In truth, he didn't want to get married. His only experience with marriage had been in watching his father and Leticia, and he had seen nothing in their relationship to recommend it. Saul Drago had been a terrible husband and a failure as a father. Leticia had performed the duties of a wife and mother, but she had never expressed joy or happiness in either role. Matt had never witnessed a happy marriage, and after his fiasco with Claire Duprey, he had decided he would never marry at all.

But now, looking down into Lacey Montana's tear-stained face, remembering how sweet she had been, the idea of marriage didn't seem so distasteful.

"Yes," he said, surprising them both. "I want to get married."

Lacey's smile was radiant. "I love you, Matt," she murmured shyly, and wondered when it had happened. She had tried not to like him, frequently reminding herself that he was a convict, but she had nursed him and lived with him, and somehow, in spite of herself, she had grown to love him.

"Lacey." He drew her close, his heart swelling with an emotion he had never felt for anyone, not even Claire. Perhaps it was love, he mused, perhaps not. But whatever it was, he planned to hang onto it.

The rain stopped that afternoon. Reluctantly, they left the shack. Lacey looked back once, wanting to memorize every line of the drab little cabin where Matt had shown her what it was like to be a woman. She smiled faintly as she gazed at the sagging roof and crooked door, the rough plank walls. Somehow the place didn't look as ugly as before.

"Where are we going?" Lacey asked as they rode away from the shack. Her stomach rumbled hungrily. They'd had little to eat in the cabin due to a lack of dry wood for a fire.

"Camp Verde's not far from here," Matt replied, thinking out loud. "We can pick up some supplies there. Could be they'll have news of the Apache."

Lacey nodded. She had almost forgotten about her father, lost as she was in the glow of Matt's lovemaking, but now she was suddenly more worried about him than ever. She had heard dreadful stories of men who had been tortured and abused by the Indians, tales of such cruelty and savagery that she had refused to believe they were true. Surely even a people as godless and fearless as the Apache were rumored to be could not be as barbaric as she had been told.

With a shake of her head, she put such thoughts from her. It was too beautiful a day to contemplate cruelty and ugliness. Better to assume that her father was alive and well until she knew otherwise.

She gigged her horse up beside Matt and smiled prettily when he glanced over at her. The mere touch of his eyes on her face made her heart sing, and Lacey thought that, except for not knowing where her father was, she had never been happier in her life. The sky was a warm vibrant blue, the distant trees were emerald green and fresh-washed from the rain, the sun overhead was the color of butter. Cinder's steps were lively, and Lacey had to hold the mare on a tight rein to keep her at a walk. Oh, but it was good to be alive!

The day flew by, and now, lying snug in her blankets beside their banked campfire, Lacey could not sleep. Her emotions were in turmoil and she tossed and turned restlessly. All she could think of was Matt and how much she yearned to be in his arms again. Her whole body longed for his touch, her lips ached for his kiss, yet she could not bring herself to call him even though she could see him sitting cross-legged beside the fire. He was staring out across the plains, a cigarette clamped between his teeth, a brooding expression on his face. His profile stood out in vivid detail, bronzed by the embers of the fire, and she thought again how handsome he was. Desire was a new emotion, one she did not quite know how to handle. She knew it was wrong of her to want Matt, knew she should not allow him to make love to her again until after they were legally wed. But she wanted him so much, and she wanted him now. If only she had the nerve to call him; but then, what could she possibly say?

Lacey let out a sigh of frustration. She didn't know much about men. Perhaps Matt didn't want her again so soon. Better to say nothing than ask for his loving and be refused.

Matt Drago took a deep drag on his cigarette, then exhaled a cloud of blue-gray smoke. From the corner of his eye, he could see Lacey tossing restlessly in her blankets. He was restless, too, he mused, restless and wanting. He had thought that once he had possessed Lacey, the desire that had plagued him would be satisfied; instead, it had only made it worse. All day, he had thought of little else. Several times he had been tempted to drag her off her horse and tumble her in the grass,

but he knew she would be shocked and repulsed by anything so crude. Shocked and
ashamed. Hadn't she made it perfectly clear
last night that she had been horrified by what
they had done?

Damn! If only he dared take her in his arms
and make love to her again. If only she wanted
him as much as he wanted her. Rising, he
walked around their camp, his eyes constantly
straying toward Lacey's inert form. He was
about to head for his own blankets when her
gaze met his. For a long moment, their eyes
met and held across the dying embers of the
fire, and Matt felt all his senses come screaming to life as the current between them crack-
led like lightning in a summer storm.

As though hypnotized, he walked toward
her, drawn by the veiled hunger in her luminous brown eyes. Kneeling, he threw back the
blankets and drew Lacey into his arms. She
came without protest, her head falling back
over his arm, her lips slightly parted, her eyes
naked with desire.

And still he hesitated, not wanting to bruise
her tender feelings toward him.

"Lacey?" The wanting, the hunger he felt
for her, was there in his voice.

She nodded, hoping Matt would know what
she wanted even though she could not say the
words.

"Oh, Lacey," he breathed, and his mouth

slanted over hers. He kissed her with all the longing in his heart, his blood turning to fire as she returned his kiss with a fervor that surprised and pleased him.

"Am I awful, Matt?" she whispered tremulously. "Awful to want you so?"

"No."

"I can't help the way I feel. I . . ." She turned away, unable to tell him how her body cried out for his touch.

"I can wait, Lacey," Matt said in a ragged voice. "We'll be at Verde in a couple of days. The chaplain can marry us then." He let out a shaky breath. "I can wait," he repeated wryly. "It won't be easy, but I can wait."

"I don't want to wait, Matt," she admitted, her words softer than the gentle breeze soughing through the trees.

"I love you, Lacey," Matt murmured hoarsely. "Lord, but I love you."

And as he kissed her once more, she had no reason to doubt it.

CHAPTER 6

They reached Camp Verde on a dismal Saturday afternoon. The post, established in 1864, was located on the west bank of the Rio Verde some thirty-five miles east of Prescott, Arizona. The camp had been built to provide protection for the Prescott mining district.

On this day, a handful of new recruits were drilling on the parade ground while, some distance away, a Negro sergeant was riding a wildly bucking mustang in a small corral. The rider was being cheered on by a half-dozen soldiers in sweat-stained Army blue.

A tall, lanky man wearing the gold bars of a lieutenant approached Matt and Lacey as they dismounted.

"May I help you?" the soldier asked.

He eyed Matt somewhat warily, Lacey thought, and wondered why.

"We're looking for a place to spend the night," Matt replied, slapping the dust from his hat. He smiled fondly at Lacey. "And we're looking for a preacher."

Lieutenant Wilson Charles McKay's glance shifted from Matt to Lacey, and he felt his breath catch in his throat as he took a good look at the young woman standing beside the stranger. She was a decidedly pretty woman, McKay realized, and he had not seen a pretty woman in a long time. Not a decent one, anyway.

The lieutenant's gaze moved back to Matt. The man was dangerous, McKay thought. There was a hint of wildness in the deep blue eyes, a wariness in his stance that belied his easy manner.

"I expect the post chaplain will be able to oblige you," the lieutenant said. "You'll have to check with Captain Slater about spending the night." McKay gestured toward a building on his left. "The captain's office is in there, first door on the left. You can't miss it." Saluting, the lieutenant pivoted on his heel and walked away.

Taking Lacey by the hand, Matt set out for the captain's office.

Captain Tom Slater was sitting at his desk, idly thumbing through a worn copy of the

Police Gazette. It was a lazy kind of day, he mused, and wondered absently what Margaret had prepared for dinner, and if Sergeant Carlisle had returned from Prescott. He grinned as a rousing cheer went up from the corral, signaling that Sergeant Leroy had topped another broomtail.

Slater laid the magazine aside as a young man and woman entered his office.

"Can I help you?" he asked, sitting up a little straighter in his chair. His deep-set gray eyes took in every detail of the couple standing before him. The man was tall and dark. The fact that he was part Indian did not go unnoticed by the captain, who had spent fifteen years in Apache country. The girl was fair and easy on the eyes. Both looked as though they'd been traveling a hard road for a long time.

A muscle twitched in Matt's jaw as he met the officer's inquiring gaze. "We need a place to spend the night."

Slater's eyes narrowed. There was no ring on the girl's hand. "You married?"

"Not yet," Matt replied easily. "We were hoping the post chaplain could help us out."

Slater nodded thoughtfully, wondering if the girl had run away from home to marry a man her parents didn't approve of. And with good reason. Slater had come to respect the Apache, but he didn't trust half-breeds, and he hated to see a girl as pretty and young as this one get mixed up with a man who would only cause her unhappiness. But it wasn't his problem.

The captain smiled. "Good excuse for a party," he said congenially. "I don't believe I caught your name?"

"Dunbar," Matt said, extending his hand. "Matthew Dunbar. And this is Lacey Montana."

Slater shook Matt's hand, but his eyes were on Lacey. He had not missed the look of confusion on her face when Dunbar introduced himself.

"I imagine you'd like to freshen up, Miss Montana," the captain remarked. "Why don't you go along to my quarters? Last house past the infirmary. You can't miss it. It's the only house with flowers in the yard. My missus would be pleased to have your company."

Lacey glanced at Matt, her expression apprehensive.

"Go along, Lacey," Matt said, giving her a reassuring smile. "I'll be along soon."

"All right. Thank you, captain," Lacey said politely. She gave Matt's hand a squeeze and left the room.

Outside, she walked slowly toward the captain's house, feeling rather like a lost lamb as she made her way down the dusty road. Several men turned to stare at her as she

143

passed by. One whistled under his breath. Another saluted her. They all smiled.

The last house was small, white, and bordered with a variety of carefully tended flowers and shrubs. Somewhat hesitantly, Lacey approached the house and knocked on the door. Whatever was she going to say?

Lacey's knock was answered by a slim woman in her mid-forties. She had dark blond hair worn in a tight knot at the nape of her neck, clear blue eyes, and skin that was tanned a deep brown from years of living under the Arizona sun.

"Yes?" the woman said in a well-modulated voice. "Can I help you?"

"I . . . Captain Slater said I should come here to freshen up."

Margaret Slater nodded as though strangers appeared at her door every day. "Of course, my dear. Won't you come in?" She stepped back so Lacey could enter the house. "I'm Margaret Slater," she said, holding out a well-manicured hand.

"Lacey Montana," Lacey replied, taking the woman's hand.

"Well, from the look of you, I'd say you'd like to bathe first and get acquainted later," Margaret Slater remarked with an amiable smile. "As it happens, I was just warming some water for myself."

"I can wait," Lacey said quickly.

"No need. The tub's in the kitchen, and the water should be hot by now."

"No, really," Lacey said. "I don't want to put you out."

Margaret Slater laughed softly. "No offense, child," she said kindly, "but I think you need a bath worse than I do."

Lacey laughed self-consciously. She did need a bath, and, in truth, she couldn't think of anything she wanted more.

"The kitchen is that way," Margaret Slater said, pointing toward a closed door. "Towels are on the table. You go on in and have a nice soak. I have a robe that should fit you when you're done if you'd like to wash out your clothes as well."

"Thank you, Mrs. Slater. That's very kind."

The water was indeed hot, and Lacey poured it carefully into the zinc tub, undressed, and stepped in. The hot water felt wonderful, and she sank down in the tub and closed her eyes, letting the heat penetrate her body, soothing saddle-weary muscles. After several minutes, she began to wash, first herself, then her hair, and then her dusty trail garb.

A half-hour later she was seated in the Slater's parlor, wrapped in a blue terrycloth robe, sipping tea from a delicate china cup.

"I can't imagine what could be keeping Matt," Lacey said.

Margaret Slater laughed softly. "I imagine Tom is pumping him for information," she said with a slight shake of her head. "Tom likes to know everything that's going on in his territory. Have you come far?"

"Yes."

"What brings you to Camp Verde? We don't get many visitors."

"We're looking for a preacher," Lacey answered, blushing prettily.

"A wedding!" Margaret said in delight. "How splendid."

Lacey nodded, liking the woman more and more.

"Would you do me a favor?" Margaret asked, leaning forward. "Would you wear my wedding dress?"

"Oh, I couldn't," Lacey protested, overwhelmed by the offer.

"It's a beautiful gown, all lace and antique satin. I had hoped my own daughter might wear it some day, but Tom and I never had any children."

"I'd be proud to wear it," Lacey said, touched by the older woman's generosity. "Thank you."

"Good. When's the wedding to take place?"

"I'm not sure."

"Would this evening be too soon? It's been so long since we had a party."

146

"I'll have to ask Matt," Lacey said uncertainly.

"Of course. Oh, here they come now."

The Slaters made Matt and Lacey feel very much at home. Margaret Slater served them a dinner fit for a king, and the four of them chatted like old friends. Matt agreed that the wedding should take place that evening, and the captain sent his striker to take care of the details.

Two hours later, Lacey was standing beside Captain Slater at the rear of the post chapel clad in Margaret Slater's wedding gown. It was indeed a beautiful dress. The neck was round and trimmed with yards and yards of delicate ivory lace. The sleeves were long, tapering to a point at Lacey's wrists. The bodice fit Lacey as though it had been made for her. The skirt, long and full, fell in graceful folds to the floor.

Standing at the altar beside the chaplain, Matt gazed at Lacey in awe, certain he had never seen anyone or anything more beautiful than the woman who was about to become his wife.

At a signal from the chaplain, the organist began to play the Wedding March, and Lacey came down the narrow aisle on Captain Slater's arm.

Lacey could not take her eyes from Matt's

147

face as the chaplain spoke the solemn words that made them man and wife. Matt was wearing a pair of black trousers and a dark blue shirt he had borrowed from one of the soldiers, and she thought, dreamily, that he was surely the most handsome man she had ever known. The dark blue shirt complemented his swarthy skin and black hair, and made his eyes glow a brilliant blue.

And then Matt was lifting her veil, taking her in his arms to bestow his first husbandly kiss. Lacey closed her eyes as his mouth closed over hers. His kiss, soft and gentle as a butterfly dancing on a rose petal, filled her with a warm inner glow.

Later there was a party in the officers' mess to celebrate. The Army cook had baked a small cake, and there was champagne and sandwiches for anyone who cared to drop by and wish the newlyweds well.

Lacey was surprised to discover that her new husband was a wonderful dancer. He twirled her around the dance floor until she was breathless. He was light on his feet for a man so big, and he knew the steps to every number the post band played.

"Wherever did you learn to dance so well?" Lacey asked curiously.

"Back home," Matt answered, smiling down at her. "Before the war."

Lacey pouted prettily. "I forgot you were from the South. I heard they were always having fancy balls and cotillions. I suppose you danced with every belle in the county."

"At least once," Matt said gravely. "And the old maids, as well."

"Cad."

"Angel."

Lacey laughed softly, her heart bubbling with happiness.

They were in the midst of a waltz when Matt saw the captain's orderly enter the room and take the captain aside. The two men spoke for several minutes, with the captain occasionally glancing in Matt's direction, and then the orderly left the room, his face grave.

A warning bell rang in Matt's mind, and he was about to lead Lacey off the dance floor when Captain Slater tapped him on the shoulder.

"Mind if I cut in?" the captain asked.

Matt hesitated only a moment. "Of course not," he said. He nodded to Lacey and headed for the refreshment table. Immediately two armed troopers fell into step beside him.

"The captain would like to see you in his office," the trooper on Matt's left said.

"Right now," added the trooper on Matt's right. He jabbed his service revolver into Matt's ribs. "Understand?"

"Perfectly," Matt answered. He offered no resistance as the two men escorted him out of the building and into the captain's office.

Moments later Tom Slater entered the room and closed the door behind him.

"Where's Lacey?" Matt asked curtly.

"Margaret took her home. Don't worry, she'll be fine."

Matt nodded warily, his eyes never leaving the captain's face.

"Search him," Slater ordered, and one of the troopers quickly ran his hands over Matt's back and down his legs.

"He's clean," the young man said confidently.

Slater nodded. He regarded Matt for a long time, his deep gray eyes thoughtful. "Drago, right?" he mused aloud. "We got a flyer on you two, three days ago. Seems the boys over at the Yuma Pen have been searching high and low for you."

Matt nodded. Outwardly he appeared calm, unconcerned, but inwardly he was cussing himself for being seven kinds of a fool. He should have known the law would have posters out on him, but he wasn't used to thinking like a criminal. Dammit, he *wasn't* a criminal.

"I thought your face looked familiar," Slater went on cheerfully, "so I had my orderly check the wanteds, and sure enough, you were there."

Matt nodded again. The captain sounded mighty pleased with himself.

"Nothing to say for yourself?" Slater remarked.

"You might have waited until tomorrow morning to arrest me," Matt said dryly.

"Sorry about that," Slater said sarcastically. "I guess your honeymoon will just have to wait."

"Yeah, indefinitely," Matt muttered. "Shit."

Tom Slater felt a brief moment of regret. It was a shame the kid had to miss out on his honeymoon. Almost, he was tempted to let the newlyweds spend the night together. But then he squared his shoulders. The man was a criminal, convicted of murder. He didn't deserve a honeymoon, or anything else but a rope. He was damn lucky they didn't hang him here and now.

Slater's gaze lifted to the two troopers standing behind Matt. "Kellog, escort Mr. Drago to the guardhouse. Stewart, you go tell Polaski to wire Yuma. Tell them we've got their missing con, and they can pick him up at their convenience."

"Polaski's in bed, sir," Stewart said.

"Wake him up."

"Yessir!"

At a prod from Kellog's weapon, Matt stepped outside and walked across the dusty ground toward the guardhouse. It was a small brick building between the infirmary and the laundry. A burly corporal stood guard.

Kellog opened a cell door and gestured for Matt to step inside. The soldier grinned impudently. It was easy to see that his prisoner had done time before. It showed in the rueful expression on his face, and in the wary hesitation of his stance.

With an exaggerated sigh of resignation, Matt took a step forward as if to enter the cell. Abruptly he pivoted on his heel and slammed his fist into Kellog's face. The private, caught completely off guard, crumpled to the floor without a sound.

Cussing softly, Matt scooped up the trooper's rifle and casually stepped outside, shutting the door behind him.

Corporal Amos Canaly did a double take as Matt Drago stepped out of the guardhouse. Belatedly he reached for his sidearm.

"I wouldn't," Matt warned, the rifle aimed at the corporal's midsection.

Canaly froze. A fine sheen of sweat beaded across his brow as he waited for the prisoner to squeeze the trigger.

"Smart boy," Matt said quietly. "Give me your kerchief and turn around."

"Are you gonna kill me?" the corporal asked, his voice quivering with fear.

"That's up to you," Matt snapped, and as the frightened young soldier turned around, Matt tapped him lightly on the back of the head with the butt of the rifle. Amos Canaly slumped to the ground with a dull thud, and Matt quickly tied the boy's hands behind his back with the kerchief, checked his pulse, and then drifted into the shadows.

He had to find Lacey, and they had to get the hell out of Camp Verde. Fast. On silent feet, he padded toward the captain's quarters.

Lacey sat on the edge of the bed in the Slaters' spare bedroom, sobbing uncontrollably. What had been the happiest night of her life had quickly become the worst. She smoothed a wrinkle from the skirt of her bridal gown, then let out a long, shuddering sigh as a fresh flood of tears spilled down her cheeks. It was so awful! Only a short time ago she had been so happy, and now Matt was locked in the guardhouse, waiting for someone from Yuma to arrive and escort him to prison. She would never find her father now, never live with Matt as his wife. Never bear his children. A wave of self-pity washed over her as she railed at the cruel hand of fate that had given her a glimpse of happiness and then snatched it from her grasp.

The sound of someone or something tapping at the window interrupted her tears. Lifting her head, Lacey glanced apprehensively toward the window. A radiant smile lit her face as she recognized Matt peering through the glass. Jumping from the bed, she flew to the window and raised the latch.

"Matt!"

"Come on, we've got to get out of here, right now!"

Lacey didn't waste time arguing. Lifting her skirts, she climbed over the windowsill and into Matt's waiting arms.

Matt swore softly as he placed Lacey on her feet.

"What is it?" she whispered anxiously, her eyes searching the darkness. Had they been discovered already?

"That dress."

Lacey glanced down at her wedding gown, now sadly rumpled. "What's wrong with it?"

"It stands out like a beacon in a lighthouse. You've got to get rid of it."

"But I don't have anything else to wear. Mrs. Slater sent my clothes out to be pressed."

"You can wear my shirt. That dress has got to go."

With a sigh of resignation, Lacey began to unfasten the long row of tiny pearl buttons that ran down the back of her borrowed gown. She had difficulty with some of them, and Matt brushed her hands away and deftly unfastened the last few loops so Lacey could step out of the dress.

"Get rid of those petticoats, too," Matt said. With a nod, she unfastened the tapes of the petticoats and let them fall around her ankles. An eager light danced in Matt's eyes as he gazed at Lacey. Her hair had come loose and fell in glorious disarray around her shoulders. Her chemise left little to the imagination, and he was sorely tempted to carry her back into the bedroom and make her his wife in a manner far more binding than a few words on a piece of paper. But there was no time for that. Not now.

"Here." He handed her his shirt, watched as she pulled it on. It covered her from her neck to mid-thigh.

"Let's go," he said urgently, and taking her by the hand, he led her toward the barn where their horses were stabled.

"Wait here," he directed. Leaving Lacey standing in the shadows, he ghosted into the dusky barn, his eyes darting warily from right to left. There was no sign of a guard, and he let out a small sigh of relief as he began to saddle their horses.

Just let our luck hold, he prayed silently, and led the horses out of the barn. A quick boost put Lacey onto Cinder's back. Then, still on foot, Matt led the horses toward the rear of the fort, giving silent thanks to the powers that be that Camp Verde was not a walled fort.

Slowly, silently, they made their way into the darkness beyond the camp. Only then did Matt swing into the saddle.

They had just urged their horses into an easy trot when a bugle began to blow.

"Damn!" Matt exclaimed. "It didn't take them long to discover we've gone. Come on, Lacey, let's ride!"

Lacey nodded as she urged her horse after Matt's. It was scary, riding through the black night, unable to see more than a few feet ahead. A low shrub, a prairie dog hole, a sudden dip in the terrain, all could spell sudden disaster when you were riding hell for leather through the dark.

The wind whipped Lacey's hair into her face and stung her cheeks and bare legs, but the fear that they might be caught spurred her on. She could not bear to think of Matt confined behind iron bars, could not imagine life without him.

They rode hard for over an hour, pushing their horses as much as they dared. Lacey's legs were numb with cold, her thighs chafed from rubbing against saddle leather, but she rode stoically on, her eyes fixed on Matt's bare back. They had to get away, and she knew she would endure any discomfort necessary to insure Matt's freedom.

The sky was turning to pale gray when Matt reined his lathered gelding to a halt. Lacey's mare slid to a stop beside him, and Matt saw that Lacey was slumped over the mare's neck, one hand wrapped in the horse's mane, the other fisted around the reins. Her eyes were closed.

"Lacey?"

Her eyes fluttered open. "I'm awake," she murmured. "Let's keep going."

Matt grinned wryly as he slid to the ground and lifted Lacey into his arms. Her head fell against his shoulder, and he saw that her eyes were closed again.

"Go to sleep, honey," he said softly.

Lacey's eyes flew open. "No, Matt. Let's keep going. I'm not tired."

"Lacey, take it easy," Matt chided gently. "The horses are tired, even if you aren't."

Lacey nodded. With a sigh, she snuggled against him and he saw that she was sound asleep. For a moment he held her in his arms, not wanting to let her go, not even for a minute. Then, with a weary sigh, he placed her on a patch of dry grass and began to unsaddle their horses. Hobbling them nearby, he spread Lacey's bedroll on the ground, then carried her to the blankets and put her to bed. Curling up beside her, he covered them with his blankets.

In minutes he, too, was sound asleep.

CHAPTER 7

She was drifting on a cloud, safe and serene, all her troubles behind her. Turning, she smiled at Matt and he took her in his arms and kissed her. His lips were warm, coaxing, his hands gentle as they moved slowly over her flesh. Gradually Lacey came awake, to realize that she was not dreaming at all.

Opening her eyes, she saw Matt beside her. He was propped up on one elbow, his free hand lightly massaging her stomach. He smiled at her, a lazy smile, and then he lowered his head and claimed her lips in a long and hungry kiss.

Warmth. Waves and waves of delicious warmth engulfed Lacey's body as Matt's mouth moved over hers. Wrapping her arms around his neck, she kissed him back, her lips parting at the touch of his tongue.

She was breathing heavily when Matt took his mouth from hers.

"Good morning, Mrs. Drago," he whispered huskily.

Lacey smiled happily. "Good morning, Mr. Drago."

Matt bent to nibble her earlobe. "We've been married one whole day," he murmured, his breath warm against her neck, "and we've not yet had a honeymoon."

"I know," Lacey said. The words came out in a breathy whisper. It was hard to think, hard to speak, when Matt was holding her close, his lips trailing kisses along her neck.

"Lacey . . ."

"Do we have time?" she asked, blushing a little. "The soldiers . . ."

"To hell with the soldiers," Matt rasped. "I want you now."

Lacey nodded shyly. She had never expected Matt to make love to her outside, in broad daylight.

The rising sun fell in muted shades of gold over Lacey's skin as Matt slowly unbuttoned her shirt and slid it over her shoulders. Her chemise came next, and then she was gloriously naked. She was his, he thought possessively, all his. Lawfully, legally his. Her skin was fair, faintly flushed under his approving gaze. Her hair was like a red-gold cloud, her lips as pink and velvety as a wild rose.

Lacey watched from beneath the veil of her lashes as Matt began to remove his trousers. He was beautiful, she thought, grinning, and wondered what he would think if she told him such a thing, for beautiful was what he was.

She went willingly into his arms, her face lifting for his kiss, her body molding itself to his as though they had made love a thousand times before. His skin was warm and firm against hers, the muscles in his back and arms taut beneath her questing fingertips. They kissed for a long, breathless time, hands eagerly exploring. Lacey gave a little gasp as she felt the very visible proof of Matt's growing desire. Strange, to think she could arouse him to such heights, she who had never known a man before Matt came into her life. It gave her a feeling of power to know she could make him tremble with desire, make his dark eyes blaze with passion, cause his lips to murmur love words as he was murmuring them now.

She basked in the love shining in his eyes, in the husky sound of his voice as he praised her beauty, in the touch of his breath upon her face. She was on fire for him when, at last, he possessed her. She reveled in his touch, in the complete sense of satisfaction that came when her body was joined with his. She forgot everything then, everything but the press of his flesh against hers, the sweet sense of wonder that swept them into a world of their own. He was hers, this wonderful man who knew her body so intimately. Her man. Her husband. Hers forever. . . .

Later, sated and content, she was on the verge of sleep when Matt's low-voiced curse sounded in her ear.

"What is it?" Lacey asked, alarmed.

"Don't move," Matt warned. "There are about thirty Indians watching us."

"Watching us?" Lacey squeaked.

"Yeah." Very slowly, Matt stood up, and as he did so he dropped his shirt over Lacey, covering her from her neck to mid-thigh.

He let out a long breath. For a fleeting moment, he thought of diving for his gun, but he knew such a move would be suicide and so he just stood there, waiting, his hands clenched in impotent fury at his sides.

The Indians snickered among themselves as they glanced from Matt to Lacey. It was easy to see what the white man had been doing only moments earlier.

Three of the warriors slid to the ground. Wordlessly they grabbed Matt's arms and tied his hands behind his back. That done, they moved toward Lacey.

She cowered on the ground as the Indians approached her. Dear God, what did they want from her? She threw a pleading glance in Matt's direction, but there was nothing he could do to help her now. One of the warriors indicated she should get dressed, and she did so as quickly as possible, her cheeks flaming with embarrassment as thirty pairs of eyes watched her slip into Matt's shirt.

Ten minutes later Matt and Lacey were mounted on their horses. Lacey's hands had been tied behind her back, her feet tied to the stirrups of her saddle. Matt was similarly bound. The Indians had not seen fit to let him dress, however, and they laughed and made obscene gestures in his direction as they rode along.

"Matt, what's going to happen to us?" Lacey asked in a hushed tone.

"Nothing good, I'll wager," Matt replied, then grunted as the warrior riding beside him struck him across the face.

"No talk," the Indian warned.

They rode until nightfall, then the Indians made camp in a gentle swale. Lacey was lifted from her horse and tied to a tree. She watched apprehensively as the Indians dragged Matt from his horse, then surrounded him, their eyes alight with mischief. One by one, the warriors struck the naked white man with the palms of their hands, and when that failed to evoke a response, they began to hit him with their knotted fists, and then with sticks, until Matt's body was covered with angry red welts.

162

Tears welled in Lacey's eyes as she watched the Indians abuse her husband. Why were they being so cruel? What was going to happen to Matt? Would they kill him? And what would they do with her?

Matt was breathing heavily as he faced the warriors, his teeth clenched, his eyes defiant. His whole body ached from the numerous blows he had received, but he never uttered a sound of pain or protest, knowing that the Indians would consider it a sign of weakness and would torment him even more just to watch him squirm.

When the warriors realized the white man was not going to whine or beg for mercy, they tired of the game. Tying him to a tree, they left him alone and went about the business of preparing a meal and lighting a fire to turn away the chill of the night. Matt sank wearily to the ground. What had they gotten themselves into?

He looked over at Lacey and gave her a smile, hoping to reassure her. She looked so scared, so pale. He tested his bonds, hoping he might be able to slip his hands free, but the ropes were securely tied, and struggling only caused him pain.

Lacey tried to return Matt's smile, but she failed miserably. She was too frightened to put up a brave front, too fearful of what the future held. Her gaze darted to the Indians, but the warriors seemed to have forgotten about their prisoners and were gathered around the campfire, gnawing on jerky and dried venison. No food was offered to Matt or Lacey, and when the Indians finished eating, they bedded down for the night, leaving two warriors to stand guard.

Lacey was so frightened, she was certain she would never be able to sleep, but soon her eyelids grew heavy and she dozed off, her dreams dark and troubled.

When she awoke, it was dawn and the Indians were breaking camp. Matt was jerked to his feet and thrust onto the back of his horse, and soon Lacey was mounted on Cinder, her hands and feet tied as they had been the day before.

They rode all that day, and the next, and at last they came to a narrow chasm that led into a large canyon. Ordinarily Lacey would have gasped with pleasure at the beauty of the canyon, for it was filled with towering trees, grass, and wildflowers. A stream gurgled merrily some yards to her left, emptying into a small lake that was as blue as the sky above. But she had eyes only for the numerous Indian lodges clustered between the sheer canyon walls.

She felt her blood run cold as a multitude of Indian women and children came running toward them, and there was much shouting and laughter as the warriors dismounted, hugging their women and children. After the first brief burst of excitement, the men began to unload the pack horses, doling out blankets and clothing and foodstuffs that had obviously been taken in several raids.

The Indian women laughed scornfully when they saw Matt, naked and helpless. Some spat at him, a few smacked him with their open palms, cursing him loudly in their native tongue.

One warrior, taller than the others, dropped a rope around Matt's neck and led him away. Lacey stared after her husband until he was out of sight. Fear for Matt was soon swallowed up in fear for her own life as a short, stocky warrior dragged her off Cinder's back and forced her to follow him into one of the crude brush-covered huts.

A plump Indian woman was nursing a child inside the lodge. She smiled at the man as he entered, then frowned when she saw the white woman.

The warrior pointed at the squaw. "My woman," he said to Lacey in stilted English. "You will do whatever she says."

Lacey nodded, too scared to reply. So that was to be her fate, she thought bitterly. She was going to be a slave.

The Indian woman did not speak English, but she quickly made it known to Lacey that

165

Lacey was at her mercy, that she had better behave and do as she was told, or be prepared to suffer the consequences.

The next few days were a nightmare. Lacey was forced to gather wood, carry water from the river, prepare meals with ingredients that were foreign to her, and do a dozen other household chores. Her new owner had a quick temper and a sharp tongue, and she did not hesitate to strike Lacey when she was displeased, which was often. Wind Woman's husband, Sun Beaver, rarely interfered. The white woman belonged to his wife. In fact, the lodge and everything it contained belonged to Wind Woman. Like all Apache men, Sun Beaver owned nothing but his weapons, clothing, and horses.

Lacey longed to talk to Matt, but she never had the chance. He was not a slave as she was. Rather, he was simply a prisoner. Dressed in a brief deerskin clout, he was kept tied outside the lodge of the man who had claimed him, much as one might keep a dog. His hands were still bound behind his back; a rope circled his neck, tethering him to a tree. He was fed scraps from the evening meal and allowed to relieve himself at dusk and dawn. Otherwise he remained tied up. Occasionally, as now, the Indian children would gather around him, pointing and jabbering away in their guttural tongue.

They had been in the Indian camp almost a week before Lacey summoned enough nerve to go to Matt. She waited until the hour after midnight when the camp was quiet and the fires had burned down to ashes; then, her heart in her throat, she crept out of Sun Beaver's lodge and made her way across the village to Matt. He was asleep, his body curled into a tight ball in an effort to keep warm, for he had no blanket to ward off the cold. Gently, she placed her hand on his shoulder and shook it.

Matt woke instantly, all his senses alert. He frowned when he rolled over and saw Lacey kneeling beside him. She was taking a terrible risk, just being there. If she was caught, she would likely be punished.

"Oh, Matt," Lacey murmured, and all the fear and unhappiness of the past six days sounded in her voice.

"I know." Matt scooted to a sitting position and Lacey wrapped her arms around his waist, her head resting on his shoulder.

Matt cursed the rope that held his arms behind his back, preventing him from taking Lacey in his arms as he so longed to do. If the days had been long for her, they had been doubly so for him. Sitting there hour after hour with nothing to do wore on his nerves. Several times a day he walked around the tree as far as his tether permitted, first one way and then the other, just to pass the time. He sweated in the sun and shivered at night, and always his thoughts were for Lacey. He watched for her constantly, occasionally being rewarded with a glimpse of her as she went to the river for water.

"Do you think we'll ever get out of here?" Lacey asked.

"I don't know, honey," he replied. "The camp is heavily guarded."

"We could try," she said. "Now! Tonight!"

"No. It's too dangerous. We'd never make it out of the canyon without being seen by the guard at the entrance."

"I hate it here. Please think of something. I'll do anything I can to help. Anything."

"I know. Here now, don't cry."

They sat together for several minutes. Matt rested his chin on the top of Lacey's head, his eyes thoughtful. He spent a good deal of his time trying to figure a way to escape, but so far no opportunity had presented itself. And Lacey only complicated matters. Alone, he would have taken any risk that would bring him his freedom, but he could not take chances that might cause Lacey harm. Her life had become more precious to him than his own.

The fragrance of her hair filled his nostrils and he kissed the top of her head and then, as she lifted her face toward him, he pressed his lips to hers in a long, hungry kiss, drinking in the taste of her as if she were life itself.

Lacey moaned softly, her mouth opening to Matt's as his kiss grew deeper and more intense. Her arms went around his neck and her body pressed close to his until, somehow, they were lying on the ground side by side. She forgot where they were, forgot everything but the fire of Matt's kisses and her own rising desire. Eyes closed, she strained toward him, her hips grinding against his, until she thought she would die with needing him.

Her hands were fumbling with the rope at his wrists when she heard an angry curse. And then Sun Beaver yanked her to her feet, his black eyes filled with wry amusement.

"If you need a man, I am here," Sun Beaver volunteered.

Anger knifed through Matt as he struggled to his feet, "She is my woman," he said through clenched teeth.

Sun Beaver shrugged. "She was your woman. Now she is my slave." Lazily he reached out and slapped Lacey across the face, hard. She reeled backward, tears stinging her eyes as she lifted a hand to her throbbing cheek.

Matt stifled the hot words of protest that rose to his lips as he stared at the bright red handprint on Lacey's cheek. He longed to strike Sun Beaver, to revile him for his harsh

169

treatment of Lacey, but there was nothing to be gained by making the Apache angry.

"Do not come near the white man again," Sun Beaver warned. "If you do, I will have him killed. Do you understand me?"

"I understand," Lacey said quickly.

With a last glance at Matt, the warrior grabbed Lacey by the arm and dragged her back to his lodge.

Matt grimaced as a handful of Apache children clustered around him. He had hoped they would grow weary of making sport of him, but it seemed a futile hope. He was the enemy, a white man, and they delighted in harassing him. Now and then one of the braver boys would dash in and strike him on the leg or across the back, counting coup, then the other boys would shriek with delight. Their childish blows rarely hurt, but the blow to his pride was tremendous. It was humiliating enough, being tied up like a damn dog, without having a bunch of half-naked little savages mocking him.

When at last the boys tired of their sport and wandered away, Matt's thoughts turned to Lacey. He wondered how she was faring. He had only seen her a couple of times since the night Sun Beaver had caught them together, and only from a distance. She seemed well enough, but there was no way to be certain. He wondered if the Apache squaw mistreated her. And if the buck had taken her to his bed. The idea of another man, any man, laying hands on his woman, his *wife*, made the blood pound in his brain and filled his heart with a cold and bitter rage. Yet he was helpless to do anything about it. And that thought was the most galling of all.

They had been in the Apache camp almost three weeks when a handful of Kiowa warriors rode in. There was a celebration of some kind that night, with a lot of singing and dancing. The women served food to the men, and when the men had eaten their fill, one of the warriors brought out a gourd of *tiswin*, which, Lacey had learned, was a kind of beer made from the heart of the mescal plant.

As the night wore on, the warriors began to gamble. Lacey watched from the shadows, her skin prickling with apprehension when she saw Matt's captor gesture toward Matt.

Later, she summoned the nerve to ask Sun Beaver what had happened.

"The white man has been traded to one of the Kiowas," Sun Beaver explained brusquely. "He leaves in the morning." The Indian fixed Lacey with a hard stare. "You remember what I said?"

"Yes," Lacey answered. "I remember."

Going to her bed, she crawled under the robes and wept softly all night long.

The following morning, Lacey watched in helpless dismay as Matt's captor handed him over to one of the Kiowa braves. Matt struggled wildly as his new owner tried to get him on the back of a horse. Lacey pressed her hand over her mouth to keep from crying out as four Kiowa warriors descended on Matt, striking him with their bows and lances until Matt was unconscious. The warriors laughed as they draped Matt over the back of a horse and tied his hands and feet together under the horse's belly.

She cried all that day, her heart aching with sorrow and loneliness. Being a slave in an Apache camp had been bad enough, but at least Matt had been there, too. Just knowing he was nearby, even though she was forbidden to talk to him, had made her plight easier to bear. And now he was gone and she was alone among an alien people.

Wind Woman threatened and scolded and finally gave Lacey a couple of swats with a stick, but to no avail. Lacey continued to sob as though her heart would break. Her father was gone, and now Matt was lost to her as well. It was simply too awful to be borne.

Lacey cried until she was dry and empty inside, and then, feeling as if she had lost all reason to go on living, she went out to gather wood for Wind Woman's fire.

Matt kept a careful eye on the countryside as they rode across the trackless prairie, grateful that his captors had allowed him to sit erect when he regained consciousness. There were a lot of miserable ways to travel, and lying on your stomach across the back of a horse had to be one of the worst.

His hands constantly worked the ropes binding his wrists in an effort to get free, but he only succeeded in making his wrists bleed and his arms weary. He shivered convulsively as the wind blew down out of the mountains, silently cursing the Indians for refusing to give him a shirt and leggings. Thorny bushes gouged his legs as his captors deliberately passed close to the spiny brush that dotted the prairie.

The second day out, it rained for several hours. The warriors rode in comfort beneath shaggy buffalo robes and coats while Matt's body was wracked with chills. His temper, always volatile, was ready to explode at the slightest provocation. He was cold and hungry and bone weary, but, more than that, he was worried about Lacey.

At noon the Indians drew to a halt in the lee of a high plateau. Dismounting, they huddled together, gnawing on jerky and pemmican, while Matt sat in the rain, his hands tied behind his back, his feet lashed to the stirrups. He glared at his captors, cursing them under his breath.

Finally one of the warriors cut Matt's feet free and pulled him from his horse. Shoving him to the ground, the Indian tossed a hunk of jerky into the mud. The message was clear: if he wanted to eat, he would have to eat from the ground like a dog.

Matt gazed hungrily at the dried meat, his appetite warring with his pride. He had not eaten in two days, yet he could not bring himself to eat off the ground. He wasn't an animal, by damn, he was a man!

The Indians watched him, amused. The white man had spirit. It would be a shame to kill him, yet that would likely be his fate in the end. A man with spirit and courage did not make a good slave. Sooner or later he rebelled, and then he was killed.

Matt sat back on his heels, his eyes blazing defiance as he glared at the warriors. And all the while his thoughts were on Lacey. She was a gently bred young woman, and though she had endured many hardships while they searched for her father, she was not accustomed to the hard work and rough life of the Apache. Would she be able to adapt to their harsh way of life? How long would it take to break her spirit? How long before some Apache buck took her for his wife? He groaned low in his throat at the thought of another man possessing her as he had possessed her, making love to her as he yearned to do, holding her close all through the night.

Some minutes later, two of the warriors grasped Matt's arms and thrust him up into the saddle. Matt lashed out with his foot as one of the Indians began to tie his feet to the stirrups. The heel of his foot caught the Apache high in the chest, knocking the wind out of him and sending him reeling backward.

It was a foolish thing to do, and Matt regretted it immediately as four warriors dragged him off his horse and began to beat him with their hands and fists. He grunted with pain as the Indians rained blow after blow to his face and midsection. Blood was oozing from his mouth and nose and from a cut under his eye when they finally let him go. Reviling him in the Apache tongue, they threw him on his horse and lashed his feet to the stirrups.

Matt rode limp in the saddle, his chin resting on his chest, his body aching from the beating he had received. He was covered with mud and blood and a growing sense of doom. Lashing out at the Indians had been stupid, he mused. So damn stupid. He had to do whatever they told him, pretend he was defeated.

Crawl, if necessary. Beg, if need be, until they were certain he was no longer a threat. Then, and only then, could he dare try to escape.

When they made camp that night, Matt huddled against a tree, seeking shelter from the wind that cut through him like a knife. His hands were still bound behind his back; his feet, bound at the ankles, were tethered to the tree. He had not eaten for almost three days, nor tasted water, and he gazed longingly at the warm fire where the Indians sat, eating the rabbits they had caught earlier and drinking water from the bladder of a deer.

Driven by a terrible thirst, he knelt on the ground and lapped at the muddy water that had gathered in a shallow puddle near the trunk of the tree. The water was gritty, but he drank it anyway, then felt the back of his neck grow hot as he heard the warriors laughing at him. One of the Indians tossed over a hunk of meat, and Matt forced himself to lean forward and pick up the meat with his teeth and eat it. Pride would not fill his empty belly, and he could not afford to let himself grow weak and sick from lack of food and drink. He had to stay strong. He had to stay alive. For Lacey's sake if not his own.

Amused by the sight of the white man eating in the mud, the Indians threw him another hunk of meat, and then another, and

Matt ate it all, swallowing the meat along with his pride, for pride was a luxury he could no longer afford.

That night, while the Indians lay warm around the fire, he shivered in the mud with only his growing hatred to keep him warm.

Three days later they reached the Kiowa camp. It was a small village situated between the narrow walls of a canyon. He counted only about twenty lodges. The women and children ran out to see the naked white man who was covered with mud and blood. They chattered excitedly as they gathered around Matt, pointing and laughing and making jokes.

The Indian who had traded three horses for Matt dropped a rope over his neck and led him to a small lodge at the far end of the village. Tying the rope to a high branch, the warrior went inside the lodge.

Alone at last, Matt sank to the ground, his back against the tree. Closing his eyes, he forced himself to relax. He would need to rest and gather his strength for whatever lay ahead.

Lacey curled up on her buffalo robe bed and closed her eyes. She was weary, so weary, but sleep would not come. Matt's image filled her mind, his dark eyes smiling at her, assuring her that everything would be all right. Where was he now? Was he still alive? Why was life so unfair? First her father had been taken from her, and now Matt.

Lacey sniffed as self-pity washed over her. She hated being a slave. She did all of Wind Woman's work, leaving the Apache woman with little to do but care for her child and visit with her friends, who all envied her because she had a white slave. Lacey was forced to cook the meals, tend the small garden behind the lodge, wash and mend the clothes, wash the baby's dirty clouts, and tidy the lodge. It wasn't fair, Lacey thought unhappily, and began to cry, even though crying was a waste of time and energy and left her eyes red and her throat sore.

She yearned to go home, and yet she had no home. She yearned for Matt, but Matt was gone, perhaps dead. She yearned for her freedom, but there was only Wind Woman and her constant demands on Lacey's time.

Despair sat on Lacey's shoulder like a carrion crow. There was no hope in sight, she thought morosely, none at all. The best she could hope for was that some Apache warrior would eventually marry her. At least then she would have a lodge of her own, perhaps a child to love.

The thought brought little comfort. She wanted a wood house with a stove and a white picket fence, not a hide lodge. She wanted Matt to be the father of her children, not an Apache warrior who would never understand her, never love her as Matt loved her.

Staring into the darkness, she made no effort to stem the tears that washed down her cheeks.

CHAPTER 8

Matt groaned softly as he sat up and stretched his legs. His shoulders were stiff, his wrists sore from the constant chafing of the rope that held his hands behind his back. Two weeks had passed, and in all that time he had not been freed of his bonds for more than a few minutes each day. The hours passed slowly, and he fretted at his captivity, and at the inactivity he had been forced to endure. Twice each day his captors offered him food and water, and twice each day Matt swallowed his pride and lapped up whatever was offered, eating it off the ground while his captor watched, openly amused.

Matt was a curiosity in the camp. The Kiowa had seen few white men up close, and they came daily to gawk at Matt, marveling at the whiskers sprouting on his jaw. The Indian men plucked the hair from their faces, and a beard was a novelty.

Scowling blackly, Matt watched the sun rise over the distant mountains. The sun. Its warmth chased the chill of the night from his body even as it chased the darkness from the sky.

His captor stepped from his lodge and dropped a hunk of venison on the ground at Matt's feet, together with a bowl of water.

Obediently, Matt began to eat. The meat was hard and cold, but he ate it anyway, knowing he would get nothing else until nightfall. He was taking a drink of water when the warrior drew a knife and cut him free.

Matt glanced at the warrior in surprise as the ropes binding his hands and feet fell away.

"Get wood," the warrior said curtly, and turning on his heel, he disappeared inside the lodge.

Matt stood up, flexing his arms and shoulders, rubbing his chafed wrists. So he was to be a slave after all.

With a sigh, he started toward the grove of trees that grew at the west end of the canyon. Several Indian women were already up and searching for wood. They stared at Matt, their dark eyes curious and resentful. He was a white man. The enemy.

Ignoring them, Matt began picking up whatever sticks and twigs he could find. He could hear the Indian women laughing at him as he walked along. Imagine, a man, even a white man, doing women's work. It was so amusing.

He had a good-sized armful of wood and was about to return to camp when he saw the gray-haired white man hobbling toward the river. Curious, Matt followed the man, noting that he limped badly and that he seemed in ill health.

The gray-haired man grimaced as he bent over to fill the waterskin. The cold weather must be hell on his old bones, Matt mused. The man turned at the sound of footsteps, his eyes showing surprise as Matt hunkered down beside him.

For a moment the two men studied each other. Then the older man smiled ruefully. "Welcome to hell, friend," he said, offering Matt his hand. "Been here long?"

"About two weeks," Matt replied, taking the older man's hand. "How about you?"

The elderly man shrugged. "I'm not sure. I've lost track of the time. A year. Perhaps two. What difference does it make?"

"Makes a difference to me," Matt said. "I don't aim to stay here that long if I can help it."

The old man laughed softly. "That's what I thought when they first captured me," he said bitterly. "I was determined to escape. I stayed quiet, kept my eyes open and my mouth shut, memorized the routine of the camp so I'd know the best time to make a break for it." He laughed again, a cold hollow sound with no hint of amusement. "They whipped me the first time I tried to escape. Beat me with a club the second time. Cut the hamstring in my right leg the third. Now I can hardly walk, let alone run. And the same thing will happen to you, you'll see. There's no way out of the canyon except through that narrow entrance. And they keep that guarded day and night."

Matt frowned. The Indians seemed to have a penchant for high-walled canyons. "I don't give a damn if the whole tribe sits up there day and night," he said fervently. "I've got to get out of here."

The old man nodded, his brown eyes filled with compassion. "Well, good luck to you, friend," he said as he stood up, the waterskin slung over his shoulder. "It was nice talking to you."

"The name's Drago. Matt Drago."

"Tom Claymore."

"Claymore!" Matt exclaimed.

"Does the name mean something to you?" Claymore asked, surprised by Matt's reaction.

"Yeah. Old Smoke Johnson used to talk about you all the time, about the shining times, he called them."

"Smoke!" Tom Claymore grinned. "Is that old buzzard still prowling around?"

Matt shook his head. "No. He was killed at Chickamauga."

"Well, there's no fool like an old fool," Claymore mused with a shake of his head. "He should have had sense enough to sit that one out. War's a young man's game."

Matt smiled. "Yeah, but he loved the South. He was proud to die for it." Matt slammed his fist into his palm. "Dammit, I've got to get out of here. Soon."

"Sounds like you've got a woman waiting somewheres," Claymore opined, chuckling.

"Yeah. She's a captive, too. I've got to find her before it's too late. Before . . ."

"Before one of the bucks takes her to bed," Claymore said knowingly.

"Yeah."

Tom Claymore nodded. "I'll help you, son," he said resolutely. "Just let me know what I can do."

Matt nodded, and the two men shook hands again.

"Well," Claymore said dryly, "back to work. The old crone who owns me swings a mean stick when she gets mad."

Matt grinned ruefully. "Woman's work is

never done," he muttered, and, picking up his load of firewood, returned to his captor's lodge.

He lay awake a long time that night. Two men just might be able to make their way out of the canyon. It would take a lot of planning and more than a little luck, he mused. Only he didn't have a plan. And he was afraid his luck had run out.

The days that followed were difficult. It was hard to be a slave, hard to obey, hard to be hungry and dirty all the time. He was still clad in nothing but a deerskin clout, still compelled to sleep outside, huddled in the dirt. The only bright spot was that he was no longer tied to a tree like a damn dog. He was grateful for that, and then angry. Damned Indians! Why should he feel gratitude because he was no longer tied up like an animal? What right did these savages have to keep him in captivity? Dammit, he'd never done anything to any of them.

Matt laughed hollowly. Anger was a waste of time and energy. In the days that followed, he found himself doing the same things Tom Claymore had done. He stayed to himself, keeping quiet, drawing no attention to his person. He watched everything that went on around him, noting what time the Indians rose in the morning, when they went to bed at night, how they spent their days. He paid close attention to the entrance of the canyon, memorizing where the guards stood to keep watch, what time the guard was changed.

Daily, he did whatever chores he was ordered to do, and daily the fact that he was a slave ate deeper into his soul, festering like an open wound. But, more than that, his concern for Lacey nagged him constantly. How was she? Was she well? Sick? Had she been abused? Raped? The last thought drove him wild. His dreams were rife with images of Lacey being forced to submit to another man's desires. The thought haunted his days and tormented his sleep, and when he could stand it no longer, he vowed to escape before the next full moon.

He had no plan in mind, only a burning desire to see Lacey again, to touch her, to reassure himself that she was still his. In the end, he decided he would simply wait until the Indians were asleep, and then head for the canyon entrance. With luck, he would be able to slip away, undetected.

Lacey stood at the cookfire, listlessly stirring a large pot of venison stew flavored with sage and wild onions and a few vegetables. She had been a prisoner in the Apache camp for over a month now, though it seemed more like a year. She had come to understand the Indians a little, and she realized they were not the godless monsters she had once thought them to be. They were just people struggling to survive the best way they could in a hostile land. The women laughed and cried and complained, the men provided food and protection, and men and women alike adored their little ones. Apache children were never spanked or slapped, but ran carefree through the village, learning by the example of others how they were expected to behave. Only when they came of age to begin the task of becoming warriors or women were the youth of the tribe subjected to discipline.

Lacey gazed into the distance. She had never worked so hard in all her life as she had worked in the past few weeks. She was up at dawn and did not retire to her bed until late at night, rarely finding more than a few minutes each day to call her own. Her hands were rough and red, the nails broken and uneven, the palms calloused. Her fair skin had been reddened by constant exposure to sun and wind. Her hair had lost its luster, but she no longer cared about her appearance, or anything else, for her worst fear had come to pass.

His name was Sky Runner. He was of medium height, with deep-set black eyes and a ready smile. He had been smitten with Lacey from the moment he first saw her, and he came to Sun Beaver's lodge every night bringing gifts: a pair of rabbits to sweeten the stew pot, a fine red blanket to turn away the cold, a necklace made of shells, a deer hide that had been tanned to a softness like fine velvet.

Lacey had tried to avoid Sky Runner, but he was always nearby, waiting for a chance to catch her alone. He fell into step with her when she went to the river for water, his dark eyes gazing at her with adoration. He never touched her, for it was taboo for a warrior to accost an unmarried woman, but he made it known in many ways that he found her desirable, and after a remarkably short time, he offered Sun Beaver six fine ponies for Lacey's hand in marriage. Such a generous offering was unheard of for a woman who was a slave, and the Apache women talked of it for days.

Lacey tried to explain to Sun Beaver and to Sky Runner that she was already married, but it didn't seem to matter. Her marriage to a white man who was, in all probability, dead was of no importance to the Indians.

Wind Woman came out of the lodge, her face set in angry lines, her shrill voice breaking into Lacey's thoughts. Where was Sun Beaver's dinner, the Apache woman demanded. What was taking so long?

With a shrug, Lacey dished up a large bowl of stew and handed it to Wind Woman. Perhaps marrying Sky Runner would be a blessing in disguise, she mused, for after she was married she would no longer have to endure Wind Woman's shrewish tongue and nagging ways, though how she would endure living with a man she did not love and hardly knew was beyond her comprehension.

Lacey filled a bowl for herself and sat down in front of Sun Beaver's lodge to eat. She could see Sky Runner in the distance. He was engaged in a game of skill with three other warriors, and Lacey could hear them shouting and making jokes as they tried to outmaneuver one another.

Sky Runner glanced at Lacey, and when he saw she was watching him, he began to try harder to win, wanting to show off his skill with bow and arrow and lance in hopes of impressing the woman he hoped to marry. He knew she did not care for him in the way a woman cared for a man, but that would change in time. He would woo her gently until she overcame her fear of him. The other warriors chided him for desiring to take a white woman for his wife when he could have his pick of the Apache maidens. She was a slave, after all. For the right price, he could likely buy her from Wind Woman and bed her as he pleased until he tired of her, and then sell her to someone else. But Sky Runner refused to demean Lacey in such a way. She was young and lovely, and he did not wish to shame her. Indeed, he wanted her for his wife, the mother of his sons.

Lacey lowered her gaze to the bowl in her lap. Sky Runner was a decent sort, for a savage, but she did not love him and she never would. How could she let Sky Runner make love to her when it was Matt whose touch she craved, Matt's lips and hands she desired?

If she had doubts and misgivings, Sky Runner did not. He was building their honeymoon lodge in a secluded glen some distance from the Apache camp. Ordinarily the bride and her mother built such a hideaway, but Lacey was not of the Apache and ignorant of their ways, so Sky Runner had taken charge. His sister, Singing Woman, was helping him. Lacey and Sky Runner would spend ten days in the honeymoon lodge alone, so they could get to know each other better. The thought filled Lacey with dread. Ten days alone with a stranger. How could she endure living with a man who did not even speak her language? How would they communicate? What if she displeased him? Would he sell her to another warrior? She had a terrible vision of being handed from warrior to warrior until, in the end, she was cast out into the prairie to die, old and alone. . . .

* * *

Tom Claymore shook his head in disbelief. "That's it?" he exclaimed. "That's your plan? You're just going to try and walk out of here and hope for the best?"

"Something like that," Matt admitted sheepishly. "Unless you've got a better idea."

"Just one," Claymore replied.

"Really?"

"Really."

"Then why the hell are you still here? If you've got such a great idea, why didn't you use it long ago?"

"The idea just came to me last night," Claymore admitted. "Listen, here's what we'll do."

"How'd you get in on this?" Matt asked drily. "You can hardly walk."

"Maybe so, but I can still ride."

"Okay, I'm listening."

"Good. There's only a quarter moon tonight. Just before midnight I'll sneak two horses out of the herd and pussyfoot it down to the canyon entrance. You start a fire behind one of the lodges at the far end of camp. Make it a big one. While everyone's busy putting out the fire, we'll make a break for it."

Matt nodded slowly. It was so simple, so damn simple, it just might work. At any rate, it was certainly worth a try. "See you at midnight, partner," he said with a grin.

"Midnight," Tom Claymore agreed, and hobbled away.

Matt Drago sat up, his eyes darting around the camp. The fires had all burned down to ashes, the dogs were quiet, the village was asleep under a dark and cloudless sky.

A quick glance at the sky put the time at just before midnight. Rising slowly, he ghosted along the edge of the camp, careful not to step on any sticks or twigs that would betray his presence. A few dogs stirred as he passed by, but he smelled pretty much the same as the Indians now and caused no alarm.

When he reached the lodge furthest from the canyon entrance, he scooped a handful of coals into a bowl, then added a handful of tinder-dry twigs. When he had a small fire burning brightly, he dumped it against the back wall of the brush-covered lodge. The wickiup caught fire almost immediately, and Matt quickly disappeared into the darkness, running for the canyon entrance. Soon the cry of "Fire!" could be heard above the crackling flames, and warriors began to pour out of their lodges, wiping the sleep from their eyes. Women emerged with babes in arms or dragging young children by the hand.

Matt ran soundlessly, keeping close to the canyon wall for cover. The whole village was awake now.

"Here."

Tom Claymore's voice reached Matt out of the darkness, and Matt turned toward the sound, his eyes searching the night.

"Hurry," Claymore urged, and Matt swung onto the back of the horse Claymore was holding for him.

"Let's go," Matt said, and they rode toward the narrow gorge that was the only exit from the canyon.

Behind them, the sky was alight with dancing flames. Two lodges were burning now, and men were running to the river, filling gourds and skins with water in an effort to douse the flames.

They were inside the passageway now. Somewhere high on the canyon rim, Matt knew there were two warriors keeping watch. Hopefully, they would be watching the fire and not the canyon entrance.

Glancing over his shoulder, Matt saw that Tom Claymore was close on his heels. They were halfway through the passage when Claymore yelled, "Go! They've seen us!"

Muttering an oath, Matt urged his horse into a gallop. Simultaneously there was the roar of a gunshot, and then they were thundering out of the narrow passageway and across the open prairie.

Matt glanced over his shoulder again and saw that Claymore was still close behind him.

There was no way to tell if the Indians were in pursuit.

As the first faint ribbons of dawn were stretching across the sky, Matt reined his heavily lathered mount to a halt in a sandy wash. Dismounting, he walked back to where Tom Claymore sat his horse. The old man's face was the color of chalk. His left side was soaked with blood.

"Sonofabitch got me," Claymore murmured weakly.

"Yeah," Matt said softly. "Here, let me help you down."

Matt gently lifted Claymore from his horse and settled him on the ground with his back against the side of the arroyo.

"You damn fool," Matt chided softly. "Why didn't you tell me you were hit?"

"There's nothing you could do," Claymore said matter-of-factly. "Guess I'll be meeting up with old Smoke sooner than I expected."

"Don't talk," Matt said. "Save your strength."

"I'm ready to go," Claymore said. "I've lived a long life, done most of the things I wanted to do . . ."

Tom Claymore's voice trailed off, and his head fell forward. Matt knew, even before he checked Claymore's pulse, that the old man was dead.

Matt sat there for a long moment staring

into the distance, watching the sun climb over the mountains, turning the sky to flame. He had not known Claymore very long, but he had counted the old man as a friend, and now he was dead.

Matt shook his head. It never failed to amaze him how quickly a life could be snuffed out. One minute you were alive, talking, laughing, dreaming, and the next you were dead, and all your hopes and dreams died with you.

Using a flat piece of wood, Matt dug a shallow hole in the soft sand, gently placed the old man in the grave, and covered him with sand and rocks.

Matt remained in the arroyo until nightfall, letting the horses rest, sleeping fitfully himself.

At dusk he swung aboard his mount and headed west leading Claymore's bay mare. The weather was cold and he cursed, wishing he had thought to steal a buckskin shirt and a pair of leggings before leaving the canyon. The clout he wore covered his loins and nothing more, and he rubbed his arms with his hands in an effort to keep warm.

That night he slept on the ground with only a cover of leaves to shut out the cold.

Dawn found him riding westward again, mounted on Claymore's horse.

* * *

The entire village turned out for the wedding. Lacey stood beside Sky Runner, clad in a doeskin dress that had been worked and bleached until it was as soft and white as velvet. Her hair hung loose around her shoulders, adorned with beads and shells. Soft moccasins hugged her feet.

Sky Runner wore a white doeskin shirt heavily fringed along the arms and back, a pair of white buckskin pants, also fringed along the outer seams, and white moccasins. A single white eagle feather was tied into his long black hair. He looked quite handsome for an Indian and a savage, Lacey mused, and felt her cheeks burn when he smiled at her. Soon she would be his wife. Even now his dark eyes were telling her that he found her desirable, that she would soon be his.

The medicine man spoke to them, the foreign words sounding harsh in Lacey's ears. Then, taking Lacey's hand in his, the medicine man made a small incision in her right palm. A similar cut was made in Sky Runner's right hand, and then the medicine man pressed their palms together.

A soft cry rippled through the crowd as their blood mingled, and then the ceremony was over. Sky Runner took Lacey's arm, gently yet possessively, and led her to where their horses stood waiting. With care, he lifted

Lacey onto Cinder's back. Then, swinging effortlessly aboard his own pony, he led the way out of the village.

Lacey's heart was beating wildly as she followed Sky Runner toward the honeymoon lodge he had prepared for them. The sun was shining brightly overhead, but the weather was cold, though not so cold as the fear in Lacey's heart. Birds were singing in the tree-tops. A deer darted across her path.

For a moment Lacey thought of trying to run away, but she knew she would never be able to outrun Sky Runner. There was no place to go, no place to hide. Endless miles of open prairie surrounded them.

Despair sat heavily upon her shoulders. This could not be happening, she thought frantically. It had to be a dream. Soon she would awaken to find herself in Matt's arms and he would laugh all her fears away.

But it was not a dream. Some thirty minutes later she was standing outside a small brush-covered lodge while Sky Runner tethered their horses to a tree. Soon, too soon, she would belong to this man who was a stranger to her.

Matt Drago sat up, awakened by the sound of horses approaching the lodge in which he had spent the night. He had traveled hard for three days, stopping late last night in what seemed to be an abandoned lodge, although it was stocked with food and blankets. Now, as he heard the sound of hoofbeats and heard the soft murmur of a man's voice, he realized he had stumbled into an Apache honeymoon lodge, and that the newlyweds had arrived.

Cursing softly, he padded noiselessly to the front of the wickiup, pressing back against the wall near the doorway. His only hope of escape was to surprise the groom, grab whatever weapon the Indian had, and run like hell.

The lodge flap swung open and a woman stepped into the dusky lodge. A warrior followed her. Had the man crossed to the far side of the lodge, Matt might have been able to slip out before his presence was discovered, but the warrior stopped just inside the entrance, his eyes riveted on the woman who was his wife.

Matt's breath caught in his throat as the woman slowly turned around to face her husband. Lacey! For a moment he could not move, could only stand there, watching as the warrior stepped forward and reached for Lacey, pulling her into his arms, murmuring to her as he held her close.

Lacey began to struggle as Sky Runner's arms slipped around her waist, and then she screamed as a dark shape materialized out of the shadows. Sky Runner stared at her for a moment, baffled by her reaction; then, realizing she was staring at something behind him, he whirled around.

It was then that Matt grabbed for the knife sheathed on the Indian's belt. Grabbed for it, and missed.

Sky Runner pulled the knife free of the beaded buckskin sheath, his black eyes glittering savagely as he advanced toward the white man who had dared to defile the lodge he had built for his bride.

Keeping his eyes on the Indian's face, Matt backed out of the wickiup. Outside, he cast about for a weapon and found none, and then there was no more time to worry about a weapon, for the Indian was there, his swarthy countenance fierce to behold, his lips drawn back in a feral snarl. The two men circled each other warily, then Sky Runner lunged forward, his knife searching for Matt's heart. Pivoting on his heel, Matt darted out of harm's way. Again and again, Sky Runner attacked, and each time Matt managed to avoid the deadly blade.

Lacey watched the two men, her heart pounding like a wild thing. Sky Runner's fury made him fearless, and only Matt's agility and surefootedness saved him from being cut to ribbons. Minutes passed, and she wondered how much longer the fight could last. How much longer could Matt stay out of reach of Sky Runner's knife?

With a harsh cry, the Apache caught Matt in a bear hug, the knife in his hand glancing off Matt's ribcage. With a grunt of pain, Matt drove his knee into Sky Runner's groin, and when the Indian stepped back, doubled up with pain, Matt drove his fist into the warrior's jaw. Sky Runner stumbled backward, his dark eyes glazed with pain, and before he could recover, Matt hit him again. Sky Runner dropped like a poleaxed ox.

Matt jerked the knife from the Indian's hand, then took a step backward, his free hand pressed against his side.

"Lacey," he panted. "Find something to tie him up with."

Lacey quickly did as bidden. In moments the unconscious warrior was bound hand and foot.

"Let's go," Matt said.

"Your side—"

"It's just a scratch. Come on, let's get the hell out of here."

"Wait," Lacey said. "We'll need food and blankets. There's plenty inside the lodge."

"Hurry."

And hurry she did. Finding a *parfleche*, she quickly filled it with food and a handful of eating utensils. Remembering that Matt was clad in nothing but a breechclout, she took one of Sky Runner's shirts and stuffed it into the bag as well. Grabbing two furry sleeping robes, she hastened outside.

Matt helped her onto Cinder's back, then handed her the supplies while he swung aboard Sky Runner's calico pony. His own horse, badly winded, was tethered in a copse of trees a short distance away.

"Let's go," Matt said, and, urging his horse into a lope, he headed south.

They rode all that day and into the night. Matt winced as the chill air closed around him, making the cut across his ribcage throb dully. But there was no time to rest now. They had to put as much distance as possible between themselves and the Indians. Sky Runner would have freed himself and returned to the village by now. No doubt the Indians were already in pursuit.

Matt frowned. There was a sleepy little town not too far away. It wasn't much, but it was too big for the Indians to mess with. If they could reach it by morning, they would be out of danger.

At midnight Matt drew his horse to a halt.

"What's the matter?" Lacey asked.

"The horses need to rest," Matt replied. His eyes searched Lacey's face. "Are you all right? Did they hurt you?"

"No, I'm fine."

Leaning from the saddle, Matt put his arm around Lacey's waist and kissed her cheek. "I missed you," he murmured. "Lord, how I missed you."

"I missed you," Lacey said. She reached out and caressed his arm, her eyes filling with love. "I didn't think I'd ever see you again."

"Lacey . . ."

She smiled at him, knowing what he was thinking. Hadn't she been thinking the same thing ever since she first saw him?

"Do we have time?" she asked.

"No, dammit. Come on, let's ride."

CHAPTER 9

It was a small town consisting of a ramshackle one-story hotel, a disreputable-looking cantina, a mercantile store, a good-sized livery stable, and a whitewashed Catholic church that boasted a large wooden cross and an ornate stained-glass window. Lacey thought the church looked out of place in such a dumpy little town. There were a few adobe houses strung out behind the church.

Matt reined his horse to a halt at the stable but did not dismount. There were only a few people on the town's dusty main street: an old man nodding in the late afternoon sun, a plump Mexican woman hanging a load of wash over a dilapidated picket fence, a boy currying a slat-sided gray gelding in front of the stable.

"What is it?" Lacey asked. "What's wrong?"

"Nothing. I'm just so damn tired of being broke and on the run."

"We'll manage."

"Yeah." Matt swung out of the saddle and helped Lacey dismount. "Come on, let's see what we can get for your saddle."

The man at the livery stable gave them a fair price for Lacey's saddle, and after leaving their horses at the barn, Matt and Lacey walked to the hotel to see about a room. Matt signed the register as Mr. and Mrs. Darbison, and Lacey laughed softly. When they had shared a hotel room the last time, they had not been married but Matt had used his real name. Now they were legally wed, and he had signed the hotel register with an alias.

They had no baggage other than what was in their saddlebags, and Lacey did not miss the speculative look the hotel manager sent in their direction as they started down the hall.

Their room was drab and dreary. The faded wallpaper had once been pretty, but was now peeling off the wall. The bed sagged in the middle; the mirror on the wall was cracked and yellow, the four-drawer oak dresser badly scarred.

Matt caught Lacey's look of dismay and

shrugged. "It won't be forever," he said. "Just until we can get a few dollars together."

"I know, but—"

"But we never had a real honeymoon and you were hoping for something a little nicer," Matt said, finishing her thought.

Lacey's cheeks turned pink. "Yes," she admitted shyly.

"Does it really matter where we are?"

Her heart beat a quick tattoo as his eyes lingered on her face. "Oh, Matt," she murmured. "Stop asking silly questions and kiss me."

"Yes, ma'am," he said, smiling broadly, and took her in his arms, his mouth closing over hers in a hungry kiss that left them both breathless.

Lacey swayed against Matt, her arms twining around his neck, her lips parting as he kissed her again. The thrust of his tongue turned her blood to fire, and she clung to him, loving the warmth of his body against her own, the way he moaned her name as his hands moved feverishly over the length of her body. She had almost forgotten the magic of his touch, and how her knees went weak while her whole being seemed to come to life.

Matt kissed Lacey again and again, seemingly unable to get his fill. It had been so long since he had held her close, so long since he had been able to hold her and love her. Slowly, his mouth never leaving hers, he began to undress her, his hands sliding sensuously over her bared flesh. Touching her, kissing her, knowing she was his, filled him with such longing he could scarcely contain it.

Murmuring her name, he lifted her into his arms and carried her to bed, his blood singing with delight as Lacey began to undress him. Passion made her bold and she stripped away his shirt and clout, her fingers brazenly exploring each inch of bronze, hard-muscled flesh. Soft sounds of sympathy emerged from her throat as she kissed his scars, and he was moved with a deep tenderness for her gentle concern.

And now they lay side by side, gazing into each other's eyes. Matt knew he had never seen such love reflected in anyone's eyes before and he felt a peculiar lump in his throat as he gently stroked the curve of Lacey's cheek. She was so sweet, so lovely, and she was his. He could not get over the wonder of it, could hardly believe that she loved him, that she trusted him.

With a wordless cry, he buried his face in the red-gold mass of her hair, his hands caressing her breasts and belly and thighs, the soft roundness of her hips and buttocks, the smooth expanse of her back. Lacey moaned softly as his hands and lips swiftly aroused her, overcome by a wondrous sense of belonging and wonder. She closed her eyes as Matt's body became a part of her, and it no longer mattered where they were, only that they were together as they were meant to be together.

Her fingers kneaded his broad back and shoulders as he moved within her, the rhythmic strokes flooding her with waves of pleasure. She arched her hips upward, wanting to be closer, to absorb him into herself so that they might always be one.

She gasped his name as his life spilled into her, filling her, satisfying her, not just physically but emotionally as well. They didn't move for a long time after, content to lie in each other's arms, reluctant for the moment to end. Gradually their breathing returned to normal and the sweat cooled on their skin.

Matt touched Lacey's cheek, his eyes warm and tender. "Someday I'll clothe you in silks and satins and build you a house that will make the rest of the world green with envy," he promised solemnly.

"If the world knew what we had, they'd be green with envy now," Lacey murmured, her fingers tracing the outline of Matt's rough-hewn jaw.

"Pea green," Matt said, grinning.

Lacey grinned back at him. "Of course, I wouldn't object to silk dresses and a big house."

"Witch," Matt teased, and began tickling her unmercifully.

Lacey shrieked, her hands vainly trying to push him away, but she was no match for his strength and he tickled her until she was breathless, and then he kissed her, his midnight blue eyes filled with love and tenderness, his lips soft and warm against hers, his breath like the sweet summer wind against her ear as he murmured her name.

In moments they were entwined in each other's arms again, their bodies seeking the sweet fulfillment only the other could give. Caught up in the wonder of Matt's touch, all thought of silk dresses and fine houses evaporated like the morning dew and Lacey knew she would be content to spend the rest of her life in that dingy little room so long as Matt was there beside her.

The days that followed were peaceful ones. The town, though small, was surrounded by several large ranches, and it was the ranch families and cowboys that kept the town alive.

Matt got a job dealing poker at the cantina, and Lacey adjusted her hours to his. They slept during the early part of the day, ate dinner at the hotel, strolled through the town in the afternoon, or spent the time making love in their room until it was time for Matt to go to work.

To pass the time, Lacey bought some material and patterns, needles and thread, and made several shirts for Matt and a couple of dresses for herself. When she grew weary of sewing, she read a battered copy of *David Copperfield* that she had found on the closet shelf.

The hours when Matt was home were the sweetest of all. Their love seemed to grow deeper and stronger with each passing day, and Lacey often marveled at the way her life had turned out. Who would have thought that she would find love in the arms of a man convicted of murder? Of course, she no longer believed Matt was guilty of such a thing. Now that she knew him, she realized he could never have killed Billy Henderson, or anyone else, in cold blood. Drunk or sober, Matt Drago was not that kind of man.

Gradually they bought a few things. For Matt, a new .44 Colt and a holster, a black Stetson, a sheepskin jacket, new boots, a pair of levis. For Lacey, a new coat, undergarments, shoes and stockings, a frilly straw hat. They got her saddle out of hock.

The winter was cold and wet. It was snow-ing the night Lacey asked about their chances of finding her father, come spring.

Matt let out a long sigh. Finding Lacey's father would likely take a miracle now. "Listen, Lacey . . ."

She had been darning a pair of Matt's socks. Now she laid them aside, her eyes searching his.

"What is it?" she asked tremulously. "Don't you think we'll be able to find him? You said the Apaches would probably return to that same general area in the spring."

"I know, but don't get your hopes up too high. Even if he's still alive, he could have been traded to another tribe. Hell, just don't get your hopes up too high, honey. This is a hard country, and the Apache are unpredictable at best. I just don't want you to get hurt."

Lacey nodded. Matt was right, of course, but she couldn't stop hoping. Hope was all she had left. She remembered how her father had always been able to make her laugh, how hard he had tried to make her happy, the rag doll he had bought her when she was eight. He couldn't be dead.

"Lacey." Matt took her in his arms and held her tight. For her sake, he hoped they could find her father, but he didn't think they had much of a chance.

Lacey remained in Matt's arms for a long time, not thinking, content just to be held, to feel the strength of his arms around her, to know that he loved her, that she wasn't alone.

That night after Matt left for work, Lacey stretched out on the bed and let her mind wander into the past. Her first memory was of her father teaching her to ride a little dapple gray pony named Cupcake. She recalled how proud her father had been because she hadn't been afraid. She had been happy as a child, secure in the love of her parents, certain that only good things awaited her in the future.

She had been twelve when her mother died. Her father had not been able to accept her death. He had gotten drunk on the day of the funeral and stayed that way for two weeks, never leaving his bedroom, eating little, saying nothing. And drinking, always drinking. When he sobered up, he sold their house, the only home Lacey had ever known, and they had embarked on a journey that was, for Lacey, a nightmare most of the time. Her father had numerous jobs in the next five years, and he lost them all because he couldn't leave the booze alone. Lacey had been ashamed of the way they had lived, of the way people looked at her, their eyes filled with pity because her mother was dead and her father was a drunk.

And then they had arrived in Arizona and her father got a job as cook at the Double L Ranch, and it seemed like all their troubles were finally behind them. She had been so certain her father would stay sober this time. She had hoped and prayed and dreamed. . . .

The tears came then and she cried herself to sleep, weeping for her father's wasted life, for the unhappiness they had shared, for the mother who had died too soon.

She felt a little better the next day. Rising early, she slipped out of bed without waking Matt, dressed, and walked down the dusty street to the church at the south end of town. The interior of the church was cool and dim. A large wooden cross loomed behind the altar. A statue of the Virgin Mary stood in one corner, a statue of St. Francis of Assisi at the far end of the chapel.

As she did every Sunday, Lacey knelt at the back pew and offered a silent prayer for her father, beseeching the Lord to keep him safe, to bless him with health and strength, to enable Matt to find the trail in the spring.

It was peaceful in the church. Later, Father Gonzalez would hold mass for the townspeople, but for now she was alone. She sat for a long time, gazing at the wooden cross, and as she studied the rough timber, she thought about the man who had died such a dreadful death, and as she did so, a wonderful sense of peace filled her heart. Everything would be all right.

She was smiling when she left the church. Everything would be all right.

It was a beautiful day, cold and clear. The sky was a hard brilliant blue. The trees were barren, the distant hills clothed in shades of brown and gray. Wrapping her arms around her body, she began to walk a little faster, eager to return to the hotel and Matt's loving arms.

CHAPTER 10

Matt Drago let out a long sigh of relief as they left the dingy little town behind. It was good to be out in the open again, out of the smoke-filled cantina, out of the dreary hotel room. He had spent the past three months dealing poker and during that time he had remembered, vividly, why he had given up gambling for a living. The hours were long, the atmosphere was sleazy and smoky, the people were, for the most part, losers who hoped to make one big score at the poker table and then retire for life. But it never happened. Gambling got in a man's blood, and sooner or later you always lost everything you'd won, and more.

Dealing for the house had paid pretty well,

though. He and Lacey were well supplied for their journey: they had clothes and food and blankets, money in their pocket. It was a good feeling.

He smiled at Lacey riding beside him. Lord, she was beautiful, and easily the best thing that had ever happened to him. The months they had shared had been like a taste of heaven, and he loved her more than he'd ever thought possible.

Lacey smiled back at Matt, her eyes warm with love. She was glad to be traveling again, glad to be away from the dirty little town where they had spent the winter. It had been hard, living in the hotel, staying alone at night while Matt worked in the cantina. She had worried about him constantly, even though she knew he could take care of himself. Still, she had not been able to keep from worrying that he might be hurt in a brawl, or killed in a gunfight. Sometimes when he came home she had smelled liquor on his breath, and a terrible fear had engulfed her. What if he began to drink excessively? What if he changed, as her father had changed?

One night she had poured out her heart to him, begging him not to drink any more. She had spoken in a rush, fearful that he might become angry, and yet needing to tell him how she felt. When the words were out, she had waited, breathless, for his reply. He had not been angry with her, as she had feared. Instead, he had promised her that he would never touch another drop so long as he lived, if that was what she wanted.

The memory of that night warmed her even now.

"How long will it take us to reach our destination?" she asked.

"Not long."

And it didn't seem long. The days were warm and sunny, the nights cool and filled with stars. And always Matt was there beside her, smiling at her, loving her. She had never been happier. He had only to look at her and she seemed to melt inside. Her heart would pound, her cheeks grew flushed, and she felt as if her whole being was drenched in liquid sunshine. She blossomed under his caresses, reveling in the way he made her feel, rejoicing in his love. His hands knew every inch of her flesh, every curve, just as she knew his. She had thought that such feelings would surely diminish with time, yet she never tired of his lovemaking, never thought of refusing his touch. Nor did she ever grow weary of looking at him. When he smiled at her, she knew she had never seen a more handsome man. She loved the color of his eyes, the way his hair curled over his collar, the texture of his skin, the spread of his shoulders, the length of his legs, the sound of his voice.

It was on a sunlit April morning when they saw the smoke. Matt reined his horse to a halt, his narrowed eyes sweeping over the landscape. A prickle of fear rose in the pit of his stomach as a dozen mounted warriors appeared out of a fold in the ground.

"Don't move," he warned Lacey. Carefully he lifted his hands away from his gunbelt.

The Indians quickly surrounded them, their dark eyes filled with suspicion and malice.

"You are on Chiricahua land," one of the warriors said in stilted English. "What are you doing here?"

"We are looking for someone," Matt replied. He studied the warrior nearest him. *Chiricahua land*, the Indian had said. These were his people. "Perhaps you can help us?"

"Perhaps." The warrior's eyes lingered on Lacey. "Who are you looking for?"

"A white man."

The warrior nodded. "We have a white man in our village. He is married to one of our women."

"How is he called?"

"He is known to us as Pale Buffalo."

"What is his white name?"

The warrior shrugged. "It is of no importance to us." His dark eyes moved over Lacey again. His own woman had been dead for two summers now, raped and then killed by soldiers who had attacked their village while

217

most of the men were away. From that day forward he had vowed to take his vengeance on every white man and every white woman who crossed his path. His eyes swept over Lacey again. One way or another, he intended to have her, to hear her cry out with fear and pain when he took his pleasure between her thighs, as River Woman had undoubtedly cried out when the soldiers violated her. He smiled inwardly as he imagined the white woman writhing beneath him, and then he looked at Matt. "Is she your woman?"

Matt nodded. He had not missed the lust in the Apache's eyes when he looked at Lacey.

"I will give you six ponies for her."

"She is my wife," Matt said. "She is not for sale at any price."

"I would have her for *my* woman," the warrior said flatly. And suddenly his rifle was in his hand, pointed at Matt's midsection. The other warriors drew their weapons as well, waiting to see what would happen next.

"Matt!"

"Keep out of this, Lacey," Matt admonished quietly. Hands clenched at his sides, he kept his gaze fixed on the warrior who seemed to be the leader.

The warrior grinned wryly. The white man was afraid, but it did not show on his face, only in his tightly clenched fists and in the sudden sweat across his brow. Killing him now would be too quick, too easy. Better to keep him alive; to let him wait and wonder when death would come, to torture him a little each day.

"We will go to the village," the warrior decided, relieving Matt of his rifle and sidearm. "Perhaps I will be able to persuade you to sell me your woman. And if not . . ." The warrior shrugged.

If not, Matt thought, *he can always kill me and take her anyway*.

The warrior grinned at Matt. Wheeling his horse around, he headed for the Apache camp.

Lacey followed Matt into the Indian encampment, her heart pounding with fear as women and warriors quickly surrounded them on all sides. Matt was pulled from his horse and tied to a stout post in the center of the camp. When Lacey tried to go to him, she was grabbed from behind and led into a brush-covered wickiup.

"You will stay here," the warrior instructed. "Do not try to leave."

"What are you going to do to my husband?"

The warrior smiled. "I am going to persuade him that it would be wise to give me what I desire."

"And if he refuses?"

The warrior smiled again. It was a decidedly cruel smile. "If he is wise, he will not refuse."

"Please let us go. We mean you no harm."

The warrior did not answer her. Instead, he turned on his heel and left the lodge.

Lacey stood in the middle of the wickiup, her mind reeling. What was going to happen to them? One minute she had been filled with excitement at the thought that they might have found her father, and the next she was in fear for Matt's life. Dropping to her knees, she peered under the lodge flap. Immediately a moccasined foot appeared in her line of vision, and then another as someone paced back and forth in front of the lodge. So, she was being held under guard.

Rising to her feet, she began to pace the lodge, her thoughts chasing round and round like mice in a maze. What would happen now? She paced until her legs ached and then she sank down on a pile of robes, intending to rest for a moment. In seconds she was asleep.

Matt's gaze wandered around the village, his eyes and ears absorbing the sights and sounds and smells of the Indian camp. His mother had been born and raised in a village like this one. He studied the women as they moved about. Had his mother laughed as those women were laughing? Had she loved

Saul Drago, or hated him because he had been a white man? If she had lived, Matt might have been raised in a village much like this one. He might never have known any other way of life.

He watched several boys who were shooting arrows at a rabbit skin pegged to a tree trunk. What would it have been like to grow up here, to have been taught from childhood to hunt and track and fight? He glanced at his skin. He was nearly as dark as the Indians. His hair was black and long. Only his eyes betrayed the white blood in his veins.

His gaze strayed toward the wickiup where Lacey had been taken. Three hours had passed since their arrival, and no one had entered the lodge. He wished he could go to her, comfort her. He knew she must be frightened half to death. And rightfully so. They were in a hell of a predicament, there was no doubt of that. He wondered what his captors would say if he told them he was half Apache. Would they believe him, or accuse him of lying to save his skin?

Matt swore under his breath as the sun moved slowly across the sky. Sweat stood out on his brow and trickled down his back and arms and legs. He longed for a drink of water, but knew he was not likely to get one, even if he humbled himself enough to ask.

Another hour passed, and another, and now

the sun was at its zenith. The village lay quiet. Warriors lounged in the shade of their lodges, gambling or chatting with their neighbors. Women put their babies down for naps. The dogs lay sprawled in the shade; the horses stood head to tail, idly swishing flies.

Matt closed his eyes against the sun's burning brightness. His whole body was damp with sweat. His throat was as hot and dry as the desert in mid-July, and he thought he might easily sell his soul for just one drink of ice cold water. The heat made him lethargic, and he longed to lie down and sleep for just a few minutes. Resting the back of his head against the post, he dozed fitfully.

At sunset the women began to prepare the evening meal. Matt's stomach rumbled loudly as the aroma of roasting meat tickled his nostrils. The Indians went about their business as though he were not there. Behind the village, a dozen young braves were engaged in a horse race. Several young girls made their way to the river for water, their dark eyes sliding curiously in his direction. Little boys chased each other around the wickiups, shrieking loudly, while doe-eyed little girls trailed at their mother's skirts, or played with dolls made of corn husks and rawhide.

An elderly squaw carrying a bowl of stew made her way to the lodge where Lacey was being held. She, at least, would be fed, Matt thought with relief.

Later that evening the warrior who had captured Matt strutted into view. He looked well-fed and highly pleased with himself, Matt thought irritably, and steeled himself for whatever was to come.

"I am called High Yellow Cloud," the warrior said arrogantly. "My bravery and wisdom are well-known among the People. I have counted many coup against our enemies. It is my wish to have your wife for my woman. I ask you once again, will you sell her to me?"

"And I tell you again, my answer is no."

High Yellow Cloud nodded, but his eyes were dark and angry. "I will come again at this time tomorrow and see if you have changed your mind."

"Don't waste your time," Matt retorted, but he was talking to empty air.

Lacey stared blankly at the entrance to the wickiup. The hours passed so slowly. She had seen no one all day except for the old woman who had brought her something to eat. Lacey had eaten ravenously, but that had been hours ago, and now she was hungry again. And thirsty. She wondered how Matt was. Were the Indians treating him well?

Rising, she began to pace the floor of the

lodge again. It was awful, not knowing what was going to happen to them. She was contemplating whether it would be wise to try and leave the lodge when the old woman stepped inside. She carried a bowl of boiled meat and vegetables in one hand and a doeskin tunic and moccasins in the other. With gestures, she indicated that Lacey should eat and then change her clothes.

Lacey nodded that she understood, and the old woman flashed a toothless grin and left the wickiup.

The food was plentiful and tasty, and Lacey ate it all and wished for more. With a sigh, she laid the empty bowl aside and picked up the tunic. It was made of cream-colored doeskin, incredibly soft to the touch. Somewhat hesitantly, Lacey slipped out of her clothes and stepped into the tunic. The bodice was a trifle snug across her breasts, the skirt fell past her knees. The moccasins were soft and comfortable.

She had no sooner changed clothes than High Yellow Cloud entered the lodge. His dark eyes moved approvingly over Lacey.

"You are very beautiful," he said. "My people will be envious when I make you my woman."

"Your woman!" Lacey exclaimed. "I'll never be your woman."

High Yellow Cloud smiled indulgently. He liked a woman with spirit.

"Where's Matt?" Lacey demanded. "Where's my husband?"

"He is well, for the moment."

"What do you mean, for the moment?"

"Do not concern yourself with him," High Yellow Cloud admonished. "Tomorrow I will have Sky Woman take you to the river so that you may bathe. Would you like that?"

"Yes," Lacey answered sullenly. It had been on the tip of her tongue to refuse, but to do so would only deprive her of something she desired. And going outside might afford her a chance to see Matt.

"Good. Is there anything you need?"

"Yes, I . . ." Lacey's cheeks turned scarlet. She badly needed to relieve herself and there were no facilities for such a necessity inside the lodge.

"What is it?" High Yellow Cloud asked, frowning.

"I need to . . . to go outside."

"Ah." Comprehension dawned in the warrior's eyes. "Come, I will take you."

"You?"

"I will not look," High Yellow Cloud assured her.

"Very well," Lacey agreed doubtfully, and followed the Apache warrior out of the lodge.

She quickly glanced in Matt's direction. He was still tied to the tree in the center of the camp. His chin was resting on his chest and he appeared to be asleep.

"Come along," High Yellow Cloud said curtly.

"Can't I speak to my husband?"

"No."

There was no point in arguing with that tone of voice, Lacey thought resentfully, and followed High Yellow Cloud away from the village toward a small copse of scrawny trees.

"I will wait for you here," the warrior said. "Do not be long. And do not try to run away. The white man will suffer for it if you do."

With a nod, Lacey walked several yards further into the darkness. Where was the white man the Apache had spoke of? Oh, if only it was her father!

Later, back in the lodge, Lacey stretched out on the robes and closed her eyes. What were they going to do? Why did High Yellow Cloud want to marry her? She was not Indian. She would never be Indian. Why would he want to marry a stranger? And Matt. What would happen to Matt if he refused to sell her? Lacey laughed hollowly. What would she do if Matt *did* sell her to High Yellow Cloud? But he would never do that. And where was her father . . .

* * *

Matt Drago lifted his head. Morning. Somehow he had managed to sleep through the night, but he still felt weary. His arms and legs felt heavy, his mouth was like cotton. And he was hungry. So damned hungry. And thirsty enough to drink the Missouri dry.

He frowned as High Yellow Cloud approached him.

"Did you sleep well, white man?" the warrior asked with a wry grin.

"Yeah," Matt answered sarcastically. "I slept like a baby."

"Have you decided to sell your woman yet?"

"No."

High Yellow Cloud nodded. "I am a patient man. But not too patient. You would be wise to give me what I want."

Slowly, stubbornly, Matt shook his head. "No."

"You cannot win," the warrior said confidently. "In the end, she will be mine."

"Never," Matt muttered as High Yellow Cloud walked away. "Not so long as I live." And that, Matt thought sourly, was High Yellow Cloud's ace in the hole. If Matt continued to refuse to give the warrior what he wanted, all the Apache had to do was end Matt's life and Lacey would be a widow. She would have little choice but to marry High Yellow Cloud or become a slave.

The sun rose in the sky and Matt's strength waned, leached away by the heat and the sweat that poured from his body. He gazed longingly at the narrow ribbon of blue that zigzagged behind the village, deeply envious of the women and children who played at the water's edge or sought relief from the heat in its clear, cool depths.

His legs grew weary of bearing his weight, yet there was no relief in sight. He could not sit down, but could only stand there hour after hour. He dozed fitfully, his dreams haunted by images of Lacey caught up in the arms of another man.

At sundown the warrior came to see Matt once again. "I want your woman," he said. "I will give you your freedom, food and water. What say you?"

"No."

High Yellow Cloud nodded sadly as he withdrew his knife from the buckskin sheath on his belt. Walking to a nearby cookfire, he heated the blade until it glowed red-hot, then returned to Matt. Lifting the white man's shirt, he laid the hot metal against Matt's stomach. A sickly-sweet odor filled the air as the blade seared Matt's flesh.

Matt gasped, the pain driving the breath from his body as his flesh recoiled from the heat of the blade.

Wordlessly High Yellow Cloud heated the

blade a second time. Matt stared at the glowing steel, his insides shrinking with fear as the Indian came toward him again.

"Your woman," the warrior said.

"No." Matt hissed the word from between clenched teeth as the heated blade touched his flesh. "I don't care if you burn every inch of my flesh from my body," he snarled angrily. "She's my wife and I won't give her up."

"I believe you," High Yellow Cloud said. He gazed at Matt with grudging admiration. "You are a brave man. Brave, but foolish. I have only to kill you to take what I want."

"If you kill me, she'll hate you forever."

"I do not need her love," the warrior retorted. "I want only to bend her will to mine, to plant my seed in her belly. I think she will give me sons. Many sons." He nodded to himself. "Prepare to die, white man. I have left you alive long enough. Tonight, she will be mine."

Matt let out a long breath, fear for his own life swallowed up in his concern for Lacey. He struggled against the ropes that held him to the post, his only thought to get free, to kill the man who spoke of impregnating Lacey as though she were nothing more than a brood mare, someone to be used and abused. And then, out of the blue, an idea formed in his mind. Squaring his shoulders, he glared at High Yellow Cloud.

"You shame our people," he said with as much dignity as he could muster under the circumstances.

High Yellow Cloud frowned. "What do you mean, *our* people?"

"I carry the blood of the Dineh in my veins," Matt declared haughtily.

"You lie!"

"I speak the truth. My mother was a daughter of the Chiricahua. She was called Hummingbird."

"The name means nothing to me," High Yellow Cloud retorted. "But since you claim to be of our blood, I will fight you for the woman."

"Suits me," Matt said.

High Yellow Cloud grinned wolfishly. No one in the village was more skilled than he with knife or lance. "We will fight," he said arrogantly. "And you will lose."

"Maybe," Matt replied. "Maybe not."

"We will fight now," High Yellow Cloud decided. "Tonight she will warm my bed."

"I haven't had anything to eat or drink for two days," Matt remarked. "How about giving me thirty minutes to get something to eat and stretch my legs?"

"As you wish," High Yellow Cloud agreed smugly. "But it will not make any difference."

The warrior cut Matt loose and said, "I will have one of the women bring you something to eat. Do not try to see your woman or leave this place.''

Matt nodded, and High Yellow Cloud went to his lodge. Alone, Matt began to stretch his arms and legs. The burns on his belly ached dully, but were of little consequence now. He walked back and forth for several minutes, and then an old woman brought him a half a dozen slices of cold venison and a small gourd of cold water. Sitting against the post, Matt ate the meal slowly, sipped the water. There was no point in gulping it down and having it sit like a hard lump in his belly.

He ate only half the meat, drank half the water, then emptied the gourd over his hands and face. That done, he rested his head against the post and closed his eyes, willing his muscles to relax.

Fifteen minutes later High Yellow Cloud dropped a knife in Matt's lap. "Get up, white man. It is time.''

With a low groan, Matt stood up. All he wanted to do was sleep. He thought briefly of asking High Yellow Cloud to postpone their fight until tomorrow, but he knew the warrior would refuse. Better to hold his tongue and retain his pride than ask a favor and be refused.

Glancing around, Matt saw that most of the Indians had gathered near the center of the camp to watch the fight. He felt his heart skip a beat as he saw Lacey standing off to one side, flanked by two Apache warriors. Of course, Matt thought dryly, High Yellow Cloud would want her to be there to see his victory.

"Now," High Yellow Cloud said, and dropped into a crouch, his chin tucked in, his knife hand held out in front of him.

Automatically Matt took a similar stance and the two men circled each other. High Yellow Cloud made several sharp passes in Matt's direction, testing the white man's reflexes and finding them fast and accurate. Wary now, he moved more cautiously.

Lacey watched, mesmerized by the sight of two men fighting to the death. She knew they were fighting over her, like two dogs over a bone, and the idea filled her with revulsion. How could she live with herself if Matt was killed because of her? How could she bear it if he had to kill a man? She longed to look away, yet she could not draw her gaze from the two men who were even now lunging at each other, knives flashing in the firelight like angry fangs. High Yellow Cloud was perhaps two inches shorter than Matt, but he was solid and strong. His dark eyes were fierce, his face set in determined lines as he lashed out at his opponent. He was clad in a loincloth and moccasins, nothing more.

Matt looked weary but determined as he

parried the thrust of the warrior's blade, and Lacey wondered how long he would be able to withstand the Apache's assault. She knew that Matt had had little sleep in the last two days, and that he was in no fit condition for a fight. She uttered a little cry of dismay as the two men came together, knives seeking flesh, and when they parted, both were bleeding from shallow cuts on their bodies. Again and again they came together, the harsh rasp of their breathing and the ring of steel striking steel rising above the cheers of the crowd.

Matt and High Yellow Cloud came together in a rush, bodies straining, muscles taut, bronzed skin sheened with sweat. Tears filled Lacey's eyes as she saw the blood oozing from Matt's side, and she glanced away, sickened by the sight of his blood and by the thought that he might be killed. Her breath caught in her throat as her wandering gaze came to rest on a handful of mounted men riding into the village. The man in front was dressed in buckskins and moccasins. His face was tanned a dark brown. An eagle feather was tied in his long gray hair. But there was no mistaking the fact that he was a white man.

"Daddy!" Darting from between the two warriors who were guarding her, she ran to her father.

Royce Montana's mouth dropped open in

surprise as he saw Lacey running toward him. Dismounting, he caught her in his arms, tears blurring his vision as he held her tight.

"Lacey," he murmured. "My God, Lacey, what are you doing here?"

"Looking for you. Daddy, stop the fight, please."

Royce Montana glanced over his daughter's head to see the two men locked in mortal combat. He recognized High Yellow Cloud immediately and assumed that Lacey's fears were for the white man who was obviously fighting for his life.

"I can't stop it, Lacey," Royce Montana said sadly. "They'll have to fight it out."

Lacey's shoulders sagged in discouragement. The fight seemed to have lasted forever, though in reality perhaps only five or six minutes had gone by. Both men had sustained a number of superficial cuts and there was blood everywhere, and still they fought, snarling like angry wolves. It was brutal and savage and ugly, and yet strangely compelling at the same time.

Lacey looked away as High Yellow Cloud's knife opened a long shallow gash in Matt's right side. For a moment she watched the faces of the Indians, baffled that they could find pleasure in the sight of two men fighting for their lives. Were the Indians so primitive, so savage, that they had no regard for human life? They cheered loudly when High Yellow Cloud drew blood, readily voiced their approval for Matt's agility when he managed to elude a brutal thrust that would have cost him his life. Dimly she realized that the warriors were not cruel or coldblooded. They valued a man's bravery and his skill with a knife, and she realized that, even though Matt was the enemy, they still cheered for his courage and cunning.

The hard clang of metal scraping metal drew Lacey's attention once again, and as she turned back toward the fight, she saw that Matt was tiring. His movements were becoming slow, his reflexes sluggish, and even as she watched, he seemed to be falling. Her hand went to her throat as High Yellow Cloud instantly moved in for the kill. And then, miraculously, Matt regained his balance. Pivoting on his heel, he drove his knotted fist into the Indian's jaw. High Yellow Cloud went down heavily and Matt was on him. Sides heaving, body bathed in sweat and blood, Matt pressed the edge of his blade against the warrior's throat.

"Live or die," Matt hissed. "It's up to you."

High Yellow Cloud glared at Matt, his dark eyes glinting with anger and humiliation. "I will live," he said hoarsely. "But know this, white man. It is not over between us. Not until one of us is dead."

"Whatever you say," Matt replied, grinning. "But if I can whip your ass after two days without food or water, just think what I might do when I'm feeling good."

High Yellow Cloud made a sound of disgust low in his throat. "You do not frighten me," he said disdainfully. "The woman will yet be mine."

"Give it up," Matt said wearily, and rising to his feet, he walked away from the defeated warrior, and away from the crowd.

"Matt! Matt, come here."

He turned at the sound of Lacey's voice and saw her standing beside a man that Matt recognized as Royce Montana. So, he mused, she was right not to give up her search after all.

Royce Montana watched his daughter's face light up as the man called Matt walked toward them. So, he thought, it's happened. My little girl's fallen in love.

"Matt, this is my father. Daddy, this is Matt Drago. My husband."

"Husband!" Royce Montana could not keep the surprise out of his voice. "When did that happen?"

"Several months ago," Lacey said. "We can talk about all that later, Daddy. Matt's hurt."

"Of course," Royce Montana agreed quickly. "Come on, we'll go to my lodge and my woman can look after him."

"Your woman?" Lacey echoed, stunned. "What woman?"

"I got married, too, honey," Royce Montana said, leading the way to a lodge near the end of the village.

Lacey stared at her father's back. Dimly she remembered that High Yellow Cloud had mentioned that the white man in their camp had married one of their women. Good Lord, Lacey thought, aghast, he's married an Apache!

Things happened in a blur after that. They followed Royce Montana into a large wickiup and were met by an Apache woman who quickly made them feel at home. Lacey watched, speechless, as the woman efficiently treated Matt's wounds, which were not as serious as Lacey had feared, then whipped up dinner for all of them.

"This is Blue Willow," Royce Montana said when they were all seated around the fire.

"Pleased to meet you," Lacey said politely, though she could not quite comprehend the fact that her father had married an Indian.

"She doesn't speak much English," Royce remarked, smiling at his wife, "and I don't speak a whole lot of Apache, but we manage to communicate pretty well."

"Yes," Lacey said dryly. "I can see that."

Indeed, it was easy to see that Royce Montana and Blue Willow were much in love. The

Indian woman was about thirty, Lacey guessed. Her hair was long and straight and black, her eyes were almond-shaped and beautiful, her face unlined and lovely.

During the next hour Royce Montana told how he had been captured by the Apaches and forced to become a slave. He had endured considerable abuse and humiliation until the day he saved an Apache child from drowning in the river. His act of heroism had earned him a place in the tribe, and he had planned to leave the Indians in the spring and return to his own people. But during the long cold winter he had fallen in love with Blue Willow and they had been married.

"I can't leave her," Royce said, giving his wife an affectionate squeeze. "She wouldn't be happy living among the whites, and I wouldn't be happy without her, so . . ." he shrugged. "I've decided to stay here." He glanced from Lacey to Matt and frowned thoughtfully. "I've seen you somewhere before, haven't I?"

"Yeah. We were traveling companions."

Royce nodded slowly. "I remember now. You were on your way to Yuma. I thought the Indians got you."

"They did, but Lacey stepped in and saved my life."

"I see."

"I can't blame you for not being overjoyed

to learn your daughter's married to a man convicted of murder," Matt said evenly, "but I didn't kill that kid. I swear it."

"You'll excuse me if I appear a little skeptical," Royce Montana replied wryly, "but every man in that wagon swore he was innocent."

"Including you?"

"No. I was guilty as hell."

"Daddy!"

"It's true, Lacey. I killed Lemuel Webster. The fact that I was drunk at the time doesn't mean a thing." Royce Montana stroked his wife's arm, his eyes haunted and sad. "It's something I'll have to live with the rest of my life." He smiled wistfully. "No more sad tales tonight," he said with forced cheerfulness. "I'm glad you're here, Lacey. You and Matt can bed down in our lodge for now. Tomorrow I'll go and have a talk with Lame Bear. He's Blue Willow's father and just happens to be one of the chiefs. I'm sure he'll agree to let you stay for a while, if that's what you want to do."

Lacey glanced at Matt hopefully. "Can we stay, Matt? At least for a few days."

"If that's what you want."

"It is."

"It's settled then," Royce Montana said. "I don't know about the rest of you, but I'm beat. I think I'll turn in."

"Sounds like a good idea to me," Matt agreed. "I'm going outside for a few minutes."

"Me, too," Lacey said, and taking Matt's hand, she followed him out of the wickiup and into the trees.

"Are you happy now?" Matt asked.

"Yes. He looks well, doesn't he? I think living with the Indians must agree with him."

"I reckon," Matt allowed, "but it hasn't done me any good. I'm sore as hell."

Lacey came to stand beside her husband, her eyes filled with concern. "Does it hurt very much?" she asked, laying a gentle hand on his arm.

"Does what hurt?" Matt asked ruefully. "The burns across my belly, or the knife wound in my side?"

"Matt, I'm serious. Are you in much pain?"

"No." He pulled Lacey into his arms and kissed her fiercely. "Lacey . . ."

"I know. I want you, too."

His mouth closed over hers again, evoking a quick response. Lacey's arms twined around Matt's neck as she pressed her body to his, loving the hard muscular length of him, reveling in the way her whole being seemed to come alive at his touch. She did not protest when he began to unlace the ties that held the tunic together, nor did she offer any resistance as he lowered her to the ground. The grass was cool beneath her naked flesh, but the gentle caress of Matt's hands and mouth quickly warmed her. Uttering a little cry of contentment, she began to undress Matt, her fingers delighting in the touch of his flesh, in his sudden intake of breath as her hands lightly stroked his thighs and belly and then boldly caressed him.

She felt gloriously alive as Matt lowered his long body over hers, and shuddered with pleasure as his skin touched her own. For a moment, time seemed to stand still and she was aware of everything around her: the smell of roasting meat and sage, the damp grass beneath her back, the twinkling stars dancing across the darkened sky, the sound of a distant drum. Her heart was beating rapidly, and she felt wild and primitive and free.

She sighed as Matt's hands roamed restlessly over her flesh. His lips claimed hers in a kiss that was long and possessive and demanding. At first, Lacey held back, fearful of causing Matt pain, but he seemed oblivious to his wounds, to everything but his desire for her, and for the urgent need to join their bodies into one flesh. She cried Matt's name as his life poured into her, moaned softly as wave after wave of pleasure washed over her, filling her with sweet ecstasy.

Feeling weary and utterly content, Matt rolled off Lacey but did not let her go. Loving her was like a balm to his body and soul, healing his wounds, easing his pain. Holding her close, he fell asleep.

"Matt?" Lacey whispered his name, unable to believe he had fallen asleep so quickly. But then, she mused, he had not had a good night's sleep for two days. Add to that the fact that he had been in a fight and wounded several times, and she supposed it was little wonder that he was exhausted. Smiling faintly, she wondered where he had found the stamina to make love to her.

She was still smiling when she, too, drifted to sleep.

CHAPTER 11

Lacey hummed softly as she gathered an armful of twigs and branches and began walking back toward her father's wickiup. Three weeks had passed since they had arrived at the Apache camp. The Chiricahua chief, Lame Bear, had agreed that Matt and Lacey could stay in the village as guests of the white man called Pale Buffalo. Matt surmised that they were not so much guests as prisoners, but they were allowed to come and go within the village as they pleased, although Matt was not allowed to carry a weapon and they had been warned not to try to leave the village.

Lacey learned a lot about the Indians in the

days that followed. She had once viewed the Apache as less than human, but now, living with them, watching them, she discovered they were a complex and fascinating people. They ate their dogs and their horses when meat was scarce, yet they would not eat the fish that were plentiful in the river because they believed that the fish was related to the snake and therefore cursed and unfit for consumption. The warriors could be cruel, savage, but they were caring fathers, capable of great tenderness and love as they played with their children. The women could be as ferocious as the men, and they often fought at their husbands' sides, yet they were loving mothers and devoted wives.

The Chiricahua were a religious people who prayed often to their god, *Usen*, the Giver of Life. There were prayers and songs for the sick and the dying, and for the dead. There were chants for planting and harvesting, songs for war and for love. Despite their warlike ways, the Indians had a great respect for life, all life. People, plants, animals, the earth itself, all were respected and revered. Each rock, each tree, each blade of grass was believed to have a spirit of its own. Blood ties were strong, virtually unbreakable. Friends were treated the same as family and were supported and protected. Tribal laws and taboos were strictly enforced; punishment was swift.

Life among the Chiricahua was different than life with the Mescalero. Lacey was not a slave now, and though the Apache way of life was rigorous, she was happier than she had ever been in her life, and that surprised her. After her last few encounters with Indians, she had never expected to feel at ease among them, yet she was learning to appreciate them as a people. She found herself singing as she worked, smiling with the Indian women, laughing with the children. Life was hard, but it was good. Her father was alive and in good health, Matt's wounds were healing beautifully, and Blue Willow had become a dear friend.

The only fly in the ointment was High Yellow Cloud. He had not yet recovered from his defeat at Matt's hands, and Lacey was sorely afraid that, sooner or later, the Apache warrior would seek his revenge for the humiliation he had suffered at Matt's hands. Often she caught the warrior staring at her, his dark eyes filled with anger and desire. He still wanted her for his woman, and the knowledge bothered Lacey greatly.

When Lacey reached her father's lodge, she stacked the wood she had collected near the door, then began to help Blue Willow prepare the morning meal. She smiled fondly at Matt, who was shaving under the amused eye of several young Apache children. Indian men did not have much facial hair, and what little they had, they plucked out.

Lacey laughed softly when Matt nicked himself and the Apache children howled with delight. Oh, but it was good to be alive and in love on such a glorious morning, she thought happily, and when Matt came to kiss her, a wave of well-being washed over her.

In the days that followed, Matt began to wear buckskins and moccasins. His skin, already brown, grew even darker. His hair, as black and straight as any Indian's, hung almost to his shoulders. Indeed, Lacey mused, he looked almost like an Apache himself.

Others in the village thought the same, and when High Yellow Cloud remarked that the white man had claimed to be the son of Hummingbird, the news spread quickly through the village. One warrior, Red Knife, was particularly interested in Matt's claim. Hummingbird had been his cousin. Her father had sold her to a white man for a new rifle and a jug of corn liquor, to the everlasting shame of his family.

Matt and Lacey were sitting outside late one afternoon when Red Knife and his entire family approached the lodge. Lacey looked at Matt, her heart in her throat. Something was wrong. Why else would so many Indians be coming toward them, their faces grave?

Matt stood up as Red Knife approached him. "Welcome to our lodge," Matt said formally. "Will you eat?"

Red Knife nodded. He sat down on Matt's right, and the rest of his family sat down behind him.

Rising, Lacey quickly prepared a plate of food and offered it to the Indians. They each took a helping, nodding their thanks.

They would have accepted whatever she offered, Lacey knew. To refuse would be impolite. She had quickly learned that the amenities in an Apache camp were just as strictly adhered to as were those in the East.

When the Indians had finished eating, Red Knife and Matt discussed the possibilities of hunting together, and then Red Knife brought up the real reason for his visit.

"High Yellow Cloud tells me your mother was of the Dineh," the warrior said, his eyes locked on Matt's.

"Yes. Her name was Hummingbird."

Red Knife nodded. Turning to those gathered behind him, he repeated what Matt had said in his own language. There was a brief flurry of excited chatter, and then all eyes focused on Matt. Their expressions were no longer sober, but warm with welcome.

"We are your family," Red Knife said, his

voice thick with emotion. "Your mother was my cousin."

Matt nodded, his heart swelling with emotion as he gazed at the men, women, and children clustered in the lodge. These people were his kin, blood of his blood.

Lacey stared up at Matt, trying to comprehend what Red Knife had said. Matt was an Indian. These people were all related to him. She was married to a man who was half Apache.

She didn't know whether to laugh or cry.

The next day, Matt's female relatives erected a lodge for Matt and Lacey to live in. Other members of the tribe brought gifts: blankets and robes, eating utensils, cooking pots, a drying rack, a pair of willow backrests.

Matt was touched by the generosity of his new-found family, and with the help of Blue Willow and Royce Montana, he put on a feast for the whole tribe. The Apache were pleased with his gesture of friendship, and Matt and Lacey became members of the tribe instead of unwelcome guests.

In the weeks that followed, Matt spent a lot of time with Red Knife, and when Lacey asked, somewhat jealously, what they were doing, Matt replied, a little sheepishly, that Red Knife was teaching him to be a warrior.

"A warrior!" Lacey exclaimed. "Whatever for?"

Matt shrugged. "If my father had stayed here, I would have been raised as an Apache. I've always been curious about that part of my heritage, always wondered what it would have been like to grow up among the Indians. This may be the only chance I have to find out."

Lacey nodded. She supposed she couldn't blame Matt for wanting to learn more about his mother's people, about the way they lived and what their beliefs were.

In a short time, Lacey saw changes in Matt. He began to pick up the Apache language with an ease that was astonishing. He learned to shoot a bow and arrow and throw a lance. He participated in many of the warrior activities, like hunting and wrestling, gambling and horse racing.

Lacey resented the time he spent away from her. They were newlyweds, after all, and his place was with her. But Matt was too caught up in the newness of belonging to be aware of her feelings, too eager to be accepted as a warrior.

Blue Willow shrugged when Lacey complained. "It is our way of life," the Indian woman said serenly. "The men do not seem to work very hard, but their games of skill and strength are a way of honing their hunting and fighting skills. They must always be ready to protect the village. A man who is burdened with gathering wood or drawing water becomes soft and lazy. We have a few men in the village who do not care for manly things." Blue Willow gestured toward a nearby lodge where a man sat near a fire. He had a baby on his lap and was grinding corn into flour. "That one never cared for hunting or fighting. He would rather spend his time with the women, caring for children, or cooking. He is a good man, a kind man, but he is not a warrior." Blue Willow threw Lacey a probing glance. "Would you prefer a man like that to the one you have?"

"No, of course not," Lacey answered quickly.

"Do not think your man loves you less because he spends so much time with Red Knife. Matt is learning who he is. I am sure he will be more attentive once he has discovered who he is and what he is."

"Thank you, Blue Willow. I've been behaving foolishly."

Walking back to her own lodge, Lacey paused to watch Matt and a handful of other warriors engaged in a lively tussle. Matt wore only a brief deerskin clout and moccasins, and she could not help noticing that he was far and away the strongest, the most sure-footed, and the handsomest man in the group. He wrestled four warriors, one after the other, and won each time.

Lacey could not help feeling a thrill of pride

as he bested the last man. He was a joy to watch. His deep blue eyes sparkled with excitement, his muscles rippled like quicksilver under his tawny skin as he wrestled the last man to the ground, then good-naturedly offered the warrior a hand up.

The Apache men were impressed with Matt's skill. Bravery, cunning, strength, and endurance were qualities that were much admired, and Matt possessed them all. Of course, there were a few Indians, High Yellow Cloud foremost among them, who hated Matt simply because he was half white. For them, that was reason enough, and nothing Matt could say or do would change it.

There were women who felt that way, too. They shunned Lacey, refusing to speak to her or acknowledge her presence. They made nasty remarks about her behind her back, gesturing and pointing in a most impolite manner. Lacey ignored them as best she could, but it hurt to know they hated her simply because of the color of her skin.

Surprisingly, she quickly fell into the routine of the village. Food was always available in an Apache camp, and the warriors ate whenever they were hungry rather than at set times during the day. Lacey kept their lodge tidy, cooked the meals, gathered wood and water, and bathed each morning after breakfast, usually with Blue Willow. She learned to make ash cakes out of ground mesquite beans, tallow, and honey. She became adept at skinning the game Matt brought home, and she learned where to find the acorns, sunflower seeds, pine nuts, juniper berries, and mesquite beans that made up a good part of the Apache diet.

The men spent much of their time hunting. Deer was the most sought-after game, and there were specific thoughts and ceremonies that preceded a hunt. The men fasted, and they were not to wash or put on anything aromatic that the deer might smell. A hunter was to be reverent and generous. The kill must be shared with others.

In addition to deer, the warriors hunted opossum, cougars, skunks, wood rats, raccoons, and cottontail rabbits. Jackrabbits were not used for food. Wild hogs and prairie dogs were not eaten because they ate snakes, which were taboo. The Chiricahua also had a strong dislike for pork, fish, and frogs, the latter two being classed with snakes. Lacey thought it strange that the Indians would eat skunks and wood rats, but not pork or fish. The badger, beaver, and otter were hunted for their fur.

As the days passed, Lacey absorbed many of the Apache beliefs and customs. The Chiricahua did not speak the names of the dead. A man did not speak to his mother-in-law. The only things a warrior owned were his horse and his weapons. Everything else, including the lodge, belonged to his wife. The Chiricahua believed that everything was alive. The trees, the mountains, the rocks and the grass, the earth and the water, all possessed a spirit. Life Giver was given credit for the creation of the universe. Feminine qualities were attributed to the earth, and in all ceremonial chants, the earth was referred to as Earth Woman. Lightning and thunder were believed to be persons from whom power could be obtained. Lightning was the arrow of the Thunder People, the flash being the flight of the arrow across the sky. According to Apache belief, the Thunder People had once acted as hunters for the People and their arrows had killed all the game the tribe could use. But, according to legend, the People had been ungrateful for the bounty they had received. The Thunder People had been offended by their lack of appreciation and had stopped hunting for the People.

Lacey especially enjoyed tales of Coyote. Often, late at night around the campfire, the old ones told stories of Coyote, who was a trickster with few redeeming qualities. Coyote opened a bag he was told not to touch, thereby bringing darkness to the world. It was Coyote who introduced wickedness to the People: gluttony, lying, stealing, adultery, and all other evil practices were first done by Coyote. Warriors who were guilty of such crimes were said to be following Coyote's trail.

Child of the Waters was the Apache hero. His mother was *Ihsta-nedleheh*, or White Painted Woman, who existed from the beginning and was impregnated by Water. Another hero was Killer of Enemies. It was believed that White Painted Woman and Killer of Enemies had once shared the earth with humans.

Matt and Lacey had been in the village for almost two months when one of the young girls started her menses, thereby becoming a woman in the eyes of the tribe. There was a puberty ritual the following night.

During the ceremony, the Apache believed that the girl became White Painted Woman. Blue Willow explained that the ceremony symbolically reproduced the creation of the earth and the creation of man, showing the girl all the stages of her future life, from childhood into happy old age. The entire tribe was invited to the ceremony, which was a costly affair. Food and gifts were given to the guests; a fee was paid to the medicine man.

The Apache shaman, Blue Hawk, was held in high regard by the tribe. It was believed that the supernatural powers were under his personal control. Medicine men who employed the spirits to cause evil were considered witches and could only be vanquished by a medicine man with greater power and purity. Blue Hawk was a man of honor and esteem.

Lacey was fascinated by the ceremony. The girl sat inside a special wickiup, clad in a magnificent white tunic and white moccasins. An elaborate headdress gave her the look of a queen granting favors. It was believed that she held special sacred powers at this particular time, that she could see into the future, that she could ease old hurts.

Later they watched the Gans dance. Lacey was awed by the dancers' grotesque black masks and wooden headdresses, and by their wild gyrations. The Gans represented the mountain spirits, which brought rain and health and the good things of life. The dancers were clad in kilts and moccasins, their bodies streaked with paint.

Lacey was surprised to learn that the celebration would last four days. Four, she had learned, was a sacred number. There were four seasons of the year, four directions of the earth.

Matt, too, was caught up in the wonder of it all. The chants, the dancing, the continual celebration and feasting were like nothing he had ever seen, and yet, somehow, it all seemed familiar. Here, in the heart of the Apache homeland, the white man's world seemed far away. He was content to sleep beneath a fur robe, to bathe in the chill water of the river, to eat wild game and ash cakes, to wear little more than a clout and moccasins.

How quickly civilization falls away, he mused as he watched the Gans cavort in the center of the village. *How quickly man returns to the wild*. He gazed at Lacey sitting beside him, her lovely face luminous in the light of the dancing flames. What more did a man need than a place to lay his head, food in his belly, a fire for warmth, and a woman to love?

The sound of the drums pounded in his ears as Lacey turned to look at him. She was Woman, eternal and primal, and he was suddenly overcome with the need to bury himself in her warmth. Her doeskin tunic did not conceal the ripe body that lay beneath. Her hair was as red as the leaping flames, her skin clear and unblemished. In the distance, the Gans danced and the sound of drums vibrated in the night, but Matt was suddenly oblivious to all but the woman beside him. She was his wife. Someday she would bear his children. He swallowed hard, the need to make love to her growing stronger and more urgent with each passing moment.

He was thinking of carrying her off to bed when there was a change in the drumming and now all the young unmarried maidens danced before the tribe, their feet moving in a slow pattern to the beat of the drum.

Matt took Lacey's hand in his. "Let's go," he whispered.

"Wait," Lacey said, smiling prettily. "I want to watch the dance."

"They've been dancing all day," Matt growled irritably.

"Please, Matt? It's so lovely."

Matt nodded. It was lovely, and if Lacey wanted to stay, he would stay.

At a pause in the drumming, each maiden left the circle to lightly touch the shoulder of the man she wished to dance with. When the drumming resumed, there were two circles, men on the outside facing in, women on the inside facing out. Slowly they circled back and forth, never touching, yet Lacey thought the dance oddly sensual and provocative.

The married couples danced next. Lacey grinned with delight when she saw her father and Blue Willow join the other dancers. It was obvious that her father was deeply in love with the Indian woman and enjoyed living with the Apache, and Lacey was happy for him. He had been unhappy for so long, he deserved to find happiness at last.

Eyes sparkling with joy, Lacey looked at her husband. "Shall we dance?"

Matt looked a trifle bemused by the idea.

Dancing was not what he had in mind. And then he shrugged. "I'm game if you are," he said, and they took a place beside Lacey's father.

The steps were simple, and Lacey and Matt quickly learned the pattern of the dance. It was nothing like a waltz or a polka or any of the other dances Lacey was familiar with, but she found it thrilling to be dancing with Matt, to look into his eyes and see his love for her shining there. The beat of the drum seemed to infuse itself into Lacey's soul, and she felt suddenly wild and primitive. The music began to move faster, and Lacey's ears were filled with the rhythmic beat of the drum and the wild pounding of her heart. As the drumming grew faster and faster, the spectators began to clap, urging the dancers on and on until, at last, the music ended.

Breathless, Lacey took Matt's arm and started back toward their place in the crowd, but Matt shook his head and led her into the darkness beyond the village. Excitement fluttered in the pit of Lacey's stomach as she followed Matt into the woods. When they were well out of sight of the camp and its occupants, Matt took Lacey in his arms and began to kiss her fervently, passionately. Lacey surrendered willingly to the onslaught of his lips, her own parting beneath the pressure of his mouth as her arms twined around his neck. A wild elation heightened her senses, and it was as though every nerve ending in her body was tuned to his touch. There was a sweet singing in her blood as his hand cupped her breast, a tingling in the core of her being as his tongue tasted hers. She was fire and he was the air she breathed. Without him, she would wither and die.

Matt groaned low in his throat as Lacey ground her body against his groin. The dancing, the primal beat of the drum, the sight of Lacey clad in a doeskin tunic, her hair flowing down her back, all had fired his desire until he felt he must possess her or perish.

His hands were urgent as he unfastened her dress, gentle as they caressed the warm flesh beneath. He kissed her deeply, his lips drifting from her mouth to the curve of her throat to her shoulder. His hands slid down her back, over her softly rounded buttocks and down the gentle curve of her hips, and each touch sent tremors of desire pulsing through him. Carefully he lowered her to the ground, needing her, wanting her as never before.

They came together in a rush, their mouths fused as everything else faded away save their need for each other.

Later, wonderfully content, Lacey smiled at her husband. "You really are a savage," she teased.

"Are you complaining?"

"No," she said quickly. "I was just thinking perhaps we should stay here forever."

"Would you be happy here?"

"I'd be happy wherever you were."

Touched by her words, Matt kissed her tenderly. He was about to tell her he loved her more than life itself when the sound of someone moving stealthily through the underbrush caught his ear. Dropping his hand over Lacey's mouth, he motioned for her to remain silent, then carefully gained his feet, his eyes and ears straining for a clue as to the whereabouts of the intruder.

He was just turning to glance toward the village when there was a sudden hissing sound past his ear, followed by a loud thwack as an arrow struck a tree only inches from Matt's head. Muttering an oath, Matt dropped to the ground. He held his breath, his eyes searching the shadows, but he saw nothing, heard nothing.

He remained motionless for several minutes, his eyes warning Lacey to keep silent, and then some inner sense told him the danger was past and they were alone.

Rising, Matt went to Lacey. "Are you all right?"

"I'm fine." She was trembling visibly. "Who was that?"

Matt uttered a short laugh. "Who the hell do you think?"

"High Yellow Cloud," Lacey said slowly.

"That'd be my guess."

"Let's get out of here before he comes back," Lacey said urgently. Grabbing her tunic, she pulled it over her head and began to fasten the laces.

"Take it easy, Lacey. He's gone. I think that was just his way of telling me he hasn't forgotten that I beat him, and that it won't be over between us until one of us is dead."

"Oh, Matt, we've got to get out of here. Right away."

"I thought you wanted to stay here forever."

"Not any more. Not if it means worrying about High Yellow Cloud shooting you in the back."

"He could have done that tonight. I don't think he's the type to backshoot me. I think maybe he just wants to keep us on edge."

"Matt, I'm so scared. Please, let's just get out of here."

"I'm not ready to leave, Lacey," Matt answered with a shake of his head. "These are my people. I'd like to learn more about them, more about myself. I feel at home here."

"All right, Matt, if it means that much to you," Lacey agreed reluctantly. "But promise me you'll be careful."

"I'm always careful. Come on, let's get back to the village."

Lacey nodded, her eyes darting from side to

side as Matt slipped into his shirt and pants. Her earlier feeling of contentment had fled and in its place stood fear. Unlike Matt, she did not think High Yellow Cloud was above sticking a knife in a man's back.

Matt placed his arm around Lacey's shoulders and they walked back to camp. High Yellow Cloud was standing near the campfire. He grinned knowingly as Matt and Lacey walked by.

Matt felt his anger rise, but held it in check. Instead of smashing his fist into the warrior's face, as he longed to do, he stopped outside their lodge and kissed Lacey full on the mouth. Then, with a smug grin at High Yellow Cloud, he took Lacey by the hand and entered their wickiup.

"Do you think that was wise?" Lacey asked.

"Probably not," Matt allowed, "but I couldn't resist it."

"Please be careful, Matt. I'd die if anything happened to you."

"Nothing's gonna happen to me," Matt assured her. "Come on, let's get some sleep. All that dancing wore me out."

"That's too bad," Lacey murmured. Provocatively she began to unlace her tunic, letting it fall slowly to the floor around her feet. "I'm not tired at all."

Matt sucked in a deep breath as his eyes traveled over Lacey's delectable body. He had spoken the truth when he said he was tired, but now, suddenly, he was wide awake. Awake and wanting.

Whispering her name, he lifted Lacey into his arms and carried her to bed.

The camp was in turmoil the following morning. Sometime during the night, the Comanche had raided the horse herd and had killed one of the herd boys.

Lame Bear called a council of war, and all the warriors and the medicine man attended. There was no question but that the Apache would retaliate. *Usen*, the Supreme Being, had not commanded his people to love their enemies, nor had he taught that a life for a life was compensation enough. For every Apache killed, many enemy lives were required. The herd boy had been cousin to High Yellow Cloud, and as the boy had no other adult male relations, High Yellow Cloud would lead the raid. Most of the younger warriors declared they would go, while the older warriors elected to stay behind and guard the village.

Lacey was horrified when Matt remarked that he was going out with the war party.

"You're kidding, aren't you?" she asked, aghast that he would even consider such a thing.

"No. Red Knife has asked me to ride with him."

263

"But they're going to fight."

Matt shrugged. "I've been in fights before."

"But not like this."

"It's something I've got to do."

"I don't understand."

"I don't either, not really." Matt smiled at her, his eyes warm with love. "I'll be all right, Lacey. Don't worry."

"But you could be killed," Lacey replied in a choked voice. "And for what? Please don't go."

"I've got to go," Matt said, taking her in his arms. "I've already told Red Knife I would accompany him. I can't back out now. He'd think I was a coward, or worse—that you ruled our lodge."

Lacey nodded unhappily. She wanted to yell and scream and accuse him of not loving her enough to stay behind, but she knew it would accomplish nothing. Matt had made up his mind to go and nothing she could say would stop him.

That night there was a war dance called *haskegojital*, which, Lacey learned, meant angriness dance. All the men who were going on the raid participated.

The war dance, or angriness dance, was nothing like Lacey had expected it to be. The men sang softly, accompanied by the low beat of a drum. They never raised their voices, since to do so in battle meant certain death.

Occasionally one of the warriors fired a gun into the air. None of the men wore paint. They wore only headbands, moccasins, and breech-clouts.

Four men started the dance, then the other warriors who intended to fight joined in. All the women at the dance were called White Painted Woman and were not to be called by their own names. The dance ended when the warriors had circled the fire four times. Four again, Lacey mused. There was a round dance after the *haskegojital*, and after that, a partner dance.

Lacey tried to resist when Matt insisted she dance with him, but he ignored her protests and drew her into the circle. His insensitivity made her angry. She did not want him to go to battle, nor did she want to participate in the dancing, which would go on all night. And yet, he looked so handsome. Shirtless, his hair hanging to his shoulders, his face bronzed by the flickering flames, she thought he looked as much an Indian as any of the others. He looked wild and untamed, and her stomach quivered strangely at the thought that he was becoming more uncivilized every day. She wished he would forget about going to war and make love to her instead.

Too soon, the night turned to day and it was time for the war party to leave. The men who were going on the raid gathered together.

Most of them were armed with bows and arrows. The bows were made of mulberry wood because it was strong and durable; the arrows were made of cane that grew in the mountains or along the river bottoms. Some of the men carried spears made from sotol stalks, or brandished war clubs. A few, including Matt, carried rifles.

A silence fell over the assembled warriors as the medicine man joined them. Lifting his arms toward Heaven, the aged shaman beseeched the Apache gods to look with favor on the forthcoming raid. When he finished his prayer, he handed each warrior a small bag of pollen, and another of herbs.

Abruptly High Yellow Cloud broke away from the other warriors. Running to his favorite war horse, he vaulted onto the animal's back and raised his lance over his head.

"Aiiieee!" he shouted. "Let us ride!"

The other warriors ran for their mounts amid cries and shouts. Matt swung aboard his horse and rode to where Lacey was standing. Like the other warriors, he wore only a loincloth, knee-high moccasins, and headband. Leaning over his horse's neck, he caught Lacey around the waist, lifted her off her feet, and kissed her soundly.

"Pray for me," he whispered, and was gone.

Lacey stared after him until he was out of sight, and then she ran to their lodge. Inside, she dropped to her knees and offered an urgent prayer to God, begging him to keep her husband from harm and bring him safely home.

Never had a day passed so slowly. Her father and Blue Willow tried to keep her occupied, but time and again her thoughts strayed toward Matt and the war party. Had they found the Comanches? Had the fighting begun?

Blue Willow told Lacey that she must use only one end of the fire poker to stir the fire until Matt returned. If she used both ends, something bad would happen to her husband. Lacey thought such a superstition was nonsense, yet she was careful to observe it. Why tempt fate? A wife prayed every morning for four days after her husband left on a raid, Blue Willow continued, and every time she took a pot of meat from the fire, she was to pray that he would be successful. Pregnant women were not permitted to handle weapons, or even step over them, for fear it would cause their owner to shoot crooked.

Lacey's father told her that the Indians believed in *inda ke'ho'ndi*, which meant enemies against power. It was a war power that came from *nayezgane*, Killer of Monsters. In the beginning, Royce Montana said, Killer of Monsters went all over the earth seeking out and killing monsters, and he was the first one to use his power in doing this.

Learning about Apache beliefs helped to pass the time, but it didn't keep her from worrying about Matt. She spent a sleepless night. Every time she closed her eyes, nightmare images filled her mind, images of Matt lying dead in a pool of blood, images of Matt wounded, killed, scalped alive.

She was up with the dawn. Dressing, she stepped outside and took a deep breath, filling her lungs with the cool fresh air. Slowly the Indians began to stir from their lodges and the village came to life. Men went to the river to bathe. Women dressed their children and prepared the morning meal. The children ran through the village, playing hide and seek.

As the morning turned to afternoon, Lacey's fears grew with each passing minute. She was gazing into the distance, praying for Matt's safe return, when she saw a warrior pause at the top of a rise some distance from the village. He reined his horse in a circle and then came thundering down the hill toward the camp, followed by the rest of a war party.

As the rider drew near, Lacey saw it was High Yellow Cloud, and she let her gaze sweep past him, her eyes searching the returning warriors for Matt.

And then, miraculously, he was riding toward her, sweeping her off her feet and onto the back of his horse. She started to ask if he was unhurt, but his mouth closed over hers in a fiercely passionate kiss that assured her he was well indeed. He drew rein at their lodge, swept Lacey into his arms, dismounted in an agile movement, and carried her into the privacy of their wickiup.

"I missed you," he murmured huskily, his lips trailing fire down the side of her neck to press against the bodice of her tunic.

Lacey felt the heat of his lips all the way down to her toes, and then he was undressing her, his hands quick and eager, his eyes aflame as his gaze lingered on her silken flesh.

He was naked to the waist, and he shed his breechclout in a fluid movement, then dropped down on their blankets, drawing Lacey with him.

He made love to her wildly, his blood hot with the need to possess her. The excitement of battle, the memory of how close he had been to death, gave him a renewed appreciation for life, a realization of how quickly it could be snuffed out. He caressed Lacey, his hands and mouth adoring her beauty.

Lacey responded to Matt's touch, not knowing what was driving him, but aware that his need for her at that moment was deeper than mere physical desire. He was wild yet tender, gentle yet masterful, a stranger and yet a well-loved friend.

Later, lying in the warmth of his arms, she asked him about the battle.

"It was short," Matt replied. "Short and bloody."

"Did you kill anyone?"

"Yeah." He spoke the word softly, regretfully.

"Oh." Lacey stared up at the smokehole, her eyes fixed on the tiny patch of blue sky. She could not imagine taking a human life, not even to defend her own. "Were you scared?"

Matt laughed softly, humorlessly. "There was no time to be scared. We rode hard and caught the Comanche just before nightfall. They were making camp when we attacked." Matt shook his head. "They fought like demons, but we had them outnumbered."

"They're all dead?"

"Yeah." Matt heaved a sigh that seemed to come from his very soul. He had killed two men in hand-to-hand combat. He hadn't been afraid at the time. His blood had been up, his heart pounding with excitement. All around him, men had been struggling, fighting for their lives, but he hadn't been aware of them at the time. His own life had been on the line, and nothing else had mattered. It was only later, when the battle was over and the ground was covered with bodies and blood, that he realized how close to death he had been, realized how close he had come to never seeing Lacey again. The Apache had left the

270

scene of the slaughter immediately, driving their ponies before them, eager to flee the vicinity of the newly dead.

"Did you . . . did you scalp anyone?" Lacey asked tremulously.

"The Chiricahua don't take scalps," Matt answered. "They fear the dead. To take an enemy scalp would be unthinkable."

"If they took scalps, would you have been able to do it?"

"I don't think so," Matt answered with a wry grin. "I don't think I'll ever be Indian enough for that."

There was a victory dance later that night, with singing and dancing and many re-tellings of the raid against the Comanche. High Yellow Cloud was lavishly praised for his part in the raid, commended for finding and defeating the enemy, and for bringing all his men safely home.

Red Knife stood before the tribe and lauded Matt for his courage in battle. The white man had fought like an enraged grizzly, Red Knife exclaimed proudly, and was therefore worthy of an Indian name.

"In the future," Red Knife declared, "he shall be known as Iron Hand." His speech ended, he took two eagle feathers from his hair and presented them to Matt.

Lacey shivered as Matt accepted the long

white plumes. Each feather represented a man killed in battle.

The dancing and singing lasted all through the night. High Yellow Cloud was the hero of the moment and his name was on everyone's lips. In addition to recovering the horses that had been stolen by the Comanche, the war party had returned with the Comanche ponies too, and these were divided among the men in the tribe, adding to their wealth.

Lacey avoided High Yellow Cloud, but she could not avoid his eyes. Always he seemed to be watching her, a waiting expression on his swarthy face. Once, when their eyes met, he grinned at her, nodding, as if to say *Soon you will be mine.*

It made her flesh crawl and she turned away, her heart pounding with fear.

In the days that followed, High Yellow Cloud was ever on Lacey's mind. No matter where she went, he was there. He never spoke to her, never approached her, but he was always nearby, waiting. He followed her to the river when she went after water in the morning, he followed her into the forest when she went after wood. If she sat outside her lodge, he took a place nearby so she was sure to see him.

Her nerves grew taut. It was disturbing, having him watching her all the time, knowing if she went for a walk, he would be there.

Even safe inside her own lodge, she felt that High Yellow Cloud was somehow watching her. It got so bad, she refused to go to the river or the woods alone, and she began staying inside the lodge unless it was absolutely necessary for her to be outside.

She didn't voice her growing irritation or concern to Matt for fear he would do something foolish, but she mentioned it to her father.

Royce Montana advised Lacey to stay calm, certain that sooner or later High Yellow Cloud would stop his silly game of cat-and-mouse and go about his own business. Lacey admitted she was probably overreacting, but she couldn't help it. She was afraid of the warrior, and all the wise counsel in the world could not change that.

Things came to a head one sunny afternoon. Taking her courage in hand, Lacey left the wickiup and headed for the river to bathe. No Apache warrior ever accosted a woman at her bath, and she was certain that even High Yellow Cloud would not have the nerve to follow her to the place upriver where the women went to bathe.

With a sigh, Lacey stepped out of her doeskin tunic and waded into the cool clear water. Closing her eyes, she drifted with the gentle current. It was good to be alone, to be able to relax and let her mind wander where it would. The sun was warm on her face, the water cool and refreshing. Tonight there would be a celebration to honor Crow Hawk's oldest daughter, who had recently become a woman in the eyes of the tribe. There would be a feast and dancing, and Lacey looked forward to dancing with Matt again.

Smiling with anticipation, she quickly washed her face and hair, soaped and rinsed her body, and started for the riverbank. Then she saw High Yellow Cloud. He was standing under a tree, her tunic in his hand.

Lacey came to an abrupt halt, her arms crossed over her breasts, her heart pounding with fear.

High Yellow Cloud smiled at her as he held out her dress.

"Go away," Lacey said. "You should not be here."

"I wish to talk to you."

"No. Go away and leave me alone."

"Come out," High Yellow Cloud coaxed. "I will not harm you."

"I'm not afraid of you," Lacey lied. "Now go away and leave me alone."

High Yellow Cloud laughed softly. "I am a patient man. Take your time."

It was then that Matt appeared on the scene. He took it all in at a glance: Lacey standing in the water, her arms covering her breasts, her eyes angry and afraid, High Yellow Cloud standing on the bank, Lacey's tunic in his hand, a waiting expression on his face, naked desire in his eyes.

With a cry of rage, Matt lunged at the warrior. Catching him by surprise, he toppled High Yellow Cloud to the ground, his fists striking the warrior's face. High Yellow Cloud recovered quickly, and the two men grappled wildly for several minutes until High Yellow Cloud slipped out of Matt's grasp and reached for his knife.

"Come on, white man," the Apache taunted. "Feel my blade in your belly."

"Coward," Matt jeered. "I have no weapon."

The warrior grinned triumphantly. Then, with a wild cry, he hurled himself at Matt, his knife arm raised to strike. Instinctively Matt threw his arm up to ward off the blow, and the blade drove into his left arm just below the elbow. Twisting, Matt wrenched sideways, jerking the knife from High Yellow Cloud's hand.

With a grunt, Matt yanked the blade from his arm and whirled around to face High Yellow Cloud. Now *he* was smiling. "Come on, Injun," he taunted. "Feel my blade in *your* belly."

Lacey held her breath as the two men eyed each other warily. Would High Yellow Cloud charge, or would he simply wait until Matt grew so weak from loss of blood that he could no longer fight back?

Matt seemed unaware of the blood dripping from his arm. His midnight blue eyes were alight with the need for vengeance, his lips pulled back in a feral snarl as he waited for High Yellow Cloud to make the next move.

Abruptly Matt lowered the knife, and a soft laugh emerged from his throat. "I knew it," he said in a mocking tone. "You are a coward."

A grin of triumph spread across High Yellow Cloud's face as he pulled a skinning knife from inside one of the knee-high moccasins he wore. With the war cry of the people on his lips, he hurled himself at Matt, and the two men crashed to the earth in a tangle of flailing arms and legs as each tried to strike a fatal blow.

Heedless of her nudity, Lacey emerged from the river, her face pale, her eyes clouded with fear as she watched the two men grappling in the dirt. This would be a fight to the death, she thought helplessly, and Matt was going to lose.

She screamed with horror as High Yellow Cloud's blade sliced into Matt's right side.

Lacey's terrified cry echoed in Matt's ears. He risked a quick look in her direction, his eyes taking in her nakedness and beauty and the concern on her face in a single glance. If he lost the fight, his suffering would be over forever. Lacey would be the real loser.

The image of Lacey living in High Yellow Cloud's lodge and sharing the warrior's bed darted across Matt's mind, bringing a sense of utter rage. From somewhere deep inside himself, Matt summoned the strength to break free of the warrior's hold. Rolling away from High Yellow Cloud, he scrambled to his feet.

High Yellow Cloud stood up, a satisfied smile on his face as he observed the wounds he had inflicted on his enemy.

"Now you will die, white man," the warrior crowed, "and your woman will be mine. But do not worry. I will keep her too busy to mourn your death."

"Matt," Lacey whispered brokenly. "Oh, God, Matt."

Slowly, deliberately, High Yellow Cloud advanced toward the white man. The fight would soon be over, and the white woman would be his. She would give him sons, he thought smugly, many fine sons.

With a triumphant cry, the warrior lunged forward, his blade driving toward Matt's heart. Matt held his ground, and Lacey screamed in despair as the Apache's blade plunged toward his chest. At the last possible moment, Matt pivoted sideways to avoid the warrior's thrust, and as he did so, he drove his knife into High Yellow Cloud's back, piercing the Apache's heart. The warrior's momentum carried him forward for several feet before he fell face down in the dirt, his knife still clutched in his fist. A long shudder wracked the Indian's body, and then he lay still, his dark eyes staring sightlessly at the ground.

Lacey ran to Matt, her arm circling his waist as he slowly sank to his knees.

"Matt, oh, God, Matt, don't die. Please don't die."

"I'm not gonna die, Lacey," Matt mumbled. "Not yet."

She was crying now, her tears staining her cheeks as she used Matt's knife to cut her skirt into strips for bandages.

"Dirt," Matt gasped. "Use dirt . . . to stop the bleeding."

"Dirt?" Lacey repeated, appalled at the idea.

"Do it."

Certain she was doing the wrong thing, Lacey took handfuls of dirt and patted it over her husband's wounds. Miraculously, the bleeding stopped.

"Old Indian remedy," Matt rasped.

Lacey nodded as she wrapped a strip of cloth around Matt's midsection.

"Lacey . . . go get our horses."

"Horses? What for?"

"We've got to get out of here."

"No. You need help, and you need it now."

"Trouble," Matt mumbled.

Lacey nodded. There would indeed be trouble when High Yellow Cloud's death was discovered, but right now Matt needed help. Her stomach churned as she recalled the amount of blood he had lost. How much blood could a man lose and still live?

"Rest," Lacey said. "I'm going for help."

Matt nodded weakly, and Lacey pulled her tunic over her head and ran back toward the village and her father's lodge. Royce Montana listened gravely as Lacey told him what had happened.

"There's going to be trouble, all right," he muttered. But they couldn't worry about that now. Catching up his horse, he followed Lacey to the river. Matt groaned as Royce lifted him onto the back of his horse.

"You'd better ride up here behind him," Lacey's father advised her. "He's liable to pass out and fall off."

The journey back to the village seemed to take forever. Lacey held onto Matt, knowing that each step the horse took was causing him pain. Blood oozed from his side and lay warm and sticky against her arm. Matt's blood. It was all she could do to keep from vomiting.

Blue Willow did not waste time asking questions when Royce carried Matt into their lodge. She quickly sent her husband after the medicine man, and while they waited for the shaman to arrive, she began to wash the dirt and blood from Matt's side. He flinched each time the Indian woman touched him, and Lacey flinched, too, her heart aching to see him in such pain. He might have been killed, and it would have been all her fault.

The medicine man entered the lodge on quiet feet. He was a short, stocky man with long gray braids and a weathered face that bespoke many years of hard living, yet his deep-set black eyes were kind. He knelt beside Matt, his hands moving lightly over Matt's wounds, and then he laid out several small pouches which contained the various herbs and poultices he used for healing.

Lacey stood beside her father, helplessly wringing her hands, as the shaman began to chant softly. He ground several leaves together in a shallow bowl, added a small amount of water, and mixed the concoction until it was a pasty yellow, and then he smeared the sticky salve over the wounds in Matt's side and arm. All the while he chanted softly, the words melodic and strangely compelling.

When he finished spreading the salve over Matt's injuries, he sprinkled sacred pollen into the fire and then, still chanting in an eerie minor key, he passed his hands over the fire, drawing the smoke toward Matt.

Lacey wanted to scream that pollen and smoke and endless chanting would not heal her husband. He needed medicine, real medicine.

"I've seen old Blue Hawk work some real miracles, Lacey," Royce Montana said, squeezing her shoulder sympathetically. "Don't be fooled and think Indian medicine men are just a lot of hokum. They've lived out here a long time. Some of those herbs are pretty effective."

Lacey nodded, but she wasn't convinced. When Blue Hawk left the lodge a short time later, Lacey knelt at Matt's side. He was breathing heavily; his face and body were damp with sweat. The wound in his side was deep, so deep. How could she bear it if he died?

Sensing her presence, Matt opened his eyes and smiled weakly. "Don't worry," he whispered. "I'll be all right."

Lacey nodded, wanting to believe him, but was so afraid. She stayed at his bedside constantly, refusing to budge, refusing to sleep. Blue Hawk returned later that night with more sacred pollen and more chanting. He applied a foul-smelling poultice to the wound in Matt's side, nodded to himself, and left the lodge. Outside, he sat near the doorway, chanting softly all through the night.

Lacey added her own prayers to those of Blue Hawk, beseeching the Lord to heal the man she loved. She would never forgive herself if Matt died. She would never have begged Matt to help her find her father if she had thought it would cost him his life.

The announcement of High Yellow Cloud's death stirred a great controversy within the tribe. His friends and family demanded that the white man be killed immediately. The shedding of Apache blood by another Apache was a strict taboo, and the penalty was death or banishment from the tribe. High Yellow Cloud's family demanded the death penalty.

Red Knife disagreed. All knew of High Yellow Cloud's desire for the white woman. The white man had done right to protect his wife from High Yellow Cloud's lust. Indeed, he had almost lost his own life in defending his woman's honor.

In the midst of all the turmoil, Lacey remained at Matt's side. Two days passed, and Lacey had not been away from Matt's bedside for more than a few minutes at a time. Now, late at night, she sat beside him, dozing fitfully, afraid to sleep for fear she might not hear him if he should awake and need her. It was after midnight when exhaustion claimed her and she fell into a deep sleep.

It was quiet, so quiet. Wondering if he had died, Matt opened his eyes and glanced around the lodge. Lacey was lying beside him, her head pillowed on her arm. Her face looked drawn and haggard, and there were dark shadows under her eyes, as though she hadn't been getting enough sleep.

For a moment he lay still, just looking at her. The pain in his side was a dull ache that could not be ignored. Life was funny, he mused. He had spent four years in the Confederate Army and never got a scratch. Now, in less than a year, he had been wounded more times than he cared to count.

He tried to shift his weight on the hide pallet, and swore under his breath as the movement intensified the pain in his side.

His muffled oath woke Lacey instantly. "What is it?" she asked anxiously. "What's wrong?"

"You look like hell," Matt rasped.

"Matt—"

"I'm all right, Lacey," he said reassuringly. "Lie down beside me and get some sleep."

Too weary to argue, she stretched out beside him, careful not to touch him lest she hurt him in some way, but Matt put his arm around her and drew her close.

"I've missed you beside me," he murmured. His lips brushed against her cheek, soft and light as a butterfly landing on the petal of a rose.

"Oh, Matt."

"Don't worry, Lacey. Everything's gonna be all right."

Lacey nodded, but in her heart she was

afraid. High Yellow Cloud's death was still causing contention in the Apache camp. There were many meetings in the days that followed. Lacey's father was not permitted to attend, but Red Knife kept them informed. The meetings were to determine Matt's future. Each warrior in the tribe was permitted to voice his opinion as to what should be done with the white man who had killed High Yellow Cloud, and when all the men had spoken, they would vote.

"It isn't just up to Lame Bear," Royce Montana explained to Lacey. "He's a chief, but he isn't the only chief. Each man in the village has a say in what goes on."

In the end, it was decided that High Yellow Cloud's death should be avenged, and that Matt's life would be forfeit. He was half Apache and he had shed the blood of a brother. Had High Yellow Cloud killed Matt, the penalty would have been the same. Lacey would be permitted to stay with her father, if that was her wish, or she could leave the village and return to her own people.

Lacey felt her heart turn to stone as her father recounted the council's decision.

"No." She shook her head, refusing to believe that Matt was going to die. They had been through so much already. Surely they deserved a chance at happiness.

"Lacey." Royce Montana's voice was soft

and sympathetic as he placed his hand on his daughter's arm.

"No!" she cried. "He isn't even well yet." Her eyes filled with tears as she looked up at her father, silently pleading with him to make everything right.

Royce Montana drew a deep breath, then cleared his throat. "You're going to have to be strong about this, Lacey," he said sternly. "If you try to interfere, you'll only put your own life in danger. There's nothing you can do."

"He's right, Lacey," Matt said. "Do what your father says."

She was still trying to comprehend the terrible turn of events when two warriors burst into the lodge and took hold of Matt. Jerking him to his feet, they dragged him outside.

Lacey started to run after Matt, but her father laid a restraining hand on her arm.

"No, Lacey."

"Let me go!"

"You can't help him now, daughter. Face it."

"Please, Papa, do something."

"There's nothing to be done," Royce Montana said heavily. "I'm sorry, honey."

Matt didn't resist as the warriors tied him to the tree in the center of camp. To do so would only anger the Indians further, perhaps goading them into harming Lacey and her father.

His gaze wandered around the village. How much time did he have left? What kind of death did they have planned for him? Something quick and merciful, or something long and lingering and painful? He swallowed hard, wondering if he had the guts to die like a man, or if he'd go out screaming and kicking and begging for mercy. How did a man know how much he could take until he had to face it? It was said the Indians never showed fear or pain in the presence of an enemy. How did they manage to exert such iron control over their emotions? Could he do the same?

Matt twisted his head around so he could see his lodge. Damn. If only he'd been able to make love to Lacey one last time. If only his side didn't hurt so damn bad. If only he'd met Lacey in another time, another place . . .

Lacey stared into the empty darkness of the lodge, her cheeks damp with tears, her heart aching. Matt was going to die unless she did something to help him. Courage had never been her strong suit, and now, when she needed it more than ever, she could feel it ebbing away. Somehow she had to free Matt, even if in so doing she would be risking her own life. It was a frightening thought. And yet, what else could she do? She could not sit quietly by and watch while Matt was killed. She simply could not. Nor could she ask her father for help. Royce Montana would try to stop her, of that she had no doubt. At any rate, her father had made a good life for himself here with the Apache. She could not ask him to jeopardize that, could not put his life in danger, too.

Rising, she made her way to the lodge flap and peered cautiously outside. The camp was dark and quiet. A lone warrior sat near a small fire, guarding Matt. The Indian seemed to be dozing. She would never have a better chance.

She quickly gathered their belongings and stuffed them into one of Matt's saddlebags. Picking up one of the rocks that shaped the firepit, she took a deep breath, let it out slowly, and then stepped outside. Carefully she made her way toward the warrior, the rock clutched in her fist, her heart pounding so loud she was certain it would wake the whole camp. Quietly, step by wary step, she crept up on the warrior.

Matt woke abruptly, unaware of what had roused him. Lifting his head, he saw Lacey stealing toward the warrior on guard, a rock in one hand, his saddlebag in the other. He shook his head vigorously, trying to warn her away. He had come to terms with his own death, had accepted it because he knew Lacey would be safe with her father. Now, because of him, she was putting her own life in jeopardy.

Lacey did not look at Matt. She had eyes only for the warrior, her whole attention focused on what she was about to do. Her hand was trembling visibly as she lifted the rock and brought it down on the back of the Indian's head. There was a muffled thud as the Apache toppled sideways to the ground.

She felt suddenly sick to her stomach as she realized she might have killed him, but there was no time to worry about that. Quickly she took the Indian's knife and cut Matt free.

"You little fool," Matt hissed, "what do you think you're doing?"

"I think I'm saving your life," Lacey retorted.

Matt grinned broadly as he took the knife from her hand and stuck it in his belt. "I think you're right," he agreed. "Let's get the hell out of here."

Matt quickly bound the warrior's hands and feet, stuffed the Indian's headband into his mouth, took his rifle, and then, like shadows, they drifted out of the village.

Wordlessly Matt led the way to the horse herd. A sharp right cross rendered the herd boy unconscious. Moments later they were riding away from the village.

"Do you think they will come after us?" Lacey asked when they were well away from the Apache camp.

Matt shrugged. "Who knows? The Apache are unpredictable creatures at best."

Lacey nodded. There was no way to tell what the Indians would do. She could only hope for the best.

They rode for several hours, then Matt dismounted and, handing the reins of his horse to Lacey, began to erase their tracks as they went along. It was a tedious job, but when he was finished, he was reasonably certain the Indians wouldn't be able to guess which way they had gone. Hopefully, finding them would take more time and effort than the Apache would wish to spend.

It was dawn when Matt lifted Lacey from the back of her horse. Unsaddling her mount, he hobbled the mare next to his own horse. Then, taking the saddle blanket in one hand and Lacey's arm in the other, he made his way through the brush until he came to a small thicket. Spreading the blanket on the ground, he took Lacey in his arms.

"That was a brave thing you did," he said gruffly. "If you'd been caught, you might have been killed."

"It was a chance I had to take," Lacey replied. "I couldn't let them kill you."

"You could have," Matt countered quietly. He gazed into her eyes, his heart filling with love and gratitude for the woman in his arms.

She was shy and soft-spoken, yet she had the heart of a lioness.

Lacey returned Matt's gaze and then, overwhelmed with happiness because they were both alive and well, she grinned up at him.

"You don't act very grateful," she said impishly.

Matt quirked an eyebrow at her. "Don't I?"

"No. If you were really grateful, you'd kiss me and—"

His mouth dropped over hers, silencing her as he kissed her again and again. Hardly aware that he was doing so, he sank to the ground, carrying Lacey with him. His kisses became more intense, more ardent, until he was on fire with his need for her. His hands roamed over her back and shoulders, caressing her satiny skin as he impatiently removed her clothing, delighting in the smooth perfection of each lovely limb.

Lacey responded to his touch eagerly, willingly, joyfully. Her hands tugged at Matt's clothing, wanting to feel his body next to her own, needing his touch. Her fingertips traced the muscles in his arms, delighting in the strength sleeping there. Her tongue danced over his flat belly and she laughed softly, seductively, as he shivered with pleasure. He was here, he was hers.

She sat up abruptly as her fingers encountered the bandage swathed around his middle. In the excitement of being with him, she had forgotten about his wound. Now she saw that there was fresh blood on the bandage. He was bleeding, hurting, and she had been so mad with desire she hadn't even noticed.

"Lacey." Matt groaned her name as she drew away from him.

"Oh, Matt," Lacey whispered, mistaking his groan of desire for pain. "I'm sorry. I didn't think . . . I mean, I forgot you were hurt."

"It isn't my side that's hurting," Matt said, his dark eyes glinting roguishly.

"Matt, we shouldn't."

"I'm fine," he assured her. "Come here, and I'll prove it to you."

Still, Lacey did not relent. As much as she wanted to make love to him, his recovery was more important. There would be other days, other nights.

"Stubborn wench," Matt muttered, and pulling her down beside him once more, he rose over her, his hands on either side of her head as his mouth plundered her.

The touch of Matt's lips drove the last shred of resistance from Lacey's mind. With a sigh, she arched up to meet him, her thighs parting to receive that part of him that made her whole, complete. Little moans of ecstasy rumbled in her throat as Matt made sweet love to her, his hands gently stroking her breasts and thighs and belly as his body joined hers, their souls almost touching as they soared to the pinnacle of rapture that only true lovers ever know.

Afterward, Matt held Lacey close, his fingertips tenderly tracing the outline of her face, drifting over her lips, down the slender column of her neck.

"You might have been killed," he muttered, the thought haunting him still. "Don't ever take a risk like that again. Promise me."

"No," Lacey said, shaking her head. "Whatever happens to you happens to me." She smiled at him, hoping to lighten his mood. "I plan to follow you right into heaven."

"Or hell?" Matt mused, grinning back at her.

"Or hell," she whispered, and surrendered her lips to his kiss.

They were traveling again at first light, crossing a flat gray desert that was covered with cacti and paloverde and greasewood.

"Where are we going?" Lacey asked.

"Tucson," Matt replied, and then he laughed. "Seems we're always starting out broke and on the run."

"We may be on the run," Lacey said, "but we're not broke."

"We're not?"

Lacey shook her head. "We've still got the money you won in that awful little town, remember?"

"Yeah, now that you mention it."

"Why are we going to Tucson?"

"We need clothes and supplies."

Lacey nodded. "And then what?"

"I've got to find out who killed Billy Henderson. If we're gonna have any kind of life together, I've got to clear my name."

"How do you intend to find out who killed him?"

"Beats the hell out of me."

"So what are we going to do?"

"Play it by ear, Lacey girl," Matt said with a light-hearted grin. "Just play it by ear."

CHAPTER 12

Some days later Matt and Lacey arrived in Tucson. It was an old town, surrounded by rolling foothills and craggy peaks. The town had been built on a low ridge along the banks of the Santa Cruz River. It was a busy place, always humming with activity. Squat, thick-walled adobe buildings lined both sides of the streets at irregular intervals. There were no sidewalks. When it rained, the mud was a foot deep.

As they rode down the dusty street, Lacey's first thought was that every building seemed to be a cantina. Women in long dresses made their way through the town, going shopping or to church. There were soldiers and businessmen and numerous children and dogs.

She wrinkled her nose as the mingled odors of coffee, grease, spicy food, chili, mesquite smoke, and dust assailed her nostrils. From somewhere came the soft sound of guitar music, but it was quickly lost in the rattle of wagon wheels and the somber wail of a mission bell.

Matt drew rein at a hotel, got them settled into a room, and then took Lacey shopping. He bought her a new dress, underthings, shoes and stockings, a lacy white parasol, a perky bonnet with pink and blue ribbons, and a pale blue shawl with long fringe. For himself, Matt bought a suit of black broadcloth, a white linen shirt, and a wine-red vest embroidered with tiny pink satin flowers. He also purchased a black, flat-brimmed Stetson, a pair of expensive black leather boots, and a gunbelt and holster, complete with a new Colt .44.

Lacey stared at him, speechless, as he donned his new finery back in their hotel room. He looked every inch a gambler. And terribly handsome. The black broadcloth molded itself to his broad shoulders and long, muscular legs; the snowy white shirt perfectly complemented his dark hair and midnight-blue eyes while emphasizing his tawny skin. She felt her heart flutter with feminine admiration. He was beautiful, and he was hers.

"I've decided the best thing to do is just

hang around the saloon in Salt Creek," Matt mused aloud. "No better place to hear the latest gossip, you know. And it's the last place anyone will think to look for me."

Lacey nodded. They had been lucky so far. Matt had spied a wanted poster on the bulletin board outside the marshal's office. It had been disconcerting, seeing his name and likeness on such a thing. Still, no one who had seen Matt before would be likely to recognize him now. His hair had grown long in the last few months. He had grown a thick moustache, long sideburns, and a closely cropped beard that made him look devilishly handsome.

Lacey slipped into her new dress and admired herself in the mirror. It was nice to be clean again, dressed like a lady instead of a wild Indian.

She frowned at her reflection as she recalled the last time Matt had worked in a saloon.

"I'm not going to sit in some crummy hotel night after night like I did the last time," she remarked petulantly.

"No?"

"No."

"Just what do you want to do?" Matt asked, though he had a terrible hunch he already knew the answer. And he was right.

"I want to be with you. If you're going to spend all your time in a saloon, so am I."

"Don't be ridiculous."

"I don't want to argue about it, Matthew Drago," Lacey said in a determined tone. "If you can pretend to be a gambler, then I can pretend to be a dancehall girl."

"But I'm not pretending," Matt pointed out dryly. "I *am* a gambler. And a damn good one."

"Well, I can be a dancehall girl. I can serve drinks as well as anyone else."

"No, Lacey. I won't have it."

"Please, Matt," Lacey said, pouting prettily. "I want to be where you are." Standing on tiptoe, she kissed him, her fingers playing in his hair. "Can't I at least try it?"

"We'll see," Matt drawled. His hand cupped her breast as his mouth traveled leisurely over her eyes and nose and sweet pink lips.

Little bursts of excitement exploded in Lacey's stomach as Matt began to arouse her. It never failed to fill her with wonder that this incredibly handsome man found her desirable. She loved to look at him, to see the desire flare in his eyes, to hear his voice grow husky with longing when he murmured her name. He had only to touch her and she melted in his arms like butter over a flame, everything else forgotten in the joy of his

297

caress, the wonder of his love, the thrill of being possessed by such a man.

Soon they were lying side by side on the bed, their new clothes piled in an untidy heap on the floor. Once, Lacey had blushed to let Matt make love to her in the light of day, but no more. She found pleasure in the sight of his masculine strength, and it pleased her to know that he found her body beautiful in return. She touched his face with her finger-tips, marveling anew that a man could be so beautiful, that she had the power to arouse him.

And then Matt was rising over her, his body blocking every other sight and thought from her mind. She craved his touch, his kiss, his caress. Only with Matt did she feel whole, complete. Always, when they were apart, she felt bereft, as though a vital portion of her being was missing.

With a sigh, she wrapped her arms and legs around his waist, holding him tighter, tighter, wanting to draw him closer until they were one flesh, one body, one soul.

Later, lying content in his arms, she knew that everything would be all right so long as she had Matt beside her.

They spent a leisurely week in Tucson. Matt bought Lacey several more dresses. They dined at the city's finest restaurant, walked hand in hand through the town, went to see a play by a traveling Shakespearean company. And on Sunday morning Lacey coaxed Matt into taking her to church.

Matt felt decidedly uncomfortable sitting on the back pew, his hat in his hand. He had not been inside a church since Leticia Drago had forced him to attend Sunday school over twenty years ago. He had never thought of himself as a sinful man, yet he knew he had done a number of things that would be frowned on by most of the people sitting around him.

Lacey was familiar with the hymns, and she had a lovely clear voice that made him feel good just listening to her. The sermon was long and dry, Matt thought, but Lacey listened intently as the preacher spoke of loving your enemy and making restitution to those you had wronged. He was glad when the service was over and they were again out in the sunshine.

Lacey seemed preoccupied as they walked back to the hotel. At the entrance to the hotel, she paused and laid her hand on his arm.

"Would you do something for me, Matt?" she asked hesitantly.

"Anything, honey. You know that." He smiled at her mischievously. "Didn't I just take you to church?"

Lacey nodded. "When I left Salt Creek to

follow my father, I stole some clothes and some food. Would you give me enough money to pay for the things I took?''

"You took that sermon to heart, didn't you?"

"Don't make fun of me, Matt."

"I wasn't," he apologized.

"I always intended to pay for what I took," Lacey said. "Will you help me?"

"Sure, Lacey."

Her smile was radiant. "Thank you, Matt."

Matt Drago grinned. He had married a good woman, he thought, pleased and a trifle amused. No doubt she would see to it that he became a righteous, God-fearing man in due time. He wouldn't mind, not really. He'd do anything she asked of him. Anything at all.

But first he had to clear his name.

Salt Creek had not changed much in their absence. It remained a thriving town, growing daily as new people made their way across the plains to settle in the West.

After getting a room at the hotel, Matt and Lacey made their way to the saloon where Matt had been accused of killing Billy Henderson. Matt was wearing his black broadcloth suit, and several women turned to stare at him as they walked down the street. Jealousy stabbed at Lacey's heart, and she laid her hand over Matt's arm in an age-old gesture that clearly said, "He's mine."

Lacey glanced up at her husband. It had never occurred to her that other women would find Matt attractive. Now, studying his rugged profile, she realized that a woman would have to be dead or blind to be immune to Matt Drago's masculine beauty and virile strength. Just looking at him was enough to set feminine hearts aflutter.

She had never realized she was the jealous type, but when Matt smiled at a pretty young woman as they crossed the street, Lacey almost choked. What was happening to her?

Matt patted Lacey's arm as they reached the Black Horse Saloon. "Nervous?"

"A little," she admitted. "I've only been in a saloon once before, you know."

"Yeah. And you remember how *that* turned out, don't you?" Matt muttered dryly. "Dammit, Lacey, won't you please go back to the hotel?"

"Matt—"

"I know, I know, you want to be a saloon girl. Dammit, what would your father say?"

"He'll never know." Lacey took a deep breath. "I'm ready."

Matt nodded grimly. What did a man do with a woman as stubborn as Lacey? "Here we go," he muttered, and stepped into the saloon.

301

The place was quiet at this time of the day. A lone bartender stood behind the bar, idly polishing a shot glass. Two men sat at the far table. One appeared to be asleep; the other was playing solitaire.

"How do we find the boss?" Lacey asked.

"I think that's him coming toward us."

Lacey smiled uncertainly as a tall man in a brown pinstripe suit emerged from the shadows.

"I'm Tucker," the man said. He eyed Matt and Lacey speculatively as Matt introduced himself as Matthew Walker and asked for a job.

"You any good with a deck of cards?" Tucker asked.

"Try me."

"I run a clean place here," Tucker said. "No dealing off the bottom, no extra aces, no tricks."

"I can deal 'em any way you like."

Tucker nodded slowly. He had always been a good judge of men, and he knew instinctively that the man was as good as he said he was. "Who's the girl?"

"My wife. Lacey."

Tucker's eyebrows shot up. "Your wife! What the hell is she doing in here?"

"She wants to work."

Tucker looked skeptical. Lacey Walker

didn't appear to be a saloon girl. "What does she do?"

Matt grinned. "She wants to serve drinks."

"That's all?"

"That's all."

J.J. Tucker frowned thoughtfully. Most of the girls in the saloon did more than serve drinks. Still, the gambler's wife was a beautiful woman. And men were always fascinated by what they couldn't have. Maybe the girl would be good to have around, just to dress up the place, give it a little class. The other saloon girls weren't bad looking exactly, but they all looked old and used compared to the gambler's woman.

"I'll give you both a try starting tonight," Tucker decided. "Eight o'clock till two. Don't be late."

Lacey patted her hair nervously as she gazed at her reflection in the mirror. She was wearing the dress Tucker had sent over to the hotel. It was flaming red, with long sleeves and a short ruffled skirt. The neck was square, provocatively low cut.

"What do you think, Matt?" she asked, pirouetting in front of him.

"I think you should stay home," he answered curtly.

"No. I'm going with you."

"Dammit, Lacey, I don't want a roomful of cowhands leering at you while you parade around in that getup. Good Lord, what would your father say if he could see you now?"

"I don't know," Lacey mumbled, but she did know. Her father would be scandalized to think of his daughter wearing such an outfit, and even more shocked to know she was going to serve drinks in a saloon.

"Well, I know what he'd say," Matt muttered, "and he'd be right."

"Matt, please let me do this. I might be able to learn something about who killed Billy Henderson."

She was right, Matt thought bleakly. A few drinks and most men would tell a pretty woman anything she wanted to know.

Some of Lacey's enthusiasm waned as she stepped into the saloon that night. It was Saturday and the saloon was crowded with cowhands and townsmen looking for a little relaxation after a hard day, or perhaps a little excitement. The air was filled with smoke from dozens of cigars and cigarettes. Men could be heard talking and laughing above the tinny notes of a piano. Several women, all clad in dresses similar to Lacey's, wandered around the saloon, serving drinks, smiling and laughing and flirting with the customers. Lacey felt her cheeks grow hot as she watched one of the saloon girls go upstairs with a middle-aged cowboy.

J.J. Tucker came through the crowd to greet them. His eyes, a cool pale green, lingered on Lacey for a long moment.

"You look fine, just fine," the saloon owner remarked. "Just wander around and take orders. I've passed the word that you're spoken for, so there shouldn't be any trouble, but who knows?" Tucker shrugged nonchalantly. "If any of the customers give you a bad time, you come to me and I'll take care of it." Tucker glanced at Matt. "You can take over for Brill at table five. Are you carrying a piece?"

"What do you think?"

Tucker nodded. "Try not to use it."

As Tucker turned away, Matt took Lacey in his arms and kissed her soundly. She was his, and he intended for every man in the saloon to know it.

Lacey blushed from the roots of her hair to the soles of her feet as Matt's lips branded her own. Breathless, she gazed into his eyes, a flutter of excitement blossoming in her belly. She had never been kissed in public except by her relatives, and a public display of affection embarrassed her even as it pleased her. There was a boisterous round of applause when Matt let her go.

The next few hours passed quickly. Matt

dealt the cards easily, his fingers nimble, his manner relaxed and friendly. He felt a sense of homecoming as he sat there with a drink at his elbow and a fresh deck in his hand. Perhaps this was where he belonged, where he was destined to spend his life, because no matter what else happened, it seemed he always ended up in a saloon with a deck of cards in his hands. He was sorely tempted to deal an ace or two off the bottom, just for the hell of it. He'd never thought to earn his living with a deck of cards again. Indeed, the short time he had spent gambling the past winter had reminded him of why he had quit in the first place. And yet, sitting there, idly shuffling the deck, he felt right at home.

He dealt the cards smoothly. He had given his word to play the cards the way they fell, and he did. As usual, the house won more than it lost, but then, that was to be expected.

No matter what was happening at his table, Matt was aware of Lacey. Once she overcame her initial nervousness and embarrassment at being inside a saloon, she handled herself well. She smiled at the customers, but it was a cool smile, not one of invitation. She frequently glanced in his direction as if to assure herself that he was still there if she needed him. But the men were polite, pleased to see a new face, and a pretty one at that. The word quickly spread that she was not one of the regular girls, and that she was only there to serve drinks, nothing more.

J.J. Tucker's eyes were frequently on his newest saloon girl. She was a comely wench, pretty as a picture but with an air of innocence that intrigued him. Her figure was nearly perfect, her face without blemish, her hair a mass of soft red-gold waves. Many a man lost a hand at poker or faro because he was watching Lacey's voluptuous curves when he should have been watching his cards. But no one complained.

J.J. also kept a close eye on the man who called himself Matt Walker. The gambler was as good as he said he was. J.J. sat in for a couple of hands, and he noted that the gambler's hands were deft and sure when he dealt the cards, and Tucker had no doubt in his mind that Matt Walker could slide an ace off the bottom as easily as off the top when it suited him.

At ten o'clock the sheriff stepped into the saloon on his nightly rounds. Matt felt his mouth go dry as Henderson sauntered over to his table.

"You're new in town," the sheriff said, his eyes going over Matt in a long, measuring look.

"That's right, sheriff," Matt replied coolly. He met the lawman's eyes, one hand on the table top, the other resting on his thigh.

Henderson nodded. "I don't like trouble in my town. If you want to stay, you'd best keep that in mind."

Matt nodded, his heart slamming against his ribs as the sheriff studied him for another long moment.

"Remember what I said," Henderson remarked tersely, and left the table.

Matt felt the tension drain out of him as he watched the lawman leave the saloon.

It was going on eleven o'clock when the batwing doors swung open and three men sauntered in. Matt felt the muscles tighten in the back of his neck. Two of the men had been in the Black Horse Saloon the night Billy Henderson died. Both had testified under oath that Matt had gunned the kid down in cold blood.

Matt watched the three men make their way to the bar. They stayed only long enough to drink a beer, and then they were gone, but Matt was satisfied. At least two of the men he was after were still in town.

Lacey glanced at the clock over the bar. Another hour and she would be finished. Her feet were killing her, yet she had rather enjoyed the work. Most of the men had treated her with respect. A few had tried to get fresh, but she had only to remind them that her husband was a very jealous man to cool their ardor. There was something about Matt that made the men wary of him, though Lacey could not put her finger on what it was. He looked the same as always to her, yet, as the night had worn on, she had sensed a subtle difference in him that she could not quite put a name to.

The thought stayed in her mind over the next few days, and she began to notice a new wariness in his eyes. He seemed tense, like a snake coiled to strike at the slightest provocation. At first she thought it was only her too vivid imagination, but then she realized that Matt was a different man when he sat behind a poker table. His senses seemed sharper, his nerves always a little on edge, as if he were expecting trouble and wanted to be ready for it. And yet, it was more than that, and Lacey realized that Matt Drago would be a very dangerous man to run afoul of. And the men who played cards with him knew it.

Lacey stifled a yawn as she carried a tray of drinks across the room. She had been working in the saloon for almost two weeks and the newness had long worn off. Sometimes she felt as though she had worked in a saloon all her life.

She smiled a cardboard smile as she placed the drinks on the table and made change.

"How about a dance?" asked one of the men. He was tall and thick-set, with sharp brown eyes and a square jaw. There was a long scar on his left cheek.

"No, thank you," Lacey replied.

She was walking away from the table when the scar-faced man gained his feet and took hold of her arm.

"Just one dance," the man insisted.

"I said no," Lacey said, her voice cold and final.

"And I said yes." Taking the tray from her hand, he pulled her into his arms and began to waltz her around the floor.

Lacey looked around for Tucker, but he was nowhere to be seen. She gasped as the scar-faced man pulled her closer, his eyes moving to the swell of her breasts.

"Take your hands off of her."

Matt's voice was hard and cold. The piano player took his hands from the keys, and the whole saloon went suddenly quiet as the scar-faced man whirled around, his arm still locked around Lacey's waist.

"Who the hell are you?" the man asked.

"I'm her husband."

"Husband! No shit?"

"No shit. Now take your hands off her."

"Sure," the man said. "I don't want any trouble."

He released his hold on Lacey, made as if to leave, then pivoted on his heel and drove his

fist into Matt's face. Matt staggered backward. The hand he lifted to his mouth came away covered with blood.

He ducked, quickly stepping out of the way as the scar-faced man lunged at him. Reaching out, Matt grabbed the man by the arm, spun him around, and slammed his fist into the man's midsection. As the man doubled over, Matt grabbed him by the hair, jerked his head up, and hit him in the mouth. A second blow to the jaw rendered the man unconscious.

"Okay, folks, show's over." J.J. Tucker elbowed his way through the crowd. He took a long look at the big man crumpled on the floor, and the expression on Matt's face. So, it had finally happened. He was surprised there hadn't been trouble before this. He wasn't surprised to find that Walker was as good with his fists as he was with a deck of cards. "Come on, break it up."

Matt took Lacey aside. "You okay?"

"I'm fine." She dabbed at his mouth with a towel. "Are you?"

"Yeah."

"My hero," she murmured under her breath.

"I told you to stay home where you belonged," Matt growled. "But you had to work in a saloon."

"And you had to be a gambler."

"Okay, okay, I surrender." Taking her face in his hands, he brushed a kiss across her lips.

J.J. Tucker cleared his throat. "Think you two could get back to work?" he asked with a wry grin.

"Sure," Matt said. Giving Lacey's arm a squeeze, he went back to his table, whistling softly.

As time went on, Lacey began to grow acquainted with the saloon's regular customers. Most of them were businessmen who stopped by for a cold beer and a few minutes' conversation before going home to the wife and kids. Cowboys from the outlying ranches came in on the weekends, eager to spend their money on good whiskey and bad girls. Lacey often saw the two men Matt had pointed out to her, the men who had accused him of killing Billy Henderson. The other man who had accused Matt never showed up at the saloon, and Matt remarked that he might have moved away, or died, or was simply out of town.

J.J. Tucker frequently took Lacey aside to talk to her, ostensibly about business, and she began to realize that the saloon owner was growing fond of her. It was a fact that troubled her deeply, mainly because she wasn't sure how to handle it. Tucker never said or did anything that could be construed as forward, yet she knew, in the way a woman always knows, that J.J. Tucker found her attractive. He was a handsome man. His hair was dark brown, his eyes pale green, as cold as the Pacific in winter. He dressed immaculately, favoring dark suits and flowered brocade vests. He wore a large diamond ring on his right hand, a ruby stickpin in his cravat. Tucker was about the same height as Matt, but Matt was all whipcord and muscle while J.J. tended to be a little on the heavy side. Despite the fact that he was unfailingly polite, Lacey did not trust J.J. Tucker. There was something about him that made her uneasy, though she could not explain what it was.

Lacey had assumed that Tucker lived in one of the rooms over the saloon, but Matt told her he owned a large house near the end of town. His sister lived there as well. She was somewhat of a recluse, people said, but Matt remarked that he had heard from one of the men that she was a little crazy in the head.

Lacey frowned at Matt. "There's something you're not telling me."

A muscle worked in Matt's jaw and his eyes grew hard. "She was engaged to Billy Henderson. They say she hasn't left the house since he was killed, not even to attend the funeral."

"Matt, it's not your fault."

"Maybe it is. Maybe I did kill the kid." He

slammed his fist against the wall. "I wish I could remember what happened that night."

"Matt—"

"I hear tell she's a pretty woman," Matt remarked, "or was before she took to hiding in the house all the time. They say she hasn't been out of that house since he died. Just sits in the parlor waiting for him to come calling."

Lacey shook her head, her heart filling with compassion for the woman who had turned her back on the world.

"She must have loved Billy very much," Lacey mused, and wondered how she would react if anything so tragic happened to Matt.

"Maybe. But people die, and life goes on. You can't change the past by pretending it didn't happen."

"I wouldn't want to go on living without you," Lacey murmured.

"But you would," Matt replied. "You wouldn't stop living."

Lacey shrugged. Who could say how they would react to something as awful as the death of a loved one until it happened?

"I don't want to talk about it any more," Lacey said.

But she couldn't put the woman out of her mind. The next time she went shopping in town, she walked to the end of the street and gazed at the large house where J.J. Tucker's sister lived. The house appeared well cared for. The paint was fairly new, the grass was green and neatly trimmed, shrubs and flowers grew near the front porch. The curtains were all drawn, Lacey noted, the front door closed against the world.

Curious, Lacey walked past the house looking for some sign of life. For a moment, she thought she saw a face at the front window, but it was such a fleeting image she decided it must have been a shadow, or perhaps her own reflection as she passed by. Somehow the thought of a woman locking herself away from the world bothered Lacey deeply, and she puzzled over it and fretted about it for days. She thought about Matt and how deeply she loved him, how much a part of her he had become. What would she do if she lost him? Would she want to go on living? Would she have the courage to face the world without him beside her, or would she react like Tucker's sister and simply withdraw from reality?

Taking her courage in hand, she brought the subject up to Tucker one night when business was slow.

"I . . . I heard some of the men talking about your sister," Lacey began somewhat hesitantly.

"Did you?" Tucker replied, his voice void of expression.

315

"Yes. They say she never goes out."

"That's right." Tucker shrugged helplessly. "I tried to cheer her up at first, tried to make her see that her life wasn't over, but she just stared at me like I wasn't there." Tucker snorted with disgust. "I tried to tell her that Henderson wasn't worth one of her tears. The little bastard, always snooping around the saloon as if he had every right to be there just because he was engaged to Susanne . . ."

Tucker broke off abruptly, his expression becoming blank. "I shouldn't be boring you with all this."

"You aren't," Lacey assured him, somewhat mystified by J.J.'s outburst. What had he been afraid Billy Henderson would find? "How old is your sister?" Lacey asked.

Tucker frowned. "Twenty-two, twenty-three, I'm not sure."

"She's so young!" Lacey exclaimed. "You can't let her waste away in that house any longer."

"Just what do you suggest I do?" Tucker demanded. "I've tried everything I can think of."

"I don't know. Would it be all right if I went to visit her?"

"You can try, but I doubt if she'll let you in."

Lacey bit down on her lip, wondering what she had gotten herself into. "She's not . . . dangerous, is she?"

"Susanne?" Tucker laughed softly. "No, she's not dangerous. Just alone."

Matt was less than thrilled when Lacey told him she was going to pay a call on J.J. Tucker's sister.

"Why do you want to get involved in that?" he asked incredulously. "Haven't we got enough troubles of our own without you going out and looking for more?"

"I'm not looking for trouble," Lacey retorted. "I just—I don't know, I can't explain it, but I feel so sorry for her."

Matt shook his head. "I don't like it, but you do whatever you think is best."

Lacey nodded. "Matt, do you think Tucker could have had anything to do with Billy Henderson's death?"

"J.J.?" Matt shrugged. "Why do you ask?"

"I don't know. I was talking to him last night and I got the impression that he wasn't very fond of Billy. He said something about Billy always snooping around the saloon and —oh, I don't know. It was just a thought."

"You be careful, Lacey. Don't be sticking your nose in where it doesn't belong."

Lacey went to the Tucker house the following afternoon. There were butterflies in her stomach as she climbed the stairs and knocked on the front door.

A minute passed. Two. No one came to the door.

Lacey knocked again, louder this time. Still no answer.

She knocked a third time, hammering on the door with her fist. "Susanne? I know you're in there. Please let me in. I'm a friend of J.J.'s."

Another minute passed, and Lacey was about to give up and go home when the door opened the merest fraction and a pair of dark green eyes peered out at her.

"Susanne?" Lacey asked. "My name is Lacey Walker, and I work for your brother."

"What do you want?" Susanne's voice was soft and raspy, as though she rarely spoke aloud.

What did she want? Lacey mused to herself. "I . . . I don't know anyone in town and I thought we might be friends."

"No, thank you," Susanne replied, her voice impersonal and polite as though she were refusing a biscuit at dinner.

"Susanne, wait, please."

"Good-bye," Susanne said, and closed the door.

Lacey refused to be discouraged. Befriending Susanne had become a goal, a mountain to be climbed, an obstacle to be overcome, and she was determined not to give up. Besides, it gave her something to do. Nights, she worked in the saloon with Matt. Days, they made love, or shopped, or tidied up their hotel room. Sometimes Matt went to the saloon during the afternoon to pass a few hours and gamble with his own money. It was during those times that Lacey made her way to J.J. Tucker's house.

Susanne always opened the door, but she never invited Lacey inside, and she rarely spoke to her for more than a minute or two. Still, Lacey thought she was making progress.

She had visited Susanne four times in two weeks and was again standing on the front porch the day Susanne opened the front door and invited her into the house.

Pleased and flustered at this unexpected turn of events, Lacey stepped into the hall. It was a lovely house. The floors were hardwood, polished to a high shine. The walls were covered with pale blue paper. The furniture was of fine mahogany upholstered in a deep blue damask woven with a delicate gold thread. Paintings and mirrors hung from the walls, suspended by silken cords.

Susanne led the way into the parlor. "Please be seated," she invited. She took a place on the sofa and indicated Lacey should sit beside her. "You are the first guest I've received in over a year," she mused.

Lacey smiled, uncertain of what to say.

"May I offer you a cup of tea?"

"Thank you, I'd like that."

Lacey tried not to stare at Susanne, but the woman was quite lovely. Her skin was very pale, her eyes large and emerald green. Her hair was the same shade of brown as Tucker's and she wore it tied in a severe knot at the nape of her neck. Her face was heart-shaped and delicate, the nose and mouth finely sculpted, her eyebrows and lashes very dark against the translucent skin. Her hands were small and dainty, graceful as she poured tea into two china cups. Her dress, high-necked and long-sleeved, was of black silk.

"So," Susanne said in that soft raspy voice, "tell me about yourself."

"I hardly know where to begin," Lacey said, and for the next hour she told Susanne of her childhood, of her father's reaction to her mother's death, of how she had saved Matt's life and fallen deeply in love with him. She did not mention that Matt's real last name was Drago, or that he had been in town before.

Susanne's green eyes were sad when Lacey finished her story. "I was in love like that once," she said wistfully. "Perhaps J.J. told you."

"Yes. I'm so sorry. I tried to imagine what my life would be like without Matt, and that's why I came here. To tell you that you can't just give up. Life is too precious, too fleeting, to be wasted."

Susanne shrugged slightly, her eyes growing moist with unshed tears. "I know that what you say is true, and I've told myself the same thing many, many times, but I just can't face the world without him." Susanne stood up, small and wraithlike in the severe black dress. "I'm a little weary now, Lacey. Thank you for coming. I enjoyed our talk."

Lacey stood up. Impulsively she placed her hand on Susanne's arm and gave it a squeeze. "Please don't stay shut up in this house any longer, Susanne. It's such a waste. You're a lovely woman. I'm sure you have much to give to others."

Slowly Susanne shook her head. "I have nothing left inside," she answered sadly. "Billy took everything with him when he died." She placed her hand over Lacey's. "Please don't come here again. It's too painful."

"I'm sorry, Susanne," Lacey said sincerely. "I didn't mean to make you unhappy. I hope you'll think of me as a friend. And if there's ever anything I can do for you, please let me know."

"Thank you, Lacey," Susanne murmured. "Good-bye."

At home that night, secure in the warm circle of Matt's arms, Lacey told him of her latest encounter with J.J. Tucker's sister.

"She sounds a little loony to me," Matt remarked.

"She's not! She's just sad and lonely. I wish there was something I could do to help her, something I could say to bring her out of herself."

"You tried," Matt said, his fingers running lightly over Lacey's arm and shoulder. "You're the only one she's let into that house in over a year. I'd call that something."

"I guess." Lacey gazed into Matt's dark blue eyes and felt a wave of tenderness engulf her. And suddenly she needed him, needed to feel his strength, to bask in his love, to know that he was hers, that he would always be hers. "Love me, Matt," she whispered. "Love me and don't ever stop."

He seemed to know what she was feeling. He made love to her tenderly, telling her with each kiss and caress that he loved her, would always love her.

CHAPTER 13

So," J.J. Tucker said, nodding. "You let her in."

"Yes," Susanne replied. "She's very nice, J.J."

Tucker nodded again. Nice was not the word he would have used to describe Lacey Walker. Beautiful, alluring, provocative, desirable. Those were the words that came to mind when he thought of her, and lately he thought of little else.

"They're very much in love," Susanne remarked. "I see them sometimes, strolling by the house. I've seen the way Lacey's husband looks at her, the same way my Billy looks at me."

Tucker shook his head irritably. "Billy is dead, Susanne. It's time you got on with your own life."

"Don't say that!" Susanne shrieked. "Don't say that word. Don't ever say it!"

"I'm sorry," Tucker said quickly. "Forgive me."

He cursed under his breath as tears spilled down his sister's cheeks and great wracking sobs shook her body. It wasn't natural for a woman to grieve over a beau for so long. Why couldn't Susanne accept the fact that Billy was dead and get on with her life? How long was she going to hide inside the house, refusing to see people, refusing to face reality? Guilt gnawed at J.J.'s soul. If only he'd been more patient. If only he hadn't lost his temper . . .

Tenderly J.J. took Susanne in his arms and patted her back. Susanne was the only person in the world he had ever cared about, the only decent thing in his life, and he had almost destroyed her.

He held her until she was calm, then helped her up the stairs to her room. He turned his back while she got ready for bed, then sat beside her, holding her hand until she fell asleep.

There was a lively crowd in the Black Horse Saloon when J.J. arrived, and he smiled, pleased. He would rake in a bundle tonight, he mused. His eyes drifted around the room. Matt was dealing poker to four men at a table in the back of the room. A heavy blue-gray smoke haze hung over the table; there was a large pile of currency in the pot. Again, Tucker felt a sense of wonder as he watched Matt shuffle the deck. The man was amazing, truly amazing. His fingers were nimble and quick as he dealt the cards.

Tucker watched Lacey approach her husband's table carrying a bottle of whiskey and four glasses. He had bought a new dress for her to wear, and she looked ravishing. The dress was black satin, low-cut, tight at the waist and flaring over her hips. J.J. Tucker felt a hard knot of jealousy form in the pit of his stomach as Lacey bent and placed a quick kiss on her husband's cheek.

Matt happened to glance up just then and his gaze met Tucker's. There was no mistaking the jealousy lurking in J.J. Tucker's eyes, no doubt that Tucker found Lacey desirable. Matt's face went hard and his eyes flashed a warning that was not lost on Tucker. With a shrug and a tight little smile, the saloon owner went to the bar and poured himself a shot of bourbon.

Matt took a deep breath. Sooner or later there was going to be trouble between himself and Tucker. He had seen the way J.J.'s eyes followed Lacey. Often when they talked, J.J. found an excuse to touch her. Sometimes it was just a brief pat on the back, sometimes he put his arm around her shoulders and gave her an encouraging squeeze when she was having a rough night. Lacey thought Tucker was just being friendly. But Matt knew better. J.J. had no interest in being Lacey's friend. He wanted her, wanted her in the way a man wanted a woman.

It was after midnight when the crowd thinned out and the saloon grew reasonably quiet. Lacey was sitting beside Mort, the piano player, chatting amiably while he played a melancholy ballad. Matt was relaxing at the card table playing solitaire when three men entered the saloon. He felt a jolt in the pit of his stomach as the men made their way to his table and sat down. They were all there, the three men who had accused him of gunning down Billy Henderson.

Matt felt his mouth go dry as he shuffled the cards.

"You're new here, aren't you?" asked Toby Pitman.

Matt nodded warily. He remembered Pitman from the trial. Pitman had been the most vocal of Matt's accusers, his words of condemnation so positive, so forceful, they had erased any doubt the jury might have had.

Pitman grunted. "You look familiar. Haven't I seen you in town before?"

"I doubt it," Matt answered. He dealt the cards, his fingers swift and sure.

Pitman grunted again. "I didn't catch your name."

"I didn't give it."

"Any particular reason?"

Matt shrugged. "I didn't think it was important."

Lige Tanner cleared his throat. "We always like to have a friendly game, that's all. My name's Lige. This here hombre is Raoul Gonzalez, and that's Toby Pitman. We work for the Rocking W Ranch. Toby's the ramrod."

Matt nodded. "My name's Walker."

They played the rest of the hand without talking much except to raise or call. Tanner won the hand, and his grin spread from ear to ear as he raked in the pot.

Matt studied the three men carefully during the next hour. Toby Pitman was a heavy bettor, and a poor loser. His eyes were pale blue and sharp in a hawklike face. He had arms like trees and the biggest hands Matt had ever seen. Lige Tanner was a young man with sandy-colored hair and brown eyes. He was a poor player, for his eyes easily telegraphed whether his cards were good or bad. Raoul Gonzalez rarely spoke. He was a conservative player, not easily bluffed out of a hand, but not given to take chances, either.

Matt caught Pitman staring at him time and again, his eyes thoughtful, and Matt knew that Toby Pitman was trying to recall where he'd seen the gambler before.

They played until one o'clock, and then, at a word from Pitman, the three men left the saloon.

Matt let out a long sigh as he watched the three cowhands leave the building. It wouldn't be long before Pitman remembered where he'd seen Matt, and then all hell would likely break loose.

"You look troubled," Lacey remarked, coming up behind Matt and placing her hands on his shoulders. "Is anything wrong?"

"Time's running out," Matt remarked. "I've got to find out who killed Billy Henderson before Toby Pitman remembers where we've met." He shuffled the cards, and each time the ace of spades appeared on top. But he wasn't thinking about cards. He was thinking about the night young Billy Henderson had been killed, trying to recall exactly what had happened. He stared at the painting on the wall behind the bar. He had been sitting at the last table in the back of the room that night, alone. Pitman, Gonzalez, and Tanner had been standing at the far end of the bar with Billy Henderson. They'd all been drinking heavily and they got louder and more obnoxious with each drink. The bartender had asked them to hold it down, but they had just laughed and told him to mind his own business. Matt recalled that Henderson had started bragging about how good he was with a gun . . .

"Matt, let's go home."

"Right." Dropping the cards on the table, Matt picked up his hat and coat and they left the saloon.

"My feet are killing me," Lacey said as they walked down the boardwalk toward the hotel.

"Why don't you quit that damn job?" Matt asked gruffly. "I hate seeing you in that damn saloon every night, watching men leer at you like you were a piece of fresh meat for sale."

"It's not like that," Lacey protested. "Most of them are very respectful."

"They may act respectful," Matt retorted, "but they're all wishing they could haul you upstairs for a quick ten minutes in the sack."

"Matt!"

"It's true and you know it."

Lacey stared at Matt, her mouth making a little moue of surprise. She had known all along that Matt didn't approve of her working in the Black Horse Saloon, but he'd never been quite so angry about it before.

"What's really bothering you?" Lacey asked.

Matt let out a long breath and some of the

329

tension he had been feeling all night drained out of him. "It's Tucker. His eyes follow every move you make."

"J.J.? He's never said or done anything out of line. Not once."

"He's thinking it, though." Matt came to an abrupt halt as they neared the alley near their hotel. "Hush," he whispered, and his voice was low and urgent.

"What is it?" Lacey whispered back.

"I think we're being followed. You go across the street and keep walking toward the hotel."

"What are you going to do?"

"I don't have time to explain now. Just do what I said."

He gave her a little push, and then, in a loud angry voice, he said, "You little tramp! If I catch you flirting again, I'll take my belt to your backside."

He started walking again, then ducked into the alley, his head cocked to one side as he listened for some sound to indicate he was still being followed.

A dark silhouette appeared at the mouth of the alley, paused a moment, and then started walking again. On catlike feet, Matt stepped up behind the man and pressed his gun into his back. "You lookin' for me?" he asked in a silky voice.

Lige Tanner shook his head vigorously. "No. I was just going home."

"Really? When did the Rocking W take up residence in town?"

Lige Tanner swallowed hard. "I wasn't going to the ranch. I was going to see my Ma. She lives over at the Adamses' Boardinghouse."

"Kind of late to be visiting, isn't it?"

"She's . . . she's been sick. I been staying with her the last couple of days."

"You're lying," Matt said quietly. "Why are you following me?"

"Pitman told me to. He told me to check the hotel register and see what name you'd used. He thinks he's seen you before and it bothers him that he can't remember where."

"Why doesn't he do his own bird doggin'?"

Tanner shrugged. "I dunno. He's my boss and I do what he says. He don't like questions."

"You were in the saloon the night Billy Henderson was killed," Matt said, jabbing his gun barrel a little deeper into Tanner's back. "What happened?"

"A stranger gunned Billy down in cold blood."

"Just like that? Gunned him down for no reason?"

"He was drunk. The stranger, I mean. It might have been an accident, I don't know."

"Move it," Matt said curtly. "Head back the way you came, and don't look back."

331

Tanner nodded, his mouth gone dry and his palms suddenly wet. Hands clenched at his sides, he retraced his steps, wondering if he was about to get a bullet in the back.

Matt stayed where he was, his eyes on Lige Tanner as the young man moved away from him. When Tanner reached the saloon, a dark figure fell into step beside him.

Matt frowned as he recognized J.J. Tucker. He didn't leave the cover of the alley until both men were out of sight.

Lacey was waiting for him in the hotel lobby, her face pale. "Is everything all right?" she asked anxiously.

"Yeah. Let's go to bed. I'm beat."

In their room, Matt touched a match to the lamp, then sat on the edge of the bed watching Lacey undress. She moved with a feminine grace that was sheer delight to watch, and he smiled faintly, knowing she was being deliberately provocative in an attempt to take his mind off their troubles. And it was working. Matt's throat went dry as she slipped out of her dress, then slid her undergarments off, slowly, enticingly, until she stood before him clad in black net stockings and garter belt. He felt his heart begin to pound as she unfastened her stockings and slid them over her legs, removed the garter belt, and then slid into bed, patting the place beside her in silent invitation.

"Hussy," Matt growled, and quickly shedding his own clothes, he slid into bed beside her.

Her skin was soft and warm, her lips eager and willing. His hands moved in the wealth of her hair, loving the way the long silky strands curled around his fingers as though they had a life of their own. He slid his hands over her back and shoulders, traced the outline of her hips and softly rounded fanny. She was here and she was his and for a few brief moments he forgot everything but the wonder of her touch and the joy of possessing her.

It was only later, when Lacey was sleeping peacefully beside him, her head pillowed on his shoulder, her arm draped over his chest, her legs tangled with his, that Matt's thoughts again grew troubled. He had been a fool to bring Lacey back to Salt Creek. If he couldn't clear his name, he would likely wind up dead or in jail. In either case, Lacey would be left alone and J.J. Tucker would close in on her like a wolf on the scent of fresh blood. Tucker. There was no doubt that the man wanted Lacey. Damn him.

Matt gazed into the darkness. Lige Tanner, Toby Pitman, Raoul Gonzalez. Which one had killed Billy Henderson, and why? That's what he needed to know, and soon. Before Pitman put two and two together and remembered where he'd seen Matt before. And what about

Tucker? Where did he fit into the puzzle? Was it possible J.J. had killed Billy Henderson? But that was ridiculous. What reason would he have had for killing Susanne's boyfriend? What reason could he have had for meeting Lige Tanner in a dark alley late at night? Questions, nothing but questions and no answers.

Tanner, Pitman, and Gonzalez showed up at the Black Horse every night for the next three nights. And every night they sat at Matt's table.

Trying to get on my nerves, Matt mused grimly. And it was working. Pitman watched his every move, his eyes wary, speculative, as he tried to place where he'd seen Matt before.

For the hell of it, Matt dealt the cards so that Pitman lost every hand. Tanner and Gonzalez kidded Toby about his bad luck until Pitman slammed a meaty fist down on the table. Tanner's drink sloshed over the side of his glass and made a dark stain on the green baize top.

"Maybe it's got nothing to do with luck," Pitman growled, his pale blue eyes boring into Matt's. "Maybe it's got something to do with who's dealin' the cards."

"You calling me a card cheat?" Matt asked, his voice mild.

"Damn right!"

"I reckon you'd have to prove it."

"I'll prove it. Let me have a look at that deck."

With a shrug, Matt pushed the cards toward Pitman, smiling indulgently as the man examined the cards one by one.

"What seems to be the trouble here?" Tucker demanded in a low voice.

Matt pushed away from the table, his hand dropping to his lap. "This man thinks I'm cheating."

"Are you?"

"Of course not," Matt replied, and the lie rolled easily off his tongue.

"If you aren't happy at this table, move to another one," Tucker advised Pitman. "I don't want any trouble in here."

"He's cheating, I tell you," Pitman insisted.

Tucker reached into his jacket and pulled out a new deck of cards. "Here, open this one yourself, Toby. It's a fresh deck. The seal hasn't been broken."

Pitman took the deck and checked the seal, then slid his thumbnail under the seal, breaking it. He shuffled the cards and dealt them. Matt almost laughed out loud when he picked up his cards. He had a pair of aces and a pair of queens. Pitman's face was livid when he lost the hand to Matt.

Later, at home, Lacey shook her head as Matt told her what had happened. "Even when he does his own dealing, he can't win,"

Matt said, laughing. "You should have seen the look on his face when I raked in the pot."

"I did," Lacey said soberly. "He looked like he wanted to kill you."

"I think he does, Lacey girl. I think he does."

"Then what are you laughing at?"

"Damned if I know," Matt said, the laughter dying in his throat.

"Matt, why don't we leave this place?"

"And go where? I can't spend the rest of my life looking over my shoulder, never knowing when someone will try and collect on that wanted poster. I can't live like that, Lacey, and I certainly can't expect you to."

"Matt."

Something in her tone of voice made his heart pound. "What is it, honey?"

"I'm pregnant."

"Pregnant!" His eyes moved to her stomach. It was still flat, and his eyes lifted to her face. Slowly he shook his head, not wanting to believe her. They didn't need a baby to complicate matters, not now. "Are you sure?"

"Yes. Please, let's get out of here now, before it's too late. I want my baby to have a father."

"Lacey, I can't leave, not now. Please try to understand."

"We could go to Kansas."

"Kansas!" Matt exclaimed. "What the hell would we do in Kansas?"

Lacey held up a letter she had received from her father that day. " 'I'm sending this to Salt Creek in the hopes it will find you there eventually,' " she read. " 'The Apache were rounded up and sent to the reservation. Blue Willow didn't like it there and so we went to Kansas.' " Lacey looked up at Matt. "He says we're more than welcome to join them. We could lead a normal life, make a home for our baby."

It was tempting, Matt mused. Damned tempting, but he couldn't spend the rest of his life pretending he was someone else, couldn't rest until he knew who had killed the Henderson boy and why.

"Please, Matt."

"I can't, Lacey," he said wearily. "I just can't."

She swallowed the sob that rose in her throat. Why was he being so stubborn? How could finding out who killed Billy Henderson be more important than the life they could have together, more important than their child? Hurt and angry, she turned away from him, tears burning her eyes.

Matt mouthed a vague obscenity as he stared at Lacey's back. Her slight shoulders were shaking as she fought the urge to cry.

337

Almost, he changed his mind, but then he thought of the child Lacey carried beneath her heart. He had to clear his name, if not for his own sake, then for the sake of his child. He couldn't go away with Lacey and settle down somewhere, always waiting for the day when a bounty hunter or a lawman might discover who he was. He couldn't live with a price on his head, couldn't let his son grow up in the shadow of his unsettled past.

"Maybe you should go to Kansas," Matt suggested.

"Alone?" Lacey asked in a small voice.

"Yeah. Maybe it would be for the best, for now."

Lacey nodded. *Don't send me away, Matt,* her heart cried in anguish. *I don't want to live without you.* "Maybe it would be for the best," she said, her voice sounding loud in her ears.

"It's something to think about," Matt said hoarsely, and wondered why he was hurting her, why he was hurting himself. She didn't want to leave him, he knew that, and he didn't want her to go. But the words had been said and he couldn't call them back. And perhaps it would be for the best. There was going to be bloodshed before the trouble between himself and Pitman was settled, and he didn't want Lacey to get caught in the crossfire.

Turning, Lacey placed her hand on Matt's

arm, determined to make him see things her way. "Matt, please forget about finding Billy Henderson's killer. We've been here for months and we're no closer to finding out who killed him than we ever were."

"Pitman killed him," Matt replied stonily. "All I have to do is find a way to prove it."

"And what if you get yourself killed in the meantime?" Lacey cried. "What then?"

"I'm sure J.J. will take good care of you," Matt retorted. "He's had his eye on you ever since the first day we arrived. And don't tell me you haven't noticed! I've seen the way you look at him."

"I don't know what you mean."

"Don't you?"

"I've never looked at anyone but you," Lacey said, her voice like frost. "And you know it."

"Like hell! I've seen how the two of you huddle close around the bar when business is slow. I've seen how you smile at him, how he looks at you."

Lacey stared at Matt, unable to believe her ears. "You're crazy," she said coldly. "J.J. has nothing to do with this."

"Doesn't he? Maybe he's just what you've been looking for. He's got plenty of money, enough to give you everything you want. Maybe you should throw in with him."

"Maybe I should!" Lacey retorted angrily. "At least then I'd have a home of my own, a name of my own!"

"What the hell does that mean?"

"We aren't even legally married," Lacey exclaimed, her anger making her reckless. "We were married under fake names, and now we're living under an assumed surname. Which one shall I give our child, Matt? The one on the marriage license or the one on the hotel register?"

"Give him Tucker's name," Matt said, biting off each word. "For all I know, the kid belongs to him!"

Lacey recoiled as if she had been struck. How could he accuse her of such a dreadful thing? She wanted to cry, to lash out at him, to hurt him as she had been hurt, but the words would not come. She felt as though an iron hand were tearing at her insides, squeezing the very breath from her body. And over and over again she heard the anger in his voice, the cruel mockery: *For all I know, the kid belongs to him.*

She waited for Matt to apologize, to say he was sorry for making such a dreadful accusation, to say something, anything, but he remained mute, his dark eyes cold and distant.

Matt swore under his breath as Lacey's face went deathly pale. He had hurt her deeply and he knew it, but it was too late to recall the words. He had never realized how deeply his jealousy ran until now, never realized the ugly thoughts that had been lurking in the back of his mind.

That night they slept apart for the first time. Lacey huddled on her side of the bed, careful not to touch Matt, though she wanted nothing more than to be in his arms, to have him kiss away her hurt and assure her that he loved her, that he hadn't meant what he said, that everything would be all right between them again. How could he be so stubborn? Why couldn't he forget about Billy Henderson? Why couldn't they go to Kansas and build a new life together? She wouldn't mind living under an assumed name if it meant a chance to live a peaceful life with the man she loved.

She stayed awake a long time, hoping Matt would relent and take her in his arms, but he remained on his side of the bed, and after a while she curled into a ball, her hands wrapped protectively around her stomach, tears coursing down her cheeks like silent rain. That was how she fell asleep.

Matt spent a restless night and woke early, his mood dark and unsettled. He glanced at Lacey, sleeping as far away from him as she could get, and he felt his anger rise anew. Why couldn't she understand how he felt? Did she have any idea what it was like to know that every bounty hunter and lawman this side of the Mississippi considered him fair game? Damn!

Slipping out of bed, he dressed quickly and quietly and went downstairs. Going outside, he leaned against the porch rail, rehashing the argument they'd had the night before. He had said some nasty things to Lacey, made accusations that were absurd in the clear light of day. He grinned wryly. She was pregnant. That took some getting used to. He had never thought of himself as the fatherly type, but the idea was suddenly exciting. He thought of waking her, of telling her how sorry he was for all the terrible things he'd said, and then he decided to let her sleep a little longer. They'd had a rough night; no doubt she could use the rest.

He was going to be a father. Grinning, he headed for the Black Horse. Early as it was, he was going to have a drink to celebrate.

He was halfway to the saloon when Toby Pitman and Lige Tanner fell in on either side of him. Matt swore as he felt the press of a gun barrel against his side.

"Just keep walkin'," Pitman advised.

"What do you want, Toby?"

"We're going to have a little talk, that's all.

When we get to the corner, cross the street and head for that old shed on the vacant lot next to Tucker's place."

Matt nodded. He felt his muscles tense as Tanner reached inside his coat and relieved him of his gun.

It was early Sunday morning and there were only a few people on the street. Pitman nodded affably to old Mrs. Adams as they passed the boardinghouse, and then they were crossing the street. Tanner unlocked the door to the shed, and when Matt hesitated, Pitman shoved him inside.

When they were all inside the shed, Tanner closed the door, then touched a match to an old kerosene lamp hanging from a nail on the back wall.

"Put your hands behind your back," Pitman told Matt.

"I thought we were just going to talk," Matt remarked as Tanner tied his hands behind his back.

"We are," Pitman replied. He shoved his gun into the waistband of his trousers, then stood spraddle-legged, his fists resting on his hips. "I'm gonna ask you just one more time. Who are you?"

"I told you," Matt answered evenly. "My name's Walker."

Pitman nodded. "I had a feeling you'd be

343

stubborn about this. Shave him, Lige. Let's see what he looks like under that beard."

With a nod, Tanner pulled a straight razor from his pocket and quickly removed Matt's beard and moustache, grinning as the blade drew blood.

Pitman nodded, his pale eyes lighting with recognition as Tanner finished up.

"Drago," Pitman muttered. "Why the hell did you come back here?"

"Why the hell do you think?"

"It was a damn fool thing to do," Pitman said with a shake of his head. "We heard you'd escaped, but I never thought you'd be stupid enough to show your face around here. Lige, go get the sheriff. I reckon he'll be pleased as punch when he sees who we've got here."

Lige Tanner looked uncertain. Then, with a shrug, he left the shed.

"So it was you," Matt said. "You're the one who killed Henderson."

"We're through talking," Pitman said gruffly.

"What I can't figure out is why," Matt went on. "He was just a kid."

"I said shut up," Pitman growled, and drawing back his arm, he drove a meaty fist into Matt's jaw.

The blow sent Matt reeling backward and he fell heavily. He uttered a hoarse cry of pain as his arm struck an axe handle, swore aloud as the weight of his body snapped the bone in his forearm.

. Pitman was leaning down to drag Matt to his feet when the door to the shed creaked open. Without looking up, Pitman called, "Lige, give me a hand here," and then he grunted softly and fell forward.

With an effort, Matt rolled out of the way. Glancing toward the door, he grinned faintly when he saw Susanne Tucker standing there with a shovel in her hand.

"Get up, quickly," she urged. "We don't have much time."

With a nod, Matt struggled to his feet and followed her out of the shed. Outside, Susanne dropped the shovel and locked the door. Matt's eyes darted warily from side to side, but the streets were still deserted and no one saw them duck around the side of the Tucker place and enter the house through the back door.

Inside the kitchen, Matt dropped to his knees, then sat back on his heels, his face damp with sweat, his arm throbbing with pain.

"What is it?" Susanne asked.

"My arm," Matt said in a tight voice. "It's broken."

"Oh, dear." She gazed at Matt, not certain

what to do next, the shock of actually venturing outside the house beginning to set in. She had seen Pitman and Tanner take Matt into the shed and she had known that Matt was in trouble. Her first thought had been one of satisfaction, and she hoped Toby Pitman would kill him. After all, Matt had killed Billy. But then she remembered that Matt was Lacey's husband, and Lacey had been kind to her. Torn between a need for vengeance and a need to help her friend's husband, she had crept out of the house, not knowing exactly what she was going to do. She paused at the shed's back window, and though she hadn't been able to see anything because the window had been boarded up, she had been able to hear most of what was said. Impulsively she had picked up a rusty shovel leaning against the wall, entered the shed, and hit Toby Pitman over the head. The full impact of what she had done left her weak and trembling.

Matt felt light-headed as waves of pain chased up and down the length of his right arm. He slid a look in Susanne's direction and wondered if she was all right. She looked worse than he felt, he thought glumly, and he felt like hell.

"Susanne?"

"What?" She looked at him as if she couldn't remember who he was.

"Do you think you could untie my hands?"

346

She blinked at him several times. Why was Lacey's husband in her kitchen?

"Susanne?"

She shook her head, then smiled uncertainly as she began to fumble with the rope binding Matt's hands together.

Matt choked back a groan as she jarred his broken arm, and then his hands were free. With his left hand, he carefully brought his right arm up, cradling it against his chest. The effort brought a fresh sheen of sweat to his brow. The bone hadn't broken the skin, but his arm was swollen and turning purple.

Susanne hovered over him, her eyes sympathetic and helpless. She had always hated to see anyone in pain, and she could see that Matt was hurting terribly. His breathing was shallow and rapid, and his eyes, as deep and dark as a midnight sky, were clouded with misery.

"Matt, you can't stay here." The words came out in a rush, as though the thought had just occurred to her. "J.J. is asleep upstairs."

"I've got nowhere else to go," Matt rasped. There was a slim chance that Tucker wouldn't turn him in, Matt thought glumly. Damn slim.

"The basement," Susanne said. "Can you make it down to the basement?"

"Sure." Gritting his teeth, Matt stood up.

"I'll help you," Susanne said. Timidly she placed her arm around his waist, and slowly

347

they made their way down the narrow stairway to the basement. Each step sent little shafts of pain dancing down Matt's arm, and he was sweating heavily when they reached their destination. Wearily, he sank down on the cold stone floor.

"I'll bring you a blanket and a candle and something to eat," Susanne said. "Would you like anything else?"

"Do you think you could splint my arm? It hurts like hell."

Susanne Tucker's face turned even more pale than usual. "No, I couldn't. I'll . . . I'll go fetch the doctor."

"No."

"Lacey, then?" Susanne suggested. She smiled at the thought of her friend. Lacey would know what to do.

"No," Matt said. "It's better if no one knows where I am just now."

Susanne nodded. "I understand, but . . . I don't know how to set a broken bone."

"I'll tell you what to do. You just do the best you can."

"I'll try."

"Good. You got any whiskey?"

"Yes. J.J. has some."

"Good. We'll need something for a splint, and some cloth to hold it in place."

"All right."

Matt looked at her, his eyes probing her face. She seemed so distant that he wondered if she really understood what he was saying. "Could you bring me that whiskey now?"

"Yes, if you like." On quiet feet she left the basement and went into the dining room.

Matt closed his eyes, willing the pain to go away. He wondered how long it would take before Pitman and the sheriff figured out where he was. He wondered what Lacey would think when she woke and found him gone.

"Matt?"

He opened his eyes and blinked up at Susanne, his mind hazy with pain.

"The whiskey?" She held out a crystal decanter filled with a clear amber liquid.

"Thanks." Moving carefully so as not to jar his injured arm, he reached for the bottle and took a long drink. The whiskey was smooth as velvet and it warmed him immediately, dulling the ache in his arm. He took another drink, and then another.

Susanne watched him with a worried expression, the glass in her hand forgotten as she watched him drink from the bottle. J.J. rarely had more than a single glass of whiskey in the evening, and that was usually mixed with water. He never drank it straight from the bottle.

Matt sat on his heels, his eyes closed, his broken arm cradled against his chest, for several minutes. The pain had been reduced to a dull ache now, and the whiskey, swallowed fast and landing on an empty stomach, had hit him hard.

"Matt?"

He opened his eyes and gazed up at her. "What?"

"Your arm. What should I do?"

It took him a moment to remember what she was talking about, and then he told her, as best he could, what needed to be done.

It was after ten when Lacey woke up. She knew immediately, without even turning her head, that Matt was gone. The room felt empty, and she was alone.

Had he left her, then? Rising quickly, she hurried to the wardrobe and flung open the door. His clothes were still inside, and she breathed a sigh of relief. Wherever he had gone, he would be coming back.

Slipping into her wrapper, she sat in the chair near the window and gazed into the street below, wondering what she would say to Matt when he returned. She had not meant to blurt out the news that she was pregnant. She had thought to tell him when they were curled up in bed, his arms tight around her, the mood between them warm and loving. She had been certain he would agree to leave this dreadful town when he knew about the baby, certain he would realize it would be best for all concerned if they went to live with her father in Kansas, away from the troubles that plagued them in Salt Creek. She tried to put herself in Matt's place, tried to understand how he felt. True, it would be terrible to know you were wanted by the law for a crime you hadn't committed, but they had been in Salt Creek for several months now, and Matt was no closer to finding out who had killed Billy Henderson than when they arrived.

She sat by the window for a long time, waiting for Matt to return. It wasn't until he had been gone for nearly three hours that she began to worry. Where could he be?

Dressing, she left the room and went into the hotel dining room. Perhaps he was lingering over a cup of coffee. But he wasn't there either, and she left the hotel and walked briskly toward the livery stable. His horse was still there, quietly munching a flake of hay. His saddle and bridle were in place as well, together with his saddlebags and canteen.

"Can I help you, ma'am?"

Lacey turned as Clyde Booker came up behind her. She smiled a greeting at the stable owner. "I was looking for my husband."

Clyde Booker shook his head. "Ain't seen him this morning, Miz Walker."

"Thank you," Lacey said, and picking up her skirts, she left the barn and walked slowly back toward the hotel. Where was Matt?

At the Black Horse, she stopped outside the batwing doors and peeked inside, but there was no sign of Matt. Back at the hotel, she sat in the lobby for an hour, idly thumbing through an old newspaper, her thoughts tumbling madly as she tried to surmise her husband's whereabouts.

At six-thirty she began to get ready for work. Surely Matt would show up at the saloon. She took pains with her appearance, wanting to look especially pretty when she saw him again. Whatever was wrong between them could be worked out. Anything would be better than facing the future without Matt. Just being without him for a few short hours had taught her that.

She arrived at the saloon a little late, breathless from hurrying down the street. Her eyes swept the saloon as she stepped inside, but Matt was nowhere to be seen. The table he usually occupied was empty.

It was then that the first real twinge of fear made itself known. Something was wrong.

"Evening, Lacey," J.J. said, coming to stand beside her. "Where's that husband of yours?"

"I don't know," Lacey admitted, and burst into tears.

Frowning, J.J. put his arms around Lacey's shoulders and led her into his private office, a large and ornately furnished room behind the bar.

Closing the door, he poured Lacey a shot of bourbon. "Here, drink this. It'll make you feel better."

With a sniff, Lacey took the glass and obediently drank it down. The whiskey burned a path to her stomach and brought a quick flush to her cheeks.

"Now, what do you mean, you don't know where he is?" Tucker asked kindly.

"I mean I don't know," Lacey said, dabbing at her eyes with the back of her hand. "When I got up this morning he was gone, and I haven't seen him all day."

J.J. Tucker's face did not change expression. It would be a shame to lose Matt Walker. The man was a hell of a dealer, probably the best J.J. had ever seen, and he'd seen plenty. On the other hand, with Walker out of the picture, J.J. would have a clear field with Lacey. A little kindness, a little understanding during a trying time, and the next thing you knew, she would be eating out of the palm of his hand— and sleeping in his bed.

Lacey gazed up at Tucker, her eyes brimming with tears. She had never been overly fond of the man, but at this moment he seemed like the only friend she had in the world.

"There, there," J.J. said, pulling her into his arms. "Go ahead and cry if it will make you feel better."

And cry she did. The tears flowed, seemingly without end, and Tucker held her all the while, his hands soothing as they patted her back, his voice soft and consoling as he assured her that everything would be all right.

"Maybe you shouldn't work tonight," J.J. suggested. "Why don't you just stay in here and relax? I'll order some dinner from the hotel later, and we can have a nice talk. Meanwhile, I'll ask around and see if I can learn anything about your husband's whereabouts."

"Thank you, J.J.," Lacey said, her voice filled with gratitude. "I really don't feel like working tonight."

"It's settled then," Tucker said, giving her a disarming smile. "You just rest awhile, and I'll look in on you later."

Lacey nodded. Perhaps she had misjudged the man. He was really very kind. For a few minutes she wandered around his office. It was expensively furnished with a large mahogany desk, an overstuffed black leather chair, a pair of brass oil lamps, a comfortable sofa, and a small bar stocked with several kinds of whiskey and a tray of crystal glassware.

Feeling weary and discouraged, Lacey curled up on the sofa and drifted to sleep.

Tucker was whistling softly when he left his office. Along about eight, the saloon began to fill and he moved from table to table, taking time to exchange a few words with his regular customers, pausing at the gaming tables to make sure everything was as it should be.

A short time later Toby Pitman entered, followed by the sheriff. Tucker frowned. Henderson never set foot in the Black Horse except when making his nightly rounds or to make an arrest.

"Evening, sheriff," Tucker said pleasantly. He glanced pointedly at the bandage swathed around Pitman's head, saw the warning in his eyes. "Anything wrong?"

"I'll say," Henderson replied tersely. "I just rode into town a few minutes ago. Been out checking on a complaint over by the Double L. Anyway, Pitman here identified your new dealer as Matt Drago."

Tucker's eyebrows shot up as he lost his usually placid expression in surprise. "Drago! The man who killed Billy?"

"One and the same," the sheriff said.

"Well, he's not here," Tucker said. "See for yourself."

The sheriff nodded. "Pitman had him dead to rights, but Drago managed to get away. We've checked the livery. His horse is still there, so we figure he's holed up in town somewheres."

Tucker nodded. "Like I said, he's not here, but you're free to look around."

"Obliged," Henderson said, and spent the next ten minutes poking into the rooms upstairs, which caused considerable annoyance to several men seeking some female companionship from the saloon girls.

Tucker stood at the bar, his foot on the rail, a thoughtful expression in his eyes. He didn't object when Henderson asked to take a look in his office, although he knew it would be hard to explain what Lacey was doing there.

The lawman threw J.J. an amused look when he saw Lacey asleep on Tucker's sofa. "So," he said, closing the door, "that's the way it is."

"Don't go jumping to any conclusions, sheriff," Tucker warned. "She was upset about her husband's disappearance, that's all. She came to me for help, and I let her take the night off. That's all."

"Makes no never mind to me," Henderson replied with a nasty smirk. "I want that murderin' bastard behind bars. I don't care what his wife does, or who she does it with."

"If I hear anything, I'll let you know."

"I'm sure of that," Henderson said with a knowing grin. "I'm damn sure of that."

"Bastard," Tucker muttered under his breath as Henderson moved away. He watched the lawman leave the saloon, then turned hard green eyes on Pitman. "Spit it out, Toby. What the hell happened?"

Pitman shrugged. "I had him tied up, and then somebody hit me from behind." Toby lifted a hand to his head. "Whoever it was knocked me out cold. When I came to, I was at the doc's and he was patching me up. He gave me something to make me sleep. I came here as soon as I woke up."

"Where's Tanner?"

"Looking for Drago."

"Why didn't you come to me first?"

"I wanted to make sure my hunch was right before I said anything to you."

"You damn fool. Now we've lost him." Tucker fixed Pitman with a piercing stare. "You didn't tell him anything, did you?"

"Of course not," Pitman said quickly.

Tucker nodded. "Get out of here. I don't want to see your face again until Matt Drago is behind bars. You got that?"

"Yessir."

Tucker rubbed his jaw thoughtfully, his eyes as cold as glacier ice. Pitman had made one mistake too many.

Lacey was sitting up when J.J. Tucker entered his office a few moments later. Her eyes were a little puffy, her hair tousled. He thought she had never looked lovelier, or been more vulnerable.

"Hungry?" he asked.

Lacey nodded. She hadn't eaten since the night before.

"Good. I ordered dinner about twenty minutes ago. It should be here soon. Would you care for a drink? Some sherry, perhaps?"

"No, thank you." She was suddenly aware of being alone in J.J.'s office. What would Matt think if he found out? She could feel Tucker's eyes watching her and she shivered, unaccountably troubled by the expression in his icy green eyes. She felt suddenly like a mouse being stalked by a cat. She swallowed hard as J.J. sat down on the sofa and took her hand in his. Gently he massaged the back of her hand with his thumb, marveling at its softness. Yes, she was vulnerable now, he thought, and the idea filled him with excitement, like a hunter about to close in for the kill.

"The sheriff was here a while ago," he remarked. "He knows who Matt is."

Fear knotted in Lacey's throat and clawed at her belly, making speech impossible. She could only stare at J.J., her eyes wide with disbelief as her worst fears came true.

J.J. patted her hand sympathetically. "They haven't caught him. Not yet. But it's only a matter of time."

"He didn't do it."

"Didn't he?"

"No."

J.J. shrugged. "Three men took the stand and swore he was guilty."

"They lied," Lacey said, her eyes begging him to believe her.

"Maybe," J.J. mused. "And maybe Matt Drago's lying when he says he's innocent."

Lacey frowned. *Was* Matt lying? Was it possible he was guilty?

"Is there anything I can do?" J.J. asked solicitously.

"No." Her voice was like broken glass, cracked and filled with pain.

"Would you like to stay here tonight?"

"I couldn't," Lacey said. "It wouldn't be proper."

Tucker nodded, his eyes warm with understanding. Inwardly he was amused. It wouldn't be proper for her to spend the night in his office, yet she didn't seem to mind working in the saloon. Strange, the workings of the female mind.

There was a knock at the door, and a waiter from the hotel dining room entered J.J.'s office. His face was impassive as he spread a cloth on J.J.'s desk and laid out a meal fit for a king.

Lacey picked at her food, not tasting anything. The sheriff knew who Matt was. It was just a matter of time before Matt was found and arrested again. The long journey back to Salt Creek, the argument they'd had the night before, it had all been for nothing.

"Lacey?"

"I'm sorry," she said, laying her fork aside. "I guess I'm just not hungry."

"I understand," J.J. assured her. "Come, let me walk you home."

Lacey nodded and J.J. stood up. Taking his coat, he draped it over her shoulders, then took her arm and escorted her back to the hotel.

He took his leave of her in the lobby, at Lacey's request. "Send for me if you need me," J.J. said. "Any time, day or night." He took her hands in his and gave them a squeeze.

"I will."

"I'll look in on you in the morning."

"Thank you, J.J. You've been very kind."

"Only concerned," he said, and, leaning forward, he brushed his lips against the back of her hand. "Try not to worry."

Lacey nodded. Climbing the stairs to her room, she stepped inside and closed the door. How empty and dark the room was, she thought bleakly, as empty and dark as the pain in her heart.

She stood there for a long time letting the tears fall, until sobs wracked her body and she fell across the bed, hurting more than she had ever hurt in her life.

CHAPTER 14

Matt regained consciousness a layer at a time, hearing footsteps moving around upstairs, feeling the dull ache in his arm, tasting the whiskey that lay heavy in his belly. The basement smelled of dampness and decay.

Opening his eyes, he saw only darkness, and he wondered how long he had been out. He'd fainted when Susanne set his arm. Glancing at it now, he saw that his arm was neatly splinted and swathed in a thick bandage, a ghostly splash of white in the darkness that surrounded him.

His muscles tensed as the basement door opened and he heard someone coming down the stairs. He breathed a sigh of sweet relief when he saw it was Susanne. She carried a kerosene lamp in one hand and a covered basket in the other.

"I brought you something to eat," she said, smiling shyly. "I hope you're hungry."

He wasn't, but he said he was just to please her. After all, she'd gone to a lot of trouble on his behalf and he didn't want to hurt her feelings.

"How long have I been unconscious?" Matt asked as she lifted a plate of steak and fried potatoes from the basket and placed it on the floor beside him.

"All day," Susanne answered. "I've been so worried."

"All day? What time is it now?"

"Almost ten."

Matt swore softly, and the mild oath brought a flush of embarrassment to Susanne's cheeks. "Sorry," Matt muttered.

Susanne nodded, bending her head over the plate to hide her embarrassment. With graceful movements, she cut the steak into bite-sized pieces so he could manage it. She had thought, because of his broken arm, that she might offer to feed him, but she knew instinctively that he would not appreciate being treated like an invalid. Instead she pushed the plate closer to him and handed him the fork.

"Thanks," Matt said.

Susanne nodded. Tucking her skirts around her ankles, she sat there, quiet and thoughtful, while he ate. He was such a big man. His skin was dark, his eyes the color of the sky at night. His hands were big, the fingers long and capable. She glanced at her own hands, small and delicate and as pale as cream, and then looked at his again, trying to imagine what it would be like to feel his hands on her face. She felt a secret longing to reach out and stroke his cheek, to smooth the lines of pain from his brow and erase the worry from his eyes. She didn't, of course. He was Lacey's husband, a stranger Susanne had taken in out of pity because he was hurt, and out of friendship for the woman who had wanted to be her friend.

"You're a good cook," Matt remarked as he laid the fork aside. His eyes held hers, and a slow smile spread across his face. "I haven't thanked you for your help."

"It isn't necessary."

"The hell it isn't," he retorted, and then grinned. "Sorry. I guess working in that saloon has made me forget how to talk around decent people."

"It's all right," Susanne assured him with a rueful grin. "J.J. swears occasionally, too." She lowered her gaze, uncomfortable beneath his unwavering eyes. Life was so unfair, she thought sadly. She had locked herself away from the world, certain she had nothing to live for, certain she would never again find a man she could love. Now Matt was here, and she knew that, with very little effort, she could love him. He was tall and strong and handsome, soft-spoken and good-hearted, everything Billy had been. Indeed, he reminded her of Billy in many ways.

Matt shifted his position on the stone floor, grunting softly as a twinge of pain went through his broken arm.

"Are you all right?" Susanne asked.

"Yeah. You did a nice job setting my arm. I'm obliged to you."

Susanne basked in the glow of his approval. His smile was warm and friendly, and a rush of envy went through her as she thought of how lucky Lacey was to have such a man for her husband.

"I'd better go," Susanne said.

"I wish you'd stay," Matt said. "It's lonely down here."

"Very well." She settled her skirts around her ankles once more and folded her hands in her lap. J.J. wouldn't be home for hours. "Shall we talk?"

"Sure."

"About what?" Susanne asked, smiling up at him.

"You," Matt said, returning her smile. "Tell me about you. What are you doing buried in a big old house like this?"

Had anyone else dared ask such a question, she would have refused to answer. But she could tell Matt because he would understand.

"My parents died when I was very young," Susanne began, her voice soft and wistful. "J.J. raised me. We lived back East until I was fourteen, and then J.J. decided to move West. There was a fortune to be made out here, he said, and he wanted his share. For a while he searched for gold, but it was hard work and he never found more than a handful of dust in two years, so we left California and started back East. When we reached Salt Creek, J.J. met a man and they went into business together. I don't know exactly what it was. Something to do with guns, I think. Anyway, J.J. made a lot of money and he built the saloon, and he's done very well. I met Billy here . . ."

Susanne's voice trailed off and she stared at Matt as if seeing him for the first time. Why was she talking to this man—this *murderer*?

"Why?" she cried, her voice suddenly filled with anguish. "Why did you kill him? He was so good to me. He loved me. Why?"

"I didn't kill him," Matt said forcefully. "You've got to believe me."

"J.J. said you did," Susanne sobbed. "J.J.'s never lied to me."

"Susanne, listen to me." He put his hand on her forearm and gave it a squeeze. "Listen to me! I didn't kill him. I swear it. But I know who did."

Susanne blinked back her tears. She gazed into Matt's eyes and knew he was telling the truth."

"Who was it?" she asked. "Who killed my Billy?"

"It was Pitman."

"Toby? Why would he kill Billy?"

"I don't know, but I'm going to find out. I can promise you that." Matt frowned. "What happened to J.J.'s business partner?"

"Someone stabbed him in the back. They found his body floating face down in the river."

"How long ago was that?"

"I don't know. Just before J.J. built the saloon, I think. I don't remember." She looked at Matt candidly. "The people in town think I'm crazy," she said. "Do you?"

The question took Matt by surprise. One minute she was torn up with grief, and the next she was asking if he thought she was crazy. Maybe she was.

"I don't think you're crazy," he answered slowly. "But I think you've grieved long enough. You're much too pretty and too young to stay locked up inside this place."

Susanne smiled, pleased by his words. "Do

you really think I'm pretty?" she asked shyly. J.J. always said so, but he was her brother and didn't count.

"You're more than pretty," Matt said, meaning it. "I'd court you myself if I wasn't a married man."

"Really?" Her cheeks grew rosy with the pleasure of his compliment.

"Really. Don't hide yourself from the world, Susanne. You should have a man to love you, children, a life with some meaning, some happiness."

"Yes," Susanne said slowly. "Perhaps you're right."

And perhaps he was, she mused thoughtfully. Perhaps she had spent enough time grieving for what might have been. Billy was gone, and he was never coming back. Perhaps, somewhere, she might find another man to love. A man like Matt Drago.

"It's getting late," she said. "I'd better go before J.J. comes home."

Matt nodded. "Thanks again, Susanne."

She smiled at him, wishing she had the nerve to kiss him good night. Instead she picked up the plate and utensils and placed them in the basket. "Sleep well," she said softly and made her way up the stairs, her long skirts swishing softly behind her.

Matt sat there for a long time, his thoughts glum. He wondered how Lacey was getting along, and what she was thinking. He wanted desperately to send her a message, to assure her that he hadn't abandoned her and hadn't meant the terrible things he'd said. But such a move would be unwise. Messages could be intercepted. Pitman might be watching her, waiting for Lacey to lead him to Matt.

Pitman. Matt rubbed his jaw where Pitman had struck him. It was sore, tender to the touch. He was certain now that Toby Pitman had killed Billy Henderson. As soon as his arm healed, he would find a way to prove it. Once that was done, Matt's life would be his own again. He would take Lacey and go to Kansas and they would settle down and make a good life together.

But first he had to clear his name.

Susanne was happy in the next two days, happier than she had been since Billy died. She had a reason to live, someone to care for. Someone to love. She knew that Matt could never be hers, that he belonged to Lacey, but she spent hours daydreaming of what it would be like to be his wife. Knowing it was impossible, she fantasied that somehow she could keep Matt in the basement forever, that she could make him love her.

She took care with her appearance and discarded her black silk dresses in favor of soft blues and greens. Her gowns were out of style now, but they suited her complexion and figure, and Matt complimented her often, telling her she was as pretty as the flowers that bloomed in the mountains. They spent hours talking of unimportant things, and Susanne felt her grief and unhappiness melt away under the genuine affection that Matt felt for her.

She cooked elaborate meals and served them on her finest china and crystal. She prepared fancy desserts, brought him J.J.'s finest cigars and most expensive whiskey.

And dreamed her girlish dreams.

J.J. Tucker, too, was not unaware of the sudden change in Susanne's behavior. She was taking an interest in life again, singing as she cooked his meals. Rich desserts began cropping up in the kitchen, their best china came out of the cupboard, her mourning clothes were replaced by bright cottons and gaily printed silks. She smiled all the time, her eyes bright and alive, her laughter again filling the house.

His sister was in love. And Matt Drago was still missing.

Susanne stared at her brother, her eyes wide, her lips white. "I don't know what you mean," she said. "You're talking nonsense."

"Am I?" J.J. asked. He leaned back in his

chair, his arms folded across his chest, his eyes riveted on his sister's face.

"Of course." Susanne stood up. Her hands, hidden in the folds of her blue linen skirt, were tightly clenched. "I'm going up to bed now. I'll see you in the morning."

"Where is he, Susanne?" J.J. demanded angrily. "I know you're hiding him some-where in the house. Where? Your room, or the basement?"

"I'm not!" She tried to keep her voice even, but it rose shrilly, laced with guilt.

J.J. stood up, his face composing itself into passive lines. "The sheriff has searched every inch of this town, every store, every house," he explained patiently. "He's looked in every abandoned building and well and even under the jailhouse porch. I talked to Pitman. He told me Drago was hurt. This is the only place the sheriff hasn't searched yet. Now, where is he?"

"In the basement," Susanne confessed in a small voice. "Please don't hurt him, J.J."

Tucker looked at his sister with something akin to scorn. "You care for him, don't you?"

"Yes."

"Well, I'll be damned," J.J. murmured, shaking his head in disbelief.

"J.J.?" Susanne's voice reached out to him, pulling him back to the problem at hand.

"The sheriff's on his way over," J.J. said. "I think you'd better go upstairs."

"The sheriff?" Susanne said weakly. "Coming here?"

J.J. nodded, and all of Susanne's daydreams vanished in that instant. She had imagined that somehow she might make Matt Drago love her, if only for a little while. She had entertained visions of the two of them sitting side by side in the dark, exchanging a kiss, a caress. He belonged to Lacey—she knew that, but she had hoped he could be hers for just a little while, until his arm healed and he was able to defend himself again.

"Susanne?"

"Oh, J.J., how could you?" she sobbed, and turning on her heel, she gathered her skirts and ran up the stairs to her room.

Matt was half asleep when he heard the basement door swing open. He sat up, a feeling of helplessness washing over him as he heard the sheriff's voice. And then J.J. Tucker and Bill Henderson were standing on either side of him. The sheriff had a gun in his hand.

"Get up," the lawman growled, and Matt was certain he had never seen such hatred in anyone's eyes in all his life.

Awkwardly Matt gained his feet. His eyes met J.J.'s, and he nodded slowly. So, he thought sourly, that's the way it's going to be. Tucker wanted Lacey, wanted her bad enough to turn Matt over to the sheriff to get him out of the way.

Tucker met Drago's glance and shrugged, his mouth turning down in a mocking smile.

"Let's go," Henderson said, and gave Matt a shove toward the stairs.

The walk to the jail seemed longer than usual. Matt glanced up at his hotel room as they passed by, wondering if Lacey was still awake.

"Don't worry," Tucker said, lighting a cigar and placing it in the corner of his mouth. "I'll take good care of her."

"You can try," Matt retorted. But deep inside he wondered how long Lacey would be able to keep Tucker at bay. J.J. was a smooth talker, and Lacey would be confused and lonely, vulnerable.

Inside the jail, Matt hesitated before stepping into the cell. It was the same one he had occupied before, he thought bitterly, and shivered as Henderson shut the cell door with a bang and turned the key in the lock.

"Beat it," the sheriff told J.J., and Tucker obligingly left the jailhouse, whistling softly.

Matt faced the lawman. "I didn't kill your boy," he said evenly.

The sheriff made a low growl of disgust

deep in his throat. "I've got witnesses," he said with a sneer. "Three of Salt Creek's finest citizens. They all identified you as Billy's killer." Henderson stepped closer to the bars, his face a mask of hate, his eyes burning like the fires of hell. "It's lucky for you that I'm a law-abiding man. If I wasn't, you'd be dead now. My wife begged me to kill you when she learned you were back in town. Got down on her knees and begged me to kill you. And her a God-fearing woman. I was tempted, mighty tempted, but I've been a lawman for twenty years and as much as I'd like to shoot you here and now, I can't do it. So you're going to prison, and this time I'm gonna see to it personally."

Matt was speechless in the face of such hatred. What could he say to convince the man he was innocent? The sheriff would never believe that Toby Pitman was the guilty party. Pitman was foreman of the biggest ranch in the territory. He was respected, a citizen of the town. Matt was a stranger, a drifter, a gambler. The perfect fall guy.

"Sheriff," Matt called out to Henderson as the lawman turned to leave the cellblock.

"What?"

"Would you send a message to my wife and let her know I'm here?"

"No." Leaving the cellblock, the sheriff

slammed the door, plunging the cellblock into darkness.

It was over, Matt thought bleakly. All over.

Lacey sat up in bed, awakened by the sound of someone knocking on her door. Frowning, she slipped out of bed and drew on her robe, and then she felt a sudden flicker of hope. Perhaps it was Matt.

She flew across the room and flung open the door, her smile of welcome fading when she saw Susanne Tucker standing in the dark hall.

"Susanne! What are you doing here in the middle of the night?"

"Matt's in jail," Susanne said. She had not meant to blurt out the news like that, had meant to prepare Lacey for the shock, but the words poured out of her mouth in a rush. "He's been hurt. Not bad. His arm's broken, and he's in jail."

Lacey's mind was in a whirl. Matt was hurt and in jail: how did Susanne know? "Come in, won't you?"

Susanne stepped into the room, and Lacey closed the door behind her.

"Tell me," Lacey said. "Tell me everything."

It was well after midnight when Susanne finished her story. She told Lacey everything from the time she hit Pitman with the shovel to the time the sheriff took Matt away. Everything but her feelings for Lacey's husband.

"Thank you, Susanne," Lacey said gratefully. "Thank you for everything, especially for helping Matt."

"You'd have done the same for me," Susanne replied.

The two women embraced, and then Susanne went home. Alone, Lacey sat on the edge of the bed, staring out the window into the darkness beyond. Matt was hurt and in jail. The thing she had dreaded had come to pass. In a day or two Matt would be sent to Yuma and he'd be lost to her.

Agitated, she stood up and began to pace the floor. What was the matter with her? She was a big girl now, not a child to sit weeping in the dark. A stagecoach would be leaving for Yuma the first of next week, and she would be on it. Yuma was a thriving town. There were undoubtedly saloons there. If necessary, she would get a job in one of them to support herself. She would be near Matt, as she had once planned to be near her father.

Needing to be busy, she dragged her suitcase out from under the bed and began packing. She didn't know if the visiting hours at the Yuma prison were once a week, once a month, or once a year, but it didn't matter. She would see Matt as often as possible. He would need to know she was nearby, waiting for him, praying for him. He would need to know that he wasn't alone.

She felt better after packing her bag. Tomorrow she would go to the jail and see Matt. The argument they had had was no longer important.

Crawling under the covers, she closed her eyes, willing herself to go to sleep so the morrow would come quicker.

Tomorrow she would see Matt.

Lacey stared at the sheriff, her eyes bright with anger and disappointment. "What do you mean, I can't see him?" she demanded. "He's my husband."

"And he's my prisoner," Henderson replied coldly. "He can't have any visitors. Now, get the hell outta my jail and don't come back."

Lacey choked down the angry words that rose in her throat. There was no point in arguing with the man, no point in making him angry.

Wrapping her dignity around her like a cloak, Lacey turned on her heel and marched out of Henderson's office. Outside, she leaned against one of the porch uprights, fighting the urge to cry. She *had* to see Matt.

Squaring her shoulders, she went to the Black Horse Saloon and knocked on the door to J.J.'s office. She had no one else to turn to.

"Lacey," Tucker exclaimed, surprised. "What brings you here so early in the day?"

"The sheriff won't let me see Matt," she answered, and broke into tears as her resolve to be strong melted.

J.J. Tucker grunted softly as he drew Lacey into his office and closed the door. His kindness and understanding were beginning to pay off, he mused. Soon she would be his. It was only a matter of time.

"Don't cry, honey," he murmured, patting her back. "J.J. will make it right."

With a sniff, Lacey lifted her head, her eyes searching his, her heart hardly daring to hope. "Can you help Matt?"

"Of course I can," he replied. And then his voice was suddenly hard and implacable, his eyes as sharp as shards of broken glass. "I have a proposition to discuss with you."

Lacey blinked back her tears, repelled by J.J.'s predatory gaze. "A proposition? I don't understand."

"I'll make it perfectly clear. I want you, and I intend to have you, one way or another."

Appalled, Lacey backed away, but Tucker's hand closed over her arm in a grip of iron.

"Listen to me," he said harshly. "You have two choices. You can refuse me, in which case Drago will go to prison for the rest of his life, or you can agree to be my mistress, in which case I'll tell Henderson who killed his son and Drago will go free."

Mistress. The very word burned her ears and made her stomach knot with revulsion. Mistress . . .

Lacey's head jerked up. "You know who killed Billy Henderson?"

"Of course I know. It happened in my saloon, didn't it? I know everything that goes on in there."

Lacey stared at Tucker as if seeing him for the first time. He wasn't kind at all. He was hard and cruel and selfish. He had known all along who killed Billy Henderson, yet he had let an innocent man take the blame, was willing to let Matt spend the rest of his life behind bars for a crime he hadn't committed.

"I'm waiting for your answer," Tucker reminded her impatiently.

"But I love Matt."

"Then you'd better accept my offer."

Lacey stared at J.J. helplessly. How could she agree to be his mistress? It went against everything she had been taught. Matt, oh Matt, she thought in anguish.

J.J. examined his fingernails. "Have you ever been to Yuma?" he asked.

"Of course not," Lacey answered warily.

"I have." His cold green eyes bored into her. "Believe me when I tell you it isn't a pleasant place. Lice-infested blankets. Scummy water and rotten food. Men locked up like animals. Whipped. Starved. And no one cares. Most of them just give up and die after awhile."

"J.J., don't . . ." Lacey shook her head, not wanting to hear more.

"It'll be hard on a man like Drago," Tucker went on. "He's a proud man, stubborn. They'll try to break his spirit, and it'll be hard on him. Damn hard."

"Please . . ." Lacey choked back a sob as she imagined Matt in such a terrible place, being whipped, starved, his body bruised, his spirit crushed.

"You can spare him all that," J.J. remarked. "It's up to you."

Lacey stared at J.J. in despair. Fleetingly she thought of pleading with him, begging him to reconsider, but she knew it would be a waste of time. J.J. was a selfish man, not caring about anyone but himself and what he wanted. And he wanted her.

"I'm pregnant." She blurted out the news in a last desperate effort to make him change his mind.

"I like kids," Tucker said with a shrug, and Lacey's shoulders slumped in defeat.

"Very well," she said heavily. "I'll be your . . . mistress. But not until my baby is born."

Tucker shook his head. "You will be my mistress starting now, this minute."

"Now?" Lacey squeaked.

"Now."

"I won't sleep with you!" Lacey said defiantly. "Not until my baby is born."

J.J. regarded her through narrowed eyes for a long moment, and then he nodded. A gambler by nature, he knew when to call and when to fold, and now was the time to fold. If he pushed Lacey too hard, he might lose the game. And he wanted Lacey in his bed more than he wanted Drago behind bars.

"Very well," J.J. agreed. "But you will move into my house today. You will do whatever else I ask, willingly, and with a smile. Agreed?"

Lacey nodded.

"Furthermore, you will divorce Drago as soon as possible."

Lacey almost laughed out loud. Divorce Matt? In all probability, they weren't even legally married, but she saw no reason to mention that to J.J. "Anything else?" she asked bitterly.

"Just one thing. If you should get pregnant in the future, we will be married. There will be no bastards in my house."

"Except for you."

Tucker's eyes narrowed as he backhanded

her across the face, hard. "Never say that again."

Lacey nodded. Her cheek hurt fiercely, but she resisted the urge to rub it.

"Once I've talked to Henderson, there can be no changing your mind," J.J. warned, his voice as hard and cold as ice. "I expect you to live up to your end of the bargain. If you tell Drago I blackmailed you into this arrangement, or try to run away with him, I'll see him dead, and your child with him."

Lacey stared at Tucker and it was like looking into the face of doom. He meant what he said. She did not doubt it for an instant. "I believe you," she whispered.

"Yes," Tucker drawled. "I think you do. Now, come here."

Lacey took a hesitant step forward, her whole being crying out in protest.

"Willingly and with a smile," J.J. reminded her.

Obediently, Lacey pasted a stiff smile on her face. Her lips were cold and unresponsive as she accepted J.J.'s kiss. The touch of his hands on her flesh made her skin crawl.

"We shall have to work on your kissing, my dear," Tucker mused as he took her arm. "Come along, it's time to go tell Drago the good news."

*   *   *

Lacey stood beside J.J., her eyes downcast, as Tucker told Sheriff Henderson that Toby Pitman had killed his son.

"Why didn't you tell me this before?" Henderson demanded, his face red with rage.

J.J. shrugged. "Let's just say I came across some new information, shall we? Toby's your man."

"Where is he now?"

"Still out of town as far as I know. He took his wife to Leadville to visit her mother. Won't be back until next month sometime."

"You're sure he's coming back?"

"Nothing's sure in this life, sheriff. You should know that."

"What about Tanner and Gonzalez?" Henderson remarked. "They testified that Drago killed my boy."

"Yeah. Well, they work for Pitman, you know. They were both covering up for him, but they've decided it's time for justice to be done."

Henderson snorted. "I don't suppose anybody else saw anything."

"My bartender."

"He refused to testify at the trial."

"He'll testify now." J.J. smiled benignly. "I guess that just about does it. Be seeing you, sheriff."

"Wait a minute," Lacey said, tugging on J.J.'s arm. "What about Matt?"

"What about him?" J.J. asked, annoyed.
"He's free now, isn't he?"

"Sheriff?"

"Not quite yet, Tucker," Henderson said. "I'm not doubting your word, you understand, but I need something a little more substantial than that before I can turn Drago loose. He stays where he is until Pitman's convicted."

Lacey glared at J.J. "You swine! You knew this would happen."

"It was a possibility," Tucker admitted. He took Lacey aside. "You'd best behave yourself, my dear," he warned in a low voice. "Especially if you want Tanner and Gonzalez to testify that Pitman killed Billy."

"What do you mean?"

"I mean Tanner and Gonzalez will say whatever I tell them to say. Without their testimony, it's Toby's word against Drago's. Who do you think a jury will believe? The foreman of a well-established ranch, or a two-bit half-breed drifter?"

J.J. was right. Toby Pitman was a well-respected member of the community, a family man with a pious wife and two children.

"It's not fair," Lacey said. "I thought Matt would be freed today. He could spend another couple of months in jail."

"Better a couple of months than the rest of his life," Tucker said. "But that's neither here nor there. We made an agreement. I've kept my part, and I expect you to keep yours or suffer the consequences."

Lacey nodded. How could she have forgotten, even for a moment, that J.J. had threatened Matt's life and that of her child?

"I thought you'd see things my way," Tucker said smugly. He gave her a little push toward the cellblock. "Go tell Drago you're leaving him to become my mistress. I want him to chew on that for a while."

Lacey's feet were like lead as she made her way to Matt's cell. She kept reminding herself that she was doing this for Matt, but it didn't make it any easier. He would hate her now.

Matt stood up, his eyes showing surprise and pleasure as he saw Lacey coming toward him. And then he frowned. She looked pale and drawn. Her eyes, usually so full of life, were dull.

"I just came to tell you that you were right about everything," she said flatly. "The baby's J.J.'s. I'm moving in with him today."

"Moving in with him?" Matt gripped the bars and glared at her, stunned.

"He asked me to be his mistress, and I agreed. I just thought you should know," she said quickly, and turned and fled before he could see her tears.

Matt's voice called after her, loud and angry.

"Lacey! Dammit, Lacey, come back here!"

She ran out of the cellblock and out of the sheriff's office, running blindly down the street until J.J. caught up with her.

"Come on," he said, his voice filled with victory. "I'll take you home."

CHAPTER 15

Matt sat at a table in a darkened corner of the saloon, his back to the wall, a bottle of rye whiskey in his left hand, a shot glass in his right.

Five weeks had passed since Lacey had moved in with J.J. Tucker. Matt had seen her several times, always from a distance, of course. Each time she had been with J.J., smiling up at him, hanging on his every word. And dressed to the teeth. J.J. had obviously spent a fortune on his whore, buying her expensive gowns of silk and satin and velvet. The first time Matt had seen the two of them together, he had drunk himself into oblivion. Now he spent his days at the Red Ace, drinking heavily in an effort to blot her image from his mind, but to no avail. He had only to close his eyes and she was there.

He tossed off another drink, his eyes dark as he thought of Lacey carrying J.J.'s child, sleeping in J.J.'s bed, returning J.J.'s caresses. It was almost more than he could bear.

One good thing had happened in the last five weeks, he mused. Toby Pitman had been found dead, ambushed on the trail between Leadville and Salt Creek.

Matt laughed softly. Pitman was dead, shot in the back by an unknown assailant, and Matt had a perfect alibi. They couldn't pin this one on him, he mused. No sir. He had been in jail at the time. There had been an inquest. Raoul Gonzalez and Lige Tanner had testified that Toby Pitman had killed Billy Henderson. Both men had been fined heavily for perjury, and then had disappeared. Gonzalez had been found dead a few days later.

Matt frowned. Pitman was dead. Why? Because he had killed the sheriff's son, or because he had been covering up for the real killer? And where was Tanner?

He swore under his breath. It was no longer any concern of his. He was free and that was all that mattered, except for Lacey. He couldn't put her out of his mind.

He had started to leave town a dozen times in the last few weeks, but he never got any farther than the end of Main Street before he turned back. He couldn't leave, couldn't leave *her*. He cursed the day he had met her, cursed himself for wanting her, for needing her. And yes, dammit, for loving her in spite of everything.

He stood abruptly, his chair clattering loudly as it slammed against the wall. He took a last drink, slammed the bottle down on the table, and grabbed his hat. Jamming it on his head, he stalked out of the saloon, and bumped into Lacey head on.

For a moment they stared at each other. She looked stunningly beautiful, he thought bitterly. Her dress was of dark blue silk. Black kid slippers hugged her feet. A diamond-studded comb glittered in her hair.

Lacey gazed at Matt, her eyes drinking in the sight of him as though she were dying of thirst and he her only hope of salvation. His very nearness made her heart skip a beat.

"Excuse me, Miss Montana," Matt said, his voice dripping with disdain. His eyes dropped to her softly rounded belly before returning to her face.

"Matt."

He gestured at the packages in her hand. "Been out spending old J.J.'s money, I see," he sneered. "Or are you spending what he pays you to be his whore?"

His words were like a slap in the face. "It's none of your concern," she replied coolly. "Good day."

"Good day," he mimicked. "Is that all you've got to say to me?"

"What else is there?"

"What else, indeed," he rasped, and, grabbing her arm, practically dragged her down the street.

"Matt, please."

"Shut up," he hissed. "Just shut the hell up!" His fingers dug into her arm as he pulled her along, not caring that he was hurting her, not caring that heads turned to stare as they passed by. Not caring about anything but the anger coursing through him like slow poison.

Lacey had to run to keep up with him, and all the while the touch of his hand on her arm was searing her flesh, making her heart beat fast and her pulse race with yearning. It was only when they were out of town and very much alone that he slowed, pulling her into the privacy of a thick clump of trees.

"*Why*, Lacey?" he demanded, his voice sharp and angry.

She stared at Matt, unable to think of a plausible lie, unable to think at all when he was so near. For weeks she had dreamed of him, yearned for him, and now he was here, so near she could smell the heady masculine scent of him.

"Why, dammit!"

"I don't have to explain anything to you," Lacey retorted. She had forgotten how tall he was, how broad, how devilishly handsome. He was wearing black pants and a dark gray shirt and he looked rugged and oh, so desirable. His eyes, dark and angry, were staring into her own as if he might find the answer there. His hair, though still long, had been neatly trimmed. He towered over her, exuding strength and masculinity, and her whole body cried out for his touch. She longed to tell him that the child she carried was his, that she hated J.J. Tucker, that the only reason she had agreed to be J.J.'s mistress was to spare Matt a life behind bars. Almost, she blurted out the whole ugly story, but J.J.'s threat held her silent.

"The hell you don't."

"I got tired of being poor," she lied. She lifted her chin and met his accusing stare. "J.J. can give me anything I want."

"Can he give you this?" Matt rasped, and before she quite knew what was happening, she was in his arms.

The packages tumbled from her hand as his mouth slanted over hers, his lips hard, his kiss brutal, and she gloried in it, sighing with pleasure as his hand moved to her back to draw her closer. His body was taut, his desire evident, and her body reacted to his with a mind of its own, wanting to be closer. She lifted her hand to his chest and unfastened his shirt, her fingers moving restlessly over his hard-muscled chest, her fingers weaving in and out of the mat of curly black hair. She pressed her body to his, feeling his heat through the layers of her skirt and petticoats.

Matt groaned low in his throat as her questing hand traveled over his chest, gradually moving lower, lower, until it was at his waist. Her mere touch was enough to drive him wild and he kissed her again, harder, longer, wanting to brand her mouth with his own. He lifted a hand to her breast, quietly cursing the layers of cloth that barred his hand from her flesh.

He drew back to gaze into her face. Her eyes were smoky with desire, her lips swollen from the force of his kisses. She didn't protest when he slowly lowered her to the ground and deftly removed her clothing, and then his own.

"Lacey." Matt groaned her name as the last obstacle between them was flung aside. She was here, her eyes glazed with passion, her voice husky with longing as she murmured his name. She was here, she was his, only his.

Their bodies came together in a rush. Lacey was on fire for him, eager for his touch, with no thought in her mind except to love and be loved. She shivered with ecstasy as he became a part of her, and nothing else mattered then, not the past, not the future, only the glorious present, and his mouth on hers. . . .

Matt let out a long breath as reality returned. He sat up slowly. He had never meant to make love to her, but just being near her had flooded his senses with desire, with memories of the days and nights they had shared before J.J. entered the picture. J.J. Matt's eyes narrowed as he glanced at Lacey's softly rounded belly, and all the tenderness he had felt for her only moments before was smothered beneath the weight of his jealousy.

"Matt, what is it?"

He stood up and reached for his pants. "Get dressed."

She flinched at the tone of his voice, the disdain in his eyes. What had happened? One minute he was making love to her as if he would never let her go, and the next he was looking at her as if she were beneath contempt. And then she saw him look at her stomach and glance quickly away. So that was it. He hadn't cared she was pregnant a moment ago, but now he was angry and jealous because he thought she had slept with J.J., that she carried Tucker's child.

Furious and hurt, she scrambled to her feet and pulled on her clothes. Damn him! Why couldn't he see that she despised J.J. Tucker? Why was he so quick to think the worst of her?

How could he have professed to love her, to believe she had loved him, and still think she would let J.J. or any other man touch her?

"You cad!" she hissed. "I never want to see you again."

Before he could form a reply, she had scooped up her packages and was walking away from him, her head high, her back rigid with outrage.

He did not follow her.

Some perverse quirk of nature took him to the Black Horse Saloon that night. He shot Tucker a wry grin as he settled into a chair and tossed a handful of greenbacks on the green-baize table top. He won over a hundred dollars on the first three hands.

Tucker sauntered over to the table as Matt raked in another pot. "Take a break, Max," he said, tapping the dealer on the shoulder. "I think I'll sit in awhile."

The man called Max left the table and Tucker slid into his chair. He opened a fresh deck, shuffled the cards, and passed them to Matt. "Cut?"

Matt cut the cards and Tucker dealt three hands: one to Matt, one to the other man at the table, and one for himself.

Matt's face remained impassive as he looked at his cards: a pair of aces, a pair of queens, and the three of clubs. He tossed the three face-down on the table. "Just one," he said softly.

Tucker's face didn't change expression as he slid a four of hearts off the bottom and gave it to Drago. The other man took three cards. J.J. took one.

Matt quirked an eyebrow at Tucker as he slid the four into his hand but said nothing.

Tucker won the hand with a full house. "Why don't you go back to the Red Ace, Drago?" he suggested quietly. "I think your luck's changed."

"There's nothing wrong with my luck," Matt retorted calmly. "I'll deal the next hand."

J.J.'s gaze shifted to the other man at the table. "Why don't you try another game, Harry? This one's closed for the night."

"I think *I'll* try the Red Ace," Harry muttered, and, sweeping his winnings into his hat, he left the table.

J.J. leaned forward, his green eyes narrowed ominously. "Why are you still in town, Drago? There's nothing for you here now. Nothing."

"There's nothing for me anywhere else, either," Matt answered calmly. "Besides, I think your sister likes me."

"You leave Susanne alone," Tucker snapped. "She's too good for the likes of you."

Matt shrugged. "Maybe. And maybe I'll ask

her to marry me, and then we'll all be just one big happy family."

"I'll see you dead first."

"Don't threaten me, J.J. You might have been able to bushwhack Pitman, but you'll never get a shot at my back. And I don't think you've got the guts to face me like a man."

The jibe about Pitman was a shot in the dark, but it hit home. Tucker's eyes widened for just an instant and his face went suddenly white, as though he had received an unexpected blow. And then his expression was bland again, his eyes opaque.

"I don't know what you're talking about," J.J. said smoothly.

Matt grunted softly. "It was you all along. You had Pitman kill Billy Henderson, and when you didn't need Toby any more, you killed him, too. Why?"

Tucker stood up, his hands clenched at his sides. "Don't come in here again."

Matt rose to his feet, his hand hovering near the gun holstered on his right hip. "You're scared, J.J. I can see it in your eyes. And when I find out what you're scared of, I'll know why Billy died."

"Get out."

"I'm going," Matt said. He backed slowly toward the door, his eyes never leaving Tucker's face until he was outside.

CHAPTER 16

Lacey stared at the note in her hand. It was written in Matt's bold scrawl.

"Good luck, honey," it read. "I hope you get everything you deserve."

She pressed the paper to her breast, feeling as though her heart would break. Matt had left town. He would always believe she had betrayed him, that her child had been fathered by Tucker. And yet, perhaps it was for the best. It had been hard, knowing that Matt was nearby, never knowing when she might run into him. How long could she pretend she didn't love him anymore? How long before she blurted out the truth, endangering not only Matt's life, but her child's as well?

Carefully she folded the note and placed it

in her drawer underneath her stockings. She never looked at it again.

Tucker could not hide his relief when he learned that Matt had left town. His eyes, as green as the sea, glinted with triumph when he looked at Lacey. She was his now, all his. When the child was born, he would make her his in fact as well as in name. And perhaps, if he played his cards right, he could find a way to rid himself of the child as well. Billy was dead and Pitman was dead, and his secret had died with them. Gonzalez had been disposed of, too, and Tanner would never have the guts to reveal what little he knew.

Tucker lit a cigar, filled with a sense of satisfaction. Next year he would sell the Black Horse and begin to cultivate a more refined demeanor. He would buy a respectable business, attend church, donate to the local charities. He would become a respected citizen, and Lacey would be his wedge into society. Once he got her pregnant, she would have to marry him. She was lovely, well-educated, obviously well-bred. No telling how far he could go with her at his side. Mayor, perhaps, then governor. With enough money and the right connections, there would be no stopping him.

Susanne refused to believe that Matt had left town without telling her good-bye. She went to his hotel room, and only then did she believe that he was gone.

With a wordless cry of despair, she sat down on the edge of his bed and wept. Not since Billy had she cared about another human being. She had grieved for Billy for over a year, certain her life was over, and then Matt had come into her life, and she had realized that she could love again. She had known, deep in her heart, that Matt loved Lacey, that he would never be hers, but she had hoped and dreamed and she had found a new reason to live.

And now he was gone, and it was as though he had never existed. Lacey had moved in with J.J. and Matt had left town.

Susanne stared blankly at the hard wood floor. She had not dared question J.J. about the sudden turn of events, nor did she possess the nerve to ask Lacey why she had decided to become J.J.'s mistress.

She kept to her room for the next several days, and gradually she realized she had never been in love with Matt Drago, though she had been attracted to him. It was just that he was the first person she had let herself care about, the first man she had been close to, besides J.J., in over a year.

For Lacey, the days and nights passed slowly after Matt left town. She spent most of her time in the house, decorating a room for her baby, which would be born in the spring. She had the room painted a soft yellow and hung fluffy white curtains at the window. She ordered the most expensive crib she could find from a mail order catalog, as well as a high chair and a perambulator. She had money now, as much as she wanted, and she spent it freely. If J.J. wanted her to be his mistress, he could pay for it. She spent hours sewing baby clothes and quilts, making far more garments than one child could ever hope to wear simply because it gave her something to do. Matt was gone, but she still had his child to live for.

She spent a good deal of time with Susanne. They went shopping together, buying whatever caught their fancy. Susanne bought a whole new wardrobe: dresses and hats and shoes, lacy parasols, delicate underwear, silk stockings. They talked about what fun it would be to have a baby in the house, and bought toys and dolls and a wooden rocking horse.

Gradually Susanne began spending less time at home, and when she was there she wore a dreamy expression and often did not hear what was being said. Eventually she admitted that she was head-over-heels in love with Robert Morrison, the new owner of the Salt Creek *Gazette*. Susanne thought he was wonderful, and when Lacey met him, she could understand why. Robert was thoughtful, attentive, and polite. He had a delightful sense of humor, a winning smile, and a strong sense of right and wrong. And it was obvious that he adored Susanne.

No one was surprised when they announced their engagement. J.J. promised to give Susanne the biggest wedding the town had ever seen, and they began to make plans immediately though the wedding would not take place until the first of March.

Lacey could not help envying Susanne's happiness. J.J.'s sister was radiant. She laughed easily, sang as she went about the house, had a kind word for everyone. She attributed Lacey's growing irritability to her pregnancy and was constantly admonishing J.J. to be kinder and more tolerant of Lacey's moods, never realizing that J.J. was the cause of Lacey's misery.

On the surface, J.J. was the soul of concern. He never raised his voice, never complained if dinner was late or the house untidy. He was constantly bringing Lacey gifts of clothing and jewelry, indulged her every whim, praised her beauty.

Only when they were alone did he let himself say what he was really thinking. And then he accused her of being a two-faced whore, of moving in with him just to save Drago's hide. Lacey was confused by his anger. Of course that was why she had moved in with him. What other reason could there have been?

And always he reminded her that she had promised to be his once the baby was born. "I'll make you forget Drago," he vowed, his fingers digging painfully into her arms, his eyes boring into her own. "You'll forget you ever knew him."

She was glad when winter came. The dark clouds and storm-darkened skies suited her mood perfectly. She spent her days sitting in the nursery, rocking gently, her hand on her swollen belly, her eyes staring out the window. It was her favorite room in the house. Her child would grow up in this room. Her child. Matt's child. She hoped for a boy with thick black hair and midnight blue eyes.

Rocking back and forth, she watched the lightning rend the blackened skies and she wondered where Matt had gone. Did he ever think of her? Had he found someone else to love?

She heard the clock downstairs chime the hour, and then she heard the front door open and knew that J.J. was home. She felt her muscles tense as she heard him climb the stairs, and then he was standing in the doorway, his green eyes glinting like shards of glass, his mouth turned down in a cruel mocking smile.

"Good evening, my dear," he said with a

sneer. "Have you no welcome for me, no kiss of greeting?"

"Welcome home, J.J."

"No kiss?"

Awkwardly she rose to her feet and pressed her lips to his. He grabbed her when she would have drawn away, his arms like steel bands around her waist.

"Willingly and with a smile," he taunted. "Remember."

"J.J., you're hurting me."

"You're mine," he growled. "Not his. Mine!"

Lacey stared up at him, seeing the jealousy blazing in his eyes, smelling the whiskey on his breath, tasting it as he kissed her again, his mouth hard and cruel as though he wanted to hurt her. She uttered a little cry of pain as his mouth crushed hers.

"I'm tired of waiting for that brat to be born," he rasped as he backed her against the wall and fell against her. "I've been patient, Lacey. Haven't I been patient? But I'm not made of stone."

She tried to push him away, but he was too heavy, too strong. "J.J., you promised!"

"You'd let him, wouldn't you? You wouldn't tell Drago no."

"J.J., leave me alone!"

He laughed harshly as he backed away from her, and for a minute she thought she had won. But then he swept her into his arms and carried her down the hall to his room and closed the door.

"You've never been in my room before, have you?" J.J. mused.

Lacey did not answer him. She was too frightened of what she knew was going to happen. Afraid to say or do anything that would make J.J. angry, she shook her head.

"It's . . . it's a nice room," she stammered.

"I want you to sleep in here from now on," J.J. said. "No more separate bedrooms."

She saw the look in his eyes and she dared not refuse, nor did she object when he placed her on the bed and began kissing her. She felt his hands fumbling with her gown, felt his mouth on hers, his tongue sliding across her lips, and she was filled with revulsion.

"J.J., stop," she gasped. "I'm going to be sick."

"It won't work," J.J. said. "Tonight you'll be mine."

With a groan, she pushed him away, then turned her head and was violently ill. Her stomach heaved until it was empty and sore, and then she curled up on the bed, hardly aware that J.J. was suddenly sober, or that he had called for Susanne. He left the room while Susanne helped Lacey get washed up and into a clean gown. Lacey sat on the window seat while Susanne quickly changed the bedclothes, then helped Lacey into bed.

"Thank you," Lacey murmured.

"Can I get you anything?" Susanne offered. "A glass of water, or a cup of tea, perhaps."

"No, thank you. I'd just like to be alone."

Susanne smiled. "You'll feel better once the baby is born. You'll see."

"Yes," Lacey agreed. How could she explain that it wasn't the baby making her ill, but J.J.'s touch?

Alone, she let the tears come. "Is this what I deserve, Matt?" she whispered to the darkness. And heard only silence in reply.

CHAPTER 17

Matt Drago smiled as he laid his cards on the green-baize table top, face up.

"Four queens," muttered Troy Blackburn. "Damn! I thought sure you were bluffing."

"Not this time." Matt plucked a five-dollar gold piece from his winnings and dropped it down the ample cleavage of the raven-haired woman sitting on his knee. "For bringing me luck," he drawled softly.

"Anytime, hombre," Consuelo replied. She ran her hand along the inside of his thigh. "Anything, anytime."

"The pot's light, Drago," complained Tom Sully. "You in or out?"

"I'm in." He threw ten dollars into the pot, picked up his cards as they were dealt to him.

He had a pair of kings, a jack, a ten, and a deuce. Not bad. He grinned as Consuelo pressed a kiss to his cheek. She was a pretty thing, with huge brown eyes and a voluptuous figure that bordered on plumpness.

"Dammit, Matt," growled Blackburn. "You gonna make love or play poker?"

"Sorry."

"Sorry, hell. You in or out?"

"I'm in." He slid another ten dollars into the pot.

"Cards?"

"Two," Matt requested. He tossed the ten and the deuce onto the table, picked up his new cards. A jack and another king. *Lucky at cards, unlucky at love.* The phrase whispered in his mind as he raised his bet by another ten dollars. He had been in this town for over a month, drinking and gambling and trying to forget a woman with red-gold hair. After leaving Salt Creek, he had wandered aimlessly from one town to another, never staying long in any one place until winter came, and had decided to hole up here for no other reason than that he liked the town's only saloon. He had been playing poker with Blackburn and Sully long enough to know that Blackburn would bet on anything, and that Sully could outbluff anybody. They were all gamblers; they all knew the tricks of the trade, and it made for some of the most exciting poker

Matt had ever played. So far, he figured he was ahead of the game by about eight hundred dollars.

Consuelo squealed with delight as Matt raked in the second pot in a row, and stuffed a handful of greenbacks into her bodice. He was easily the most handsome and most thoughtful man she knew. The other girls in the saloon were jealous because he never paid them any attention, never took them upstairs. Of course, he never took Consuelo upstairs, either, but he let her sit on his lap, and he showered her with hugs and kisses and cash. All in all, it was a very satisfying arrangement. She had tried many times to lure him into her bed, but he always refused. That mystified her, for he was obviously a virile man, one who liked women. And he liked her, she was certain of that.

She smiled as he kissed her cheek. "How about bringing me a beer?" he asked, and she slid off his lap and walked to the bar, swinging her hips provocatively in case he was watching her. Maybe tonight, she mused. Maybe tonight.

Matt played poker until well after midnight; then, pocketing his winnings, he took his leave of Blackburn and Sully, kissed Consuelo good night, and left the saloon.

It was raining outside, a cold steady drizzle

that had turned the streets to mud. Pulling his hat down over his face, he hunched into his coat and walked down the dark street. As always, once he was alone his thoughts turned to Lacey. No matter how far he rode, no matter how much he drank, he could not forget her.

Lacey. He remembered how she had ridden at his side, uncomplaining, while they searched for her father. He remembered her tender concern when he was hurt, her shy sensuality the first time they made love, her courage in the face of danger and death. His need for her was a constant gnawing ache, a pain that refused to be dulled by time or distance. He had loved her as he had never loved anyone, and she had betrayed him in the arms of another man.

Damn. Why couldn't he forget her? Abruptly he turned on his heel and walked swiftly back to the saloon. Consuelo was sitting at one of the tables, talking to a couple of the saloon girls, when Matt grabbed her by the arm and hauled her, none too gently, to her feet.

"Come on," he said tersely, and headed for the rooms above the saloon. It was time to forget Lacey, time to get on with his own life. He had been acting like a lovestruck boy long enough.

Consuelo's huge brown eyes were shining

with anticipation as Matt closed the door and took her in his arms. His kiss was hard, brutal, but she didn't mind.

Matt kissed her for a long time, his hands playing along her ribcage, down her hips, over her buttocks. His nostrils filled with the scent of her, and even as he wrinkled his nose against her cheap perfume and the smell of beer and tobacco smoke that clung to her, he was remembering Lacey. She had smelled clean and sweet, like roses on a summer day.

With a groan of despair, he carried Consuelo to the bed and hastily removed her clothing. Her skin was light brown, smooth, plump, and all woman. He didn't resist when she began to undress him. He needed a woman, any woman.

She moaned softly as he caressed her, her lips softly yielding, her hands sliding across his broad back. She arched her hips upward, inviting him to take her.

Matt swore softly as he gazed into Consuelo's eyes. He had thought to find relief in the arms of another woman, but it was no use. He might spend his lust between Consuelo's plump thighs, but he could never satisfy his need for Lacey in another woman's arms. Not if he lived to be a hundred.

"What is it, hombre?" Consuelo purred, her voice deep and husky, her eyes glazed with passion. She reached for his arm as he started to rise. "Where are you going?"

"I wish to hell I knew," Matt muttered. He dressed quickly, tossed Consuelo twenty dollars, and left the room.

Where are you going?

Consuelo's question haunted Matt as he rode out of town the following morning. Where *was* he going? He was tired of living from day to day, tired of smoke-filled saloons and lumpy beds in cheap hotel rooms. So damned tired.

It was a cold, windy day when he left another two-bit town behind. He rode with no destination in mind, letting the horse pick their speed and direction.

He wound up in a dismal little town south of the border. The place had little to recommend it other than the fact that he'd never been there before.

He'd been there almost a week, drinking and gambling in the town's only cantina, when Lige Tanner walked through the swinging doors. It took Matt a few minutes to recognize the man. Tanner had grown a full beard and a moustache. His hair was long and unkempt, his eyes wary.

"How's it going, Lige?" Matt asked.

Lige Turner whirled around, his hand reaching for his gun, his eyes wild. He swallowed hard when he felt Matt's gun jabbing him in the side.

"I'm surprised you're still alive," Matt mused. "My grandmother could've beat that draw."

"What do you want, Drago?" Tanner asked. His voice was scared, like his eyes.

"Thought I'd buy you a drink."

Tanner looked suspicious. "Why?"

Matt shrugged. "I thought I'd buy you a drink, and you'd give me a little information."

"I don't know anything," Tanner said quickly.

"Why'd Pitman kill Billy Henderson? You were there that night. I want to know what happened."

Tanner shook his head. "I don't know nothing."

Matt eared the hammer back on his Colt. "Who are you protecting, Lige? Who are you afraid of?"

"Nobody, honest. Please, just let me go."

"It was Tucker, wasn't it? Pitman pulled the trigger, but it was Tucker who wanted Billy dead. And I happened to be in the saloon at the time, dead drunk, so Pitman pinned the murder on me, and you and Gonzalez backed him up. Right?"

"I don't know what you're talking about."

"Don't you? Let's go outside."

"Why?"

Matt grinned wolfishly. "There's too many witnesses in here. I don't want anybody to see me kill you."

"Wait a minute, dammit . . ."

Matt nodded. "Now you're getting smart. Why'd Tucker want Billy dead?"

Lige Tanner swallowed hard. He was looking death in the face and he knew it. J.J. Tucker was miles away, but Drago was here, now, holding a gun to his ribs.

"Billy got nosey," Tanner said, the words pouring out of his mouth. "He started wondering where J.J. got the money to build the Black Horse. Billy fancied himself quite a detective. He was taking a course by mail, thought he was Sherlock Holmes or something. He started asking questions of some of the old-timers, snooping around where he didn't belong. He found out who J.J.'s partner had been and, hell, I don't know how he found out, but he discovered that J.J. and his partner had sold guns to the Indians. I guess that went on for quite a while, until Salt Creek started getting civilized. J.J.'s partner turned up dead soon after that, and J.J. built the saloon."

"How'd you find out all this?"

"Billy told me one night when he'd had too much to drink. I happened to mention it to Pitman, and I guess he told J.J. I never knew Pitman was going to kill Billy. It all happened

413

so fast. Billy was drunk that night, bragging about how he was going to be a big man in town. He was fast-drawing his gun, showing off. He challenged Pitman to draw against him to see who was fastest. Their guns were supposed to be empty, but the next thing I knew, Billy was dead. Pitman slipped something into your drink when the bartender wasn't looking, and when you passed out, he fired a round from your gun and called the sheriff."

Matt grunted softly. "So this all happened because J.J. didn't want people to know he got his start running guns to the Apache?"

"Yeah. People don't look kindly on those who sell guns to the enemy. I guess J.J. was afraid the townspeople would string him up, or run him out of Salt Creek."

"Why'd he kill Pitman?"

"I don't know. Me and Gonzalez, we got scared. He headed home to El Paso, I think. I been running ever since."

"Gonzalez is dead."

Tanner's face went chalk white. "Are you sure?"

"I'm sure." Matt drummed his fingertips on the bar top. He could understand why Tucker hadn't wanted anyone digging around in his past. A lot of the local citizens had lost friends and loved ones during the Indian wars. People had long memories where things like that were concerned. But, more than that, Matt suspected that J.J. had been afraid Susanne might discover he'd hired Pitman to kill Billy. That was why he had killed Toby. He didn't want to see his sister's adoration turn to hatred, couldn't take a chance on Pitman going to court and spilling everything he knew. Only one question remained.

"Who killed Pitman?"

"I don't know."

"Don't know, or won't say?"

"I don't know. I swear it."

Matt slid his gun back in the holster, his eyes thoughtful. "Thanks." He tossed a silver dollar onto the bar. "Buy yourself a drink."

"Obliged," Tanner said. He turned to order a drink from the barkeep. When he turned around again, Drago was gone.

CHAPTER 18

It was Susanne's wedding day, and J.J. had spared no expense. Everyone in town had been invited. Following the ceremony, there would be a lavish reception in the town hall. J.J. had hired a six-piece orchestra all the way from St. Louis. There would be food and champagne, and a wedding cake almost three feet tall. Susanne's dress was exquisite. Made of heavy white satin, it had a high neck and a long swirling skirt that swished when she walked. The sleeves were full near her shoulders, gradually tapering to her wrists. The bodice was adorned with hundreds of tiny seed pearls set in an intricate design. It was, Lacey thought, a gown fit for a queen, and

Susanne looked like royalty when she put it on.

Lacey glanced in the mirror. Her own dress was of a deep rose pink silk. It had a square neck and a high empire waist that helped conceal her thick waist.

She placed a hand over her swollen belly, smiled as she felt her child's lusty kick. The baby was due in a few short weeks, and she could hardly wait to cradle the child in her arms. It would be a boy, she was certain, a tiny version of Matt that she could hold and love.

Matt. Her love for him had never wavered or diminished, nor had a day gone by that she didn't think of him. Where was he now? Had he left Salt Creek for good? The idea of never seeing him again still hurt, even after all these months.

She heard the clock downstairs chime the hour. Soon it would be time to go to the church. She could hear Susanne moving about in the next room. It had been painful, helping Susanne get dressed, seeing the happiness that radiated in her eyes. J.J.'s sister was so young, so beautiful, and so happy. Her whole being fairly glowed with the knowledge that she was loved.

"I thought I loved Matt," Susanne had confided to Lacey earlier that day, "but I know now it was just infatuation. Robert is everything I ever dreamed of."

Lacey wanted to be happy for her future sister-in-law, but it was hard to smile when her heart was breaking, hard to know that Susanne was facing a life of happiness with a man she loved while her own life was filled with such misery. And dread. Her child was due in less than four weeks. And already J.J. had started to remind her that he intended to consummate their bargain as soon as possible after the baby was born. He had come close several times, and Lacey had cringed when he touched her. His kisses filled her with revulsion, the touch of his hands on her breasts sickened her. And yet she had promised to be his . . . his whore if he would get Matt out of jail. J.J. had kept his end of the bargain. He reminded her of that at least once a day. Soon she would have to fulfill her part of the bargain. But she would not think of that now.

With a sigh, she peered at her reflection in the mirror. She looked fat and ugly and unhappy, she thought critically. Perhaps it was just as well that Matt could not see her now.

She whirled around as she sensed someone behind her, gasped when she saw Matt standing near the open window. Mouth open, eyes wide, she stared at him, wondering if he were real, or merely the ghost of her heart's desire.

"Matt." He looked well and prosperous. His boots were new, his black trousers and dark blue shirt were of good quality. A gray silk kerchief was loosely knotted at his throat. He wore a black Stetson pushed back on his head. A hand-tooled gunbelt was snugged around his lean waist, the holster holding a pearl-handled Colt .44.

His eyes, as cold and blue as a winter sky, moved over her in a long sweeping glance. Her hair was piled on her head in a mass of elegant curls, her face pale despite a touch of rouge on her cheeks and the paint on her lips. But it was the expression in her eyes that caught at his heart. They were dull and life-less, as if all the joy she had ever known had been crushed from her spirit. He almost felt sorry for her, but she had made her bed, so to speak, and if she now regretted her choice, it had nothing to do with him.

"Matt." She whispered his name again, her eyes riveted on his face, his beloved face.

He gestured at her dress. "What's the occasion?"

"Susanne's getting married."

"Anybody I know?"

Lacey shook her head. "His name's Robert Morrison. He's the editor of the Salt Creek *Gazette*." Her voice grew wistful. "They're very much in love."

"I hope she'll be happy," Matt remarked quietly. "She deserves it."

"And what do I deserve?" She had not meant to speak the words aloud, but they spilled out of her mouth of their own volition, sharp and edged with bitterness.

"What's the matter, honey?" Matt asked sardonically. "Hasn't J.J. given you everything you wanted?"

Lacey bit down on her lower lip, stifling the urge to tell Matt that he was all she had ever wanted. If only she could pour out her heart, tell him why she had moved in with J.J., tell him that the child she carried was his. But J.J.'s threat to kill Matt and her child kept her mute. She knew J.J. better now, knew he would not hesitate to kill Matt at the slightest provocation.

"Answer me," Matt said curtly. "Hasn't J.J. made you happy?"

"Of course he has," she lied. She lifted her hand in a gesture that encompassed the room and its furnishings. "I have everything I could possibly want."

Matt cocked his head to one side. She was lying. He could see it in the haunted sadness of her eyes, hear the pain in her voice. He passed a hand over his jaw, his expression thoughtful. It had been a mistake to come here, a mistake to see her again. He had thought himself well rid of any feelings for her.

During the past winter he had come to terms with the past and set a course for the future. He had learned why J.J. had killed

Billy Henderson, and the knowledge was of no importance except that it meant he was a free man again. There was no point in airing J.J.'s dirty linen, nothing to be gained by ruining Susanne's image of her brother. It was all in the past and best forgotten. As for the future, he was going home, back to Virginia to see if he couldn't make a new life for himself. But something, some shadowy emotion he could neither define nor ignore had driven him to Salt Creek. He had to see Lacey one last time, no matter how much it hurt.

He had not expected it to hurt quite so bad.

Hands clenched at his sides, he took a step toward her. "Are you happy, Lacey?" His voice was soft, raw with pain. "Is this what you wanted?"

"Yes," she exclaimed. "How many times do I have to say it?"

He took another step toward her, his heart aching for the misery he saw reflected in her eyes. "Lacey."

"Go away." She took a step backward, knowing she would lose all self-control if he so much as touched her.

He watched her, confused by the changing play of emotions on her face. What was she afraid of? She was reaching out for him, not with her arms, but with her soul. He could feel the unhappiness in her, see it on her face.

Without warning, he closed the distance

421

between them and took her in his arms, his mouth dropping gently over hers, his arms sliding around her waist. He had forgotten how perfectly her body fit against his. He lifted a hand to her hair, his fingers removing the pins so that the heavy reddish-brown mass tumbled down her back in a riot of waves. He inhaled the fragrance of her hair and skin, let his lips wander over her nose and eyes before returning to her mouth.

Lacey swayed against him, the blood singing in her veins as she returned Matt's kiss with all the love and longing in her heart. Her body gloried in the hard maleness of his, her nostrils filled with the scent of horse and leather and man. Her man. She belonged to Matt, body and soul, in a way she could never, would never, belong to J.J. or anyone else.

Matt drew back a little, his eyes searching hers. "You don't love J.J.," he said slowly. "You never did. Why, then? Why'd you move in with the bastard?"

Fear and reality returned as soon as his lips left hers. "I do love him," Lacey said, not meeting Matt's gaze. "I'm just happy to see you, that's all."

"Happy, hell. You're hungry for me."

She did not deny it.

"Lacey, come away with me. Now."

It was tempting, so tempting.

"You want to, I know you do." His lips

nibbled at her ear lobe, slid down her neck, trailed fire as they returned to her mouth, suddenly hot and hungry and demanding. His tongue probed the delicate recesses of her mouth, making her body tingle with desire, making her feel warm and alive for the first time in months. She pressed her hips against his maleness, heard him groan low in his throat as his hands slid down to her buttocks and drew her closer still.

"I love you, Matt." She murmured the words against his neck, knowing she had to say them or die. "I never stopped."

"Then why, Lacey? For God's sake, tell me the truth."

"By all means, my dear. Tell him the truth."

Lacey gasped at the sound of Tucker's voice. She twisted out of Matt's arms, her face as white as J.J.'s linen shirt, fear congealing in her heart as she saw the gun in J.J.'s hand.

Matt did not move. Through narrowed eyes, he glanced from Lacey to J.J., his gaze lingering on the Colt in Tucker's hand. It was cocked and ready to fire.

"Go ahead, my dear," J.J. said with a sneer. "I guess the man deserves to hear the truth before he dies."

"J.J., please, I'll do anything you say. Just let him go."

"Tell him," Tucker demanded.

"Matt, I . . ." Lacey licked her lips, hoping

423

he would believe her. "I moved in with J.J. to keep you out of prison. He said if I became his mistress, he'd tell the sheriff who killed Billy. It's as simple as that. I never loved him. Never!"

"Go on," J.J. urged. "Tell him the rest."

"The baby . . . it isn't J.J.'s. It's yours." Lacey gazed intently at Matt, trying to guess what he was feeling, what he was thinking, but his face was impassive, his dark eyes empty of expression. "I did it for you!" she cried. He had to believe her, she thought desperately. He couldn't die thinking she had been unfaithful. Oh, God, he couldn't die!

Slowly Matt turned to face Lacey. For a moment he was angry with her, more angry than he'd ever been in his life. All these months he had hated her for being unfaithful. He had cursed the day they met, dying a little every time he thought of her carrying another man's child.

But it was his child. His anger dissolved as he gazed into Lacey's clear brown eyes, and he felt a rush of love more powerful than anything he had ever known. She had sold herself to a man she didn't love to keep him out of prison.

"Lacey." There was a wealth of emotion in his voice as he murmured her name. His eyes moved to her swollen breasts, to the bulge of her stomach barely visible beneath the concealing folds of her gown. A child slept there. His child. A child he would never see.

Tears welled in Lacey's eyes as she felt the force of Matt's love reach out to her. "I never slept with J.J." She turned cold brown eyes toward Tucker. "And I never will."

"That's where you're wrong, my dear," Tucker said, his smile smug and sure. "I intend to seal our bargain tonight." J.J. raised the gun a little higher. "Where do you want it, Drago? In the front, or in the back?"

"What the hell difference does it make?"

"None, I guess," Tucker mused with a wry grin.

"Just one thing. Why'd you kill Pitman? You owe me that much."

Tucker shrugged. "He knew too much. I couldn't trust him to keep his mouth shut once he was locked up. You must have guessed that."

"And that's why you killed Gonzalez?"

J.J. nodded.

"What about Tanner?"

"I'll find him," J.J. said confidently.

"It never stops, does it? You killed Pitman to cover the fact that you killed Billy Henderson. And then you had to kill Gonzalez."

"And Tanner's living on borrowed time," Tucker said. "Just like you."

There was a choked sound from the doorway. J.J. didn't turn around, but Matt glanced past Tucker to see Susanne standing in the doorway, her face as white as her wedding gown.

"What does he mean, J.J.?" she asked, her voice brittle. "What does he mean about you killing Billy?"

"Nothing, Susanne. Get out of here."

"What does he mean, J.J.?" she repeated, her voice rising. "Tell me it isn't true."

"He's lying," Tucker said flatly.

"Matt?" Susanne's eyes were wide, bright with unshed tears. "Lacey?"

"It's true," Matt said. "J.J. had Billy killed because Billy was prying into things that didn't concern him."

"Damn you, Drago," J.J. hissed. His finger tightened around the trigger, taking up the slack.

Lacey screamed, "No!" and lunged toward Tucker, her hand reaching for the gun, just as Susanne hurled herself at her brother.

"You killed him!" Susanne shrieked. "You killed my Billy. I'll never forgive you!" She pummeled Tucker's back with her fists.

There was a loud explosion as the gun in J.J.'s hand fired. Lacey screamed as the bullet meant for Matt struck her in the chest. The sound of the gunshot was still in the air when Matt drew and fired. His bullet struck J.J. square in the heart.

Time moved in slow motion after that.

Tucker stood upright for a moment, a stunned expression on his face as his gun fell from his hand.

Susanne began to cry as her brother slowly sank to his knees and then pitched forward and lay still.

But Matt had eyes only for Lacey. She lay in a crumpled heap on the floor, her face drained of color, a crimson tide staining the bodice of her dress.

"Get a doctor," Matt cried hoarsely. He tore the kerchief from his neck and pressed it over the dreadful wound in Lacey's chest, appalled at how quickly the gray silk turned red with blood.

"J.J. . . ." Susanne whimpered her brother's name.

"He's past help," Matt said curtly. "Please, Susanne," he implored. "Go get the doctor."

With a nod, Susanne rose to her feet and ran from the room.

"Lacey." Matt called her name, begging her not to die. But she only lay there, as still as death. Clutching her hand in his, he willed his strength into her. Time and again he glanced at the door. Where was the doctor? What was taking so long?

After what seemed like hours, the doctor entered the room, followed by Sheriff Henderson. The sawbones carried a large black bag; Henderson held a gun.

The doctor didn't waste time examining Tucker. The man was obviously dead. He knelt beside Lacey, his face grave as he quickly determined the extent of the injury. The bullet had passed cleanly through her body. Fortunately, no major damage had been done. Opening his bag, he began to treat the wound.

"I'll take that gun, Drago," Henderson said curtly, and Matt handed it over without a word, too concerned about Lacey to argue.

Henderson pulled a pair of handcuffs out of his back pocket and tossed them to Matt. "Put 'em on."

Matt slipped the cuffs off, his eyes never leaving Lacey's face. She was moaning softly. "Is she gonna be all right, doc?" he asked.

"It's too soon to tell. The bullet missed her heart, but she's lost a lot of blood. And she's in labor." The doctor finished bandaging the wound, wiped his hands, and stood up. "Bill, help me get her on the bed."

Henderson glanced at Matt, then holstered his gun. Drago wasn't going anywhere.

Gently the two men lifted Lacey and placed her on the bed. She groaned, her hands clutching her belly, her head moving back and forth on the pillow.

"I'll wait outside," Henderson said. He picked up Tucker's gun and tossed a blanket over J.J.'s body before leaving the room.

Matt stood beside the bed as the doctor undressed Lacey, then covered her with a sheet.

Susanne entered the room a few minutes later, followed by Robert Morrison. They had stopped at the church to postpone the wedding, saying only that an emergency had arisen. Leaving a church full of people to wonder what had happened.

Susanne looked at Matt, and then at Lacey. And then at the blanket-draped body of her brother. This was all J.J.'s fault, she thought sadly. She had adored him all her life. Too late, she realized she had idolized a man who never existed.

"How's Lacey?" Susanne asked.

Matt shrugged. "She's lost a lot of blood. And she's in labor."

Susanne nodded. She felt so calm. Why wasn't she crying? J.J. was dead, her whole life should be shattered. "I didn't tell the sheriff," she said, seeing the handcuffs on Matt's wrists. "He was having a cup of coffee with Doc Bradley when I got there."

"It doesn't matter," Matt said. He winced as Lacey cried out, her voice thick with pain as his child struggled to be born. "Hang on, Lacey," he begged. Kneeling beside the bed, he took her hand in his and gave it a squeeze.

"Matt, I want Matt."

"I'm here."

Her eyelids fluttered open. Her eyes were dark with pain and fear. "Matt, I'm so afraid."

"Don't be. Everything will be all right. I promise."

"It hurts," she whimpered. "Everything hurts. Why? What's wrong with me?"

"The baby's coming," Matt explained.

"But it's too soon!"

"Relax, honey, just relax."

"I can't. It hurts." She began to cry softly as a contraction knifed through her. She clung to Matt's hand, her eyes fixed on his face, her grip loosening as the contraction passed. There was a pain in her chest. She frowned as she looked down and saw the bandage wrapped around her upper body. "What happened?"

"You've been hurt. Tucker . . ." Tears stung his eyes, and he swore softly. It was his fault she'd been shot, his fault she was in such pain. If he'd stayed away from her, none of this would have happened.

"He shot you," Lacey said. "I remember now." She searched Matt's face. "Are you all right?"

"I'm fine. The bullet missed me and hit you."

Before she could absorb that, another contraction hit her, and then another.

"I think you'd best leave the room, Miss Tucker, Mr. Morrison. And you, too, Drago."

"I'm staying," Matt said.

"We'll go," Morrison said. He took Susanne by the hand and started for the door. "We'll be downstairs if you need us."

The doctor looked at Matt speculatively. "Have you ever delivered a baby before?"

"No."

"Think you can work around those cuffs?"

"I'll manage."

Things moved quickly after that. Lacey was lost in a world of pain as her baby made its way into the world. It was Matt who caught the child as it emerged from the womb, and he cried unashamedly as he stared at the tiny scrap of humanity cradled in his hands. It was a boy, with a thatch of thick black hair and smoky blue eyes.

The doctor cut the cord, quickly examined the baby, pronounced it as healthy as could be expected seeing as how it was almost a month premature, and then turned back to Lacey. She had passed the afterbirth and was bleeding profusely.

Matt held his son, freshly washed and wrapped in a blanket, while the doctor fought to save Lacey's life. Sometime during the long night, Susanne came in and took the baby, but Matt hardly noticed. He refused to leave

Lacey's side. A short time later Morrison brought Matt a plate of food and a cup of coffee. Matt drank the coffee but left the food untouched.

"You should eat," the doctor advised. He gestured at his own plate with his fork. "It's good, and you need the strength."

Matt shook his head. He was vaguely aware of Susanne moving in and out of the room as the hours passed. It was near midnight when Susanne went to bed. The doctor fell asleep in the chair beside the window, but Matt stayed at Lacey's side. Her face was pale, so pale, her lips almost blue, her hands cold.

He knelt by the bed, his dark eyes haunted and sad. "Don't die, Lacey," he begged in a choked voice. "Please don't die. I need you. Our son needs you."

He was still awake when dawn brightened the horizon. Dr. Bradley woke with a start, stood up, and placed his stethoscope to Lacey's chest. When he looked at Matt, there was little hope in his expression.

"I've done all I can do," Bradley said. "It's up to her now. All we can do is pray." He moved quietly around the room, gathering his instruments. "Call me if there's any change."

"Yeah. Thanks, doc."

Henderson entered the room as Bradley went out. "Let's go, Drago," he said gruffly. "I've got work to do."

Matt shook his head. "I can't leave her."

"And I can't sit around here all day to keep an eye on you. Miss Tucker can let you know if anything happens."

"What are you holding me for anyway, sheriff?" Matt asked brusquely. "I killed J.J. in self-defense."

"Maybe, maybe not. It's up to a jury to decide."

"Ask Susanne. She was here. She saw the whole thing."

"We'll still need a trial."

Matt let out a sigh of exasperation. "Dammit, Henderson, I'm not going anywhere. I've got a brand new baby to care for and a wife who's . . . Dammit, I won't leave her."

"What's going on in here?" Susanne asked. She glanced from the sheriff to Matt. "You're making too much noise. The baby's asleep, and Lacey needs her rest. If you must argue, go outside."

"Susanne, tell him I shot J.J. in self-defense. Maybe he'll listen to you."

Susanne glanced at the bloodstain on the bedroom floor. During the night, Robert had removed the body. She wondered absently if they would ever be able to wash the blood from the wood.

"Susanne?"

She looked at Matt and then at the sheriff. "It was self-defense." She blinked back her tears. "J.J. was going to kill Matt. His shot went wide because I hit his arm, and the bullet hit Lacey instead. Matt fired his gun in self-defense."

Henderson nodded slowly. She was telling the truth, he had no doubt of that. Everyone knew how much she had loved J.J. She wouldn't lie about how he died.

With a sigh of regret, Henderson removed the handcuffs from Matt's wrists. "Don't leave town, Drago," he muttered. "Good day, Miss Tucker. My condolences about your brother."

"Thank you, sheriff."

Susanne smiled wanly at Matt, then followed Henderson out of the room and closed the door.

CHAPTER 19

The sound of a baby's cry penetrated the mists of darkness that sheltered her like loving arms, standing between Lacey and the pain that waited to claim her.

A baby, she mused. *Why, there's a baby in the house!* She tried to remember whose baby it was, but the darkness closed in on her again, wrapping her in black velvet oblivion.

She seemed to be sinking deeper and deeper, drowning in layers of blackness. *Just let go*, a voice whispered, softly enticing and persuasive. *Just let go*.

It was Death's voice, soft and seductive, coaxing her to turn her back on life, on pain, to surrender to endless peace and forgetfulness.

Just let go. She felt herself slowly sinking deeper into the nothingness of infinity and she lacked the strength to resist.

"Lacey!"

A voice pierced the darkness, a voice filled with unbearable anguish.

"Lacey!" It came again, calling her back, begging her not to die. A man's voice. A familiar voice.

With great effort, she drew away from the all-encompassing darkness as the voice sobbed her name again and again.

Matt. It was Matt's voice, calling her back from the brink of eternity, begging her not to leave him.

He was crying. The thought tore at her heart. She loved him so much, and he was crying. Her Matt, so big, so strong, so endlessly sure of himself, crying because of her.

It was more than she could bear.

She struggled against the web of darkness, fighting her way toward the light, toward the sound of Matt's voice.

A low moan escaped her lips as the darkness withdrew, leaving her at the mercy of the throbbing pain in her chest, the weary ache in her body. It was an effort to open her eyes, but worth the struggle. Matt's face was the first thing she saw. His dark eyes were shadowed and sad. There was a three-day growth of beard on his jaw.

"Lacey," he breathed. "Thank God."

"You look terrible," she murmured weakly.

"And you look beautiful." Gently he kissed her cheek. "I thought I'd lost you."

"I heard your voice calling me," Lacey said, her brow furrowed as she tried to remember. "I heard your voice and I knew you were crying, and I couldn't bear to think that you were unhappy." She looked up into his face, his beloved face, and then she frowned. "Matt, I heard a baby cry."

"It was your son. Our son."

Lacey placed her hands on her stomach. It hadn't been a dream, then. "Where is he? I want to see him."

"I'll get him." Rising, Matt kissed her cheek, squeezed her hand, and kissed her again before he left the room.

He returned moments later carrying a tiny blanket-wrapped bundle. Reverently he placed the child in Lacey's outstretched arms, shed tears of joy and gratitude as he watched Lacey count each tiny finger and toe.

"He's beautiful," she murmured fervently. "He looks just like you."

Matt let out a long sigh of contentment, certain he had never seen anything more wonderful than the sight of Lacey cradling their son.

Lacey smiled up at Matt, warmed through and through by the love she saw reflected in his eyes. "Come and sit with us," she invited, patting the bed beside her. "Daddy."

Matt sat beside Lacey, his arm around her waist. "Daddy. That takes some getting used to."

"Oh, Matt, isn't he beautiful?"

"You are." His arm tightened around her waist. She looked so pale, so thin, and so beautiful.

"Have you named him?" Lacey asked.

Matt shook his head, marveling at the way the baby gripped his finger. "No, I was waiting until you were better. I thought maybe you should decide."

Lacey gazed into her son's face. He was so beautiful, so perfect, a living, breathing miracle of her love for Matt.

"I think we should name him Matthew Royce Drago, after his father and grandfather. Oh, Matt, won't Daddy be surprised!"

Matt nodded, his gaze meeting Lacey's over the top of their son's head. Slowly they came together, their lips meeting in a joyous kiss that was filled with all the love and promise the future would hold.

Epilogue

Lacey sat on the grassy riverbank, her bare feet dangling in the sun-dappled water. Beside her, Matt Jr. slept peacefully on a blanket, his thumb jammed into his mouth, his knees drawn up under his chest. He was a darling baby, with wavy black hair, dark blue eyes, and tawny skin. No other child ever born was as cute, as smart, as beautiful.

The past was finally behind them. There had been an inquest following J.J.'s death. Susanne had testified that Matt had shot her brother in self-defense, and the case had been closed. The funeral had been the next day. Dr. Bradley had refused to let Lacey attend, and for that she had been grateful.

Six weeks after her son was born, the

doctor pronounced her well enough to get out of bed. Two weeks later, Susanne married Robert Morrison in a quiet ceremony. Matt and Lacey left for Kansas the next day. There, in a quaint country church, they repeated their wedding vows. Royce Montana had given the bride away, Blue Willow had been Lacey's matron of honor.

Now, only a few months later, they had a home of their own in a lush green valley not far from where Lacey's father lived.

She smiled as Matt came to sit beside her, her heart beating faster at his nearness. How handsome he was, and how she loved him!

Her heart filled with tenderness as she watched Matt stroke their son's downy cheek with a calloused thumb. What a picture they made together: her husband, so tall and dark and handsome, and her son, a tiny replica of his father.

She sighed as Matt slipped his arm around her waist and drew her close.

"Happy, honey?" he asked.

"So happy," she murmured, and knew she would ask nothing more of life than to have her son safely by her side and Matt's midnight blue eyes gazing lovingly into her own.

"So happy," she said again, and lifted her face for her husband's kiss, a kiss that was as fervent as a prayer, as warm as the summer sun, and as beautiful as the love they shared.